A KING OF MASKS
AND MAGIC

LISA CASSIDY

National Library of Australia Cataloguing-in-Publication Entry

Creator: Lisa Cassidy

Publisher: Tate House

ISBN: 9780648539254

Copyright © 2020 by Lisa Cassidy

Cover design: Jessica Bell

Map design: Oscar Paludi

Music and lyrics: Peny Bohan

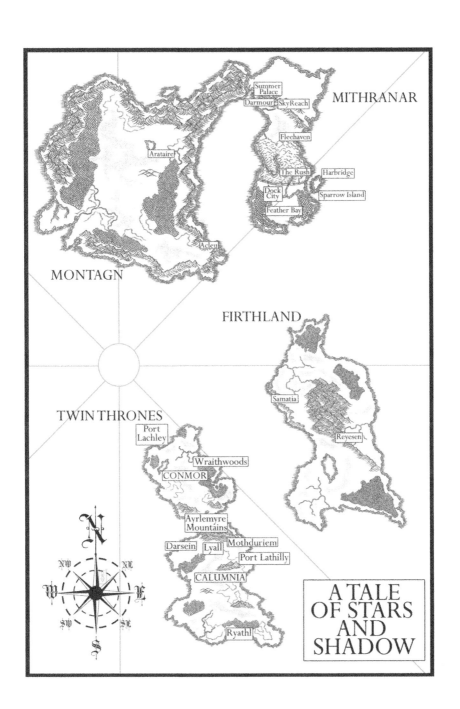

MITHRANAR

Summer Palace

Darmour · SkyReach

Fleehaven

Arataire

The Rush · Harbridge

Dock City · Sparrow Island

Feather Bay

Acleu

MONTAGN

FIRTHLAND

Samatia

TWIN THRONES

Port Lachley

Reyesen

Wraithwoods

CONMOR

Ayrlemyre Mountains

Darsein · Lyall · Mothduriem

Port Lathilly

CALUMNIA

Ryathl

A TALE
OF STARS
AND
SHADOW

CHAPTER 1

*E*verything hurt. All the time.

Which was technically a good thing.

The fact he could actually *feel* the constant aching of the slowly-healing bones in his left leg meant that the swelling around his spine was lessening. Or so Tiercelin said.

And Cuinn trusted Tiercelin. The winged healer currently working on his leg—with a look of furious concentration on his face —had been tireless in his efforts to heal the awful wounds Cuinn had sustained from being buried in a mine cave-in while trying to escape Vengeance. Most days ended with Tiercelin's brown skin ashen from exhaustion, his hands trembling and shoulders slumped. But he never gave up.

Not that they'd talked in detail about what had happened yet. For days upon days, Cuinn had been unable to do anything but lie there and ride out the agonising pain, not to mention the subsequent fever and illness that came with an infection in his leg. Sometimes he thought it had only been the presence of his Wolves—their unyielding concern and determination to protect him—that had pulled him through.

There was always one of them on guard outside his door, and

those not on guard made regular appearances to bring meals and drinks for both prince and healer. Cuinn had heard Halun on more than one occasion quietly insisting Tiercelin get some rest.

The obvious bond between the five men both warmed him and made him achingly lonely at the same time. He'd never had that. Not with anyone except Raya, and she was long gone.

Then had come the morning when he'd felt alert enough to ask where exactly they were, curious about the scent of salt and ocean on the breeze through his window. Staying in a house owned by a friend of Talyn's had been Tiercelin's answer. Cuinn had yet to meet this friend, which was probably deliberate given Talyn had brought him here to hide.

And he couldn't ask more because she'd been gone by then—off on some important business his fevered brain hadn't quite managed to grasp when she farewelled him—and the Wolves didn't seem to know any more about the friend or the house. He hoped she'd be back soon. He missed her. He wasn't worried about her though. No, that would be the height of foolishness... Talyn Dynan wasn't a woman you worried about.

And he was sliding back into delirium.

Cuinn cleared his throat. "Did you ever imagine, when we were boys and I was ignoring you because you were too young to be of notice, that we'd end up here one day?" He was seeking a distraction. Herbal tea helped a little, but once the fever had faded and he'd regained his mental alertness, oftentimes conversation was the only way he could distract himself from the constant pain aching through his body. Or from thoughts of what had happened before leaving Mithranar.

They'd come so close to death. Talyn. Her Wolves. Him. The thought tore into him each time it surfaced. And Vengeance was still out there. Still murderously angry and hungering for their twisted version of revenge.

"Not for a second." Tiercelin chuckled, sparing him a glance before returning his focus to where Cuinn's leg had been broken in two places.

A faint dizziness spread through him—the result of the healer using Cuinn's own energy to help with the healing. Unlike other winged folk abilities, healing magic drew upon both the practitioner and the patient. It could be dangerous for both.

"What's the prognosis? Amputation?" He managed a smile.

"Not at all. In fact, the bones are beginning to knit together nicely. Soon I'll need to get you up on your feet to start rebuilding the strength in your legs."

A heavy silence fell over the room. Tiercelin had spoken casually, gaze still on Cuinn's leg, but there had been a time when they both doubted Cuinn would ever walk again.

"What you've done for me..."

Tiercelin waved a hand. "My job is to protect you, Prince Cuinn."

"I saw something, after I was caught in the rockfall." He frowned, trying to put words to his experience. "It felt like I went somewhere, as crazy as that sounds. Green fields. A bright blue sky—brighter than I've ever seen. And then it vanished. Maybe I was just hallucinating."

"You weren't," Tiercelin said softly. "I was fortunate to be able to bring you back from there. That place exists very close to death."

Silence filled the room as Cuinn processed the depth of what Tiercelin had done for him, the power he must have. "Tiercelin, I owe you my life. You should be head of the healers."

"I'll leave that to Jystar." Tiercelin spoke of his eldest brother—the man who'd taken the position of Mithranar's head healer after his predecessor's violent murder. Her killer still hadn't been found, but had probably been Vengeance. That unspoken thought resounded through the room for a moment, but neither was willing to broach the subject. Tiercelin only smiled warmly. "I'm a Wolf."

Cuinn sagged back against the pillows, shifting in a vain attempt to get comfortable. Lying in bed so long meant that apart from the constant pain, there was also the growing discomfort of being unable to move or exercise.

But Tiercelin had just told him he would walk again. Without that, he would still have been able to fly, but it would have been limited and difficult. This was everything he'd hoped for.

He began humming under his breath, a wordless tune, but one he threaded with his song magic, telling Tiercelin in a way that words never could how grateful and relieved he was.

The healer's work faltered, and tears welled in his grey eyes. "You're welcome, Prince Cuinn," he whispered.

LATER THAT DAY a knock at the door woke him from a restless nap. He stared around, blinking—the room was empty. "Come in!"

Corrin entered, bowing in a way that made Cuinn itch. "We received a letter from your brother, Your Highness. One of Captain Dynan's Aimsir friends delivered it this morning."

He really wished they would all stop bowing and calling him that. He hated the title, hated that good men who'd risked their lives for him twice now felt like they had to treat him differently, like he was more important than they were. That couldn't be further from the truth.

"Finally. On a scale of furious to downright murderous, how bad is it?" Talyn had helped him write a letter to his family in one of his brief lucid moments after first arriving in Ryathl. It told them he'd gotten bored on Sparrow Island—where Anrun Windsong had promised to inform them Cuinn was going—and left to visit the reputedly beautiful south-eastern coastline of Calumnia. Talyn had picked one of the most expensive inns in Ryathl as a delivery address for replies, then had one of her friends check there regularly for any responses.

Doing what he'd done without telling them—not just leaving, but visiting a foreign country without approval—was extreme, even for the selfish, indolent prince image he'd carefully cultivated. But it had been necessary. He braced himself for Mithanis's furious words.

"Actually, it's from Prince Azrilan."

Cuinn winced. "Worse than downright murderous, then. Mithanis must have been too rigid with fury to manage a coherent word."

Corrin cleared his throat, stifling a smile. "Prince Azrilan commends your desire to travel, but suggests it's time to return home."

"How polite of him." Cuinn winced as a cramp stabbed through his right calf. "I suppose we'd best write back."

"Later, Your Highness." Corrin hadn't missed his wince. "When you feel better."

He huffed a pain-edged laugh. "I ache, I hurt and I feel ill most of the time because I have to eat, even though I'm not hungry because I can't move from this bed. Let's just get the letter written—see if we can't stall Mithanis from doing something annoying like coming after me."

"I'll get some parchment and quill."

"Any word from Captain Dynan?" He'd prefer Talyn's help with the letter. He'd prefer she was there irrespective of the letter, actually, because he missed her. More than was good for him. But there it was.

"Not yet. Though I expect she's reached Port Lathilly by now on that amazing horse of hers." He smiled. "I'm glad she's gotten the opportunity to visit with Sari's husband and son."

That's right. She'd gone to see Roan and Tarquin. Cuinn promptly relinquished his desire for her to return, hoping she'd take as long as she needed.

"What about Theac? And your mother and sisters?" Corrin had filled him in on Theac's engagement to his mother and he was delighted for both men.

"Just one letter from Theac. He's as grumpy as always, but I think he worries about us," Corrin said. "He says everything is fine back home, and Evani is settling into life in Dock City well."

"Jasper hasn't eaten anyone yet?" A wave of mournfulness washed through him. He understood Talyn's decision to leave Jasper behind— that with Cuinn so sick and unable to control the tawncat he was a danger to others—but he missed him badly. Cuinn no longer doubted any of the old stories about the creatures of the forest under the citadel possessing an uncanny intelligence. Not only had Jasper somehow known Cuinn was in trouble after Vengeance had ambushed him, the tawncat had tracked him down, killed his guard and then led Talyn and the Wolves to him after he'd been cornered.

He didn't understand it. Couldn't explain it. But it didn't matter.

Jasper was his friend, and that was all he cared about. He shook himself, trying to dislodge his sadness. "Have Theac and your mother set a date for the wedding?"

Corrin smiled. "Mam would like it to be soon, but I don't want all the preparations left to her while I'm away. So, we're thinking a month after we return. Mid-Sevenmonth. Hopefully before the rains of monsoon season start proper."

"Bring extra parchment," Cuinn said. "You'll write to her and Theac today and confirm that date. I'll be home by then, Corrin. I promise you."

Corrin bowed. "I'll be back shortly, Your Highness."

Corrin's footsteps moved away and Cuinn sank back against the pillows, closing his eyes and trying to breathe through the pain, summoning the energy he'd need for writing the letter.

He would have to begin working even harder on his recovery. He had to get well so he could go home before Mithanis started asking too many questions. His brother wouldn't tolerate anything that might seem like a threat to his power, his influence, or his right to be named their mother's heir. If he even started to suspect Cuinn was up to anything but partying in a foreign country…

And then there was what the dying Vengeance man had said, that the prince of night was pulling their strings, helping them sow chaos in Dock City in a bid to overthrow the winged rulers.

If that was true, Mithanis was an even greater enemy than he'd ever imagined. Not to mention that amidst the fever and pain he also remembered Talyn telling him she'd promised the Callanan a conversation with the Shadowhawk back in Mithranar. The details were hazy—something about a deal she made—but he trusted the reason was a good one.

Dealing with any of that seemed so far beyond his capability the thought made him ill. He would take it one step at a time. Tiercelin would make him well again.

And he wasn't completely alone anymore.

CHAPTER 2

*L*aughter and raucous conversation filled the room as Talyn made her way between the crowded tables, part of her keeping an eye on where she was walking, the other part seeking out and noting the locations of the Kingshield guards discreetly posted around the inn.

Ariar Dumnorix, Horselord of the Aimsir, sat at a table at the back of the room, booted feet resting on the wooden surface beside his hat, chair leaning back dangerously. His tangled blonde curls glinted red in the light of the lantern above his head and his luminous Dumnorix eyes flashed bright blue with laughter at something one of his companions—judging from their motley attire and the hats scattered over the table, they were his Aimsir captains—said. When he saw her approaching, his eyes shone even brighter, and he swung his legs off the table and stood up in one smooth movement. "Cousin!"

"Ariar." She grinned, allowing him to sweep her into a bone-crushing hug. Several years older, he was nonetheless her favourite Dumnorix relative. She suspected the feeling was mutual.

"Six thrices, what brings you here? I thought you were in Mithranar."

"Can we talk?"

His bright smile faded. Within moments, he'd spoken to his companions and led her out to the inn's back deck, where his King-shield guard made quick work of clearing out those enjoying Port Lathilly's fading summer warmth. The view from the deck took in the city sloping down towards the clogged harbour, the lanterns of the guards manning the city's wall bobbing back and forth. Such a familiar sight. It hurt less than it once had, but the bittersweet ache was still there.

"What happened?" Ariar demanded once they were alone. "Are you all right?"

"I ran into a bit of trouble in Mithranar," she said. "The gang I've been investigating there—they call themselves Vengeance—came after me and the Wolves."

He frowned. "It was bad enough you had to come home?"

She sucked in a breath. The last thing she wanted to do was lie to her cousin, but there were secrets that weren't hers to share. "I'm here with my talons, partly because we needed to get out of Mithranar for a while."

"You're holding back." He said it without accusation.

"I am, and I'm sorry. I can't tell you the full truth of why I'm here, but you remember the conversation we had after my father's funeral? About sharing what we know?"

"I do." His blue eyes were sober, trusting her. "Tell me what you can."

"I connected Vengeance to the assassination attempt on Queen Sarana and a series of murders in Dock City. Did the First Blade pass that on to you?"

Ariar nodded. "She did. Along with something about political murders and the gang somehow acquiring a Shadow mercenary. I'd have doubted what I heard if it hadn't come from you, Cousin."

"I'm aware of how it sounds." She huffed a breath. "They came after me and my Wolves. We turned the tables on their ambush and questioned one left alive." His screams of pain were seared on her memory, but what burned even deeper was the information he'd shared. A lot of it hadn't made sense, but one particular piece had. "He told me Vengeance's purpose was to sow discord and discontent in Mithranar."

"For what purpose?"

"Overthrowing the winged rulers." She lifted a hand. "Before you ask, all I could get out of him was that someone was pulling their strings, giving them resources, tactical advice, that sort of thing."

Ariar's face turned grim. "Who?"

"He named Prince Mithanis. But that doesn't quite fit for me. His one and only ambition is to be the next king of Mithranar, and he doesn't need to overthrow his mother to do that. He's essentially guaranteed to be named heir. He just has to bide his time to inherit a stable country."

"Maybe he's impatient. Sarana is still relatively young, no?"

"Maybe, but Mithanis is already powerful and influential, and he's an impulsive, angry man." That was Cuinn's take on his eldest brother, and what she'd seen of him fit with that.

"So not patient enough to tiptoe around with a long-term play like this?" Ariar said. "You're worried, aren't you? Whatever you know that I don't, it makes you concerned."

She sighed, wishing she didn't have to keep it from him. Her information would make a lot more sense to Ariar if she could tell him that a Callanan informant had reported Montagn was using Vengeance to lay the groundwork for an invasion of Mithranar. Only the fact that her uncle hadn't passed the information on stopped her. She had to follow her king's wishes on this. "Yes. Have you learned anything more here?"

"I wish there was something I could tell you." Ariar ran a frustrated hand through his curls. "We hit a dead end on tracking the brigands that killed your father, and Ranar and his Callanan haven't found any more leads on the Montagni we arrested in the mountains."

"Brigand activity is still unusual?" she asked.

He let out a long breath. "It's quiet. Quieter than it's been in a long time. Most of my captains think it's a response to their attack on your parents—that they've withdrawn until the fallout has died down."

That made sense. But Ariar didn't look convinced. Still—she didn't see how brigand activity could be connected to Montagn's intention to invade Mithranar.

"You said your talons are in Ryathl. Did you ride all the way here just to tell me that?" he asked, changing the subject.

"I wanted to see Roan and Tarquin too," she said, looking away.

Sari roused. *"Liar."*

In the day following their arrival in Calumnia, Talyn had constantly doubted her decision to take Cuinn such a long way from Mithranar's winged healers. She still did. His injuries had taken a terrible toll and the rough sea journey hadn't helped matters. Infection had set into his broken leg, leaving him feverish and ill.

Tiercelin had repeatedly insisted Cuinn needed fully trained and more experienced winged healers. But Cuinn's fear of his brother was as real and true as anything she'd ever seen before, and so Talyn had reluctantly conceded to his wishes to remain.

And then, abruptly, it had been too much. Too much guilt and worry and anxiety. Not to mention the heavy weight of all the secrets she was keeping. Mithranar was in danger and she couldn't tell Cuinn, couldn't tell anyone. Sari's loss still tore at her every day, not to mention the more recent loss of her father, and her guilt over Cuinn being hurt so badly on her watch was too much like the guilt she still carried over her role in Sari's death.

"It's not the same, Tal. He actively hid his identity from you. You didn't have all the information you needed to protect him properly," Sari said. *"And my death wasn't your fault."*

She knew. Finally, she had accepted that, but healing remained a process.

"And if you hadn't worked it out, if you hadn't gone into those mines after the Shadowhawk, he'd be dead now."

"And if he hadn't thrown me clear of the rockfall—"

"He saved you." Sari's warm approval filled her up, making her smile. *"You know, having a new partner wouldn't be—"*

"*No!*" Talyn said it so savagely that Sari disappeared as if she'd never been there. The idea of having a new partner was unthinkable, utterly, utterly unthinkable.

"Talyn?" Ariar sounded puzzled.

"Sorry." She managed a smile. "It was a long ride here, I drifted off for a moment."

"Then go and get some rest. Are you staying with Roan?"

"Yeah, just for a week or two. I'll have to get back soon."

"Come and see me again before you leave. I'm going to be here in the city for a while given how quiet brigand activity has been lately." He sighed. "At least it gives us some breathing space to plan more strategically. I'd like to get rid of them once and for all."

Talyn pushed off the railing and gave him an affectionate punch in the arm. "If anyone could do that, you could. It's good to see you, Ariar."

"You too, Cousin."

SARI STIRRED as Talyn strolled through the winding streets of Port Lathilly towards Roan's home, enjoying the warm air and the sea breeze rifling through her long hair.

"*I miss nights like this,*" Sari said, then, "*I think you should have told Ariar about the Callanan informant.*"

"*If the Montagni ahara found out this person was informing to the Callanan, they'd be dead in a heartbeat. And then we'd lose all insight into the ahara's plans. It's my uncle's decision to tell Ariar, not mine.*"

"*And Cuinn?*"

"*I can't tell him for the same reason. He would want to warn his mother, and if Montagn learned that Mithranar was preparing for an invasion... the informant would be in danger.*" An edge of frustration filled her voice.

"*I suppose. What are you going to do if Montagn invades Mithranar?*"

"*It's not going to come to that. I'm going to go back and take out Vengeance.*"

"*Which might stall the ahara's plans. But it's not going to stop them.*"

Talyn didn't reply. Sari was right. But she didn't have an answer to

Sari's original question. She should. Her answer should be an unequivocal confirmation that she would return home to the Twin Thrones to do whatever she needed to do to help protect her family, her home, in case Montagn's ambitions spread wider than just Mithranar.

But those words... family... home... they didn't just mean the Twin Thrones and the Dumnorix to her. Not anymore.

ALMOST A FORTNIGHT LATER, Talyn returned from taking Tarquin on a long ride outside the city to find Ariar leaning casually against the back gate of Roan's home, holding a piece of folded parchment in his hand.

"This can't be good," she said, reaching down to take the letter. The seal had been broken, but the crossed swords pressed into the amber-coloured wax was still visible.

"We've been summoned," he said, sparing a wink for Tarquin. Sari's son beamed.

"Sh...oes," Talyn muttered, only just catching herself from swearing in front of the boy. "When did this arrive?"

"This morning. Aimsir courier—one of my fastest scouts based in Ryathl." Ariar sighed. "A clear sign we're expected back just as quickly."

They headed into the back garden, and Ariar helped Tarquin jump down before Talyn slid out of the saddle.

"Can I rub her down?" Tarquin asked eagerly.

Talyn glanced at FireFlare—the mare seemed relaxed enough after a long gallop, and she'd been around the boy all day. "Sure. Just remember what I told you. Don't stand behind her, and she doesn't like sudden movements."

"I'll be careful, I promise."

"You'll have him wanting to be an Aimsir next." Roan appeared from inside the house, paint flecking his shirt and trousers. He straightened abruptly when he realised who was with her. "Your Highness, I'm sorry, I wasn't expecting you."

"Nothing wrong with your boy becoming an Aimsir." Ariar chuckled. "It's good to see you, Roan. I'm afraid I've come to steal my cousin away."

"A summons from the family." Talyn scowled, showing Roan the letter.

"Oh dear." He made a sympathetic face.

"We'll leave in the morning." She glanced up at Ariar for his agreement, then crumpled the parchment and tossed it into the garden.

"Would you like to stay for dinner, Lord Ariar?" Roan asked. It wasn't an unusual occurrence. Back when Sari had been alive, Ariar had occasionally joined them for dinner. Still, it made Roan awkward, and Ariar knew it.

"I'm honoured that you ask, but unfortunately I have dinner scheduled with Lord Seinn's regional lackey this evening. No doubt he wants to complain once again about his supplies not receiving enough protection when travelling through the mountains." Ariar made a face.

Talyn grinned without guilt. "That sounds delightful. We'll be thinking of you."

"Your empathy warms me, Cousin. I'll be here at dawn to collect you," Ariar said. "Bye Roan. Tarquin—you're doing an excellent job there, lad."

The boy lifted his hand in an excited wave as Ariar left, closing the gate behind him.

Talyn looked at Roan. "Pasta for dinner?"

He grinned and wrapped an arm around her shoulders to give her a brief hug. "It's been great, having you stay."

"It might be a while before I can do it again." Once she was back in Mithranar, she'd be going after Vengeance with everything she had. Her life there was dangerous—not only because of Vengeance—and it was going to become even more so.

And no way would she be walking away from Cuinn's protection for long trips back to the Twin Thrones. Not now that she knew who he was.

"We're not going anywhere." His voice was tinged with sadness, but he smiled as he tossed her a tomato. "Now, start chopping."

So she did, part of her focus on making sure she didn't cut her finger slicing tomatoes, the rest thinking furiously on what could have prompted such an urgent summons for her and Ariar to travel back to the capital.

CHAPTER 3

Cuinn grunted with effort, the muscles of his right arm trembling as he braced almost all his weight on the wooden crutch Halun had carved for him.

But he was on his feet, both of them.

Tiercelin's smile was wide. "Now take a step, Your Highness. Just a little one."

Gathering himself, Cuinn leaned his weight on his right, uninjured leg, and tried to step forward with his left. It was unbelievably hard, using what felt like all his remaining strength, but he managed a sliding half-shuffle.

"One more."

Cuinn took a breath, and with a grunt of pain, tried again. His breath escaped him in heavy pants and sweat slicked his skin, just from two little steps. He kept his wings half-furled, using them to help his balance, thanking everything his use of them hadn't been affected by his injuries. Pain flared sharp and unrelenting through his leg.

But he was walking. With most of his weight on the crutch, yes. But walking.

Applause burst out from where Halun stood guard at the door.

The big man's wide smile stretched the slave tattoo across his left cheek. As usual, he didn't need words to convey what he was thinking.

He managed a faint smile for Halun before returning his attention to Tiercelin.

"Two more steps," the healer instructed. "Then back to bed. I'll work on your leg, then we'll do it again in a few hours. We'll increase the distance every day."

"I'll do whatever you tell me to," Cuinn promised. Despite the pain, despite the exhaustion that left nausea curling his stomach.

Because they all knew the deadline they were working to. They had to be back in Mithranar before his departure stretched too long and Mithanis started to wonder what was really going on. And he had to be healthy enough to talk to two Callanan warriors. If they were anywhere near as fierce and intelligent as Talyn, his performance was going to have to be flawless.

"One step at a time," Tiercelin urged. "Two more steps today. Let's go."

Cuinn gritted his teeth, took a breath, and forced himself to take another step.

And another.

One step at a time.

A HALF-TURN LATER, when he was collapsed on his bed, sick with exhaustion, pain throbbing through every single muscle in his body, a knock sounded at the door. He called out, and Corrin and Andres filed in. Both wore bright smiles.

"Halun told us you were on your feet." The normally professional Andres forgot to address him by title in his excitement. Even his perfect soldier's stance was ruined as he shifted from foot to foot.

"And Tiercelin says he's astonished at your recovery," Corrin added, for once looking just like the young man he still was. "He says there are few people who have the strength for what he's been putting you through."

"Tiercelin is full of it," Cuinn said, but some of his pain momentarily faded. "Should I expect Zamaril to burst in here any moment with trumpets and a song?"

Corrin chuckled. "He's on guard right now, but I'm sure he'll be in later."

"In the meantime, we have something we thought might help." Andres opened the door wider and gestured for whoever was outside to come in.

Two servants appeared, lugging a harpsichord between them. Cuinn stared as they carried it over to a spot by the windows.

Corrin cleared his throat. "We thought now that you're up and about you might like to play a bit, have something to fill your time when Tiercelin's not in here."

"It belongs to Lady Carmalla." Ever polite, Andres still refused to call her by her first name. Cuinn assumed she must be the friend of Talyn's whose house he was staying in. "But she didn't mind us moving it in here—she says she rarely uses it."

"I..." Cuinn cleared this throat, tears welling in his eyes. Music. They'd brought him music. In some ways that was even more wonderful than being able to walk again. "You have no idea. Thank you. And please thank Lady Carmalla too."

Corrin bowed. "We'll leave you to rest. We're all going to start leaving our windows open though, hoping to catch the music when you play."

Cuinn laughed. "In that case, I'll play loudly."

Both men left, closing the door quietly behind them. There was a movement at one of the windows, then Zamaril stuck his head in. "No trumpets and a song from me, but if you'd like to play while I'm on guard duty, I won't be complaining, Your Highness."

"Noted, Zamaril."

"Oh, and congratulations on the walking thing."

Zamaril disappeared before Cuinn could reply, and he sank back on his bed. He still felt sick and sore. But there was a smile on his face despite all that.

He'd work as hard as he needed to, no matter the pain.

So that he could go home. With Talyn and these Wolves at his back, knowing everything that he was... well, there were things he might be able to do that he couldn't before.

He must have drifted into a doze because the next thing he knew he was opening his eyes to the shadows of dusk sliding across the room. A knock sounded at the door, presumably what had woken him.

"Come in." He hated the grogginess in his voice and braced himself for the pain from his leg as he pushed himself up against the pillows so that he was sitting rather than lying.

The door opened to reveal an unfamiliar man wearing a familiar black uniform. Crossed swords depicted from a hundred amber stars were stitched into the dark material over his heart, and a sheathed sword hung from his waist. He was older, maybe his mother's age, with greying hair and rough-edged features.

For a moment he froze, then remembered he was in hiding and summoned his languid prince demeanour. "You're Kingshield," Cuinn said lazily. "One of Talyn's friends?"

The man's mouth twitched, like a smile was trying to escape. "I'm First Shield of the Kingshield, yes. And this is my house you're staying in."

Horrified, Cuinn dropped the act and sat up even straighter, then winced as pain shot through his leg. "I'm so sorry, Sir. I didn't mean to—"

"A prince apologising to a soldier?" the man asked dryly. "Wonders never cease."

Again he hesitated, but if Talyn trusted this man enough to bring Cuinn here, then Cuinn probably didn't need to pretend around him. Besides, if he wanted the First Shield to keep hosting him, it would be best not to antagonise him by acting like a spoiled idiot. "You've given me shelter and safety, sir. I owe you a lot more than an apology."

"You really mean that." The First Shield settled himself on a chair near the bed, gaze thoughtful. "Interesting. I'm Lark Ceannar, and you're Prince Cuinn Acondor. Let's at least pretend to adhere to the rules of rank and propriety and have you call me by my name."

Puzzlement nagged at him once his shock began to fade. Surely

Talyn had actual friends she could have requested help from—like the Aimsir collecting his mail—so why had she brought him to the First Shield's home? "All right."

"Talyn is on her way back," Ceannar said. "I wanted to let you know, and to meet you properly. I've been weighing up whether I should or not."

Unease. Reluctant admiration. Guilt. All three emotions were coming off Ceannar, who was presumably unaware of Cuinn's song magic. "Why?"

"Your Wolves tell me that you're back on your feet." Ceannar didn't answer the question. "They're a fierce lot, aren't they?"

"They aren't mine, they're hers," Cuinn said bluntly. "And they protect me because it's what she wants."

Ceannar's eyes narrowed. "I watched them training the other day. They're as good as any Kingshield guard under my command. Was that *sabai* I saw them using? The First Blade would have a fit if she knew."

Cuinn wasn't sure how to respond to that. "I'd like to thank you, for giving me shelter. I promise I'll be gone as soon as I can."

"Much like your Wolves, I agreed to shelter you here because it's what Talyn Dynan wanted." Ceannar rose abruptly to his feet. "It was nice to meet you, Prince Cuinn."

"And you, First Shield."

Cuinn's puzzled gaze remained on the door well after it had closed behind Lark Ceannar. The First Shield didn't want him here, that was clear, but less clear was why. He hadn't sensed any dislike from the man, only uneasiness and guilt.

Whatever the reason, it didn't matter. Cuinn wanted to be gone too. Out of this room and this bed and back to his home where the air was too thick and the dawn smelled like flowers. Where he could wait until his full health returned, until Mithanis calmed down from his inevitable fury, and then...

Well, then he could go back to helping his people.

CHAPTER 4

*B*y the time FireFlare's hooves flew down the northern road into Ryathl, Greylord and Ariar matching them stride for stride, Kingshield vainly trying to keep up behind, Talyn had been away from Cuinn and her talons for just over a month.

The promise she'd made to the First Blade of the Callanan—a meeting with the Shadowhawk in Dock City in return for telling the First Shield everything about Vengeance and Montagn—loomed large in her mind, the source of the anxiety crawling under her skin.

Cuinn had looked so ill when she left… would he be healed enough to return to Mithranar in time, and, even more importantly, would he be strong enough to use his glamour? She couldn't reveal to the First Blade that the Shadowhawk and Prince Cuinn of Acondor were one and the same man. That was a secret too deadly for anyone to learn. Too many already knew.

But worrying wasn't going to help anything, and in the meantime, she had a direct summons from the king to deal with, so she put her anxiety about tightening timeframes aside and focused on the coming meeting with her family.

Which quickly replaced the anxiety with a rush of guilt.

Her father had been killed only a few months earlier, and his sudden death had been a devastating blow for her and her mother. Talyn had never seen Alyna as lifeless as she had been in the days surrounding Trys Dynan's funeral. Afterwards, her mother had made a formal return to the Dumnorix family and the court of the Twin Thrones.

The Dumnorix protected their own fiercely, and Alyna would have been well supported in the months since Trys's death, but having her daughter nearby would have made things easier too.

Yet Talyn had gone back to Mithranar after the funeral, only to walk straight into a trip to the SkyReach and an attempt on her and the Shadowhawk's lives—in the process realising that the Shadowhawk was actually Prince Cuinn Acondor, third prince of Mithranar and distant Dumnorix relative.

She huffed a breath, torn between guilt and relief that she would get to go back to Mithranar soon. That was the life she wanted, the life she was learning to live again without Sari. She didn't have a Callanan partner at her back anymore, a best friend who knew her every thought and shared her every burden. But she did have six Wolf talons and a Shadowhawk. And sixty other Wolves who were loyal and fierce and good-hearted.

"Good exchange, I say."

"You would." Talyn paused. *"I'd take back what we had without hesitation, Sari."*

"But you don't need to," she said cheerfully. *"You had me for all those years, and now you get them too."*

That was one way of looking at it. A way that, admittedly, was becoming easier to think about accepting.

Despite how unequivocal Aethain's note had been about Talyn and Ariar coming to Ryathl *this very instant,* Talyn was nonetheless astonished to find two Kingshield guards posted at the northern city gate waiting for them. Greylord was half a stride ahead as Ariar and Talyn reined in, sharing a look of mingled surprise and annoyance.

"He didn't?" Ariar greeted Noar, a man Talyn had once trained with, with a look of horror.

"I'm afraid His Grace did, Horselord." Noar saluted respectfully. "Two of us are posted at each of the city gates. We're to ask you to go straight to the palace without stopping."

The second Kingshield had already vanished, presumably running to the palace to inform the king of the Twin Thrones that Talyn and Ariar had arrived.

"I'm so sorry." Talyn's face burned with embarrassment. Kingshield guards were elite fighters—drawn from across the Twin Thrones' various fighting forces—not babysitters. "It can't have been fun standing here all this time just waiting for us."

"It hasn't been too bad." He gave an amiable shrug in the way only an ex-Aimsir could. "And loitering here is a nice break from drill."

"We'll go straight to the palace," she promised.

Noar saluted, shot her a grin, then jogged off in the direction of the Kingshield barracks.

"Go after him and get yourselves some food and rest," Ariar called to the captain of the Kingshield detail milling behind them, before turning to Talyn and lowering his voice. "What did Uncle think we were going to do, stop at a brothel on the way to the palace?"

Her laugh was half-hearted. "I hope nothing bad has happened."

His face turned serious as they urged their horses into the Ryathl city streets. "Me too. Something is going on, though."

"It can't be anything good," Sari said dubiously.

Talyn's stomach knotted. She couldn't agree more.

TALL AND AUSTERE, long raven hair flowing down her back, Alyna Dumnorix stood waiting as Talyn and Ariar were waved through the front gates and into the wide, circular courtyard of the Ryathl palace. Three Kingshield guards hovered protectively nearby, causing Talyn to lift an eyebrow in surprise as she slid out of the saddle—her mother had always refused having her own Kingshield detail.

Alyna's gaze raked over Talyn before the coolness faded from her face and she smiled and opened her arms.

"Mama." Talyn hugged her tightly. "I'm sorry, I probably don't smell great, we've been on the road for days."

"Ah. You're going with smelling bad over 'so sorry I came home and didn't visit you straight away'?" Alyna raised an eyebrow in a mirror image of her daughter. The only difference was the colour of their eyes—dark violet versus deep sapphire.

Talyn winced. "I'm sorry about that too," she said, meaning it. "But you know I wouldn't have left without visiting you."

"Alyna, lovely to see you." Ariar swept in, neatly saving Talyn from the awkwardness. A chuckle escaped her mother as she hugged Ariar.

"How are you, Mama?" Talyn asked once they'd broken apart.

"Getting along well enough." Alyna linked their arms together and Ariar fell into step with them. "You were with Roan and Tarquin?"

"I was." Talyn jerked her thumb in Ariar's direction. "And this one."

"You're forgiven." Alyna squeezed her arm. "You look better, Talyn. Truly."

You don't. It was on the tip of Talyn's tongue, but she swallowed the words. Her mother's skin was drawn taut over her cheekbones and shadows lingered under her violet eyes, suggesting she wasn't sleeping. But if there was anything more soul-destroying, more painful, than losing a Callanan partner, it was probably losing a beloved husband. Her mother needed time. Time and love. So Talyn simply squeezed back. "I assume we're going to see Uncle. What in six thrices is going on?"

Alyna's mouth twitched. "He's in a lather to see you both, but I haven't a clue why."

Who had told any of them about Talyn's arrival in Ryathl? It must have been the First Blade. Or maybe some of the Kingshield guards who'd spotted her at the barracks when she'd visited Ceannar on their arrival from Mithranar had talked and it had gotten back to one of the Dumnorix.

"I didn't rat you out." Ariar lifted his hands in the air when she turned a questioning gaze on him.

Alyna fixed Talyn with a look. "After we've seen Aethain, I hope you're planning on filling me in on what's going on with you and why you're here?"

Talyn hesitated, and her mother didn't miss it. Her voice transitioned from lightly amused to demanding in the space of a heartbeat. "Talyn? What's going on?"

"Let's just see what Uncle wants, and we can talk about it later."

"We'd better." Alyna's tone left no room for argument.

THEY WERE SHOWN into the king's presence immediately. The speed of it *could* be explained by the fact they were family, but Talyn was certain that wasn't it. You didn't post the Kingshield to every gate in the city just because you were keen to know the instant your relatives arrived.

Aethain Dumnorix was alone in his private sitting room, and he rose to meet them, dismissing both Kingshield guards inside the room with a sharp gesture. "Talyn, Ariar, thank you for coming so quickly. It's good to see you."

"And you." Ariar hugged him. "You've got us in a fervour of anticipation, Aethain. This is the first time I can remember actually wanting to be in Ryathl."

Aethain shifted his gaze to Talyn. "I'd have hoped to see you sooner."

She winced at the soft rebuke. "I'm sorry, Uncle."

"What's this about, Aethain?" Alyna asked, sounding impatient.

The king's amber gaze lingered on Talyn's mother, and then Ariar, for a long moment before he seemed to come to a decision and waved them all to chairs by the unlit fireplace. Before taking his own seat, he crossed to the open windows allowing in the summer breeze and closed them both. Talyn observed this behaviour with growing unease.

"Where's Aeris?" she asked after Aethain's son, trying to stall.

"Or Allira and Soar?" Ariar added, naming the remaining members of the Dumnorix family. "This is starting to feel suspiciously like a family meeting."

"Aeris left for Samatia last month. He'll be fostered with Warlord Hadvezer for the next few years. Allira travelled with him for company, and Soar is occupied on another matter."

Ariar's gaze shifted to Talyn, then Alyna, before he leaned against the fireplace instead of taking a chair. "Sober tone of voice noted, Uncle. I'll put my serious hat on. Tell us why we're here."

Aethain didn't prevaricate, but merely shifted his gaze to Talyn. "My summons to you and Ariar was prompted by a visit from Lark Ceannar."

"*Oh, shiiiiii—*"

Talyn cut off Sari's voice as she fought to keep a straight face. Ceannar had told the king who Cuinn was—there was no other reason her uncle would have summoned her and Ariar so precipitously. Or why he had dismissed his guards from the room and closed all the windows before having this conversation.

She should have seen this coming.

"He explained everything to me," Aethain continued. "Including why multiple First Shields have kept the knowledge secret."

"*Everything as in the Shadowhawk thing too?*" Sari's voice wondered.

"*Shush!*"

"Dare I ask?" Alyna glanced between them, eyebrows raised.

"You wanted to know what was going on with me," Talyn muttered, struggling to meet either of their gazes. "He's about to tell you."

"The youngest prince of Mithranar is a Dumnorix," Aethain said. His voice remained mild, but Talyn inwardly winced in anticipation of what was coming. "One with an arguably stronger claim to the Twin Thrones than mine. Talyn, I understand Ceannar's motives, and those of the First Shields before him, but I want you to explain right now why you didn't come to me the moment you were told."

She tried not to shift in her seat, tried to ignore Ariar staring open-mouthed at her, but failed utterly. "The First Shield swore me to secrecy."

"You are not Kingshield and haven't been for months," Aethain said flatly, voice cold and angry now. "You are Dumnorix, you are family. It was your duty to come to me with this. You are no fool, and you know the implications of it as well as I do—for me, *and* my son."

"Uncle..." Talyn started, stopped, took a breath. "Ceannar's reasons for the information being kept secret seemed reasonable, and I didn't feel like I was in a position to decide that the information *should* be shared."

"You are Dumnorix. That is all the position you need."

"Not really." Talyn bore up under his withering glare. "Mama left everything but the name, and that carried to me. I am only a warrior. I hold no influence, decision-making power or status at court."

"Cousin," Alyna spoke, saving Talyn from whatever response Aethain was about to make—it didn't look like a particularly happy one. "Will you explain this properly to Ariar and I? I don't understand."

"Yes. I'm utterly intrigued." Ariar's eyes were bright. "A secret cousin?"

"I think Talyn knows it best of all." Aethain's jaw tightened. "Explain."

Straightening her shoulders, she told her mother and Ariar everything Ceannar had relayed about Cuinn's bloodline, leaving out only his identity as the Shadowhawk. If Ceannar hadn't passed that on to Aethain, then she judged it safer for Cuinn to keep that a secret. By the time she'd finished, Alyna's face was white with shock. "So that's why you were sent to Mithranar by Lark? Not for the Callanan, but to protect this prince."

"Actually no." She wanted to tell as much truth as she could. "The Callanan mission was real—they wanted me to investigate a criminal there. By fortunate timing, the queen of Mithranar reached out to Uncle and the First Shield to request a Kingshield liaison in Mithranar to train their WingGuard in protection. The Callanan request provided a good cover for the First Shield to agree."

"Who else knows about this?" Alyna asked.

"Cuinn's mother, the queen. I think she's always known about

Cuinn's relationship to us." Talyn swallowed, wincing in anticipation of their reaction. "Her request for a Kingshield wasn't about training her WingGuard. It was about seeking protection for Cuinn."

Aethain's face turned to granite. Alyna shot Talyn a disapproving look. Ariar whistled.

"I think you all need to understand the context." Talyn made her voice firm. "Cuinn is no threat to us. He's known in Mithranar as a playboy prince. He parties and drinks and beds every pretty woman that crosses his path. He's also illegitimate and has two legitimate elder brothers." She was skirting perilously close to a lie—but being the Shadowhawk didn't make Cuinn a threat to the Twin Thrones.

Still. Now she was lying to everyone. Lying to Cuinn and the Wolves about his heritage and the threat to their country, and lying to her family about who Cuinn truly was. Such a tangle. It made her head ache, but she wasn't able to reason her way out of it, only to stick to what felt right.

"That might be true now, but what of any children he has?" It was Alyna who pointed out the obvious.

"They will be Mithranan and unaware of their Dumnorix blood. The Twin Thrones are stable—everyone respects your rule, Uncle, and the right of Aeris to rule after you. That isn't going to change." She continued before anyone could protest, throwing the king's earlier words back at him. "And Cuinn is Dumnorix, Uncle. That makes him one of us. It makes him *family*. He deserves our protection."

"From what? Why did you bring him here?" Aethain demanded. "Lark wouldn't give me any details, he insisted it was your story to tell."

Shit. She cleared her throat. How best to make her family understand without them finding out Cuinn's secret? "Can I ask for complete discretion before I answer your question?"

Her mother nodded, face unreadable. Ariar waved a hand. Aethain's mouth thinned. "Go on."

"Prince Cuinn was badly injured around the same time that I learned from one of my informants in Mithranar that there was a threat to his life. I judged he was vulnerable, that I couldn't protect him properly without understanding the threat better, so I thought it best to remove him from the situation." Her uncle's expression told her that she was far from convincing him, so she added more truth. "The threat may originate from within his own family, along with senior WingGuard officers."

"Injured how?" Alyna demanded.

Talyn inwardly swore at her mother's sharpness. For this she would have to lie, and it was one of the hardest things she'd ever done. But if she told them the truth about how Cuinn was hurt, she'd have to tell them he was the Shadowhawk. And as much as she loved and trusted her family, she couldn't risk more people knowing. "In an accident in their mountains. He got drunk and went skimming when he shouldn't have."

"And you're certain of the threat to him?" Aethain asked.

"I am."

Aethain stood, expelling a harsh breath as he spent a few moments pacing the floor. "Talyn, you know I respect you and your abilities. Shia Thorineal has never spoken so highly of any Callanan under her command. More, you are family. Given that, I accept what you're telling me."

Talyn's shoulders relaxed. "Thank you."

"I think it's best if we don't attempt to keep Cuinn's presence in Ryathl a secret," Aethain continued. "It will only look odd if we shroud his visit in mystery. I don't intend to broadcast it, but for anyone who asks, he's simply here on a personal visit to explore Ryathl, not in any formal capacity on behalf of the Mithranan crown."

Alyna nodded. "And since it's not an official visit, that explains why he's not staying at the palace. We'll say we asked the First Shield to make his home available for the prince and his personal guard to stay in. That won't look overly odd either—Lark has one of the nicest residences along the coast."

"And Talyn, you and Lark can make sure nobody gets sight of the prince until he's recovered enough to mask his injuries," Aethain finished. "Does that suit?"

It was a neat solution. Mithanis knew Cuinn was in Ryathl, and by the king of the Twin Thrones treating his presence this way, it would corroborate the claims Cuinn had made in his letters that he was only there to enjoy the beaches. "It does. Thank you."

"I'll have to come out and visit him, of course, observe the diplomatic niceties. Sarana will question it if I don't," Aethain said.

Talyn winced. Alyna caught it. "If he's truly in danger, the best way to keep Cuinn safe is to make everything appear normal," she said. "I imagine you fear Cuinn's brother might consider him meeting us a threat... but won't they question it if we don't make the usual diplomatic overtures?"

"You could write to Queen Sarana once he's gone, Uncle," Ariar suggested. "Use all the usual flowery language but make it clear you think Cuinn is a bit of a useless fool."

"That would work really well." Talyn's shoulders relaxed. Sarana might panic at the idea of Cuinn meeting his true relatives, but a letter like that would soothe any fears Mithanis might have. "Thank you, all of you."

"We are your family, Talyn. But I want Cuinn gone the moment he's recovered enough to do so," Aethain warned.

"Understood."

He rubbed a hand over his jaw, still looking troubled. "Lark told us that Cuinn is unaware of his parentage. Is that true?"

"Yes," Talyn said. The admission made her uncomfortable, as if she were somehow betraying Cuinn by hiding the truth from him. Maybe she was.

"Good." Aethain leaned forward, mouth a thin line. "He *never* knows. Am I clear, Talyn?"

Something inside her strained at that. She didn't want to promise it, even though she understood the necessity. "Don't you think he deserves to know?"

"We are Dumnorix," Alyna reminded her. "It's not about what we deserve. It's about what's best for our people. And Cuinn knowing who he is would be a dangerous thing. I know you see that."

She nodded, unable to say the words even though her mother was right.

"I find I agree." Ariar looked troubled. "At least with things unsettled as they are now."

Aethain's amber gaze landed on her. "Talyn, what you said before, about having no influence or power. Your mother has returned to court. That changes things for you."

Talyn stared between them, jaw tightening. "I don't see how. If I want in, I'll tell you and you can marry me off to the nearest powerful lord's son. Otherwise things stay as they are."

Aethain rubbed at his temples, as if a headache were looming there. "It's not that simple. I'm increasingly uneasy with you being a member of Mithranar's army. If it weren't for your work against Vengeance, I'd insist you return at once. And one day you will have to make a choice like your mother did."

"Then when I find a handsome ship's captain, I'll let you know," she said lightly, trying to dispel the solemn mood that had filled the room. Ariar was looking everywhere but at her, but Alyna was nodding along to everything coming out of Aethain's mouth. It made her deeply uncomfortable.

"That won't be your choice, and you know it," Aethain said quietly. "You've put yourself in a difficult position, Talyn."

She stood, anger rising despite herself. "You and the First Blade put me in that position by forcing Ceannar to send me to Mithranar in the first place." She met her uncle's gaze unflinchingly. "Now, I've ridden for days. I don't want to be rude, but I'd really like a hot bath and a change of clothes."

"You're staying at Ceannar's home with Prince Cuinn?" Alyna asked.

She nodded. "I am captain of his guard, after all."

"You are right that Cuinn is family. He can never know, I insist on that, and if I have my way, nobody else will ever know." Aethain paused. "But I consider by allowing you to remain with his protection detail, I have done my duty by him."

She didn't argue, even though the truth was he was allowing it because of his concerns about Montagn, not because of his duty to Cuinn. Still, at this point he was probably giving her more flexibility than she had any right to expect. After all, Aethain was king. He had to do what was right for the Twin Thrones. "Thank you."

"There is a limit to what I will allow," he warned, echoing her thoughts. "You belong here. Don't forget that."

She glanced at her mother, who smiled. "You know it too, so don't pretend you don't."

Talyn didn't want to get into that, so she simply smiled back. "Do you have time for dinner tonight before I head out of the city?"

"I'd love to. I'm already late for a meeting with Lord Seinn to discuss an issue with trade ships being held too long in Port Lathilly, but I'll meet you in my quarters in a full-turn or two? Why don't you use my bath and steal some fresh clothes from my closet while you wait?"

"That sounds perfect," Talyn said, hugging her mother before Alyna left the room.

"Am I free to return north, or was there more you wanted?" Ariar asked the king.

Aethain's gaze shifted to Talyn, then back to Ariar. "Actually, there are things we need to discuss with the First Blade. I'd appreciate if you could stay a few days."

"This relates to Talyn's work in Mithranar? Because I damn well should be in the loop on that," Ariar said, voice mild despite his firm words.

"If you can trust me with what's going on, you can trust him," Talyn added.

"I'm aware of that," Aethain snapped. "Ariar, you'll be here tomorrow morning, please. I'll have the First Blade here too."

Ariar beamed. "Aye."

"Does my mother already know?" Talyn asked quietly.

"No." Aethain let out a troubled breath. "Not because I don't trust her. But after Trys's death, I didn't want her to be worrying about you being in danger in Mithranar."

Talyn reached out to squeeze his arm. In that moment, he wasn't the king of a powerful kingdom, he was merely a worried relative. "That's not what we do, Uncle. We don't protect each other from things we are strong enough to face. We don't hold each other back."

He smiled, amber eyes lightening. "Ariar, bring Alyna with you in the morning."

Ariar nodded. "Burn bright and true."

"Burn bright and true," Talyn and Aethain spoke together.

CHAPTER 5

*S*he ended up sleeping on her mother's couch after they'd shared dinner and talked late into the night. But as soon as dawn lit up the horizon she was riding out of the city and along the coast to Ceannar's estate, a sea breeze whipping around her and Fire-Flare and taking the edge off the already warm morning.

Eagerness and worry filled her. Eagerness to see her Wolves and Cuinn—she'd missed them more than she cared to admit during her time away—and worry for Cuinn's health... for facing all of them with the secrets she held.

After stabling FireFlare she walked around the side of the house towards the back courtyard. Surrounded by greenery, its southern end had a shoulder-high stone wall separating Ceannar's estate from an unending vista of calm, turquoise ocean.

The thought came to her that maybe one day, when she was too old to fight anymore, a place just like this, by the water, might be nice —nothing but the sound of the waves washing ashore in the distance and the occasional call of a seabird.

"That won't be your choice, and you know it." Her uncle's words from the day before came back to her, and a shudder rippled down her

spine. Pushing aside gloomy thoughts, she stretched, took a deep breath of sea air, and wished she had a cup of kahvi in her hands.

She'd just come through the gate when she caught the sound of laughter on the morning breeze. Heart leaping, she looked towards the source of it.

Corrin stepped into the opposite end of the yard, his back to her, tossing a ball in his hands, his laughter still ringing out. The worry that had been wound tight inside her uncoiled on a small exhalation of breath. Her youngest talon wouldn't be sounding so light-hearted if anything had gone wrong in her absence. If Cuinn wasn't okay.

Zamaril appeared next, his narrow features more reserved as he reached out to catch the ball and shove it playfully into Corrin's chest. They scuffled for a moment, before their attention was caught by Halun and Andres coming through the gate after them.

Corrin tossed the ball to Halun, calling out something Talyn couldn't hear. Halun caught the ball, dropped it and kicked it back. At a word from Andres, all the Wolves' attention quickly turned to the person following him through the gate.

Cuinn.

On his feet.

She bit her lip, the relief that flooded through her at the sight close to overwhelming. The prince moved slowly, leaning heavily on a walking stick, but he was upright. Tiercelin paced protectively at his side.

She kept watching, drinking it in, as Cuinn limped heavily across the courtyard, his silver-white wings spread wide to either side to help him balance.

He must have sensed something of her relief and pleasure because he looked up suddenly, green gaze cutting straight to hers. They stared at each other a moment—his Dumnorix blood clear as day to her now he wasn't hiding himself behind glamour and song magic—and her hands curled at her sides, her breath escaping her in a rush. For a moment it didn't matter that she couldn't tell him about the threat from Montagn or his true bloodline, or that she'd lied to her family about his identity as the Shadowhawk.

Those were problems for another day.

Right now... he was all right. And that meant everything.

Smile stretching across her face, she walked towards them. Halun lifted his arm in a delighted wave. Andres's perfect posture straightened impossibly further.

"Captain!" Corrin's eyes lit up. "When did you arrive?"

"I just rode in," she said.

"It's good to have you back," Zamaril said. There was a slight stiffness to his bearing, but the words were sincere. She gave him a warm nod. Demoting him for his rogue actions in Montagn—stealing Halun's niece from the ahara and putting them all in danger—had been the hardest thing she'd ever done as a commander. It was also the easiest decision she'd had to make. Only time would tell if the thief accepted it.

"It's good to see you, Captain Dynan." This rich, musical voice belonged to Cuinn.

"And you." She was pleased to see that the luminous glow had returned to his emerald eyes, and the pallor of sickness was almost completely vanished from his skin. All at once she was enveloped with his delight at seeing her—his song magic in use—and she felt an answering pleasure sweep through her. "You're on your feet," she said warmly.

Cuinn motioned to the healer. "I am, thanks to Tiercelin."

"I wouldn't have been able to do half as much if you hadn't been such a determined and brave patient." Tiercelin smiled at Talyn. "Welcome back, Captain."

"Have you had breakfast yet?" Cuinn asked her. "I'm not allowed until I've completed my morning walk in this courtyard, so we could eat together."

Her stomach rumbled at the mention of food—she'd been too nervous with worry to eat before leaving the palace, and now her relief at the sight of Cuinn left her feeling like she could eat a horse. "That sounds great."

Pleased surprise lit up his green eyes at her quick acquiescence, and he stepped forward, stopping only when Tiercelin placed a cautionary hand on his arm. "Be careful, Your Highness. No quick moves, remember."

"I remember, Tiercelin." Cuinn sounded momentarily snappish, but nonetheless slowed his forward movement.

Talyn fell into step with him as they made their slow way to the other side of the yard, the Wolves falling in around them in a traditional protective formation.

"Is everything well, Captain?" Cuinn asked.

She hesitated, tried to think of how to answer that honestly. "At this very moment, seeing you so recovered... yes, everything is well."

"But there are things to discuss," he said, determination rippling over his features.

Taken aback—she'd never seen determination on Prince Cuinn Acondor's face before—she simply said, "There are. But I think we can enjoy breakfast first."

CEANNAR WAS ALREADY EATING when Cuinn and Talyn arrived. Breakfast had been laid out in a terrace that ran along the eastern wall of the main house. The wooden trellis that fenced off all but the southern length of the courtyard was covered with colourful white and blue flowers that gave off a sweet scent. The open edge of the yard looked straight to the estate's wall and the ocean beyond.

A wary look filled the First Blade's expression when he saw Talyn. "Captain Dynan, you're back."

Inwardly she smiled—he looked like a man awaiting a particularly nasty form of torture. "I am. It's good to see you, sir."

His eyebrows shot upwards. "You're still talking to me?"

"You did what you felt you had to." After having a night to think on it, she wasn't angry at Ceannar. After all, he was First Shield to Aethain, and his ultimate loyalty had to be to his king, not her. He'd simply done what he felt was right. She took the seat opposite him, trying not to make it obvious that she was keeping a careful eye on the gingerly sitting Cuinn. The glare the prince shot in her direction indicated she failed.

"Am I missing something?" Cuinn asked.

"Our host leaked to my family that I'm here," she said lightly. "I was sent a message in Port Lathilly with strict orders to return immediately."

Cuinn's eyes narrowed, as if he were putting pieces together. "And the First Shield knows your family because he's responsible for protecting them. Because I was right when I guessed you were a member of the Dumnorix family, wasn't I?"

Talyn's glance brushed over Tiercelin—the Wolf standing in the space between Cuinn and Ceannar—and he gave her a little shrug in return. They'd kept her secret. Another example of their fierce loyalty to her. For the first time, it made her uncomfortable. Ceannar remained silent, suddenly paying increased attention to his plate of food.

"Captain?" Cuinn pressed.

"Yes, you guessed right," she said softly. And he'd done it on the very first occasion she'd met him as the Shadowhawk. At the time it had astounded and unsettled her, how quickly he'd put it together, but now it made more sense. He'd already interacted with her as Prince Cuinn, and no doubt his song magic told him all kinds of things she'd prefer he didn't know.

His gaze pierced her. "How closely related?"

"My mother is the king's first cousin. He's my... uncle of sorts," she said.

Cuinn placed his fork down carefully, lined it up with his plate. She wished she had his magic, so she could tell what reaction he was currently holding back in favour of a more diplomatic one. "And the fact you just announced it within hearing distance of the five Wolves keeping watch tells me they already know."

"They do." It was going to take some time to adjust to the fact this indolent, spoiled prince had the same sharp brain as the Shadowhawk. Andres had been the last to find out about her heritage, but she'd told them all one by one, after her father's death.

His mouth tightened. "Why did they send you to Mithranar?"

She sat back, her turn to direct a pointed look—at Ceannar. He could dig them out of this one. Besides, the Shadowhawk had already guessed most of it. "Tell him, sir. About the Callanan request. He deserves that much."

Ceannar cleared his throat. "Your mother requested a Kingshield guard to assist in training her WingGuard in close protection, Your Highness. The answer was going to be no, despite the rich payment in izerdia she offered—the Kingshield only exist to protect the Dumnorix. However, our Callanan First Blade asked me to reconsider, as a favour. She wanted someone to investigate a criminal figure known as the Shadowhawk."

Cuinn's entire body turned rigid and he spun to Talyn. "You *told* him."

Not for the first time she cursed his song magic—presumably it was obvious to Cuinn that Ceannar knew who he was. "I did. The First Shield is a man I trust implicitly, Prince Cuinn, at least with this. You know I wouldn't have told him otherwise."

"I won't betray your secret, Your Highness. I haven't." With those last words Ceannar gave Talyn a little nod. She relaxed slightly at the confirmation he hadn't told her uncle the full truth. "As to your first question, Talyn was chosen to fulfil your mother's request because of her Mithranan heritage, but also because she'd previously been Callanan."

Cuinn lifted a hand to rub over his eyes, and a sudden wave of hurt mingled with despair hit her like she'd been slapped in the face. It vanished as quickly as it had come, suggesting he'd reined the emotion in immediately. "So I was right. You didn't really come back to help the Shadowhawk. You returned to investigate me for the Callanan?"

"Not exactly," she said. Part of her wanted to ask everyone to leave, so she could have this conversation with Cuinn alone, but the rest of her felt the Wolves deserved to hear it too. "Like the First Shield says, I initially went to Mithranar tasked to learn more about the Shadowhawk. That's why I tracked you down. I reported back and then I went home. That would have been the end of it…"

"But?" Cuinn asked softly. The terrace had gone still and quiet.

"After I came home, the First Blade told me they needed to know more, not just about the Shadowhawk, but Vengeance too. The Callanan were convinced you..." She glanced at Cuinn, looked away. "...were part of the gang. They asked me to use the cover I'd already established in Mithranar and go back, infiltrate your network and gain access to Vengeance."

"You came back to spy on me." He couldn't hide the misery in his voice, and it shocked her so much she hesitated before speaking again. By then it was too late, he was already levering himself upwards. "I think I've lost my appetite."

She shot to her feet, the words spilling out before she consciously made the decision to speak. "I never truly thought you were working with Vengeance, but I would do anything to protect my home, including investigating a criminal gang that could be a potential threat. But none of that matters anyway. The real truth is that the First Blade's request suited me, because what I wanted more than anything else, after two years of feeling nothing but grief and aching despair, was to go back to Mithranar and be a Wolf. To help the Shadowhawk."

The words ended with a single, gulping breath. More honesty than she'd breathed—even to herself—in a long time. It left her shaken, raw. It resounded through the quiet morning, striking everything still. She didn't say any more. Cuinn's magic would tell him the truth of her words.

"They helped you," Cuinn said quietly, wonderingly.

"They taught me how to live again." She couldn't look any of them in the eye, could barely keep her gaze steady on Cuinn's face, but it was another truth they deserved to hear. Ceannar didn't seem to know where to look. And Cuinn... his understanding reached out to her, a soft touch, then he took a deep breath, tried to hide a wince, and gingerly sat back down. "Talons, please join us."

Andres cleared his throat, but none of them seemed to know how to respond to that request. Talons didn't eat with princes and Dumnorix family members. Talyn still couldn't look at any of them.

"Sit down." The prince waved an impatient hand. "There's enough food here for an army."

"I'll make sure to pass that compliment on to my cook," Ceannar said dryly.

That seemed to break the tension. One by one the Wolves took seats around the table. Talyn resumed hers, taking several moments to lift her eyes from the tabletop. By then, her men were serving themselves food and the attention had shifted away from her.

"Did you enjoy visiting Sari's family, Captain?" Cuinn spoke conversationally, as if the past few moments had never transpired.

"I did. Very much."

"I wish you'd stayed with them longer. There is really no need for you to be here—it will be a few weeks yet before I'm walking right."

Zamaril coughed and Cuinn seemed to realise what he'd said. "I just meant—"

She waved him off, mouth curling in a smile. "I would have, but the family summons was not to be ignored."

"Captain, given your agreement with the First Blade to allow her people to talk to the Shadowhawk, I assume they no longer suspect he is a member of Vengeance?" Tiercelin spoke a few moments later.

She hesitated in responding, toying with the food on her plate, not sure how much to reveal and how much to hide. She hated lying to her Wolves.

"They have accepted my assurances that the Shadowhawk is not part of the gang," she said eventually. "But the Callanan concerns about Vengeance are genuine. In fact, they're serious enough that I've agreed to keep working for them in Mithranar."

Ceannar coughed, clearly uncomfortable she was discussing Callanan operations in front of foreigners, but she ignored him.

"That's why you agreed to let them talk to the Shadowhawk?" Cuinn asked.

"Yes." Sort of. Not really. But she couldn't tell him the real truth—that she'd bargained the Shadowhawk for the First Blade briefing Ceannar on the full Montagni threat, so that he would help her in turn with sheltering the badly hurt Cuinn. Ugh, it was such a tangle of lies and secrets, and she hated it. She buried the guilt before it rose strongly enough that Cuinn would sense it.

"I don't pretend to understand why the Callanan care so much about a criminal gang in Mithranar, no matter how violent or capable, and no doubt there is more information I'm not privy to." Cuinn's look told her he knew very well she was hiding things. "But Vengeance is a serious problem, particularly given what we were told about their goal of causing instability in my mother's rule. Having Twin Thrones assistance with the problem—even if it's only an undercover Callanan operative—is welcome." He spoke with an easy authority none of them had ever seen before, hidden as it had always been behind his playboy glamour. It checked her. She kept forgetting Cuinn was a man she didn't really know at all.

"Dangerous would be a better way of putting it, Your Highness," Tiercelin pointed out. "If your mother or Prince Mithanis learned the captain was working for the Callanan, or that we were helping her, we all know what the consequences would be. There certainly wouldn't be any *welcoming* involved."

"With all due respect, our job is protecting you, Prince Cuinn," Andres said in his quiet way, siding with Tiercelin. "Not helping the Callanan or hunting criminals. And Vengeance now thinks the Shadowhawk is dead. They won't come for him again—the Wolves have no further need to be involved."

Talyn had to stop herself shifting in discomfort. Ceannar picked up a piece of toast and began chewing vigorously. Vengeance weren't just a criminal group. And the threat they posed wasn't just to the Shadowhawk. Dammit, she *hated* having to keep all these secrets.

"I disagree, Talon Tye. If Vengeance's true purpose is to sow unrest and dissent in order to topple my family's throne, then that places me, a prince of that family, under threat," Cuinn said. "Not to mention Vengeance were also after the Wolves. We can't assume they won't come after you again."

"We need to be careful about what the man I tortured told us," Talyn interjected. "I resorted to that because the mines were about to collapse around us, but stabbing someone in the privates isn't a reliable method of getting accurate information. The fact he claimed Prince Mithanis was behind Vengeance is proof of that. Your brother is a certainty to be nominated as heir—he has no need to create dissent to take power."

Cuinn frowned slightly. "That all makes sense, but look at what Vengeance has done so far—murders in Dock City, an assassination attempt on my mother, likely murdering several powerful winged folk... then the operation they mounted to ambush us in the mines? They're too active, too well-resourced, not to have some specific goal in mind." He raised his hand and began ticking off fingers. "Lose a queen, and you get a power vacuum, no matter how temporary. Murder influential winged folk without repercussions, you create unease amongst the ruling elite. Rile up the humans enough that they start thinking about acting against their rulers... more instability."

He was right, having summed it up exactly as she would have were she in his position—he just didn't know that it was *Montagn* looking to exploit that dissent. That the Callanan informant claimed the ahara wanted to take Mithranar. But she still didn't understand how Mithanis fit in, or why the dying Vengeance member had told them the prince of night was behind the group's activities. Why tell part of the truth and lie about Mithanis?

"*I think we're missing a piece, something that links together the two things he told you.*"

"*You think all of it was the truth? He was in a lot of pain, Sari.*"

"*I know, but... someone is directing Vengeance, and the First Blade's information indicates that it's Montagn. But who specifically is in Mithranar pulling their strings?*"

And it wasn't just the Callanan informant that linked Vengeance to Montagn. The man she'd tortured had a Montagni slave tattoo hidden under the copper masks the group wore. Only Cuinn had seen it, and neither of them had mentioned it to the Wolves. Because of Halun, the entire wing was sensitive to the topic of slaves.

"*That's a good question. Also, Vengeance isn't a new gang—they know their operating ground too well and they had numbers enough for the assassi-*"

nation squad and the ambush on us. Yet their activities only started a year or so ago. What changed?" Talyn mused.

"Maybe a new leader?"

"Or someone in their leader's ear. Someone whispering on behalf of Montagn."

"Like a prince of night with song magic?"

"And that's where you lose me. There is no obvious motivation for him to destabilise a country he wants to become king of." Even so, Talyn resolved to have a longer conversation with Cuinn privately. The Shadowhawk likely knew the gang, even if he wasn't aware of it.

They were all looking at her, waiting for a response to Cuinn. She shrugged. "Either way, I think we can all agree that Vengeance needs to be destroyed."

Corrin's eyebrows shot up. "That's what the Callanan have tasked you to do?"

She nodded.

A silence fell over the table. Understandably, none of her talons looked pleased with this announcement. The situation was growing more complicated—well beyond the scope of a protection detail—and placing them all at more risk.

"I won't be involving the Wolves." She tried to reassure them. "And your safety will always be my primary consideration before I do anything. I promise you that."

Zamaril looked thoughtful. Talyn wondered what he was thinking, but didn't press. If he had something to say, he'd tell her when he was ready. Cuinn didn't say anything either, but the look in his green eyes was as thoughtful as Zamaril's as he turned back to his food.

"You ever going to acknowledge the other thing your captured prisoner said?" Sari enquired.

"His mumbling about someone wanting to protect me, or keep me out of it, or whatever that was?" Talyn gave the equivalent of a dismissive mental shrug. "That made even less sense than the Mithanis thing."

"It's odd though. I don't like it."

"We have far bigger knots to untangle, Sari, I'm not wasting my time on that."

A sigh. *"Same old Talyn. Careless with her own safety."*

"Not careless. Just well able to take care of herself."

"If that's what you'd like to call it."

Talyn ignored her and dug into her breakfast with renewed enthusiasm. Worrying about the future could come after her eggs and toast.

CHAPTER 6

*T*alyn spent the following weeks pushing herself and the talons hard, sharpening their edge, making them stronger and faster and fitter. The intense practice time saw steady improvement in their already formidable capabilities. Zamaril had reached such a level of skill with his sword that he sorely tested her each time they sparred. It wouldn't be long before he'd be beating her in a duel of swordsmanship. Corrin wasn't far behind.

Shia would be green with envy if she saw either of them in action. Talyn smiled each time she thought of it.

Tiercelin spent long stretches of each day with Cuinn. The effort both were putting into Cuinn's recovery was impressive and both looked exhausted and pale most of the time. For this reason she decided to hold off talking to Cuinn about how his work as the Shadowhawk might provide insights about Vengeance until he was stronger.

It was odd, adjusting to being around the real Cuinn Acondor, a man who was neither an overly-intense human criminal nor playboy prince, but parts of both, with intriguing hints of something else… something she suspected might be a natural instinct for ruling. Whatever it was though, it was buried deep, so deep she wasn't even sure he was aware of it.

And while it was evident that he found quiet joy in finally being able to be himself with Talyn and her talons, she wondered sometimes whether, after hiding and pretending for so long, he knew exactly who his real self was either.

"TIERCELIN SAYS I'll be ready to go soon." Cuinn scraped up the remains of his plate, forking it into his mouth. His appetite had begun to return, something that pleased the healer—and the rest of the highly observant Wolves—to no end.

She nodded. "And your glamour?"

"My magic wasn't affected by the fall." He shrugged. "I'll be fine to meet with your Callanan, Captain. Dock City is home territory—they won't guess a thing, I promise."

A smile curled her mouth. "They're going to love you."

He waggled his eyebrows at her. "Doesn't everyone? I'm disgustingly beautiful."

"Not as the Shadowhawk you're not." She snorted, almost spitting toast crumbs onto her plate. "Then you're boring and scruffy. I can't believe I never saw through it."

Ceannar glanced at Talyn. "Will the Callanan be sending more warriors to Mithranar to support you?" The First Shield seemed to have given up any pretence of being uncomfortable with Cuinn knowing Callanan business. Now he was focused on the fact a Dumnorix family member was set to undertake a highly dangerous mission far from any Kingshield protection.

"The First Blade hasn't offered, but I would turn her down if she did," Talyn said. "It's bad enough two Callanan are travelling there to speak with the Shadowhawk. Tiercelin was right the other day—Prince Mithanis needs to be considered, and how he would respond to Callanan interference in Mithranar, especially if there was any hint that it was at Prince Cuinn's instigation. His safety is my priority."

"No it's not," Cuinn said mildly. "You might not be Callanan anymore, but you're still Dumnorix, which means your priority is keeping the Twin Thrones safe."

He was right. But it didn't feel *entirely* right. She shifted in her chair, trying to come up with a response, but was saved by the sound of the bell at Ceannar's front gates ringing. Andres appeared a moment later, eyebrows raised in question. "Are you expecting visitors, First Shield?"

He shook his head.

"I'll go." Talyn rose. Not only was it an opportunity to escape a suddenly uncomfortable conversation, she wanted to be the first to greet whoever this was.

"I should come too. It will look odd otherwise," Ceannar said. "It would be best for you to stay here, Prince Cuinn."

"I'll stay put, I promise." Cuinn began piling more eggs onto his plate.

She glanced at Andres. "Keep Prince Cuinn and the Wolves out of sight until I tell you different."

He saluted. "Will do, Captain."

The gates were being opened by Ceannar's steward when they reached the entrance courtyard. A group of riders waited beyond, kicking up a cloud of dust as they urged their horses through the opening. All wore the night-black of the Kingshield.

That could mean one thing only—a Dumnorix was visiting. Immediately she tensed. Ceannar threw her a look, as if to say *this is your fault.*

"You're the one who told them I was here," she muttered.

She scanned the riders for a familiar face, her gaze first alighting on Ariar. He hadn't spotted her yet, though, his attention on a conversation with the captain of his Kingshield.

"Well, they aren't here for me," Ceannar said cheerfully. "I'll leave you to your greetings and warn my housekeeper to prepare for guests."

She glanced after him with a little smile, amused by his desire to escape, but her attention was torn away as one of the riders detached from the pack. His long hair was braided Bearman-style and his skin tanned an even deeper brown than usual from the sun. Instead of the Kingshield black he wore simple leathers akin to the niever-flyers of his homeland.

"Tarcos." Her mouth dropped open in surprise at the sight of the Firthlander prince. "What are you doing here?"

"*Uh oh.*" A hint of glee edged Sari's words.

"*Shut up,*" Talyn muttered, discomfort twisting her insides. She'd almost completely forgotten that she'd decided to end her relationship with Tarcos the next time she saw him. Not to mention his presence at Ceannar's estate was an added risk to Cuinn. Tarcos was no fool and she didn't want him sensing anything amiss.

He dismounted, smiling widely before wrapping his arms around her. "Talyn, it's wonderful to see you."

They hugged tightly—it *was* good to see him—and by the time they parted Ariar was making his way over with a relaxed, loose stride. "Cousin!" He wrapped an affectionate arm around her.

"Ariar. What brings you here? I thought you'd have escaped Ryathl by now," she asked.

"I'm here to visit you, obviously." Ariar threw a grin at Tarcos that was matched in a slightly quieter way. The Firthlander prince kept his thoughts and feelings to himself, but it looked like the two men had become fast friends during Tarcos' recent stint with Ariar in the mountains. He was also perceptive, and offered them both a little bow. "I'll see to our horses, Ariar."

Once Tarcos was gone, some of Ariar's merriment faded. "Sorry."

"What were you thinking?" she hissed. "Cuinn meeting Dumnorix family members is one thing, but a Firthlander prince too?"

"I heard your concerns loud and clear, Talyn, but Tarcos asked to come with me when I mentioned I was visiting you. It was either let him come, or be all weird and mysterious about why he couldn't." Ariar shrugged. "He already knows Cuinn is here. At least this way he doesn't get the idea anything odd is going on."

"You shouldn't have come at all."

"You didn't seriously think I'd go back north without meeting Cuinn, did you?" He rolled his eyes when her expression didn't soften.

"I'm sorry, truly. I didn't realise Tarcos would be so insistent on coming. Maybe you should have visited him already." Amusement flashed over his face. "He's quite smitten with you, Tal."

Talyn winced inwardly. He had a point. Wanting to keep a low profile, she hadn't left the estate in the weeks since arriving, but she should have made a visit to the palace to talk to Tarcos and stave off any curiosity about Cuinn.

"And you too, it seems," she deflected quickly. "You've become good friends."

"He's a good man. A little too serious at times, but good. He'll make a decent future warlord of Firthland."

"Oh, is that what Uncle is expecting? Clever of him to send Tarcos to spend a few months with you, then, wasn't it? It certainly won't hurt to have the next warlord of Firthland a close friend of a Dumnorix prince."

Ariar grinned. "Says the Dumnorix woman courting the next warlord of Firthland! Uncle has to be practically salivating at that potential match."

"We're not courting." She huffed her breath in frustration at Ariar's teasing, and changed the subject, linking her arm through his. "Come on through and I'll introduce you to Cuinn."

Ceannar must have guessed at the reason for Ariar's visit and warned Cuinn and the Wolves. By the time Talyn showed Ariar through, the breakfast meal had been cleared away and Cuinn was on his feet, the Wolf talons hovering protectively around the edges of the terrace.

Ariar's eyebrows shot skyward as they entered, and he let out a long whistle. "Will you look at those wings!"

"Impressive, aren't they?" Talyn chuckled, remembering how she'd felt the first time she saw a winged person. She stepped forward, opening her mouth to make introductions, but Ariar was already striding past her, offering a friendly hand to Cuinn. "Prince Cuinn Acondor, I take it?"

"That's right." Cuinn glanced between Talyn and Ariar as he limped over, taking Ariar's hand and shaking briskly. This visit had surprised him. "Judging from those eyes, I'm guessing you're another of the famed Dumnorix family?"

"This is Prince Ariar Dumnorix, my cousin," Talyn said.

Ariar dropped Cuinn's hand and let out another whistle. "I'm not sure I approve. Could it possibly be that there is someone alive more beautiful than me?"

Cuinn laughed, a rich musical sound that had the Wolves and Talyn smiling and Ariar's eyes widening further.

"I hope you don't mind me coming to stay a day or two? I was in Ryathl for some deathly boring meetings and needed something to do to break the tedium. Spending a day or two getting to know a foreign prince seemed like just the thing," Ariar said. "I do promise I am the most interesting and entertaining of the family."

Cuinn smiled. "Are you claiming that you're not as stubborn and serious as Captain Dynan?"

"I'm quite the opposite." Ariar chuckled as Talyn scowled.

"Am I interrupting?"

Ariar and Talyn turned as Tarcos hesitated at the terrace entrance, his brown eyes wide as he stared at Cuinn.

"Not at all." Ariar waved him over. "Prince Cuinn, this is Lord Tarcos Hadvezer. He's one of Warlord Hadvezer's nephews."

Tarcos offered his hand. "You're the prince Talyn has been guarding?"

"That's right," Cuinn said easily. His prince persona was perfectly in place, the faint hint of glamour flawless, removing all of Talyn's concerns that he might not be strong enough to deal with the Callanan. Now, even though she knew the Shadowhawk lurked behind that mask, it was impossible to see it. "It's nice to meet you, Lord Hadvezer."

Ariar huffed a breath. "All these titles are getting on my nerves. Do you mind terribly if we dispense with formalities, Prince Cuinn?"

"Not at all. Tarcos, are you here to stay as well?"

Talyn stiffened slightly in surprise. Cuinn hadn't waited for Tarcos's agreement before dropping his title, and she was sure she hadn't mistaken the slight edge to his voice as he asked the question.

"I am, actually. Talyn isn't home very often," Tarcos said amiably. "I'd like to spend as much time with her as possible before she leaves again."

There was nothing wrong with Tarcos's words, but they made her uncomfortable nonetheless. She really needed to talk to him in private. Judging from Cuinn's expression, he hadn't liked them much either, though he hid it well beneath a bland smile.

"Good." Ariar nodded in satisfaction, glancing at Talyn. "Do you think Lark would mind if we broke open his cellar? It was a dusty ride out here, and I could use a drink."

"YOU LOOK TROUBLED," Tarcos commented, glancing over at her. The two of them had saddled up, leaving Cuinn and Ariar to each other's company, to take a long ride. Since Ariar's arrival the day before, the two princes had gotten along enormously well. Ariar's relaxed attitude and natural curiosity meant he'd conversed as eagerly with the Wolf talons as Cuinn, and they'd all gone to bed the previous night leaving Ariar and Tiercelin in the kitchens talking through the fine details of how Aimsir abilities might have some magical source.

She'd suggested the ride to Tarcos at breakfast, partly because she'd been comfortable leaving Ariar alone with Cuinn, but also because she'd been keen to get Tarcos away for a while. As much as Ariar and Cuinn had instantly clicked, it seemed the opposite between the Firthlander and Mithranan prince. They were painfully polite to each other, but she could sense the underlying tension each time she looked at them, and wondered at the source of it.

"You also have to talk to Tarcos, which you haven't done yet."

"Patience is a virtue." Talyn sniffed.

"Oh, is that what it is?"

"Just juggling a few different things at the moment," she said aloud. So far their conversation had remained deliberately light, but it seemed Tarcos had picked up on her underlying worries. "Since you asked though, what's your problem with Cuinn?"

He gave her a look, like that was the strangest question he'd heard in a while. "You're surprised that I don't think much of him? He's a pretty airhead, Tal. Tell me he's at least had one serious thought in his life?"

"That's harsh," she said, stung. Not that she could blame Tarcos. Cuinn wasn't overplaying the drinking, partying prince persona like he did in Mithranar, but it was the one he'd been wearing since Ariar and Tarcos's arrival. Ariar, who had much the same streak running through him, didn't seem to have a problem with it. But of course rigidly honourable Tarcos would.

"I can't understand why you went back for that," he said mildly.

"I've told you. It wasn't for him." She shook her head, looking to change the subject. Time to try and figure out a way to start the conversation about ending their relationship. Not because she'd stopped liking or respecting Tarcos, but because she was no longer interested in a relationship with him. Things had changed too much. Aethain's words had scared her too much. It was time he knew that. "Enough about me, anyway. I've been meaning to ask, how are you doing?"

"What do you mean?" He brought his horse closer.

"The First Blade mentioned your uncle has been having some trouble with sentiment running against the Twin Thrones."

"There's a nice, clean segue into discussing your relationship." Sari snorted.

"Shut up."

Tarcos let out a long sigh. "It's strongest amongst the niever-flyers, though the Bearmen and Armun are affected too. But I told you already, they're just restless young warriors who dream of restoring the honour of the old days, when we ruled ourselves."

"You effectively *do* rule yourselves," she pointed out.

"That's easy to say when it's your kingdom that holds ultimate sovereignty over us," Tarcos said. "You Dumnorix might not pull on our leash now, when you don't need to, but that doesn't mean you won't."

She frowned. "Tarcos, don't tell me you agree with them?"

"I'm saying I understand where they're coming from." He wore his most serious look, warm eyes steady on hers. "I'm a prince of Firth-land. I need to understand the concerns of *all* my people. You agree with that, surely?"

She did. It was an admirable quality and one she shared. But they'd gotten well off track. She opened her mouth to change the subject back to them, but he spoke before she could.

"Speaking of, my uncle has informed me that he intends to name me heir," Tarcos said quietly, pride warming his brown eyes. There was something else there, too, a deep satisfaction and joy that almost vibrated from him with its intensity.

"This is what you really want," she said, understanding properly for the very first time. She knew he'd thought about it, liked the idea of being heir, but she hadn't guessed how badly he wanted it.

"It is."

"Then I'm happy for you." She reached over to squeeze his hand. "Am I going to have to start addressing you as Warlord Hadvezer?"

"Not yet." He smiled, but it quickly faded as he brought his horse even closer. "I wanted to ask—"

"Six thrices!" She swore in surprise. Ceannar's estate had come into sight, and the exterior of the walls was crawling with dark-clad figures. Kingshield.

"Talyn, what..." Tarcos's voice trailed off as he saw what she did. "Is that Kingshield?"

"I think so." She urged FireFlare into a gallop, Tarcos not far behind.

Her uncle must have come for his promised visit.

The approach of their horses was noticed, of course, and a King-shield captain came out to meet her and Tarcos. "King Aethain and your mother arrived earlier, Captain Dynan," he said briskly. "We've met before, if you remember. I'm Captain Dunnil."

"They're both here?" she asked, startled again. At Tarcos' confused glance, she smoothed the surprise from her face and tried to appear relaxed.

"Quite the family reunion." Sari chuckled.

"Yes, Captain."

"Right." She smiled, finally remembering her manners. "And of course I remember you, Captain Dunnil. You taught protection formations when I first joined the Kingshield. They were some of my favourite classes."

"I'm glad you thought so," he said. "I spoke with Prince Cuinn's guards when we arrived. If you're happy, I'll continue to coordinate with them while we're here?"

"That sounds fine."

"Thank you, Captain," he said politely, then left.

Talyn and Tarcos rode into the entry courtyard, and Tarcos offered to take FireFlare and get her settled in the stables. "Best I not intrude on your family gathering."

"Thanks. I'll see you later?" They still had to talk, after all.

"Count on it." That warm smile filled his face again.

All thoughts of a difficult conversation with Tarcos faded from her mind as Talyn headed for the main house.

"This should be fun," Sari said gleefully.

"Not quite the word I'd use."

Why had both the king and her mother decided to come—when they must have known Ariar was already here? If Mithanis got wind of this somehow...

"How?" Sari asked practically. *"You've seen the WingGuard—don't tell me you think the Acondors have a half-decent spy force?"*

"No... but I wouldn't put anything past the prince of night."

"I think you're becoming infected by Cuinn's fear of his brother to the detriment of common sense. Sarana remains queen in Mithranar and she knows who her son is."

"You're right. But his Dumnorix blood is supposed to be a secret from Cuinn too, remember?"

And Talyn hadn't thought to warn them about his song magic.

CHAPTER 7

$\mathcal{T}$he Dumnorix family was eating on Ceannar's terrace, where they had a clear view of the sparkling ocean. The First Shield gave her a firmly unhappy look as Talyn appeared—presumably unimpressed that he was playing host to four Dumnorix and their full Kingshield details—and she gave him a little shrug in response. She wasn't the one who had invited them all here.

Alyna rose from the table. "Talyn."

"Mama." Talyn hugged her tightly, before stepping back to study her mother's face. During the long dinner they'd shared weeks earlier, it had been clear Alyna was working hard to appear like she was fine.

But she wasn't, and that was even clearer now in the bright light of day. Alyna had aged since the death of her husband—her once raven hair now had streaks of grey through it, and those violet eyes had lost some of their luminous Dumnorix glow. It made Talyn miss her father even more deeply. She'd hoped that her mother's grief would fade with time, but the pain was still evidently there.

"You still grieve me, Tal, and he was her husband."

"Not just her husband. She gave up everything for him and never regretted it once."

"She loved him."

"I don't think I have that kind of love or devotion in me." She couldn't imagine it. Had always struggled with understanding it in her mother. What single person could compete with living the life she loved?

"It's good to see you again so soon." Alyna gave her another quick hug before sitting down.

"Uncle." Talyn greeted Aethain. His return smile, full of genuine pleasure at seeing her, indicated some of his anger had faded.

"Come over and have something to eat, Tal." Ariar waved her to the chair next to his. "We just started. There's plenty of food left."

Cuinn sent her a quick smile of greeting across the table. Sitting amongst them, he couldn't have been a starker contrast to the sober Dumnorix guests with his golden beauty and great silver-white wings.

Fortunately, easy conversation carried throughout the meal without much input needed from Talyn. She ignored the occasional questioning look Cuinn threw her way, internally cursing his blasted magic. Who knew what he was picking up from the Dumnorix ranged around him—she could hardly warn them about his magic in front of him without making it obvious they were all hiding something. Her discomfort increased, a tight ball of anxiousness forming in her stomach.

As far as she could tell, Aethain seemed interested simply in getting to know Cuinn a little better. He was polite, cordial, but distant, like any ruler meeting a foreign prince. Ariar gamely filled any awkward gap in conversation, winning her eternal gratitude. Alyna didn't speak much either, and as soon as she'd finished eating she excused herself, claiming she was in the mood for a walk.

Talyn clutched at the first excuse to present itself for leaving the gathering, and leapt to her feet. "I'll come with you, Mama."

They strolled companionably through the back courtyard before eventually stopping at the low wall that looked down over the white sand of the beach below. The house was some distance away, and they were completely alone.

Her mother was silent, seemingly wrestling with something, so

Talyn tried to lighten the mood. "What do you think of Cuinn?" she asked, leaning closer so their shoulders touched.

Alyna shrugged. "He's not like us, you know."

"What does that mean?" Talyn asked carefully.

"He's not a Dumnorix, not really." There was an edge to Alyna's voice. "He's too pleased with himself, too spoiled. He doesn't have the steel that we do. I don't feel that tug of connection, either."

It was the exact same response Tarcos had had. Cuinn didn't know any of them, and he was accustomed to protecting himself with his false persona. He was probably confused as to what they were all doing there and judged it best to keep himself hidden. She would have done the same.

"It's there," she said. "The connection, I mean. It took me a long time before I picked up on it though, and it's different to the one we all feel with each other. Strange, but distinctive. And there are reasons for the way Prince Cuinn behaves—he's had a very different life than us."

"I suppose it just makes me wonder why you went back there," Alyna said. "I can't understand what's so important about him that makes you want to leave your home and family to go and lead his guard detail."

"It isn't about him," Talyn said simply. "It's about the Wolves. I've been able to do something worthwhile in Mithranar, I've made a difference, even if it's a small one." She paused—she wanted her mother to understand. "And above all, it was about learning to live again. Mithranar gave me the distance and space I needed to start healing."

"Keeping a spoiled playboy alive gave you purpose?" Alyna asked sharply.

Talyn scrambled for a better explanation. "No. You know I was doing work for the Callanan there too. I still am."

Alyna sighed, a troubled look filling her face. "Aethain filled me in. I just wish you were here, where you belong. I worry for you."

"You forget that I have Mithranan blood too, from Da," she said gently. "You could argue that Mithranar is my home as much as Calumnia is." She'd never quite thought about it from that perspective before... but it was true.

Something hardened in her mother's face. "Yes, well, while you've been in Mithranar, the Callanan have been investigating your father's death," she said shortly, finally turning to face Talyn.

Talyn swallowed, taken aback by the abrupt change in topic. Ariar had told her there was no news, so she hadn't raised it, not wanting to bring up what had to be a painful topic for her mother. "Have they discovered something? Why didn't you tell me?"

Alyna took a deep breath. "I hadn't planned on coming here with Aethain. But we learned something a couple of days ago, and Aethain agreed it was important enough that I be here to tell you... important enough to outweigh the risk of all of us converging on Prince Cuinn at once."

Dread took hold of Talyn in an icy grip. Some instinct warned her this wasn't going to be good. "What is it?"

Alyna reached into her tunic and pulled out a long, thin object wrapped in cloth. Her hands trembled slightly as she held it out to Talyn. Talyn took it with a frown, unwrapping the material. Inside lay a single arrow with blood crusted on its point.

The arrow that had killed her father.

It must be. Her mother wouldn't have shown it to her otherwise. The sight of her father's blood made her sick to her stomach. She looked up from the arrow to her mother. "Why do you have this?"

"It's the arrow that killed him," she said quietly. "It's evidence."

Talyn's gaze dropped back to the arrow, and she studied it more carefully, trying to hide the trembling of her hands. Sari had been killed the same way, an arrow just like this through her heart... she ruthlessly pushed those memories away. Her father deserved better.

It had been carved from ash wood, a usual type for arrows given the commonality of ash trees throughout the Twin Thrones, but there were markings on the shaft that indicated it had been custom made for someone. The arrowhead was a simple iron point, the feathers fletched in black and blue, nothing fancy, but again, indicative of being unique to a particular archer.

"It's longer, sturdier than an Aimsir arrow," she murmured. "Consistent with being shot from a longbow like we guessed. But I don't understand what the big revelation is?"

"Do you remember Tirigan?"

She sucked in a breath, nodded. "He was one of the Callanan with us that day, when Sari was shot. I think he was the one who covered me with his shield while I was trying to…" She cleared her throat, biting her lip at the sharp clawing of grief in her chest. "What about him?"

"Shia recently assigned him to the group of Callanan investigating Trys's death." Alyna paused, took a steadying breath. Talyn's dread deepened—few things in the world could make Alyna Dumnorix hesitate. "Talyn, Tirigan recognised that arrow. He'd seen one just like it before."

"Where?"

"It's identical to the one that killed Sari. The same colour fletching and carvings on the shaft."

"How…" Talyn shook her head, her mother's words hitting her like a punch to the stomach. "What are you saying? You think the same archer killed Sari and Da?"

"Maybe. We don't know." Alyna reached out, squeezed her arm. "We're looking into it, I promise."

"But… it was random. We sprung an ambush because we went in too quickly." Talyn was talking too fast, but she couldn't stop, her thoughts crashing into each other. "And Da, they were aiming for you, not him. A targeted attack. It's different. It has to be, doesn't it?"

"We don't know anything." Alyna stepped closer, violet eyes soft. "It could be a coincidence, that the brigand involved in the ambush on you and Sari was also sent to kill me."

"What if it's not?" Talyn was suddenly finding it hard to breathe. Her chest twisted into knots, unwelcome memories trying to push into her thoughts.

Alyna didn't hesitate this time. "Then maybe it wasn't an ambush on your Callanan unit... maybe it was an attempt to get you, Talyn."

"Why?" Talyn spun, running a hand through her hair. "Why is someone coming after us? And who? It doesn't make any sense!"

"Believe it or not, I know exactly how you feel," Alyna said softly, and the realisation cut through the panic Talyn was descending into.

She nodded, swallowed. She needed air. Space. Time to think. "I'm sorry, Mama. We'll talk later."

Abruptly, she turned and walked away.

A LONG WALK alone along the beach didn't help her unsettled mind or the panic she was barely keeping at bay. She didn't believe the arrow was a coincidence, didn't believe it for a second, even though logic told her it was possible, even likely.

But why were the brigands suddenly interested in killing her and her mother? Why not the Dumnorix who held power? And Sari's death had been well over two years ago—why such a gap before going after Alyna?

"Maybe the link isn't there—maybe it's a coincidence?" Sari suggested.

"There you are!" She hesitated, then, *"I'm so sorry, Sari. If you died because..."*

"I'm dead, Talyn, and this voice is only a small piece of me left with you," Sari said. *"And if my death was so that you could live... then you know I'll take that bargain any day."*

Talyn bit her lip, fighting back tears. *"I don't think it was a coincidence."*

"Maybe they came after you and your mother because the other Dumnorix are too hard to get to with their Kingshield guards? You and your mother never had a protection detail."

"Maybe." She let out a breath. *"But what could anyone hope to achieve by killing either of us?"*

"That's the question, isn't it? Find the motive—find out who gains from you both dying—and you'll find who did it. Or who paid the brigands to come after you."

"*But I can't.*" The panic surged again. "*I have to go back to Mithranar. I have to deal with Vengeance, and I can't leave Cuinn vulnerable right now, and—*"

"*Talyn, stop! You don't have to do it yourself. Trust your mother, trust your fellow Callanan.*"

All right. That settled her slightly. Knowing this... knowing what happened, it might help work out what was actually going on. If there was anything to be found, the Callanan would find it. She trusted their skill.

Eventually she turned and walked back towards the residence—it had grown late and the place was dark, soft strains of music drifting on the night air from Cuinn's open window. Judging by the sharp reduction in Kingshield guards crawling all over the estate, Alyna and Aethain had left to return to the palace.

She stopped for a moment to listen. He was playing a gentle tune, one that was neither mournful nor cheerful, but as with all his music, it calmed her.

Eventually the notes died away, leaving only the sound of the waves crashing on the shore and the chirping of the night insects. Talyn lingered a while longer before eventually making her way inside and to her room.

Her thoughts were so busy it took her a moment to realise someone was sitting in the chair by the window. Cuinn.

"I guess your creepy Shadow powers are back too," she said dryly, shutting the door. She'd expected Tarcos to be there—but of course he would be waiting for her to make the next move. He was thoughtful with her like that. Guilt twisted through her; she still hadn't talked to him. "Please don't tell me you snuck away from the Wolves?"

"Captain, this place is surrounded by Wolves and Ariar's Kingshield. I don't think I'm in any particular danger sneaking from my room to yours. And my ability to use the darkness to hide is not creepy."

"It is when you use it to sneak into people's rooms." She rubbed at her aching temples. "Why are you here, is something wrong?"

"We both know that despite my attempts to prove otherwise to everyone back in Mithranar, I'm no fool, Captain," he said quietly. "What's with the sudden parade of Dumnorix through poor Ceannar's house? Ariar made sense—your uncle sending a lesser prince to come and do the diplomatic niceties. But then the king *and* your mother? The emotions between you reek of suspicion and secrets. You're hiding something from me and I want to know what it is."

Talyn walked across the room, sliding down against the side of her bed and stretching her legs out towards the wall, letting her head fall back to rest against the soft covers. Cuinn remained in the chair to her right. Moonlight shone through the uncovered windows, lighting everything in a silver glow.

"The fletching and other markings on the arrow that killed my father were identical to the one that killed Sari," she said eventually. "The Callanan just found out... it's why my mother came with Aethain. It was just going to be him, a diplomatic courtesy, but she wanted to be the one to tell me."

"You're serious?" The accusation that had been on his face vanished in a flash. Something like sorrow replaced it... for her, for how she must be feeling.

She took a steadying breath. Even after so much time had passed, speaking aloud about what had happened that day was painfully hard. "One of the Callanan who was with us the day Sari died recognised it."

Cuinn leaned forward. "I don't know what to say."

"Instinct tells me it's not a coincidence, even though I desperately want to believe it was, but it doesn't make any sense. What if it's my fault... what if Sari and Da are both dead because of me?" she whispered. The grief she'd been holding back since her father's death swept through her, as if something inside, a shield maybe, had torn loose. Cuinn's expression deepened into shock and dismay.

A sob escaped her. She had thought she was coping with her father's death, but now it was clear her grief still ran deep. She couldn't stop the tears, even though part of her was horrified to be showing such weakness in front of Cuinn.

Then a light melody filled the room. It settled around her like a blanket, not attempting to erase her grief, but somehow lightening the depth of it, making it quieter, more bearable. Her sobs eased, the tears slowing to a stop.

When she came back to herself, it was to find Cuinn sitting inches away from her, humming softly, eyes closed. His healing leg was stretched out, the other curled underneath him in a way that couldn't be comfortable.

His eyes opened to meet hers, green and bright in the dim room. She was taken back to the Shadowhawk's apartment, when she'd first returned to Mithranar and told him about the death of Sari, of the grief and guilt she still carried. How she'd felt his simple under-standing from across the room. It had reached her then, slipped behind her emotional shields and eased her pain, and it did the same now.

"I know the pain you feel. I'm sorry, Talyn," he murmured.

Suddenly awkward by how close he was, how intimate the conver-sation had become, she sniffed and shifted away, scrubbing furiously at her eyes. "I'm sorry," she muttered, "I didn't mean to cry in front of you."

He smiled. "Never be sorry for allowing yourself to grieve. But let me ask you something. On the ship here, you told me about Sari, how she's still with you... does she blame you for her death?"

"No. The idiot is happy that she might have saved my life that day," Talyn muttered.

"And your father? If he knew he'd taken an arrow meant for your mother, or even for you?"

She swallowed, scrubbed at the tears on her cheeks. "The same."

"It will never be easy," he said. "But maybe it will help if you think about it from that perspective."

It did. It didn't stop her from missing them terribly. But it made their deaths more bearable.

"Thank you," she said.

His green eyes scanned her face as if looking for something but not finding it. "Will you stay and help with the Callanan investigation?

Because if that's what you want, you should. Don't imagine you have any obligation to me or the Wolves."

She took a deep, shuddering breath. "I'm still… I'm still healing, you know? And there's Vengeance to be dealt with—that's important, Cuinn, and I'm in the best position to do it. But it doesn't stop me feeling horribly guilty for not staying even though I know there are good people working on it, including my mother."

He looked away suddenly, like he didn't want her to see what was on his face. She caught no hint of his emotion, indicating he was shielding tightly. A brief silence fell. It took her a moment to realise this was the first time since the avalanche that they'd had an opportunity to talk alone without him being fevered and sick. She'd told him about Sari still being in her head on a particularly bad day in an attempt to cheer him, and had half-hoped he hadn't remembered.

"I owe you an apology." She sat up straighter and wiped away the remaining wetness on her face. "All those times I was horribly rude to you… here I was thinking you were a spoiled brat who did nothing but play sport and bed women, and you were really running about as the Shadowhawk."

"To be fair, I still did spend most of my time playing sport and bedding women." He shifted, leaning back against the bed beside her, wings tucked in tight, wincing as his healing leg straightened further. "And occasionally I ventured out to do something that would annoy my mother and brothers. Don't paint me as a hero, Captain."

"You also went out of your way to make me dislike you."

"I couldn't risk having you suspect me." His tone was pensive. "I realised very early on how smart you are."

She lifted an eyebrow. "With how quickly I found you?"

"A sharp reminder that I had grown sloppy pitting myself against the WingGuard." He met her eyes. "Will you tell me the truth? About why they all came here."

And there went the lighter mood.

She forced herself to meet his eyes. "I can't."

Hurt flashed over his face and he looked away.

"I made a promise, and I can't break my word. It's not my secret to tell." She tried to explain, but the words sounded hollow, *felt* hollow.

The warmth that had been between them—a bubble of confidence and trust she hadn't even realised was there—shattered as he lifted himself awkwardly to his feet. He limped for her door, and she tried to think of something to bring him back, to try and fix what she'd just broken, but there was nothing, only more lies.

He reached the door in silence, but paused there. "It's time to go back to Mithranar. I spoke to Ceannar this morning—he's helped make arrangements. We'll leave tomorrow evening."

"Cuinn, wait." She stood, her voice stopping him as he turned the door handle. "If we're going home, I need to ask something of you."

He didn't turn around. "What?"

"No more wearing masks around me. No glamour, no emotional manipulation to make me think or believe things about you. If I'm to keep you safe, I need to know the real you, the man behind all those masks."

His hand tightened on the doorknob. "No one has seen beyond my masks for so long that I'm not sure where the glamour ends and the real me begins anymore."

She'd suspected as much. "Just be honest with me. Don't pretend."

"Be honest with you while you're keeping secrets from me. And more than one, if my magic is right." Surprisingly there wasn't any bitterness in his words. He finally turned towards her. "But maybe that's fair enough. Perhaps I need to win your trust, Captain, so that you can trust me. I'll do as you ask."

Guilt seared her. "Thank you."

With a little nod, he was gone.

Rubbing at her temples again—her headache had only gotten worse after her conversation with Cuinn—she flopped into the bed.

"Talyn?"

"What?" she muttered aloud.

"You just referred to Mithranar as home."

· · ·

UNABLE TO SLEEP, and thoroughly ignoring Sari's comment and its implications, Talyn went down to the stables and saddled up Fire-Flare. The night was warm, and a long gallop helped clear her head. The mare enjoyed it just as much as she did and the both of them were much more relaxed as they cantered slowly back into Ceannar's home, waving to the Kingshield guards on the way in.

She was surprised to find Ariar awake and leaning against the wall by the door of the barn, staring up at the stars. His hand lifted in greeting. He followed as she dismounted and led FireFlare inside, watching quietly as she began unsaddling the mare.

"Can't sleep either, huh?" he said eventually.

"Not tonight," she admitted, hauling the saddle off and hanging it on the wall. "No late-night conversation with Tiercelin?"

A smile flashed over Ariar's face. "I like your Wolves. And they adore you."

"They do not," she scoffed.

"They do." He cocked his head. "You and I are very much alike."

She raised an eyebrow. "How's that?"

His smile widened. "Look at you! Riding in well after midnight, dusty, clad in a riding jacket and torn breeches, escaping all your cares on a long ride, just you and your Aimsir mare."

She sighed. "Is there something wrong with any of that?"

"It's just not very princess-like."

Talyn chuckled. "I'm not a princess. My mother abdicated any political connection to the family."

"I think that's been un-abdicated now," he said dryly. "It has truly helped her, going back to court, being near us. But I also think she enjoys it."

A comfortable silence fell as Talyn slowly began grooming her mare. FireFlare relaxed completely, eyes drifting closed.

"Don't you miss it?"

She looked up. "What? Being an Aimsir?"

"Not just that. Being out in the saddle, being a Callanan warrior, all of it."

Talyn used the rhythmic strokes of the curry comb to distract herself from the rush of emotion Ariar's question summoned. "Always." She managed the word, forced the rest out. "The day that Sari died was the day I lost the life I loved. I would do absolutely anything to have that life back. *Anything.*" She took a deep breath, palms spread over FireFlare's warm hide. "But she's not coming back. So I have to find another life, even though I know it will never be the same."

Ariar was silent a moment, considering that, then said, "I like Cuinn too. He's a good sort."

She looked over with a smile. "You're the only one here who seems to think so."

"I told you." He waggled a finger at her. "We're alike, you and I. We don't quite fit the mould."

"You could come to Mithranar. We could use a warrior of middling skill like yourself."

He laughed. "No, I've found my place in the mountains hunting brigands. I dread the day I'm too old for that."

"You'll never be too old for that." She snorted. "You'll take an arrow at ninety-five, desperately trying to stay in the saddle while that stallion of yours races down a perilous hillside."

Ariar's smile faded. "The First Blade told your mother and I everything. Generally I make a habit of not worrying over things, but this…"

"Me too." She put the comb away, turned to face him. "Did they tell you what they want me to do in Mithranar?"

"They did. If anyone can pull it off, it will be you." He met her gaze, no trace of doubt or concern in his sky-blue Dumnorix eyes.

"It might not stop anything."

"Whatever comes, we'll be prepared to meet it," he said, though the troubled look on his face warred with his confident tone.

"Cuinn wants to leave tomorrow." She opened the stall door and stepped out. "So I guess it will be a while before I see you again."

"Yeah, I'm riding out in the morning. A message came from one of my captains in Port Lathilly. We'll go early, before dawn." He offered a sad smile. "Don't make it too long before you visit again, and take care of yourself in Mithranar. You're my favourite Dumnorix, Tal."

She reached up to hug him tightly. "Farewell, Cousin."

"For now." He smiled his bright smile at her, then let go.

Determination coalesced in her chest as she watched him walk away. She would deal with Vengeance, wipe them out, then she would do whatever it took after that to keep her home safe.

Both her homes.

CHAPTER 8

Cuinn had apparently announced his planned departure over dinner the previous night. She woke the next morning to find Corrin lingering at her door, wanting to check that she was comfortable with them all going back to Mithranar so soon.

"It's Cuinn's decision to make," she'd told him. "But I think he's going to be fine."

"So do I," Corrin said, digging his hands in his pockets. "I'll be glad to see Theac and the Wolves again, Captain, and I miss my home. But going back, it's…"

"I know." He hadn't needed to finish his sentence. "Now we know exactly how much danger he's in." And how much danger Mithranar was in. "Come on, let's go eat some breakfast. I want to talk with you all about the return trip."

She and Corrin were heading towards the kitchen where the Wolves usually ate when Tarcos found her. "Can we talk?" he asked. "It won't take long."

Her heart sank. After her conversation with Ariar the night before it had been too late—and she hadn't been in the right frame of mind— to go to Tarcos. But she had to talk to him before she left. "We do need to talk. I'll catch up with you later, Corrin."

Corrin saluted and continued to the kitchen alone.

Talyn followed as Tarcos led her into the nearby garden. It was a warm morning and the sun was bright. A slight breeze rustled through the bushes as they strolled along one of the pebbled pathways.

"I missed you last night," he said, coming to rest against the low brick wall of the estate boundary, brown eyes solemn.

"I'm sorry." She glanced away, annoyed with herself. She should have done this days ago.

"Hey." He reached out to catch her hand. "Don't apologise. You know I'll always give you what you need."

She straightened her shoulders, met his gaze. "Tarcos, we need to talk."

"We do." A serious look stole over his already grave features. Her heart sank. "I'm going to be named heir. I want a family, stability, all of that."

Unease flared through her. "Tarcos—"

"I want that life with you. It's always been you." His hand tightened on hers. "I want you at my side as consort."

She tried not to stiffen. "I've never promised you any of that."

"And I've never asked." His voice took on a formal tone. "But now I am. Will you marry me, Talyn? Your family won't protest the match—a Firthlander prince is the perfect choice for a Dumnorix princess. My uncle won't dispute it either, I've already spoken of it with him."

She took a deep breath. "I wish you hadn't. Tarcos, I can't marry you. That's not the life I want."

His face and voice gentled. "Is it about Sari? Because I hope you know I'm willing to give you whatever time you need to heal. I'll wait until you're ready."

"No." She gently tugged her hand out of his, hating the disappointment and hurt rising in his eyes. "Tarcos, I care about you. But I don't want to be consort to a warlord and I don't want marriage. I never have. You know that."

He swallowed. Her heart clenched. He was upset, deeply so, even though little of it showed on his face. Not wanting to see his pain—

knowing she was the cause of it—she glanced away, trying not to feel awkward but failing miserably.

Her gaze fell on Cuinn, limping down the path towards them—on his morning walk, of course. He insisted on walking everywhere until his leg was stronger, even though Tiercelin had been encouraging him to keep his flight muscles strong too. Abruptly she felt guilty, though that was ridiculous. Tarcos saw the direction of her gaze and true anger rippled across his dark face.

"You're saying no to me because of him?"

"Of course not!" she said, indignance rising up to swallow her discomfort. "Tarcos, I'm not… I'm not in love with you. I care about you, and I respect you, but I'm not leaving my life to marry you. I don't want to marry anyone. All those things you just listed… family, stability, I don't want any of that." She wouldn't last a half-turn in that life without restlessness making her want to crawl out of her skin.

He frowned. "I don't understand. We've been building towards this for years. I am a Hadvezer prince. You are a Dumnorix princess. We are a perfect match."

Something flashed in his eyes then that made her take a step back, cold sliding through her chest. "Tell me this isn't because I'm Dumnorix."

"What isn't?" he asked impatiently.

"You courting me, us becoming lovers. Tell me that didn't happen because you thought I would be a good political match for you?" She stared at him. It couldn't be, surely? He couldn't have been planning this the whole time.

"I love you. I want you as my wife. We've been together for years. That's what this is about. I don't understand why you're suddenly baulking."

"Then you haven't been listening to me," she said, trying and failing not to get angry at the stubbornness in his voice. "I've never promised you anything more than a casual relationship. Not once. And if you knew me at all, you would know this is the last thing I want."

His jaw tightened. "Please think about it. Maybe after some time, you'll—"

"No." She cut him off gently. "It wouldn't be fair to leave you hanging. You need to find someone who will love you like you deserve."

"I want *you*." His voice came out rough-edged and angry. "I'm sorry, I don't mean to be like this, but I've been waiting for so long. You are all I imagined."

"I didn't realise you had such different expectations. You never said anything."

"I thought it was clear."

"It wasn't," she snapped, patience fraying.

He stared at her. "Were you paying any attention at all, these past years? After everything that's happened, I thought you would eventually come home, stay here, be the Dumnorix you were born to be."

"Then clearly I wasn't paying any more attention to your wishes than you were to mine," she said coldly.

The angry words rippled around them, fading into a weighted silence. They'd never fought like this before, never, and the conversation had an unreal quality about it. Tarcos's expression softened from anger to something like helpless frustration. Before she could think of anything more to say, he abruptly brushed by her, striding away along the path towards the beach.

She didn't turn to watch him go. Instead she looked up the path to where Cuinn had been approaching. He'd vanished too.

Shit.

Sari piped up. *"That was awkward."*

"Did I miss something? I thought I'd been clear with him."

"You never promised him anything. But you've known for a while now that he was getting more serious."

"I know, but he's behaving like I just ruined his life. He doesn't love me like that. I know he doesn't. I wouldn't have stayed with him if he did."

"Right, because that would have totally scared you off."

Her mouth tightened at Sari's implication. *"That's unfair."*

"Sorry. I was joking... mostly." Sari hesitated. *"I never wanted you to be with him."*

"*Oh really?*" Talyn tried to distract herself with humour. "*You don't think Tarcos and Roan would have gotten along?*"

Laughter trilled through her head. "*Poor Roan wouldn't have known what to make of that hulking brute. And Tarcos's painful politeness would have grated my nerves to no end.*"

Talyn frowned, coming to a halt. "*You're being serious. I know you gave him a hard time when we first met, but... you truly never liked him? Why didn't you ever say anything?*"

"*It wasn't my place to tell you who you should sleep with.*"

"*You were worried. That I'd marry him and join court. Leave the Callanan,*" Talyn said in realisation.

A long silence in her head, then, "*Maybe. And I was so worried that my fear would somehow influence you against it, and I didn't want to hold you back if that's what you wanted.*"

"*Sari. I never wanted it. Not for a single second. Especially not while you were still with me.*"

"*I know that now.*"

It turned out Cuinn had only gone a little way back up the path and was sitting on a bench by the wall, left leg stretched out before him.

"Eavesdropping, were you?" she asked, still snappish with fading anger, both at Tarcos and Sari, for holding so much back from her.

"Couldn't hear a thing from here," he promised. "But that Firth-lander prince is pretty intimidating. I thought I'd better stick around in case you needed help."

She couldn't help it. Her breath huffed out in a laugh. "And what exactly would you have done if he'd attacked me? Thrown your crutch at him?"

"I've got good aim." Cuinn levered himself to his feet, wings flared for balance. There was no wince at the movement now, not even a grunt of effort. He wasn't back to full strength yet, and his leg still looked stiff, but he was essentially walking without needing to rely on the crutch he still carried. All her remaining anger vanished at the sight.

"I think what you've accomplished here... the way you've done everything Tiercelin has asked, and not given up, not even once, no matter how hard it was or how much it hurt. I think that's one of the most impressive things I've ever seen," she said quietly.

"How could I do otherwise?" he said. "After everything you and the Wolves have done for me?"

She looked away, unfamiliar emotion tight in her chest. "I was planning to talk to the Wolves over breakfast about our trip home. I assume you'd like to join us?"

"Now that I don't need to pretend around you, I'd like to be more involved," he said. "You know that I always cared, even when I had to pretend not to?"

"I do." She cleared her throat. "But that will be difficult, back in Mithranar."

Some of the light in his face dulled, but he didn't try and disagree with her. He was silent as they made their slow way to the kitchens, though.

AFTER BREAKFAST, Talyn saddled up FireFlare and galloped the distance into the city. It was the last opportunity she'd have for a long time to ride her mare, and she already felt guilty enough about not staying in Calumnia to leave without a final visit to her mother.

Before going to the palace, however, she spent some time with Leviana and Cynia at an inn popular with Ryathl's Aimsir. Both Callanan were delighted to see Talyn, and they dived straight into conversation, catching up on what had happened since they'd last seen each other.

"Tarcos wants to marry you?" Leviana looked delighted.

"I told him no." Talyn chuckled as Leviana's face fell. "I have no interest in getting married."

"You sure your refusal hasn't got something to do with that delicious Mithranan prince?" Cynia teased.

"No, it hasn't." A startled laugh of amusement escaped her at the idea. "How do you even know what he looks like anyway?"

"We don't." The partners shared a grin. "But the way you describe him... he *sounds* delicious."

"I'm pretty certain I've never described him that way," Talyn said dryly. "But it's kind of true."

They all laughed.

"Actually, we have some news for you too." Cynia turned serious. "The First Blade summoned us yesterday."

Talyn lifted an eyebrow. "Do tell."

"She's sending *us* to Mithranar to interview the Shadowhawk." Leviana jumped in excitedly, ignoring her partner's warning look. "We'll get to work together."

"I see." Talyn sat back in her chair with a sigh.

"Don't hold back your enthusiasm," Cynia said dryly.

"She doesn't trust me," Talyn said bluntly. "So she's sending two of my friends to ensure I follow through on my promise."

"Actually, that's not it at all." Leviana scowled. "Lord Ariar requested it."

A smile spread over Talyn's face.

"Don't grin like that." Cynia scowled. "Do you have any idea how annoyed the First Blade is with us for being the Horselord's sudden favourites?"

"Sorry." Talyn lifted her hands in the air. "Ariar is just looking out for me. He knows how good you are, and he wants to make sure I'm protected. It's a compliment to you both."

"Yeah, yeah," Leviana grumbled, but the glower on her face faded as a smile struggled to break free. "I'm excited about getting to see Mithranar."

Cynia tried to smile, but a troubled look quickly covered it. She lowered her voice. "Lord Ariar insisted the First Blade tell us everything. About Vengeance, the informant, all of it."

Talyn relaxed further, wishing Ariar was here so she could hug him. "I can't tell you how glad I am not to be the only one with this secret."

"I never imagined we would ever face another war." Leviana's voice dropped to a murmur.

Talyn forced reassurance into her voice. "We'll make sure it doesn't come to that. What are your plans?"

"We've got a ship booked in a week's time," Cynia said. "Given Leviana's family background, we'll be travelling as small-time merchants looking for new trade avenues. Levs knows enough to make us look and sound legitimate."

Talyn nodded. "Wait two days after you arrive, then go to a place called the *Kahvi House* in the Market Quarter. The owner's name is Petro. Find an innocuous reason to talk to him, then tell him you're a friend of Talyn's. Let him know where you're staying and he'll get a message to me. I'll warn him to look out for you." She directed a pointed look at Leviana. "Dock City is a very different place to anything you've experienced before. Once you've spoken to Petro, wait for me to contact you, and in the meantime just focus on living your cover."

"You make it sound like we're walking into a nest of brigands or something," Cynia grumbled.

"You pretty much are if you come to the notice of the wrong people," Talyn said. "Trust me on this."

"Easily done." Leviana reached across the table to squeeze her hand. "I really wanted you to come back to the Callanan, Tal. I still do. But I want you to be happy most of all. And I'm glad you've found a new life for yourself."

"Thanks." Talyn squeezed her hand back, then lifted her ale, excitement bubbling up in her chest. "Here's to working together in Mithranar."

AETHAIN WAS out of the city, so Talyn and Alyna shared lunch in her mother's quarters, tacitly agreeing not to talk about anything important, instead laughing over the latest court gossip and enjoying their time together. Eventually Talyn rose to leave, and Alyna walked her to the door.

Talyn hugged her mother tightly. "I'm okay, Mama."

Alyna's violet gaze scanned her face, reassuring herself Talyn was telling the truth. "We'll do everything we can to find the brigand archer. I promise you."

"I know you will." Talyn forced a smile. "Will you farewell Uncle for me? And say hello to Aeris next time you write to him. I'll miss you all."

"I wish you weren't going." Alyna sighed.

"I'll be back one day," Talyn said. "And I'm sorry, for not being here for you. I wish I could, I just…"

Alyna framed her face with both hands. "All I ask is that you remember your family, Talyn. Remember your duty. Burn bright and true."

"Burn bright and true," she promised. "Always."

CHAPTER 9

*U*nable to remain in the cramped cabin of the ship any longer, Cuinn limped out into the narrow walkway beyond his door and contemplated the stairs leading to the deck. A hint of salty air drifted down to him, promising space and sunlight, and he summoned his determination.

He could do stairs.

Taking it one step at a time, he eventually manoeuvred himself to the top, surprising the Wolf talon on guard there.

Andres frowned. "Your Highness, can I help?"

His leg ached bitterly, but the Wolf didn't need to know that. "I just need some fresh air, Talon Tye. No need for you or the others to follow me around like I'm a lost puppy. Nobody's going to attack me in the close confines of this ship."

Andres bowed his head. "We'll keep our distance."

He limped away, putting more weight on his healing leg than he should to avoid Andres getting the impression he needed help. Pain stabbed through him when his leg protested that show of pride, but he ignored it and pushed on.

He would get there.

The sea breeze whipped through his hair, and he extended his wings with a sigh of relief—the sensation of the air sliding through his feathers was pure delight. He considered calling for Tiercelin and taking a flight with his Wolf protector, but his attention was caught by the sight of Talyn at the prow, expression closed as she stared out at the ocean beyond, and all thoughts of a flight faded from his mind. As always with her, he got the distinct impression she was caught up in some internal battle.

While he normally used his magic constantly as Prince Cuinn, an instinctive protection just like his glamour, a warning system of sorts to tell him if anyone suspected the falseness of his indolent prince façade, it was of little use around Talyn. She was a master of cool self-control, which she wielded just as skilfully as he wielded his glamour. And on the brief occasions when he *could* read her, it was usually annoyance at him, or very rarely, a deep aching grief that burned and made him want to run away and cry.

And her masks hid secrets too. Frustration surged, but he fought it down. Talyn Dynan's honour, her innate devotion to her family—and by extension the Twin Thrones—was important to her. If she'd sworn to keep a promise, she wasn't going to break her word for him.

No matter how badly he wished she would.

Shaking his head to dispel maudlin thoughts, he limped over to join her. She noticed him coming long before he got there, of course, but said nothing and continued staring out at the ocean—allowing him to approach without the pressure of her watching.

Eventually he reached the railing and braced his hands on it, mostly to take some weight off his aching leg. His spread wings allowed him to easily stay balanced on the rocking deck while the breeze whipped around them. "You got your sea legs pretty quickly," he commented.

"What can I say?" She shrugged. "Callanan balance. What about you? You look like you're moving around on this deck pretty well. Where's your walking stick?"

He tapped his nose secretively and bent low to whisper. "It's my magical powers."

She laughed. It made her sapphire eyes sparkle. He tried not to be entranced. Failed miserably. "More like it's those enormous wings of yours. You winged folk are such cheats."

"Hah. You've clearly never tried swimming with wings." He couldn't help but smile at her good mood. "But you're right. Winged folk have natural balance. That's probably where you get yours from too."

Talyn started at his words. He didn't miss it. She was most definitely of winged folk blood—he'd guessed it the moment he met her, and she'd related the limited information her father had passed on about his winged folk blood in one of Cuinn's less feverish moments during the long ship journey to Ryathl. It made him curious about who her father was, and why he'd left Mithranar and never returned. Why he'd barely told her anything about himself.

But as usual, she wouldn't talk about anything remotely painful, instead changing the subject. "Can we expect a welcoming party when we arrive?"

The question sobered him, ugly knots of anxiety rearing in his chest and stomach, tightening so fiercely it was a struggle not to let on how her words affected him. "In my last letter I assured Mithanis I'd be home within the month, so no doubt he's got Falcons keeping an eye on all ships arriving from the Twin Thrones."

Her eyes studied his face, making him feel utterly exposed. His instinct was to draw on his glamour, project a lazy indolence to hide behind, but he'd promised to be honest with her. So instead he gritted his teeth and subjected himself to that piercing gaze.

"We will keep you safe," she promised.

"I know you'll try," he said, equally serious.

Her face turned thoughtful as she pondered that. "Theac told me once that Mithanis is the reason Montagn hasn't made any serious attempt to take Mithranar, not only because he has powerful magic but because he and Azrilan are linked to Montagn by blood. Is that true?"

"Partly." Cuinn shrugged. "Mithanis is an undeniable deterrent. It's no secret how powerful he is, and what a strong king he'll be. It's not all about him—no Montagni ahara ever tried to invade us before my mother's marriage into the Manunin family, after all—but his and Azrilan's familial connection is an important consideration." Seeing the question forming in her eyes, he continued. "I can't tell you for certain why they've never tried invasion in the past, but part of it is because the WingGuard, under the Ciantar, used to be a much more powerful entity than it is today."

She frowned. "What is a Ciantar?"

"*Who* is the Ciantar." Cuinn relaxed as the conversation moved away from his brothers. "After the Acondors, the Ciantar family were the most powerful nobles in Mithranar. Lord Ciantar sat on the Queencouncil and commanded the WingGuard. The Falcons might be lazy and incompetent now, but that wasn't always the case. Ravinire tries, but he doesn't have the influence and power the Ciantar family had, and so he's caught between my mother and my brothers and the rest of the Queencouncil."

Curiosity leaked from her, bright and infectious. "There's nobody with that name on the Queencouncil now. What happened to them?"

He took a breath. "My mother executed the entire family for treason, and she'd only just been crowned when it happened. Every single one of them. She's always refused to tell anyone exactly what they'd actually done. It's been kept a closely held secret."

"What... nobody knows the specifics of why she had them executed?" She stared at him.

"I'm fairly certain Ravinire knows at least part of it, and Mithanis and Azrilan know everything," Cuinn said. "But officially? All my mother ever announced was that the Ciantar and his family had committed treason against the crown."

"Do you know?"

"Not much. Azrilan told me once it had something to do with the previous Shadowhawk. When he was caught, he must have given up their names as helping him," Cuinn said. "Or she found out some other way."

Shock and realisation spread over her face. "That's why you took the old Shadowhawk's name?"

"My mother thought by murdering an entire family she'd gotten rid of the Shadowhawk." He smiled bitterly. "It gave me a perverse sense of satisfaction to throw it back in her face."

Talyn let out a breath. "So your mother could decide anyone—including the most powerful family in Mithranar—has committed treason and execute them with impunity? As could Mithanis, once he is king?"

"Or is formally named heir." He gave her an easy smile to hide his unease. "Exactly, Captain."

"So a winged family was helping humans back then?" she mused.

"Maybe." Cuinn wasn't certain. "If Mother wanted the Ciantar family gone for some other reason, she may have fabricated or over-exaggerated their link to the Shadowhawk."

They turned back towards the ocean, each lost in their thoughts for a few moments. Thinking of what his mother had done had his anxiety returning, fisting in his chest, almost choking off his breath-ing, despite how much he hated feeling this way. The part of him that desperately wanted to be home again fought bitterly with the part of him that was terrified to step foot back in the citadel.

His whole life had been a constant battle to appear unthreatening, to make sure nobody found out what he was doing, to stay out of Mithanis's way. And now it was going to start all over again. A cold sweat broke over his skin at the thought. All he wanted was for the hiding to end.

"Are you ready for this?" she murmured, as if sensing his distress. "Magically, I mean—after your injuries, do you have the strength to go back to pretending all the time? It's going to be more important than ever, especially in the beginning, to convince everyone you really have just been on a trip."

Despair flitted across Cuinn's face and he couldn't have hidden it even if he'd wanted to. "Do you know how much I hate pretending, how worthless it makes me feel? Especially now."

"Especially now?" She frowned.

"Yes," he wanted to say. *"Especially now you're here, and I have the Wolves. I want to be me, just me. No more hiding."* But he couldn't tell her that. She didn't want to know that he thought she was the most

wonderful thing to happen to Mithranar in a long time, that he thought… he cut himself off ruthlessly. "It's exhausting," he said instead. "And it only grows harder the longer I have to do it."

Understanding flashed in her eyes, but he watched as she pushed it away and firmed her voice. "My primary concern is your safety. You've been protecting yourself this whole time, and while I understand how hard it is, you have to keep doing it."

He nodded and summoned what fading strength he had left. It was time to broach the subject of the Shadowhawk with her. He'd been waiting till he felt stronger, till there was time, but if he was honest with himself, he'd been avoiding it too. "I concede that point, but there's something else we need to discuss. You and the Wolves have been assuming that just because it's safer to let Vengeance keep thinking the Shadowhawk is dead, I'm going to go back to Mithranar and sit idly by and do nothing."

Something flashed in her sapphire eyes, but her self-control masked the emotion from him. "And you're telling me that assumption is wrong? Cuinn, you can't do anything foolish."

"Can't I?" he demanded, growing angry. Good, anger would give him the strength he needed to face her down. "Because I'm the prince and you're the WingGuard captain in Mithranar, Talyn. You don't give me orders."

"Cuinn—"

"Since Raya's death, I have been unable to sit by and do nothing. Do you understand me? And that isn't going to change because I got hurt," he said.

"Are you telling me you're going back to being the Shadowhawk?" She looked him dead in the eye.

"Not immediately. Not while I'm still healing, still recovering my strength. And not until Mithanis calms down from his inevitable rage at my absence," he said. "But after that… the humans still need my help. And I plan to give it to them."

"Then you're a fool," she snapped. "Because Vengeance will come after you again the moment they know you're still alive. And next time they might succeed."

His mouth tightened. "They might, but that doesn't change anything. I've had Falcons and City Patrol hunting me for years. I know how to hide, and I'm not going to let fear stop me from helping my people."

"I—"

"Don't even try and argue with me on this. You are no different, Talyn Dumnorix," he said fiercely.

Something flashed over her face and she turned away. "We'll discuss it once you're well again."

She wasn't conceding, not for a second, she was just delaying the inevitable confrontation. That was fine. He was too weary to keep pushing her right now.

"Fine," he said tersely. "My leg is aching. I'm going to go and rest."

It was late afternoon two days later when their ship rounded the heads and entered Feather Bay. He hadn't spoken to Talyn again—he'd kept largely to his cabin aside from regular strolls around the deck to continue building his strength and a handful of flights with Tiercelin to stretch his wings.

Anxiety and fear had taken a fierce hold of him by the time he got out of bed that morning, the sound of the Wolves sparring on the deck above doing nothing to ease it. If anything, they only reminded him of the danger he was about to walk into. Eventually he couldn't lie there any longer and limped up on deck.

Talyn and Corrin were huddled at the port railing down near the stern, sipping at steaming mugs and presumably admiring the sight of the citadel illuminated by the morning sun. Judging from the snippets of conversation floating to him on the breeze, they were talking about Theac's wedding.

"Your Highness." Corrin saw him first, straightening into a perfect soldier's stance. "Good morning."

"Corrin." He smiled. "You must be excited to see your mother and sisters."

"I am, Your Highness."

"The Wolves are excited too," Cuinn said. "About the wedding." He often caught flashes of it with his magic.

Corrin beamed. "If you'll excuse me, Captain, Your Highness. I'd best finish packing up."

"Thanks, Corrin," Talyn murmured. She'd barely been paying attention to the conversation, her eyes firmly fixed on the citadel in the distance.

The talon hesitated, glancing between them before leaving. "We'll be ready for this."

Cuinn nodded, trying to allow himself to be reassured by the man's words, but failing miserably. Talyn said nothing, still watching the citadel. He swallowed. The fight they'd had was forgotten, over-taken by his fear and anxiety about what faced him.

"I'm scared," he said quietly.

"I can understand that."

"How pathetic does that make me?" He couldn't look at her. His eyes were fixed on the ground and his shoulders were hunched in shame. "I can't even face my own brother without being so terrified I feel ill."

"Do you remember last year when I first came to Mithranar?" she asked. Her voice was cool, unruffled. "It wasn't long after that when intruders were spotted in the citadel, and you told me you could feel Zamaril's terror as he guarded your roof door?"

He blinked at her apparent change in subject, and it took a moment to recall. "Right. I asked you to speak to him. After that, his fear faded. I've always been curious about what you said."

"He was terrified, white and shaking," she said quietly. "I told him that the true meaning of courage is to be absolutely terrified of some-thing, yet do it anyway."

He huffed a breath. "I know that already. I was the Shadowhawk for years knowing that if I was caught, I would be killed—and while that scared me, I still did what I did because it was important. But now, after what happened, I'm terrified I can't be strong again—I feel vulnerable, exposed. I can't help it. I'm a quivering mess."

She said nothing for a long time, and eventually he looked towards her, where her hands rested against the railing. They were white-knuckled, as if holding in some inner torment. He held his magic at bay, instinctively knowing she wouldn't want him to pry.

When she caught him looking, she lifted her eyes to his. "Until recently, there wasn't a day that passed since Sari's death that I wasn't terrified I'd never be what I was again, that I was permanently broken. I know what inadequacy is, Cuinn."

He reached out, sliding his hand over hers where it rested on the wood. Her skin was cold under his, but she didn't pull away. "I don't know what you were before, Captain, but I'll tell you now that I've never met anyone braver, or stronger, than you."

She cleared her throat, huffing a laugh. "You're being nice to me."

"No, I'm being truthful." His words tripped over themselves in their earnestness. He needed her to believe him, needed to do *something* to alleviate the pain that was still there deep inside her. "If Sari saw you now, she'd be beyond proud to see what you've accomplished. Your Da would feel the same. I know that with more certainty than I've ever known anything."

She went still for a breath-holding moment, then she moved, flipping the hand that lay under his palm over, entwining their fingers. He returned her grip just as fiercely.

"We can do this," she said. "Both of us. Together."

He swallowed. He didn't want to be any less strong than she was—he would fight with everything he had to be that strong. "Okay, Captain."

His voice seemed to break the spell, and she stiffened slightly, unclasping her hand from his and shifting away. He caught a flash of awkwardness, embarrassment, and underneath that, self-chastisement. For a moment he was frozen, the brief touch having roused all manner of emotions, but he tried to snap himself out of it. She was so controlled that any collapse of that control never failed to fluster her, and if he teased her now she would shut off completely and he didn't want that.

So he changed the subject. "Will you ask one of the Wolves to take my walking stick?" he said. "I don't want to show any weakness in front of Mithanis."

She frowned. "Can you walk that far?"

"I'll have to fly in," he reminded her. "Or it will look odd." He'd just have to hope he could stick the landing without betraying his weaker left leg.

Tiercelin dropped out of the sky then, grey wings spread wide, saluting to both of them. The other talons approached at the sight of him. "Theac is ready and waiting at your tower, Your Highness."

"And the ship's boats are ready to take the rest of us in, Captain," Andres added.

Cuinn turned to Talyn. "No need to make an unnecessary show of strength. If Mithanis is planning a welcoming party, I don't want to throw my guard in his face. Take your time arriving."

"I agree. Tiercelin will escort you up." She eyed him. "You ready?"

He looked at the Wolves. Disciplined, strong, and trained by her.

Then he looked back at her and nodded. "I'm ready."

CHAPTER 10

Cuinn flew directly from the ship to his tower, hoping to have the opportunity to settle in before Mithanis or his mother inevitably summoned him. But those hopes were dashed miserably as he dropped out of the sky above his tower to see Mithanis waiting for him on the bridge leading over to it. The prince of night was alone, his Falcon detail hovering a good distance off.

Cuinn fought the urge to glance over at Tiercelin as he landed, ignoring the quick, stabbing pain in his leg. The Wolf was a solid presence just behind and to his left. He couldn't see any other Wolves around though—had Mithanis ordered them away?

"Mithanis." Cuinn summoned a breezy smile. "It's good to see you. I was away so long I almost missed your sullen face."

The prince of night wasn't trying to hide the anger vibrating from him, and Cuinn didn't fail to notice that his brother's right hand rested on the hilt of the knife in his belt. Mithanis's short-cropped dark hair emphasized the hard lines of his face and his gleaming dark eyes. His magic hung around him like a perfectly tailored cloak, ready and coiled to strike.

The prince of night used his song magic as a weapon, constantly and without thought, in the same way Cuinn used his to hide. But because Mithanis didn't have to hide from anyone, his magic was a much blunter force.

"Where have you been?" Mithanis demanded.

Cuinn tried to loosen the rigidity of his shoulders. There was nothing he could do about the sweat beading his forehead. At least the air around them was stiflingly warm. He offered a languid shrug. "I've been travelling." Mithanis's mouth tightened dangerously and Cuinn hurried on. "You know where I've been—I sent you letters, plenty of them."

"You went to the Twin Thrones." It wasn't clear whether Mithanis was asking a question or making a statement. Cuinn decided to take it as a question.

"Just Ryathl. Did you know they have the most wonderful beaches? Absolutely picturesque. And the women there, well... let's just say I had a wonderful time." Cuinn let his smile widen into a leer. He knew how to do this, how to use a touch of glamour and song magic combined to project a façade that fooled everyone around him. It was second nature.

Mithanis snorted in disgust. "Beaches? Women? You've been gone for three months. You vanished without a word to any of us. Not even you are stupid enough to think that's acceptable behaviour."

Cuinn conceded that with an apologetic sigh. "I only intended to be away a week or two, that's why I just left you and Az a note. But the weather was so nice, and I was enjoying myself so much, I just lost track of time. I'm sorry. I know I should have come back sooner."

Mithanis kept tight control of his expression, but contempt flashed briefly in the depths of his dark eyes. Good, contempt was what Cuinn wanted. It meant Mithanis bought his story. "Who did you see there?"

The question was delivered with deceptive mildness, but Cuinn didn't miss the danger in it. This was what Mithanis was most interested in knowing. "I briefly spoke to King Aethain, if that's what you're asking. He seemed to feel the need to visit me even though I wasn't in Ryathl in an official capacity. I tell you what, that man is so stiff I wonder if he's ever able to sit down."

"And what did you talk about?"

"The weather. SkyRiding. It was all a bore, I tell you." Cuinn matched his words with an irritated roll of his eyes.

"Where's the rest of the pathetic human guard you took with you?" he said softly. "Fall overboard or get lost in the Calumnian wilderness, did they?"

Cuinn thought back to that night in the mines. How they'd saved his life twice now.

And he was angry.

He looked around with a puzzled expression. "I seem to recall five of my *pathetic* human guard soundly defeating Azrilan's *elite* warriors in a game of alleya some months ago."

Mithanis's face darkened. Cuinn glanced over his shoulder at Tiercelin. "I also think you may have a problem with your sight, Brother. Not all my Wolves are without wings. Talon Stormflight, am I mistaken?" He glanced at Tiercelin.

"Certainly not, Your Highness." Tiercelin bowed his head politely.

Mithanis's gaze switched to Tiercelin, lips curling in another sneer. The healer had managed the perfect pitch of deference, trained from birth to do so, but Cuinn was struck with the sudden terror that he might become another target of his brother's. He shouldn't have opened his mouth. He was fool.

"Speaking of which, what have you done with the rest of my wing?" Cuinn spoke in an effort to draw Mithanis's attention back to him. "I'm astonished they haven't draped themselves all over me like a too-warm blanket the moment I landed."

"I wanted to speak with you alone." Mithanis gave another smile that did not reach his eyes. "We will discuss your behaviour later as a family. This isn't done, Cuinn."

Cuinn wanted to hold his gaze. To try pushing back in a way he never had before. But nothing had really changed. The threat Mithanis posed to his Wolves hadn't changed. So he flashed a beaming smile. "I can't wait."

And then Cuinn walked past his brother, heading for his front door, gritting his teeth through the pain of walking without a limp.

"Cuinn?"

He turned, summoning the bored puzzlement back to his expression.

"Ensure your captain goes to see Ravinire as soon as she appears from wherever the rest of your rabble are."

There was an implied threat in those words that had Cuinn's banked fury raging again, but Talyn could handle Ravinire—she already planned to go and see him as soon as the Wolves were settled back in their barracks.

"I'll try and remember to tell her." He waved a hand. "But before you order her executed or something equally unnecessary, do keep in mind that I ordered her to come with me to Ryathl. She protested every step of the way, I assure you."

"What I choose to do with WingGuard officers is none of your concern, or interest—as you've regularly pointed out," Mithanis said smoothly, leaping into the air as he did so.

The second Mithanis was in the air, rustling sounded and Wolves appeared from all directions. Cuinn stared around him, astonished. He'd had no idea they were all there, but the way they'd been positioned... if Mithanis or his distant Falcon detail had tried anything, they'd have been dead before they got a step towards Cuinn.

"Welcome home, Your Highness." Theac strode across the bridge before stopping and saluting smartly.

"Theac." A grin tumbled over his face, the rush of delight at seeing the grizzled features of Talyn's second threatening to bowl him over. "You are a sight for sore eyes."

"You're looking well." Theac cleared his throat. Behind his habitual scowl Cuinn could feel the man's delight at his obvious recovery.

"Blame Tiercelin." Cuinn winked. "Captain Dynan is on her way up with the other talons. I assume your detail is taking over my guard?"

"That's right," Theac said. "Will you be staying in?"

"For a while. Thank you, Theac." He wanted to say more, but he couldn't, not with twenty-odd Wolves watching this whole conversation.

"Your Highness." He saluted and turned to bark orders to his detail.

Cuinn turned to Tiercelin. "Get me inside. I need to sit down before I fall down."

HE COLLAPSED onto the lush sofa in his tower as the last of his strength gave out. His body trembled all over and he had sweated through his shirt. Even worse was the stabbing pain pulsing through his left leg.

At least he'd managed to get inside before Talyn arrived or Theac saw his weakness.

A moment later and all his exhaustion and pain was temporarily forgotten as a blur of black fur and claws flashed past his peripheral vision and he found his lap full of tawncat.

"Jasper!" he murmured, sliding an arm around the animal and hugging him close. The tawncat pressed against him, yowling softly, a rough tongue scraping over the side of his face. And then he was gracefully leaping off Cuinn to land at his feet and remain there, green eyes staring up at him.

Cuinn's eyes widened. Jasper had grown remarkably over the past months, and was now comparable with a larger-sized dog... a muscular, vicious dog. A wide grin spread over his face. "I missed you."

Jasper tossed his head.

"Your Highness?"

Jasper's eyes slid over to fix a warning glare on Tiercelin.

"Just give me a moment, Tiercelin." He winced as he re-settled himself on the sofa, the pain and weariness flooding back with a vengeance.

The winged Wolf leaned down and gently lifted Cuinn's leg so that it rested on the table in front of the sofa. Cuinn's head fell back against the pillows, and he concentrated on breathing through the pain while Tiercelin disappeared for a few moments. When he returned, he lifted Cuinn's leg again to slide cushions underneath it. "How are you doing?" the healer asked, crouching before him.

Cuinn swallowed, certain he'd gone deathly pale. "Just give me a few minutes to rest and I'll be fine."

"You did too much."

"I was not going to show any weakness in front of Mithanis," Cuinn gritted out.

Tiercelin said nothing further. Instead he began using his magic on Cuinn's leg. After a short time of the healer's gentle, rhythmic hand movements, the pain began to dull and new energy seeped through him. Lethargy followed, and he dozed until Tiercelin woke him with a touch. "Here, drink this."

Cuinn took the mug and sipped at the contents. "Thank you."

"The herbs in the tea should help the physical pain." Tiercelin rose lithely to his feet, wings flaring for balance. "How do you feel otherwise?"

Cuinn looked away, not wanting to talk to Tiercelin about how terrifying it had been to face his brother. How even now, in his own quarters, he didn't feel safe. How rivalling all of that fear was guilt and shame—that once again he hadn't been able to stand up to Mithanis.

Tiercelin cleared his throat. "Do you want me to get Captain Dynan?"

Cuinn looked up sharply. "Why?"

Tiercelin settled a knowing gaze on him. "It just seems that when the captain is around, your spirits are higher."

"I'm fine, and I certainly don't need a babysitter," he snapped.

Tiercelin nodded, unoffended. "I need to report to the barracks. I'll be back this evening to work on you again. Theac's detail is surrounding the tower, so you're safe in here."

"Thanks." He lifted his gaze to the healer's, anger gone as quickly as it had come. "For everything. I wouldn't be here without you."

Tiercelin bowed his head and upper body—a single, graceful movement, wings half-unfurling, arms outstretched, in a gesture of respect the winged folk used with an Acondor royal.

A bow Cuinn had never once received in his life.

Shock flooded him. He'd never considered, not for an instant, being a true prince of his country. It had never been an option. When he'd courted Raya, proposed to her, he hadn't done it with the intention of claiming his birthright. Even then he'd known it was Mithanis's position alone.

By the time Cuinn stopped staring, slow to work out how to respond, Tiercelin had gone, the door closing softly behind him. Jasper leapt onto the sofa beside Cuinn, curled up, head resting on Cuinn's leg, eyes focused on the door. Contentment emanated from the tawncat.

A few minutes later Theac entered, two more Wolves visible through the gap before the door swung shut.

"Captain Dynan and the talons are back at the barracks, Your Highness." Theac gave him a friendly nod before going to take up a guard position in one of the higher levels.

Cuinn leaned back against the sofa, taking deep breaths in an effort to relax, his hand stroking Jasper's soft fur. The sweat was clammy on his body and he longed for a bath, but didn't have enough energy to summon a servant to draw one. Nor could he afford a servant to see him like this.

Questions and thoughts swirled around and around in his mind; were the Wolves good enough to keep him safe? What was Talyn hiding from him? Should he have just done the smart thing and stayed in Ryathl where he could live his life in safety?

No. He belonged here. He was a prince of these people and even if he couldn't act like it, there were things he could do to help them. So he needed to get strong again. Let Mithanis's temper calm down.

And then he could start helping once more.

Eventually he fell into a fitful sleep. He awoke with a start when a loud knocking came at the door. He was still shifting into a more upright position when Theac stomped down the stairs and strode over to the door. The Wolf cautiously glanced out the window, then relaxed the hand on his axe when he saw who it was.

"Prince Cuinn, it's your mother." Theac hesitated. "I can tell her you're sleeping."

"You're willing to tell the queen of Mithranar to go away?" Cuinn raised an eyebrow. "You Wolves *are* brave. No Theac, you'd best let her in. Just give me a second."

He arranged himself on the couch in what he hoped looked like a casual sprawl, then straightened his shirt and pants. Annoyed to be moved from his comfortable spot, Jasper let out a snarl and dropped to the floor. Cuinn was careful to remove his leg from its resting place and arrange it in a more natural position. A hint of glamour magic removed any sign that he might be hurt or unwell.

Theac waited until he was ready, then opened the door. He bowed low as the queen walked in, then stood guard at the open entrance, face impassive.

"Cuinn, where have you been?" his mother snapped without preamble.

"I told you, Ryathl." He threaded impatience into his voice. "Mithanis has already been here demanding the same thing. Did neither of you read my letters? I wrote them precisely so you wouldn't yell at me when I got home."

Fury lit up her pale eyes. "You didn't tell me you were leaving, nor where you were going. That is completely unacceptable."

"Yes, yes, Mithanis has already lectured me on that too," he muttered. "I'm sorry. I left on impulse, and I was enjoying myself and lost track of time."

The queen's face softened as she sighed. "Cuinn. What is going on?"

He met her eyes. His mother loved him, he didn't doubt that, but she couldn't—or wouldn't—protect him from his brother either. She was a strong queen and a powerful song mage. She held her throne with an iron grip, and she wasn't stupid. She knew the strength and ambition of her eldest son.

And she did nothing about it.

Not for Azrilan, and not for him. Sometimes he thought he hated her for it, but that emotion was always fleeting and superficial. Instead it mostly just made him feel even more lonely. It was one of the reasons he'd proposed to Raya so young—to have someone in his life who loved him, who put him first... it had been a heady feeling. And just as quickly as he'd found that, it had been ripped away.

Teaching him a valuable lesson. Lonely as it may be, it was less painful to not let people get close to you.

"Why did you go?" she pressed when he said nothing.

He shifted to ease his leg, trying to make the movement look casual. He didn't have the energy for a long, drawn-out conversation with her, not one where he'd have to keep lying convincingly. So he tried to think of a way to distract her, throw her off course, send her away in a huff.

"Who was my father?" he asked. He hadn't asked that question since childhood, eventually growing weary of her utter refusal to tell him anything. And given his father's complete absence from his life, once he'd grown older, he'd stopped caring about who he was. But he hoped asking the question now would provoke the same response, and she'd leave him alone.

Her face tightened and a wave of reluctance brushed around him— her magic seeking to dissuade him from asking more. As always, unwilling to show her the skill with which he wielded his own magic, he let it wash over him without comment. "Why would you ask me that now?"

He shrugged. "Surely you don't think it's odd that I would want to know who my father was."

"You never cared much before," she said flatly.

Underneath her words... was that *panic* he was picking up? Why? Some of his exhaustion fell away as interest took hold. He'd never imagined that the identity of his father might be important, might actually mean something. He'd always just assumed he'd been a pretty winged man from a less important family who'd briefly taken her fancy. "Maybe now I do."

Another flare, this time of terror, that she hid quickly and smoothly. "Cuinn, it really doesn't matter."

He sat up straighter, abandoning the pretence at flippancy. "I'm starting to get the impression it does. What are you hiding?"

The emotional fear and panic was even briefer this time, before his mother sighed in faint irritation with a skill so sublime Cuinn wasn't sure if he'd imagined the turmoil that preceded it. She glanced around the room a moment before seating herself across from him. "Who did you see in Ryathl?"

He frowned. In her question there had been a flicker of something. Evasion. A desire for him not to connect something. But what? "I already told Mithanis. The king did the diplomatic niceties."

It was her turn to fake the casual shrug, tossing her long golden hair over her shoulder for good measure. "I haven't seen any of the Dumnorix since they visited after Aethain's coronation. Is he as severe-looking as I remember?"

"He is. Why did you request a Kingshield guard for me?" He threw the question out as a test.

There was no visible reaction as she shrugged again. "I asked for a Kingshield to help train the WingGuard in personal protection. For all of us."

"That's a lie," he accused. "Talyn Dynan didn't train the Wing-Guard, she trained my personal guard detail, and don't even try and tell me Ravinire did that without your approval. The man doesn't sneeze without your say so. You know what Mithanis is capable of. That's why you asked for a Kingshield guard. For me."

"You're exaggerating. Your brother is ambitious, yes, but that doesn't make him the evil monster you seem to think he is."

"That's just what you want to believe," he said, upset. "You have no idea what it's like for me. What happened…"

"What are you talking about?" she asked sharply.

"Nothing. It's nothing." He sank back into the couch. "Mother, I was bored, and so I went travelling for a while. Really, it's not a big deal."

"If you can't see that a prince of Mithranar disappearing for three months is a very big deal, then you're more foolish and immature than I thought you were," his mother snapped, rising to her feet.

"Yes, well, I wouldn't want to ruin your assumptions about me." He muttered. Part of him realised she'd neatly deflected the conversation about his father and wanted to push her on it, but he was just too exhausted and heartsick.

She strode for the doorway, wings flaring in agitation, before pausing and looking back at him. He didn't know what he read in her eyes, but thought it might be disappointment.

"I loved your father, Cuinn. We had only a short time together, but I loved him; it was nothing like what I had with Mithanis and Azrilan's father. I had so hoped that the child I shared with him would be..."

He stared, thrown utterly off balance by her sudden honesty. "What?" he asked in a whisper.

"Nothing," she said equally softly. "You'll be at family dinner tonight, Cuinn."

And then she was gone.

Theac closed the door behind the queen and then turned to him, clearing his throat. "Prince Cuinn—"

"Leave me alone, Theac." Cuinn waved him off, desperately not wanting the man to see him break down. "Please, just go."

"Your Highness." He left quietly, closing the door with a soft click.

Jumping back onto the sofa, Jasper yowled softly, one paw reaching out to bat Cuinn's shoulder. He swallowed, refusing to allow the tears to fall. His mother's disappointment had hit him harder than he wanted it to.

Why was she so terrified of him knowing who his father had been? And why had he never seen that fear in her before? Because he hadn't cared to, he realised. Because he'd been so focused on hiding and working as the Shadowhawk that he hadn't bothered to notice anything about his mother aside from the fact that she wouldn't protect him from Mithanis.

And now he discovered she'd *loved* his father. Why hadn't she married him, if that was the case? With two heirs already, it wasn't like she'd needed to make another strategic marriage.

She'd *loved* his father.

Cuinn wasn't sure what to do with that knowledge. Had his father loved her? Loved *him?* Weariness crashed down over him. Right now he was too physically and emotionally exhausted to try and work any of it out. So he curled up on the couch, Jasper burrowed into his side, and closed his eyes.

CHAPTER 11

*T*heac was waiting in the drill yard of the Wolves' barracks, a chaotic alleya game going on behind him, when Talyn and her other talons came through the gate.

"He's safe?" she asked immediately.

"Secure in his tower with my detail after a happy reunion with that vicious tawncat of his," Theac assured her. "I'll head straight back there, I just wanted to say hello first."

She grinned. "It's good to see you, Theac."

"And you." His habitual scowl faded into a smile.

A brief hubbub ensued as Halun, Andres, Corrin and Zamaril greeted Theac with enthusiasm, stoically ignoring his glares and muttered complaints about hyperactive children.

"All is well here?" Talyn asked quietly once the talons had dispersed to go and greet their details.

"It has been," Theac said. "Either Windsong did a good job shielding us from any fallout, or there wasn't much of one, because it's been a quiet few months. Too quiet, if you ask me. I haven't seen the man for weeks."

Unease stirred. "You haven't? No orders, nothing like that?"

"No. We've trained every day, continued the volunteer escorts of the human servants at night, and otherwise kept quiet and unobtrusive. Ravinire told me that in your absence there was no expectation for me to attend his weekly captains' meetings—and that was the last I saw of him, too."

She let out a breath. She'd expected more of a reaction than that, even if Ravinire and the princes believed Cuinn had forced the Wolf talons to travel with him.

Theac brightened a little. "Prince Cuinn looked better than I'd expected."

"He's still doing a lot of pretending, but he and Tiercelin have worked a marvel together," she assured him.

"Good, I was worried." Theac's expression darkened momentarily before clearing. "I'd best get back to my detail. Can we talk more later?"

"Definitely. There's a lot I need to tell you." She stopped in the midst of turning away as a thought occurred to her. "How are Kiran, Liadin and Lyra?"

"No change in them that I can tell," he said of the three winged Wolves that had learned of Cuinn's Shadowhawk identity when helping to rescue him from the cave-in. "If you ask me, they're happy as fish in a pond."

"Thanks. We'll talk later."

After exchanging a series of boisterous greetings with the Wolves playing alleya in the yard—she'd missed them more than she realised —Talyn headed up to her quarters. Her nose wrinkled at the faint musty smell that hit her as she stepped inside her door.

She crossed the room and threw open the door in her glass wall. It was a characteristically muggy day outside, but a sluggish breeze flowed in, and she took a deep breath, the smell of fresh flowers filling her nose.

She'd missed that smell. Even missed the thick, soupy air.

Leaving the opened door, she went up to her bedroom and placed a tin cup on her windowsill. Speaking to Savin was a priority. He would no doubt be wondering what had happened to prompt their sudden departure from the SkyReach and she would need his help with Vengeance.

Anticipation already seeped through her, like the effect of a fine wine. They were finally back in Dock City.

It was time for a little vengeance of her own.

Her rooftop garden was as wild as she'd left it. Far below were the tops of the trees of the forest under the citadel, and if she strained her eyes she could see the top of the marble wall to the south. Closer were the spires and turrets of the palace, gleaming white in the sun.

Above, the coloured wings of the winged folk flashed and glittered as they flew the thermals. A moment's envy stabbed her as she watched them at flight—it must be marvellous to be able to swoop through the skies on a day like this.

"You're winged folk. You could grow your wings," Sari noted.

"And have to re-learn balance, agility and fighting with such an encumbrance?" Talyn shook her head. *"No thank you very much."*

She savoured the peace of the garden for a few more moments, then turned reluctantly to go back inside.

It was time to see Ravinire.

SHE'D DECIDED to sound out the Falcon before approaching Windsong. He would give her an indication of exactly how angry everyone was about Cuinn's sudden absence. After all, Windsong had effectively let them go. She hoped the fact he still apparently had a head on his shoulders was a positive sign.

Not that the Falcon wasn't going to be more than a little upset she'd left without telling him. She just hoped she could talk him down from whatever furious cliff he was likely currently perched on.

The moment she presented herself at Ravinire's spacious offices, one of his Falcons told her to go straight through. She braced herself, took a breath, and stepped inside.

"Captain Dynan." Ravinire rose from his chair, gave her a look. "At least you didn't make me chase you down."

Talyn saluted. "Sir."

He gave her a harder look, his expression warning her that feigning surprise as to the reason for the censure she was about to receive wouldn't be well received. "I have questions for you. Starting with, where have you been these past three months?"

"In Calumnia, sir. As I understand it, Prince Cuinn made you aware of that fact." She kept her tone even and polite, giving him the straight truth without hedging. She was going to have to start lying soon, and it would go down better if she started the conversation with honesty.

"Why wasn't I informed prior to your departure?"

"The decision to leave was a sudden one, sir."

"I'm aware. Windsong sent word the day you left. That doesn't answer my question." His voice was dangerously quiet.

She and Cuinn had already discussed how to handle this. Lumping all the responsibility on him was the best course of action—it fit with his irresponsible persona and hopefully removed enough blame from Talyn and her talons that no serious punitive action would be taken. So she cleared her throat. "Prince Cuinn insisted on leaving immediately, sir. He gave me little time to tell anyone."

The Falcon's jaw hardened. "So let me get this straight. You decided to depart the country entirely, with Prince Cuinn and several of my WingGuard, and not let me know where you were going, or that you were even leaving?"

Ravinire's obvious fury was intimidating. She refused to let on that she was affected by it. "It was Prince Cuinn's choice to go, sir. I merely ensured he was protected for the duration of his journey. I made Flight-Leader Windsong aware."

"He tells the same story."

She almost started in surprise. Ravinire thought both she and Windsong were feeding him a story?

"Why did Prince Cuinn suddenly decide to travel to Calumnia?"

"You'd have to ask him that, sir." An evasion, and he caught it, anger rippling across his face. Damn.

"What you did is unacceptable. I don't care what Windsong did or didn't know. What gives you the right to take Prince Cuinn anywhere without speaking to me first? Especially since you knew full well the queen knew nothing about it."

For a moment she stood uncomfortably, working out what to say. Ravinire wasn't buying Cuinn's sudden desire for travel as an excuse, so she had to double down. "Sir, Prince Cuinn made his wishes clear. He was drunk at the time, and honestly, I thought we would change his mind once he sobered up. He didn't. The best I could do was the message I sent once we docked in Ryathl."

Ravinire nodded and sat back, releasing her gaze. Talyn let out an inwards breath of relief. It was short-lived.

"Just to be absolutely clear, Captain, I don't care how urgent, or how drunk the prince is. I expect you to notify me immediately before leaving Mithranar. The fact that you didn't remains utterly unacceptable. Am I clear?"

"Provided it doesn't compromise his safety, yes, sir."

A heavy beat of silence.

Ravinire leaned forward, resting interlinked hands on the desk before him. "And there we get closer to the truth of it, I suspect. You took him away because you thought he was in danger."

She swallowed. "I already told you. It was his decision, not mine."

"I am responsible for the protection of the royal family. I need to know of all possible threats to any member of that family, Captain." True anger edged the Falcon's voice.

"Just like you gave me all the information I needed when I first came to Mithranar?" She tried for polite and barely managed it. Ravinire had been an obstruction since she'd first arrived, refusing to trust her or give her the information she needed to keep Cuinn safe. His anger was beginning to chafe at her patience.

Ravinire rose, wings spreading wide behind him as he leaned forward to stare her right in the eyes. "We both know Prince Cuinn will not lift a hand to help you if I send you packing, Captain Dynan. Windsong is already gone. From now on—"

Shocked, she interrupted him. "I'm sorry, sir. Where has Flight-Leader Windsong gone?"

"He was stripped of his rank and sent back to the SkyReach to rejoin the flight of Falcons we keep posted there," Ravinire said evenly. "On the orders of a highly displeased queen. Nor did the prince of night take kindly to his younger brother's little jaunt, or Windsong's inability to prevent it."

Dread curled through her chest. If Mithanis had sent Windsong packing then... "Why aren't you kicking me out?"

"I was going to," he said bluntly. "The queen stayed my hand. I vehemently disagree with her decision and she won't stick her neck out for you again. She can't afford to. I hope you understand that."

"Yes, sir." Talyn spoke with as much sincerity as she could. Her ongoing presence in Mithranar was contingent on her having a position in the WingGuard. Defeating Vengeance would be impossible if she was sent home. She had to do better at swallowing her anger.

"Siran Brightwing has been promoted into the vacant flight-leader's spot." Ravinire's look made it clear this was also Prince Mithanis's decision. "But from now on, you will report directly to me. I want daily copies of every guard schedule you make, and I want to know if Prince Cuinn so much as steps a toe out of the palace *before* it happens. You fail to do either of those things, even once, and you're gone. Am I clear?"

Talyn bore up under his merciless stare. "Yes, sir."

"Get out of my office."

Talyn saluted and left.

FEELING THOROUGHLY CHASTENED, Talyn went down to join the Wolves in their mess for dinner. They were happy to have their captain and talons back home, and typical of Mithranans, a small group pulled out instruments after eating, and music and song filled the hall. It eased the anxiety and tension that had been building in her all day.

"This is home, Sari. At least, it is for part of me," she admitted.

"I know, Tal." There was a hint of sadness in her partner's voice that made her frown.

"What is it?"

"*Nothing. I just worry for you.*"

"You look serious, Captain." Theac came to sit beside her, a mug of cider in one hand, tray of food in the other, interrupting her mental conversation. "How did it go with the Falcon?"

"He's furious," she said. "We were closer to disaster than you realised—it sounds like Windsong and the queen shielded us from the worst of it. You haven't seen Windsong because the queen stripped him of his rank and sent him packing to the SkyReach. One more step out of line and he's going to put me on a ship home."

Theac's face darkened. "We'll have to be even more careful."

Except that she couldn't. She had to start hunting Vengeance under Ravinire's nose without involving the Wolves.

Well, she'd always enjoyed a challenge.

A comfortable silence fell between them as Theac ate, but once he finished, he pushed aside his tray and looked at her. "What do you want to do about Zamaril and his detail?"

Talyn sighed. It hadn't been necessary for an immediate replacement with the Wolves remaining behind in Mithranar with Theac, but now they were home, Zamaril's detail needed a talon. "I welcome your thoughts on that."

"I'll take him into my detail," Theac said. "Less humiliating for him to report to me since I'm the most senior officer in the wing after you. And I'll transfer Vanton from my detail into his old one to even the numbers. Then I thought perhaps myself or Andres could take on an extra detail for a while."

"You want to give Zamaril the opportunity to earn it back, rather than promote someone into his place." She considered that. "Do you disagree with what I did?"

"Wouldn't matter if I did," he said loyally. "But no, I don't. I would like to give the lad another chance though."

"Give the extra responsibility to Andres." Theac's idea made sense, and she wasn't sure any of the other Wolves were ready for command yet anyway. "He's the most experienced leader here and he can handle it. You're already busy as my second."

"Aye, I'll get it done."

A rush of affection for him swept through her and she reached out to lay a hand lightly on his shoulder. "I wouldn't want anyone else with me, Theac."

He scowled. "Halun spoke to me earlier, about your plans regarding Vengeance."

"Good. Any issues?"

"None. The way I see it, Prince Cuinn isn't safe until Vengeance is gone."

A brief ruckus sounded at the mess entrance as Andres' detail filed in after finishing a shift. Kiran and Liadin were with them, both doubled up in laughter, no doubt at something Kiran had said.

When Liadin spotted Talyn sitting with Theac, he nudged Kiran and both young men headed their way. Kiran diverged briefly to drop by the table Lyra was sitting at. Theac rose as the three winged folk arrived at their table, leaving them to it.

"We haven't said a word, Captain. Not to anyone," Lyra spoke in an undertone.

"Figured you should hear that from us straight up," Liadin added.

"Why not?" Talyn asked bluntly, keeping her voice low so their conversation was hidden under the chatter of Wolves. "Don't misunderstand me, you're both in this wing because I trust and respect you, but you're winged folk. You must have some conflicted feelings over learning who he is."

They glanced at each other, Liadin answering first. "I joined the Wolves because I wanted to be a warrior, and I'd always been prevented from joining the WingGuard because I didn't have warrior magic. But it wasn't just that. When I saw how the talons fought together in the alleya game at Monsoon Festival last year, it changed something for me. It taught me that maybe winged folk aren't so superior after all. More, I wanted to be a part of something like that—a real team, with trust and respect and friendship."

"We *were* conflicted at first," Lyra said honestly. "But what the prince was trying to do—by helping the humans… it made us realise that he sees all of us together, not just the winged folk, as his people.

It's like the Wolves, just on a bigger scale. And when we talked about it, well…"

"That's the country we want to be part of too," Kiran said quietly, all traces of his usual joking demeanour gone. "It's the country we want to help build."

"Thank you for your honesty," she said, ignoring the unease his words inspired. Cuinn wasn't as useless as she had made it sound to Aethain; without even trying he inspired loyalty. "I won't insult you further by asking you to continue keeping the secret."

"We understand the danger," Lyra agreed. "And we're sworn to protect him."

"And one day that might be even more important than it is now—keeping him safe," Liadin added. The implication in his voice was clear; he thought that one day, Cuinn could be king. It was dangerous thinking, too dangerous, but she didn't have the heart to tell them that day was unlikely to ever come.

So she merely nodded. The three of them rose from the table, saluted, and walked away. She didn't watch them go, instead staring at her plate, her mind awhirl. While their clear loyalty was a weight off her mind, their words had been dangerous. She hoped they never spoke them aloud to anyone else.

THE FOLLOWING MORNING, Talyn left her talons drilling the Wolves and had Zamaril and Tiercelin—in command of Cuinn's morning detail—meet her in the garden at the base of Cuinn's tower. They were both there when she pushed through the gate, peering upward at a group of winged folk cavorting in the sky.

All snapped to attention when Cuinn appeared, floating down from above. Talyn smothered a smile. He looked better than he had the day before—less drained, more colour in his cheeks. She hoped it was real and not more glamour.

"Good morning." He greeted them, landing with only a slight wince. "Captain Dynan, care to tell me the reason behind this little garden party?"

"We're going to improve your security," she said. Now that she knew who Cuinn was, now that there was no need for pretence, she could do the things she'd always wanted to do. Namely, make it close to impossible for a Shadow—with or without a tawncat—to get inside his tower. "Zamaril, show me how you would get in."

The thief flashed a grin before immediately climbing the drainpipe up the outside of the tower. He stopped at the first floor window and studied the lock for a few seconds. Everyone watched. "It would take me more time to tie my shoelace than to get inside this window," he called down.

Lovely. "What about the others?"

He clambered up higher. "The same. They all only have basic locks and none of them are in use."

Talyn thought for a moment, then called out to the nearest Wolf. "Tirina, go and find one of the WingGuard blacksmiths. I want bars installed on those windows."

Cuinn cleared his throat. She arched an eyebrow at him, but he said nothing. Tirina saluted and leapt into the air, scarlet wings flashing in the sunlight.

"If we bar the windows, would you still be able to get in?" she called up to Zamaril.

"No." He shook his head. "Not without filing through the bars, and that would take hours. Too long to hover on the outside of a building without being noticed by a Wolf guard."

"Winged folk warrior magic could melt through iron bars in under a minute," Tiercelin pointed out.

"Silently?" Talyn raised an eyebrow.

"Of course not. It would be very loud, like an explosion going off."

"In that case, giving the prince and his guards plenty of fore-warning that someone was trying to get inside?"

"Well, yes." He shrugged sheepishly.

Talyn turned her attention back to Zamaril. "What would be your next option for entry?"

"The hatch that leads down through the roof," he said promptly.

"There's already a bar on the inside of that hatch," Talyn said. "Where would you go next?"

"How am I supposed to get any fresh air into my rooms?" Cuinn asked with raised eyebrows. "With everything barred up like a prison."

"There's a novel idea. Leave your windows and doors open for fresh air," Talyn said. "At the same time, you can hang out a sign inviting any would-be assassins inside for tea."

Cuinn's grin widened in amusement. "Who put salt in your oatmeal this morning, Captain Bad Mood?"

Talyn ignored him, trying hard not to roll her eyes. "Zamaril?"

"The front door would be my last option, but there are always Wolves stationed there. As long as they're not asleep, it would be impossible to sneak past them."

If her Wolves were falling asleep on duty then she had much bigger problems. Still, there were other, more sophisticated methods for subduing guards. Poison, for instance. "If you had some way of getting past the Wolves on the door, how would you get through?"

"It depends on how heavy the door was and what sort of lock was on it." Zamaril shrugged.

"So we're going up then?" Cuinn spread his wings. "I'll meet you all at my front door."

Tiercelin followed the prince into the air. Zamaril and Talyn walked out of the garden and found their way to the corridor that led to the bridge across from Cuinn's tower. Cuinn and Tiercelin waited for them at the front door. The prince was bent over the lock, studying it. When Talyn and Zamaril approached, he straightened and looked at them with a woebegone expression.

"I suppose you're going to want to bar my front door as well?" he asked.

Talyn barely managed to smother a smile. "It might be difficult for you to ever get in or out of your tower if we barred the front door too, but at the very least you are going to have to start locking it."

"Well, it could be a good time to invest in a Montagni iron mine." He sighed.

"And just think," she murmured as Zamaril bent to peer at the lock. "You'd be alive to enjoy all the profits."

"The lock is very simple, Captain." Zamaril straightened. "It would take me seconds to pick it, or smash through it with something heavy enough."

Talyn looked at him a moment. "We install a better lock then. One that couldn't be readily picked?"

"I know of those," he said. "I'll go down to Dock City this afternoon and get some."

"Good. We'll do that, and replace the door with one made from thicker, hardier wood."

Cuinn crossed his arms and leaned back against the railing of the bridge. "Well, at least we're going to have the profits from my newly purchased shares in that iron mine to fund all this."

She arched an eyebrow. "Money is a problem for you, *Prince Acondor?*"

"*Six thrices, Tal, are you* flirting *with him?*" Sari's delighted voice rippled through her mind.

"*Of course I'm not,*" she hissed. "*Go away!*"

"My mother controls all of the family's fortune." Cuinn shrugged. "I get an allowance."

"I'll go in with you for the shares to the iron mine, Your Highness," Zamaril said, a smile twitching at the corners of his mouth.

"Deal." Cuinn clapped him on the shoulder. "We'll split the profits fifty-fifty."

Talyn was momentarily struck by the interplay between Cuinn and his Wolf guard. Zamaril was clearly warmed by Cuinn's treatment of him—the prince had a magical charm that when used with sincerity was almost overwhelming. Cuinn, on the other hand, seemed to think nothing of his easy comradery with a lowly human guard.

That was dangerous. Anybody could be watching.

She gave him a look. Cuinn ignored it. The same look directed at Zamaril had the thief clearing his throat and stepping away.

Tirina appeared a few moments later with the smith, and she and

Tiercelin both disappeared when Cuinn did, bored at the prospect of watching windows being measured for bars.

"Captain?" Zamaril asked.

"Yes?" She switched her attention from the door to her talon.

"I'm not leaving."

"What?" She frowned.

He straightened his shoulders. "Ever since you demoted me, you keep looking at me like you're afraid I'm going to get so upset I'll leave."

She hesitated. "I don't truly think you're going to leave."

"You made a call. You're our captain. You need to own that."

She lifted an eyebrow at him. "Are you trying to demonstrate that you've learned what it takes to be a leader?"

He hesitated, then shook his head. "Truth is, Captain, if you put me in the same situation now, I'd do the exact same thing all over again."

"Zamaril." She huffed an exasperated breath.

"It's your fault," he said, but there was no bite in his words. "You dragged me off the streets and gave me a life. A family. You made me trust them, believe in them, and you made them do the same for me. I'd do anything for Halun, or Corrin, or Theac. Even Tiercelin." His voice turned soft, sincere. "I'd risk being kicked out of the Wolves for any of them."

"I didn't make anyone do anything. You did it for yourselves. I hope you realise that." She sighed. Zamaril was far more suited to being a Callanan warrior than talon of a protective detail. If only he'd been born in the Twin Thrones. "And while I understand the sentiment… as a leader in this wing, Prince Cuinn has to be your first priority."

He said nothing to that. A silence fell between them. Eventually Talyn turned away. "You'd best go see about those locks. I've got morning drill to get back to."

CHAPTER 12

*C*uinn found it impossible to sleep, and not only because of his still sore and healing body. Coming home had dropped him straight back into the realities of his life in Mithranar.

So when night descended and the usual *need* to go out into the streets of Dock City began itching under his skin, he couldn't lie still. He'd been away for months—his contacts would be wondering where he was, and who knew how many shipments of basic supplies had been appropriated by the Falcons... the frustration was inescapable. But Wolves stood at every entrance, no doubt paying extra attention on their talon's orders. Corrin, tonight.

Tossing and turning under tangled sheets, he tried to relax, to tell himself to calm and sleep. His body needed the rest.

But he couldn't.

Jasper gave a protesting yowl and relocated to the floor, where he promptly fell back to sleep.

Eventually Cuinn gave up trying to sleep and tried to come up with a solution instead. If he couldn't help the humans as the Shadowhawk for a while, maybe he could do it as Prince Cuinn. It would be risky, but so was acting as the Shadowhawk. He'd need to toe a fine line—try and effect change without doing enough to make Mithanis feel threatened.

The idea was terrifying.

But he had glamour, and song magic. None of his family knew his strength or depth of skill at either type of magic. And he wasn't a fool. He could do it.

It was either this, or nothing. And nothing wasn't an option.

The knock at the front door below startled him. He heard the soft murmur of Corrin's voice, then footsteps up the tower stairs. A human then.

"I'm not going to walk in on something I don't want to see, am I?" a dry voice asked from behind the closed bedroom door.

He couldn't help it. A wide smile spread over his face at the sound of her voice. He shoved back the covers and swung his legs around to the side of the bed. "Depends on whether you want to see my stunningly beautiful visage, Captain Dynan."

A snort, then the door swung open. Her gaze scanned the room, the practiced glance of a trained warrior. She only turned to him once she'd satisfied herself there was no danger inside.

"Sit." He waved her to the chair by the windows. Assuming this was a discreet visit given the late hour, he didn't light a lamp. "What brings you by?"

"How's the leg?" She pointed, refusing the seat and leaning against the windowsill instead. A scowl crossed his face at the sight of the bars on the windows. They'd been installed the day before and he'd endured endless sniggering from Irial and his other friends ever since.

"Still sore when I land on it, but otherwise getting better every day." He mirrored her posture, leaning against his bed, wings easing out comfortably to either side.

"Up for a chat about the Shadowhawk?"

"I've been trying and failing miserably to sleep," he admitted. "So a chat about anything works for me right now. We could even talk about different types of manure, if you like."

A little smile crossed her face. "Perhaps next time."

"Is this about the Callanan visit? I assume they'll be here soon."

"No, actually." She crossed her arms. "When I was talking to the First Blade back in Ryathl, trying to convince her you weren't a member of Vengeance, I asked what had made her think that in the first place." Talyn hesitated, and he got a hint of more secrets. There was something there, something she was keeping hidden. He tried not to let it upset him.

"What did she tell you?" he asked, letting her off the hook.

"She didn't have specifics, but she did say their information indicated that you worked with the group. I think that's why they assumed you were a member."

"That's pretty vague."

"I know." She shrugged. If there was more, she wasn't going to share. "But I want to talk it over with you. You have helpers in each quarter, right?"

He nodded. "I have a single contact in each quarter, and each uses a different way of communicating with me. They lead a cell of sorts, other residents of that quarter who help out when they can. I try to use a different cell each time to lessen the chances of them getting caught or recognised."

"How organised are they?" She frowned. "You make it sound like they operate on a fairly ad-hoc basis."

"Exactly. Most of them are dock workers or shop owners or servants up here. They're not full-time professional criminals."

"That doesn't sound much like Vengeance. And none are different from the others?"

He stiffened, realisation freezing his blood in his veins. "Flea-biting shit!"

Her eyebrows shot skyward. "Did an Acondor prince just use Dock City vulgarity in front of me?"

"Saniya's network!" He shot to his feet, not even feeling the ache of his healing leg at the sudden movement. "*They're* different. Very different."

Talyn's eyes narrowed, sapphire turning cold with that icy focus she had when she was focused on a target. "She was the one who gave you information about Vengeance when the murders started?"

"Yes. I've worked with her for years. They're professional, organised, don't make mistakes, and although I only ever deal with Saniya, I've always wondered who they were." He frowned. "They don't use violence, though. I wouldn't work with them if they did."

"They don't use violence that you know of," Talyn pointed out. "And if they are as professional as you say, they wouldn't let you see it, because they need the supplies you steal for them."

That stung. "You think they've been manipulating me?"

"What does your magic pick up from Saniya when you interact with her?"

Cuinn thought about it. "She's a bit like you, actually. A master of self-control—doesn't let her emotions get the best of her, so they don't flash to the surface where my magic can easily sense them. But occasionally I've picked up a hint of deep-seated anger."

"Towards the winged folk?"

"Maybe." He ran a hand through his hair. "When emotions are so well-hidden, it's impossible to tell what the source of them is. If I've been helping Vengeance all this time…"

"There are still a lot of questions." She pushed off the wall, came closer to him. "You've been working with Saniya for years, yet the murders only started a year ago, right? The assassination attempt on your mother was after that. So if they are Vengeance, something changed."

"A new leader, or some sort of influencer, like the man you tortured implied," he said quietly.

"Your brother? Working with Saniya? Would you really miss something like that?" She sounded dubious, and he felt the same way. They were missing something.

Talyn's head came up suddenly. "When we were ambushed last year, it was on the way to meet Saniya, wasn't it? She knew where we would be that night."

He nodded. Guilt seeped into his chest and squeezed hard. "I'm sorry."

"Don't be," she said softly. "None of this is your fault."

"When are we going to talk about what else that man you tortured said?" he asked. "About you… that whoever was pulling Vengeance's strings wanted you left alone?"

"That makes even less sense to me than the bit about Mithanis being behind it all," she admitted. "I truly have no idea."

"I don't want you to ignore it. If someone has been trying to protect you, that protection is over now."

"It was over when they tried to bury me in a mine cave-in. I'm not afraid of Vengeance, Cuinn." Irritation threaded her voice.

Of course she wasn't. Danger didn't scare her, it exhilarated her. He let out a sigh. "Okay, so what are we going to do next?"

"I'd like to be more confident of this theory—one thing that sticks for me is that by coming after you, Vengeance have cut off their source of supplies. Either they found another source or they're less professional than we'd judged." Talyn smiled a little. "If Saniya *is* Vengeance, she thinks you're dead. So let's keep it that way, and we'll re-visit the discussion once you're well and Mithanis is over his temper tantrum."

Hope flared. "You mean that?"

"It's like you said, Cuinn. I'm not in charge of you." Apology flashed over her face. "I'm sorry I tried to be."

"You're just trying to do your job. I know that." He met her gaze. "But I need you to understand I can't do nothing."

"I understand it far better than you'd think." She chuckled at some inner knowledge he didn't have.

"You're really going to go after them, aren't you?" He wasn't sure whether he was excited or terrified by the idea.

"We can't afford to be reckless if we're going to do a thorough job in wiping them out." A fierceness edged her voice that sent a thrill through him. "But they tried to kill me, my Wolves. You. You'd better believe I'm going after them."

She moved for the door then, waving him a good night. She was gone before he thought to tell her of the decision he'd made. What he was going to do until he could be the Shadowhawk again.

He stared at the window for a while, turning their discussion over in his mind. Saniya. Part of him could easily believe it of her—that cool mask of hers hid ruthlessness, not compassion like it did in Talyn —while the rest of him struggled to accept that a group he'd worked with for years was secretly a violent gang. How could he not have seen it?

It was only then he noticed that Jasper, curled up on the floor, hadn't issued a single snarl or hiss at Talyn's presence. In fact, he seemed to have slept through the entire encounter.

"So she's okay now, huh?" he asked the tawncat.

Jasper snored on.

Sighing, he dropped back onto the bed.

He was going to have to try and get some rest if he planned to attend Queencouncil tomorrow.

THE DOUBLE DOORS of the Queencouncil chamber echoed loudly as they opened to admit Cuinn. Pausing momentarily to take the weight off his left leg, he scanned the room. His mother sat on a backless chair at the head of a table placed in the centre of the large space, directly beneath the golden sunlight streaming in from the clear glass windows above.

Pretty. But damnably hot. One of the litany of reasons he'd often used for his aversion to attending Queencouncil sessions. At least a sluggish breeze coming from the open space in lieu of a fourth wall— the opening looking out over several lower levels of the citadel—took some of the edge off the heat.

He'd arrived slightly late for the weekly meeting, timing it deliberately to prevent his mother or Mithanis throwing him out before everyone arrived. If either wanted to do that now, it would have to be in front of all the Queencouncil members.

All the lords were present, along with Ravinire, Mithanis and Azrilan. The musical hum of debating voices that had filled the room faded at Cuinn's entrance. Those sitting with their backs to the door looked around in surprise, wings rustling.

He couldn't hide the limp entirely yet, but it was minor enough now that it could be explained away, so he walked in with apparent confidence, Halun at his side. He steadfastly ignored the big man's repeated pointed looks—Halun didn't need words to make Cuinn aware he didn't think this was a good idea.

He'd taken pains with his appearance, not wanting to lose the playboy façade entirely, but aiming to at least look sober enough his mother wouldn't have an obvious excuse to kick him out. So he'd cut his hair shorter than it had ever been, but not quite short enough to be described as neat, and forsaken his usual glamorous clothing for a simple blue jacket and cream breeches. His wings hung loose and relaxed from his back.

"Good morning," he greeted the room. "I apologise for being late."

There was a slight rustling as Halun's detail took up positions around the chamber, ignoring the sneers from the Falcons already there, attention firmly focused on their charge. Cuinn ran his eyes over the attendees as they worked out how to respond.

Charl Nightdrift, responsible for the kingdom's trade, worked closely with Tiercelin's father, Jurian Stormflight, whose responsibilities included the northern mines and izerdia extraction. Both were firmly Mithanis's men and looked forward to a healthy boost in power once Mithanis took the throne.

Beside them was Ausul Goldfeather's eldest son, the too-young and rather intimidated-looking Tirin Goldfeather. Treasury responsibilities had been taken away from him given his youth and inexperience and handed instead to Eril Blacksoar. And then there was Dirsun Swiftwing, nominally in charge of Mithranar's relationships with other countries and the only winged noble who left Mithranar with any regularity.

Completing the council was the Falcon, sitting beside the queen but looking oddly out of place... smaller, somehow. It occurred to Cuinn that his mother had chosen the wrong loyal ally to be her Falcon—something told him Windsong would have managed this room with ease.

The counsellors tried not to look like they were staring. All waited awkwardly for either Mithanis or their queen to say something. His mother didn't seem overly bothered by Cuinn's arrival—in fact, she looked tired. His eldest brother's displeasure at Cuinn's appearance leapt across the room, obvious for any song mage nearby. Azrilan wore a little smile.

"You're limping," Mithanis noted sharply, his tone making the words an accusation.

"Sprained my ankle in an alleya game last night." Cuinn shrugged. "It's nothing." He walked towards the table, keeping his movements languid so as to hide his limp as much as possible. Mithanis took his slowness as a deliberate ploy to annoy the room and his jaw clenched, his quiet seething loud and clear to Cuinn's magic.

"What is it, Cuinn?" His mother's voice sounded as cool and strong as always, despite the weariness tugging at her eyes. "We're in the middle of Queencouncil, as you well know."

"I apologise." Cuinn stopped at an empty chair at the end of the table, directly opposite his mother—and furthest from Mithanis. "I've come to sit in. Please, continue with what you were discussing."

"You've never attended one of these meetings before, little brother," Azrilan said, that small smile still on his face. Cuinn couldn't quite tell if Azrilan was being nice to him, or if his middle brother didn't like his presence any more than Mithanis did.

"I am a prince of Mithranar," Cuinn said calmly. "I have the right to be here. I won't cause any problems."

"What do you imagine you could contribute to these meetings?" Mithanis asked. "You don't know anything about the running of this country."

By now, the councillors' gazes had turned to either their shoes or the papers on the table before them, clearly uncomfortable. There was no steel in any of them. It was a powerful reminder of how much influence Mithanis and his mother had over the council.

Sarana cut in. "Enough, Mithanis. He has the right to be here, and I'd rather not waste any more time debating the point. I won't tolerate any games or disrespect while you are here, Cuinn. Is that clear?"

"Very." He nodded firmly, placed his hands in his lap, and pasted an interested expression on his face. He kept it in place as the discussion resumed and sat quietly, gaze casually roaming the room.

There were few shadowy spots in the well-lit chamber, and therefore nowhere for an assassin to hide. Cuinn hadn't announced his intention to come to the meeting, and he trusted the Wolves to protect him if anything happened. He forced himself to relax with a deep breath.

Movement in the gallery above caught his attention—Mikah was up there, still and silent. The movement had been Talyn joining him. Cuinn couldn't quite make out her expression at this distance, but doubted it was pleasant.

He made a note to tell Halun off later for being such a tattle-tale.

When his gaze returned to the table he found Mithanis watching him steadily, dark eyes unreadable. Cuinn offered a non-threatening smile and returned his attention to the discussion—a proposed raise in taxes for the population of Dock City.

Once the lords had given their views, Mithanis joined in. It had been his idea to institute the new taxes, and it wasn't taking much to convince the council. The queen spoke little, but Cuinn didn't doubt she was taking in everything that was being said.

Voices grew louder as the counsellors dissented on where the money from the new taxes would go. Nightdrift and Stormflight wanted to use it to build new merchant ships to increase their izerdia, wood, and copper exports. Blacksoar disagreed, arguing the money was needed for work on sections of the citadel that were falling into disrepair. Swiftwing looked bored. Tirin Goldfeather tried to say something but was cut off by Blacksoar. Ravinire remained silent—not bored like Swiftwing, but out of his depth.

In the middle of this debate, Mithanis and Azrilan shared a glance, and Azrilan turned to Cuinn. "Surely all of this chatter about taxes must be boring you, little brother. Do you have any views you'd like to share? Maybe then we could move on."

The discussion fell off, the lords glancing uncertainly between the princes, not sure if Azrilan's question had been serious or not. Cuinn took a steadying breath, slowly uncrossing his legs and sitting up. "Well, since you asked, I don't see a good reason for increasing the taxes in the first place."

All eyes turned to stare at him. He had no focus or energy left to read their emotions. Instead every bit of himself was used to fix that polite, considered look on his face, giving an appearance of relaxed comfort in the face of their combined attention.

Mithanis gave Cuinn a hard look. "Shadowhawk activities continue to disrupt our supply chain and izerdia extraction. The WingGuard have yet to catch him, and after a promising start Windsong proved a spectacular failure on that score. We need a better way to neutralise him and his people. Increasing the tax is a suitable punishment for the humans supporting him."

Cuinn frowned. "I was told the Shadowhawk hasn't been active in months."

"His network remains active," Azrilan drawled. "It was never just one man. Which makes taxing the humans even more sensible. Hopefully it will force them to cease supporting and sheltering him."

"Raising the taxes will only increase discontent among the humans. You risk more of them joining the Shadowhawk's network. The overwhelming majority of humans in Dock City have nothing to do with the Shadowhawk—why punish those humans who have done nothing wrong?" Cuinn used every bit of skill he had to keep his tone mild and non-confrontational, adding a hint of confusion to his emotions. Nothing there to threaten Mithanis.

"He has a point, Your Highness." Tirin Goldfeather took advantage of the brief silence that followed to finally get a word in. A flicker of astonishment went through Cuinn that the young man would choose to speak up on this topic. Tirin flushed a deep red as the entire table turned to him, before looking apprehensively at Mithanis.

"The humans must be punished for the Shadowhawk's ongoing attacks on our property. Increasing the tax will be a deterrent to those who haven't joined him yet," Mithanis said.

"I disagree," Cuinn said calmly.

"Excuse me?"

Even from a distance, the cold anger on Mithanis's face was intimidating. Cuinn held onto his calm and unruffled expression with a white-knuckled grip. He used a hint more glamour to make himself appear as non-threatening as possible, kept his voice light and casual. "You're planning to increase the taxes by an amount that will cripple many families. It will make them angry and upset. They'll turn to the Shadowhawk, who will offer them a chance to do something about it. We might find that even more supplies are stolen than before."

"If that happens, we'll impose more taxes," Azrilan said. "The humans will eventually get the message and stop helping the Shadowhawk."

"We know a lot more about this than you do. You'd do better to keep your ill-conceived comments to yourself," Mithanis added.

Don't push too far.

Fear and anger in equal parts surged through him, and he let the fear win. Nodding, he conceded and sank back into his chair, miserable and ashamed of himself. Mithanis returned to arbitrating between the lords as to where the money from the taxes would be spent.

Not one member of the council considered discussing Cuinn's views further.

Mithanis's solution was neat and left the three disputing parties happy, reminding Cuinn that apart from his irrational hatred of the humans, the prince of night was no fool when it came to ruling.

Cuinn remained quiet for the remainder of the meeting and his opinion was not requested again. It was probably for the best, though it chafed him. There were several points of discussion where he had ideas he felt would lead to a better outcome—it surprised and shamed him at the same time.

He'd always dismissed having any part in ruling Mithranar as too dangerous, too risky. He'd never considered that he might actually be good at it, or have something to contribute. It was hard to escape the sinking feeling that he'd wasted most of his life in the guise of a criminal who'd done far too little to affect any serious help for half of his countrymen.

Once it was over, Cuinn made no attempt to talk to any of the lords, leaving them huddled in small groups around the table. Halun's Wolves deployed around him as he emerged from the meeting chamber into bright sunlight and humidity. Rather than flying back to his tower, he set off at a walk, unsurprised when Talyn fell into step beside him.

"That was dangerous," she said in an undertone. "Why didn't you warn me last night?"

"To be honest, I forgot to mention it until after you were gone."

"Prince Cuinn—"

"No." He raised a hand to stop her. "I know you're trying to keep me safe. Once again, however, I am putting my safety ahead of every-body else."

Irritation flashed in those sapphire eyes. "Prince—"

"If I can't be—" He cut himself off, realising where they were and dropping his voice. "I will find another way to help until I'm fully recovered, Captain. Those taxes will cripple families. I had to say something. I will continue to do it carefully, and in a way that does not make Mithanis feel threatened. That will have to be enough for you."

He spread his wings and took flight before she could respond, Halun's winged Wolves scrambling to follow. He was too angry—at himself, at the world, at everything—to keep talking to her and risk saying something he'd regret later.

He'd barely returned to his tower when Willir knocked at the door with a summons from his mother. He huffed out a laugh. "That didn't take long."

His Wolf detail was changing over from Halun's group to Andres's, so Cuinn satisfied himself with a dirty look at the big human for his snitching, then informed Andres they were off to see his mother. Halun's expression remained utterly unremorseful.

Liadin and Kiran hovered close by for the short flight over to this mother's quarters. It was hard to miss the increased sense of protec-tiveness emanating from the two winged Wolves who now knew his true identity, though they hadn't spoken a word to him about it.

While he and Talyn had both trusted Theac to keep a close eye on them while they were in Ryathl, Cuinn had nonetheless fretted over the long-term risk of them knowing. Winged folk surely had to have different feelings about the Shadowhawk than the humans. He'd worried enough to have no compunction using the full force of his song magic to read them—and Lyra—the first time they'd been in his guard detail since returning to Mithranar.

But all he'd picked up was that increased protectiveness, a genuine desire to keep him safe. No anger. No frustration. No sense of betrayal. He trusted his magic enough to believe it, but it surprised him nonetheless. And then there had been Tirin's astonishing agreement with Cuinn's view in the Queencouncil meeting earlier.

Maybe all winged folk weren't like the ruling lords. Maybe some were better.

He dismissed all thoughts of his Wolves as he landed on the balcony outside the large reception room of his mother's quarters. He rarely saw into the more private rooms beyond—couldn't even remember spending much time in there as a child.

Arched windows high in the walls let in the afternoon sun, and a faint breeze drifted in from the opened doors at one end of the room, breaking some of the stuffiness of the air. His boots made no noise on the plush carpet as he stepped into the room and limped towards his mother and elder brother, who were huddled together over a round table covered in maps.

"I was summoned," he announced, dropping languidly into a chair in order to rest his leg.

"What was this morning's behaviour all about?" Mithanis snapped, turning towards him.

Cuinn lifted his eyebrows. "What behaviour?"

"Don't play stupid. You know what I'm talking about."

"I'm taking an interest." Cuinn idly toyed with the buttons of his jacket. "I had nothing to do for a few full-turns, and I was bored. I came to the meeting and offered my thoughts. Is there something wrong with that?"

"You were bored?" Mithanis's jaw tensed.

Cuinn smiled brilliantly at his elder brother. "Yes. Bored. A sprained ankle rather limits the list of fun things to do."

"Do you hear this inanity, Mother?" Mithanis turned to the queen.

"Cuinn, I do wish you could be bored in a more productive manner," his mother said. "Providing ignorant opinions at Queen-council is not something I will tolerate in the future."

"I'm sorry." He sighed, looked at Mithanis. If he wanted to keep going to Queencouncil, he needed to convince his brother he wouldn't be a problem. "You will be heir and king, and I will never dispute that. I couldn't think of anything worse than being king, honestly. But I am still an Acondor prince, and I'd like to help you, Mithanis. You don't have to listen to what I say. Not ever. I'd just like the opportunity to help."

Mithanis was rightfully suspicious. "Since when?"

"I did some soul-searching on my travels." He offered a not entirely insincere wince. "Now, don't expect me to stop the women and the parties and all that, but I realise as a prince I should be doing more."

"You're serious." Mithanis appeared genuinely taken aback. Cuinn hid his smile.

"I am. But if we could keep the boring 'kingdom running' business to a minimum, like no more than a full-turn each week, I'd appreciate it."

Mithanis glanced at their mother. She gave him a little nod. Mithanis shrugged and turned back to Cuinn. "Fine. Just try and sound informed. And don't ever show up drunk."

Cuinn saluted. "Yes, sir!"

Mithanis's face darkened, but he said nothing.

Cuinn smiled at him, then shifted his glance to his mother. "You wanted to see me? Was it just to disapprove about my showing up at Queencouncil?"

"Actually, no, and your sudden interest in helping your brother and I is convenient," Sarana said. "Mithanis and I have been discussing ways in which you could be of more use to us."

His heart thudded, but he forced an amused smile onto his face. "Really? And what have you come up with?"

"You will marry," Mithanis said.

Cuinn reeled, years of practice the only thing allowing him to keep the shock from his face. Instead, he only showed amusement, letting out a peal of laughter. "That's hilarious, Brother. You really are funnier than I ever thought."

His mother turned an ice-cold look on him. "I have tolerated your idle ways because your brothers have taken your share of the work. Now, however, is an opportunity for you to do something to help your country. And you're the one who just sat there and told us you wanted to do more."

"I meant attend the occasional boring meeting and contribute even more infrequently." He forced down his growing panic and hoped his expression served to convey distaste rather than horror. "Who am I to marry?"

"Ahara Venador's daughter."

The confusion that registered on Cuinn's face was genuine. "A human? Our children might never be recognised as winged folk. How would that help the crown?"

It happened, of course—his grandfather had taken the risk in marrying Sarana to a Montagni noble. The advantages of strategic marriages for winged nobles sometimes outweighed the potential for their children to be humans. But he didn't understand why *this* woman... and why now.

"It would strengthen our alliance with Montagn," Mithanis said smoothly. "As you have two elder brothers, there is no need for you to provide heirs. Kaeri Venador is a daughter and the youngest child, so she will never inherit, but we have it on good authority that she is the ahara's favourite."

Cuinn flopped back down to the couch with a half-amused, half-irritated sigh. Inwardly, he struggled to work out what was going on. Mithanis and his mother had come up with this together, it seemed, which meant both saw advantages to it. His mother's face was expressionless as she watched him, but her magic was subtly urging him to agree—each time she opened her mouth he sensed it.

It served Mithanis's purpose well for Cuinn to have no heirs, but to form such a strong alliance with Montagn through Cuinn didn't make much sense. Maybe that was what his mother sought, however —an alliance for him that didn't threaten Mithanis, but might hold his elder brother back from acting against Cuinn. The ahara probably wouldn't take kindly to his son-in-law meeting a bad end.

"Cuinn?" Mithanis snapped.

"I'm not marrying a girl I've never met. What if she's ugly?" Cuinn shuddered. "The ahara always keeps Kaeri away from my entourage whenever I visit."

"A meeting will be arranged." Mithanis's lip curled in distaste. "And don't worry, by all accounts, the woman is beautiful."

Cuinn struggled to mask his unease. He couldn't marry this woman, beautiful or otherwise. There were so many reasons he couldn't marry her, but for the life of him at that moment he couldn't think of a single one to articulate to his mother and brother.

Unbidden, an image of Raya filled his mind; his childhood friend and then lover, the only woman he had ever considered marrying. Since her death, marriage was something he'd never wanted or thought about. It was simply too dangerous, for him and whoever he married.

"Cuinn?" This time it was his mother sounding exasperated.

"Sorry." Cuinn forced his attention back to the present. "What?"

His mother looked at him, her sincerity, her concern, obvious in her magic. She was worried, more worried than he'd realised. "I need you to do this."

He frowned. "What is it that's worrying you so much?"

Mithanis sent Sarana a quelling look, but she waved him off. "We still haven't caught whoever was behind the noble murders. The lords pretend everything is fine, but they're scared."

"There hasn't been another killing since Flightbreeze, but that's just making the families more anxious. They're afraid of another murder at any moment," Mithanis said reluctantly.

"And when you add that to the fact the Shadowhawk has been active for years now without being caught, we need to give the court something to reassure their fears. Restore their trust in us," Sarana said.

"Assuming the Shadowhawk isn't behind the murders," Mithanis said pointedly.

"Ravinire has conclusively demonstrated that the murders were conducted by more than one individual." Sarana spoke with the air of someone who'd had this argument before. "It was a group, and a well-resourced one."

Cuinn's ears perked up. He hadn't realised his mother and Ravinire no longer believed the Shadowhawk was behind the murders. "And you're thinking a stronger alliance with Montagn will reassure everyone."

"You've felt it, haven't you, Prince of Song? The fear?" Mithanis asked mockingly.

He had. The air of uneasiness was tangible, particularly in the palace. He'd brushed it aside, been too caught up in calming Mithanis's anger, rebuilding his strength, working out how to be helpful without returning to the Shadowhawk yet. And now he could feel it in his mother and brother... fear that this might be something that could undermine their absolute authority over Mithranar. "I suppose. I tend to ignore things that bore me." He shrugged.

Mithanis sighed in disgust.

His mother turned away too. "You can go, Cuinn."

"I'll see you at dinner later." Cuinn rose from the couch. As he left the room, all his thoughts focused on what had just happened. They wanted him to marry.

Frustrated, he took a breath and cleared his mind, banishing all the worry. He would think of something to prevent this marriage or to change his mother's mind. That shouldn't prove too difficult.

He hoped.

CHAPTER 13

Talyn—cloaked and hooded despite the warm air—waited under the awning of a closed café across the street from the ramshackle building the Shadowhawk's apartment was housed in.

One of her talons had gone down to Dock City each day since returning to Mithranar, and the day before Corrin had come back with word from Petro.

Cynia and Leviana had arrived.

Halun—who'd been on Cuinn's guard shift that night—had consulted with the prince, then visited Petro earlier in the day with a time and place to meet. Talyn had deliberately let Cuinn choose the meeting location. He knew Dock City far better than she did and she wanted to make sure they would be meeting at a place where nobody would pay any attention to them.

She wasn't waiting long before Cuinn appeared, easing the anxiety crawling through her. Having him sneak out of the citadel without a guard wasn't ideal, but it would be even riskier if they were seen leaving together. Besides, he'd done it hundreds of times before without incident. She had to trust that. Trust him.

Tonight he wore just his glamoured human visage. It wouldn't do for someone to spot the masked Shadowhawk and for word to get back to Vengeance that he'd been seen alive in Dock City.

She studied him as he approached, noting how flawless the glamour appeared and how his limp had all but vanished. His stride was relaxed, but watchful, like anyone else walking the streets of the Poor Quarter after dark. A voluminous cloak shrouded his form and helped hide the wings at his back.

"Are you going to let me get more than two words out before cutting me off and flying away this time?" she demanded once he reached her. It had been over a week since the Queencouncil meeting he'd attended, and she was still annoyed at how he'd brushed her off when she'd tried to speak to him afterwards.

He winced. "Yes."

"If you'd have let me finish, you would know I wasn't trying to stop you going to the meetings. I told you I wouldn't decide what you can and can't do. I was just going to ask you to let me or Theac know in advance next time."

He let out a breath, remorse filling his face. "I'm sorry. I just assumed you were angry at me again."

She let it go. It had been a fair assumption—she'd always been angry at him in the past, and it would take time for both of them to adjust now she knew who he really was. "You're doing better," she noted.

"I'm feeling better every day." A smile curled at his mouth. "My leg hardly ever hurts anymore, and my energy levels are increasing, thanks to getting back to playing alleya."

"I'm glad to hear it." They started walking through the dark back-streets, Talyn following Cuinn's lead. "You not warning me aside, I thought it was an interesting Queencouncil meeting."

"It was." He was slightly out of breath, even though he tried to hide it. He'd lost a lot of conditioning during his convalescence, and his limp required him to exert more effort to pretend he could walk normally. Mentioning it wouldn't make him stop, though, so she kept a quiet eye on his movements instead—if he began looking too distressed, she'd come up with an excuse to rest.

"You made your point well," she said.

His smile flashed in the moonlight. "Didn't you just love the expression on Mithanis's face?"

Ah. So he'd chosen to go with making light of it. She wasn't going to. "No, I didn't," she said flatly. "The expression on his face worried me."

"I think we're here," he said, stopping near the entrance of a nondescript inn. She joined him in lingering by the shadows of the wall, ensuring they hadn't been followed. They would wait until Leviana and Cynia arrived, ensure *they* hadn't been followed, and then go inside to meet them.

Silence descended, and she warred with herself before heaving a soft sigh. "You did well. Your words were considered but non-threatening and you conceded when Mithanis began growing too agitated."

"Thank you," he said, gifting her a small smile.

"The fact that none of them listened... that they couldn't see the sense in what you were saying." She shook her head. "I honestly don't understand how your country hasn't fallen apart by now."

"Money and magic, Captain. And ignorance regarding the humans aside, my mother is a clever, shrewd ruler. Mithanis too, when he's not blinded by anger." He shifted. "You can't just show up every time I go near Mithanis, you know? He's not a fool and he'll start to wonder why. Trust your talons."

She nodded. Easier said than done. But it was partly the reason she'd not gone to see him since the meeting. She didn't want anyone to notice that things might have changed between Cuinn and his Wolf guard.

Not to mention she was now so busy with paperwork to satisfy Ravinire's demands that she hadn't had time to see him even if she'd wanted to. Cuinn glanced at her, presumably catching her wave of annoyance.

"I was just thinking about the mountain of paperwork Ravinire has buried me under as punishment for disappearing for three months," she explained.

"It could have been a lot worse," he said soberly.

She frowned at the heavy mood that seemed to have sunk down over him. Even his smiles so far tonight had seemed more for show than genuine. "I heard you were summoned into the queen's presence after the Queencouncil meeting. I take it she was not pleased." She nudged him playfully, trying to lighten his mood. "Did she threaten to send you to your room without dinner?"

Instead of chuckling as she'd expected, Cuinn froze, glancing away from her. She frowned. "You okay?"

"I'm fine." But his words were clipped. He shook his head. "No, she wasn't pleased."

"Andres tells me Prince Mithanis was there too," she probed, concerned now. "Did something happen?"

"Not really." He shrugged. "They said something about marrying me off to make use of me, but it was nothing."

"Marriage?" Talyn chuckled, amused at the idea. "That would severely limit one of your favourite activities, I imagine."

"You are hilarious," he muttered. "And your Callanan are late."

"Not yet they're not." She studied his face, trying to understand what had upset him. Abruptly she realised, and guilt twisted sharply in her stomach. She reached out to touch his arm. "I'm so sorry, Cuinn. I forgot about Raya. I didn't mean to make light of that."

He turned towards her, face softening. "Captain, I—"

Movement caught her eye, and she shifted her gaze, catching Cynia glancing briefly in their direction before she and Leviana headed into the inn. "They're here."

Cuinn nodded. "Then let's go."

CUINN HAD CHOSEN the location well. In fact, it was so dim—and smoky—in the bar that it took several minutes of searching to find Leviana and Cynia ensconced at a table by the far wall. Talyn didn't hug them in greeting like she wanted to, but gave them a warm smile of acknowledgement.

Cuinn settled in the chair at her side, pushing the hood of his cloak back to reveal his human face. Talyn kept hers on—it wouldn't do for the captain of the Wolves to be spotted here.

"You made it," she said briskly. "How was the ship journey?"

"Rough." Cynia made a face. "Levs was seasick the whole time."

"I was not," her partner said indignantly. "Not for all of it, anyway."

Talyn chuckled. "Levs, Cynia, as promised, this is the Shadowhawk."

Cuinn smiled widely and offered his hand. "Ladies, it's a pleasure."

Talyn shot him a scowl—he was supposed to be an edgy and overly-intense criminal, not the smoothly charming prince of Mithranar. He merely winked at her.

Leviana looked him up and down. "You have a real name to go with that super mysterious criminal identity?"

"Nope."

"I'm guessing you chose this place?" Cynia coughed for effect, making a face at the smoky air.

"It's one of my favourites. Now, Captain Dynan tells me she promised to offer me up on a serving platter for Callanan interrogation. Shall we get to it?"

"I did *not*—" Talyn abruptly cut herself off when she realised he was needling her. "Just answer their questions, and do it quickly. We shouldn't linger here too long."

Leviana and Cynia were good at what they did. They took turns asking questions, the other watching the Shadowhawk carefully for any hint of deception. They caught several occasions when he held information back and probed further each time.

Talyn sat silent at his side. She'd passed all this information to the First Blade already, Cuinn was merely confirming it. And there were no lies. He wasn't linked to Montagn. When Cynia asked him about Vengeance, he glanced at Talyn before responding. "There are several gangs that operate throughout the Poor Quarter. My suspicion is that Vengeance has settled into Dock City in the same way. I can't tell you any more than what Captain Dynan already has."

"We think we might have a lead on which gang," Talyn said, appreciating that he'd left it to her to decide how much to tell them. "Firming that up is my first priority. I'll let the First Blade know as soon as I do."

Leviana sat back in her chair, gaze firmly on the Shadowhawk. "What do you make of Montagn?"

"I don't think about it much at all." He gestured out the door. "You've seen what it's like here. The only thing the Shadowhawk is interested in is helping improve the circumstances for humans in Mithranar."

"And talking about himself in the third person," Cynia muttered.

Talyn smirked.

The two Callanan partners shared a glance, then Cynia leaned forward. "And if we asked you to help us? To learn more about Vengeance?"

"No," he said firmly.

Talyn glanced at him. His arms were crossed firmly over his chest, mouth set in a stubborn line.

"We could pay you," Leviana offered. "You can't deny that Callanan financial support could only help your efforts on behalf of the humans."

"Shia sent you here to recruit him?" Talyn snapped into the silence before Cuinn could respond, furious on his behalf. "Without talking to me?"

"It doesn't matter." Cuinn shrugged. "The answer is no. I don't work for anyone. I work alone."

"But—" Cynia tried.

"Asked and answered," Talyn said tightly. "Do you have any more questions for him?"

"Talyn, we have our orders. You know that," Cynia said.

Cuinn shot her an amused look. She ignored it.

Leviana frowned. "We're not trying to horn-in on your territory. You can run him as your informant, Tal."

"It's not that. I—"

"I'm right here, ladies." The Shadowhawk lifted a hand. "I'm not interested in being anybody's informant, to be clear. Any more questions? It's late, and I have work to do."

Talyn sat back as the partners shared another glance, then Cynia looked at her. "We'd like a second meeting. That will give us time to process what we've learned tonight and identify any follow up questions."

"I'm happy to do that." He glanced at Talyn. "Vengeance is a nasty group, and they've already caused a lot of damage. I'm reassured by the idea of you Callanan doing something about it, even though I have no idea why you care so much. It's just that my priorities are elsewhere."

"Understood." Leviana nodded. "And thank you for talking to us. We'll contact Tal when we're ready for the next meet."

Talyn rose to her feet. "We should go."

"Be safe, Tal." Cynia smiled.

THEY LEFT the Callanan drinking in the bar and moved quickly through a series of back alleys until Cuinn brought them to a halt at the back of an empty store.

Cuinn's brown human eyes raked her. "They're worried about Vengeance. A lot."

"So am I."

"What are you not telling me?" Frustration filled his voice and stance. "I can feel the secrets inside you, Talyn, despite how well you master yourself."

She lifted her hands helplessly. "If I could tell you, I would."

"You always have a choice. You're choosing loyalty to them over us." Cuinn sighed. "And I understand that. The Twin Thrones is your home, you're a Dumnorix. But it worries me, because I care about my people just as much as you do, and I know these secrets affect *my* country. You wouldn't be holding back otherwise."

Torn. She was constantly torn. Mithranar faced a potentially existential threat and she could do nothing to warn them. Not without losing the Callanan informant who was keeping the Twin Thrones safe. "I'm doing everything I can to help without breaching my duty," she said quietly. "And hunting Vengeance is a part of that."

He let out a breath. "What about your Shadow contact, is he still a no-show?"

She shook her head. They'd been back in Mithranar nearly two weeks and Savin hadn't made a single appearance, despite her leaving a cup on her windowsill every day. She was starting to wonder whether he'd been recalled to Firthland for a different posting. Odd that Shia hadn't mentioned that though.

"Should we be worried?"

"I don't think so. Shadows can take care of themselves. He might be off on an assignment. Or maybe he's been recalled back home."

He turned away. "On my way to meet you tonight, I went past a few places. There were several unanswered messages for the Shadowhawk. My network is wondering where I went, what happened. I've missed several important shipments."

"That's a good thing," she said gently. "It means there's nothing to contradict Vengeance's assumption that you're dead."

He eyed her. "You keep talking about the fact Vengeance thinks I'm dead. But what about you? They wanted you as much as me, and you're quite obviously still alive."

"Indeed." A smile flashed over her face.

A brief light lit his eyes. "You want them to come for you."

"It's better than waiting until you're back to full health and I find a way of hunting Mithranan citizens without Ravinire losing his mind and kicking me out of the country." A hint of urgency tugged at her. She didn't know how much time they had before Montagn moved against Mithranar. For all she knew, they had everything in place already and didn't need Vengeance any longer.

"Yes, well, be careful what you wish for. Vengeance have proven clever—they may not come at you directly. They framed me for a councillor's murder, remember?"

He was right. "I'll be careful."

Cuinn took a breath. "I should go."

She didn't like it. Didn't like how he'd retreated from her, but she sensed his need for it, and empathised with it far too well to keep pushing. So she just nodded. "Thanks for tonight."

He disappeared into the dark before she could say anything further.

CHAPTER 14

*A*s Theac and Errana's wedding approached, the days passed uneventfully. There continued to be no sign of Savin, and discreet enquiries from her talons when they were in Dock City identified no obvious Vengeance activity either. No murders. Nothing. The Wolves ensured they always went into the city in pairs or larger groups, but all trips occurred without incident.

The quiet made Talyn itch.

The plan to have Vengeance come after her was a sound one, and she wasn't afraid of them, but the complete lack of activity was unsettling. Without it, there was no way to identify if they were rebuilding after the ambush attempt in the SkyReach or had withdrawn to plan another big attack. Or, as Cuinn had suggested, were planning something more insidious.

"I hate to say it, but each time they've come at you directly, you've won. And easily," Sari said. *"If they're even halfway clever, they'll be looking to try something different."*

Talyn agreed. Which would make her using herself as bait useless. *"If they haven't made a move by the wedding, I'll change things up. I'll go after them."*

To distract herself from her uneasiness, she concentrated on the

Wolves, advancing their *sabai* and weapons' skills as quickly as she dared, filling her days with making them as lethal a guard force as was possible.

If Vengeance did come again, they'd find a merciless foe.

Ravinire's weekly captains' meetings were a trial. He had been unremittingly cold since their return, and not even dutiful completion of all the tedious administrative tasks he'd set her changed his attitude. That was fine. She wasn't in Mithranar to win Ravinire's affection, or even trust. She only needed to ensure he didn't grow angry enough to kick her out. But he was always watching now, and she had no doubt she was operating under a very short leash.

The same applied for Windsong's replacement, Brightwing, who was much more like Iceflight than Windsong, and who was clearly also Mithanis's lapdog. He generally steered clear of her given Ravinire's orders she report directly to him, and that worked fine for both of them.

The other captains mostly ignored her, but some of the contempt had faded from their attitudes. It was almost as if they'd gotten so used to her now that summoning the effort to be horrible was too much. One new face at the captains' meetings—Tarlen Ironfeather—she recognised as one of the Falcons who'd helped the Wolves search for survivors after the avalanche in Darmour.

When she asked around, she learned he'd been promoted into Brightwing's spot after his rise to flight-leader. On Ravinire's recommendation. It reminded her that while Ravinire was largely ineffectual, he did what he could.

Mindful of Cuinn's warning, she stayed away from the Queen-council meetings he attended, but ensured she sought immediate updates afterwards from whichever talon was in charge of his detail. They always sounded impressed with the way Cuinn attempted to moderate the more extreme suggestions made by his brothers or the councillors, but never in a way that overtly undermined the queen or Mithanis.

"I think Goldfeather is the least unlikable of the lot," Corrin said one night. Talyn often gathered with her talons in their private common room of an evening. It was a good opportunity to discuss the events of the day and manage any minor issues in the wing, but most of all she enjoyed spending time in their company. And even though Zamaril was no longer a talon, he still joined them. "Even if he doesn't often come out and say it, you can tell from his body language he often agrees with Prince Cuinn's points."

"He's too young to have any impact," Tiercelin said dismissively. "And if he keeps it up, he'll never get enough respect from the other lords to have any influence on the council."

Talyn shot him a disapproving look.

He merely shrugged. "It's the way things work here. I'm just stating fact."

"I hate how things work here," Sari grumbled.

"You and me both." Her uncle didn't have to gain the support of his senior lords before making decisions, although he only had power to rule on areas that affected both Calumnia and Conmor.

As if reading her mind, Tiercelin asked, "Does King Aethain have unlimited power?"

"Over certain things," she said. "Like decisions relating to the defence of the Twin Thrones or choosing when to go to war. Relations with other countries. Approval or veto over Firthland's proposed actions. And if the lords in charge of the day to day running of Calumnia and Conmor have a dispute they can't resolve—which happens a bit—the case is submitted to my uncle. His ruling is final."

"No wonder the Firthlander warlord is having problems then," Halun commented.

"What do you mean?" Talyn asked. "My uncle rarely intervenes. He gives the warlord free rein to rule as he sees fit. He's never once vetoed one of his decisions."

"Yes, but he could if he wanted to," Tiercelin pointed out. "Your uncle might be the best king ever, but what will his son be like, or his son's sons? What if they decide to take a more active role in governing Firthland?"

She opened her mouth, closed it.

"The way I see it," Theac weighed in, making her turn to him in astonishment. "The war happened generations ago, no? So the Firth-landers alive today, they've done nothing to act against the Twin Thrones. Their parents didn't either. So why keep punishing them for something their ancestors did?"

"When did you all suddenly get so political?" she managed.

"We all felt hopeless when you first came here, Captain," Corrin answered for them. "But you taught us that small things can matter. And it opened our eyes a bit. We ask more questions now."

"I don't," Zamaril grumbled. "But Tiercelin won't shut up with all his chattering about how things are different elsewhere and whatnot."

Talyn settled uncomfortably back into the couch, seeking a way to change the subject. Her Wolves' questions still lingered in her mind, unsettling her. She didn't have good answers for them.

She wondered if her uncle had ever considered those questions.

"This is why I'm just a warrior," she said eventually. "I don't want to have to think about all that stuff."

They all stared at her, as if she'd just said the most ridiculous thing they'd ever heard.

"What?" she demanded.

"Oh, nothing, Captain." Theac hauled himself to his feet. "I'm going to get some more tea. Anyone else want some?"

A WEEK before Theac's wedding, Talyn and Cuinn met with Leviana and Cynia for the second time. This meeting was more relaxed, with the two Callanan mainly covering a few smaller details.

"We've been doing some discreet looking around," Cynia confided. "But found nothing specific on Vengeance apart from a lot of rumour and fear."

"You won't get much more than that as outsiders," Talyn agreed. "My plan was to wait for them to come after me—they think they've killed the Shadowhawk but they wanted me dead too. But so far nothing."

"You've only been back a few weeks," Cuinn murmured. "Maybe they're still planning."

Leviana scowled. "That idea doesn't fill me with sunshine and light."

"Me either," Talyn said. "And I don't want to sit around doing nothing for much longer. One of my talons is getting married next week. If they don't come out of the shadows before then, I'll change up my plans."

"We're going to be here a few more weeks, First Blade's orders," Leviana said. "So if you need help, reach out."

"I will," Talyn said, and she meant it.

"You've got a plan," Cuinn said, reading her easily.

She did. Cuinn was growing stronger every day, and Andres reported that Mithanis had seemed relatively calm at the last council meeting Cuinn had attended. She suspected that once Theac's wedding had passed, Cuinn would insist on going back to the streets. Once the Shadowhawk was at large again, he could reach out to Saniya, get her to meet them. This time Talyn would be prepared for an ambush. And once she had Saniya in a room, well, then she could ask her questions. Having two Callanan at her back could be useful. "I've got some thoughts, yes. In fact, Levs, Cynia, let me know before you leave?"

Both Callanan looked thrilled that Talyn might actually consider enlisting their help. "We will. And the First Blade made it clear that our return could be flexible if we identified a need to stay," Cynia said.

"Good," Cuinn said quietly.

Talyn glanced at him, frowning, but he was staring at his mug of ale. His heavy mood hadn't lifted much in the past weeks, and at this second meeting with the Callanan he'd been much more the brooding criminal.

Leviana's glance flicked between them. "Tell us more about this wedding, Tal? There's nothing I love more!"

She smiled. "The Wolves are all very excited."

A faint smile flashed over Cuinn's face too. "You realise most of Dock City is just as excited?"

"Really?" Cynia asked. "Why?"

"Because the Wolves saved half the city when we had flash floods last year. Then they beat Prince Azrilan's personal Falcon detail in a very public alleya game they were set up to lose," Cuinn said matter-of-factly, ignoring Talyn nudging him sharply in the ribs. "And most recently they helped save many lives after an avalanche in the north."

The Callanan stared at Talyn, clearly unsure as to whether the Shadowhawk was having them on.

"He's right. Mostly," she muttered.

"The Wolves are an emblem of hope for the humans of Mithranar," Cuinn said softly. "And it was Talyn who created them."

"You didn't mention that in your letters," Leviana said pointedly. "I can't imagine the Acondor family thinks well of it."

"They don't," Talyn said flatly. "And there were consequences. But none of that has anything to do with the Callanan. I'll send a message through Petro if I need you, and you'll do the same before you plan to leave?"

Cynia and Leviana shared a look that communicated both their unease at Cuinn's revelation and tacit agreement not to push Talyn on it. Yet. "We will."

ON THE DAY of the wedding, Talyn rose early, wandering past a mostly empty mess on her way to the talons' common room. Those Wolves not on the current guard shift or assigned to afternoon shift had been given the day off—and every single one of them had risen at dawn to go down to Dock City and help decorate the Town Hall for the event.

It never failed to warm her how they all looked out for each other. From five original guards to sixty strong, that hadn't changed.

"It's you, Talyn. You know that, right?"

"They did it for themselves."

"You just keep telling yourself that," Sari muttered. *"And I'll just keep knowing different."*

Theac sat alone in the common room, an uneaten bowl of oatmeal sitting in front of him while his hands fidgeted nervously in his lap. Andres's detail was on shift, with Tiercelin taking over later in the morning for the duration of the ceremony and celebrations.

144

The other talons were probably getting ready. Halun and Zamaril would be standing up for Theac at the ceremony, and both had been nervous about looking smart enough for the occasion. She was certain Theac wasn't going to notice what they were wearing.

"Nervous?" she asked, taking the chair opposite him.

"No," he said quickly, then tugged at his collar. "Is it hot in here?"

"It's always hot in here." She smiled. "Theac, you're going to be fine."

"What if I'm an awful husband? What if I can't look after Errana and her girls properly?" He scowled, words almost falling out of him in his anxiety. "I mean, I'm not exactly husband material, am I? I'm rough and ill-mannered and I used to drink too much and—"

"You're loyal and steady and strong and you'll protect her and those girls with everything you have," Talyn finished. "You're a good man, and a great second. I couldn't do half of what I do without you."

His eyes searched her face. "You mean that, lass?"

"I do," she said firmly. "Anyway, you should feel fortunate you're not Aimsir."

"Why?" he asked suspiciously.

"Aimsir weddings are a little on the… exuberant side. Once the vows are spoken, the couple is doused with celebratory wine." She grinned in fond memory of the handful of Aimsir marriages she'd attended. "The partying usually lasts a couple of days, too, lots of loud music and dancing. Many sore heads afterwards. It wouldn't suit you at all."

"So that will be your fate one day, huh Captain?" He managed a smile.

She snorted. "I doubt my uncle would accept anything less than a proper court wedding. For that reason alone I am comfortable never marrying."

The door opened, and two Wolves stepped inside, Leta and Kiran from Andres' detail. Their alert demeanour indicated that Cuinn was with them. Sure enough, the winged prince came in behind them, his eyes searching the room until they fell on Theac.

"Talon Parksin, I'm glad I found you here."

"Prince Cuinn!" Theac scrambled to his feet beside Talyn.

Cuinn smiled. "I just wanted to drop by and offer you my congratulations and best wishes."

Theac's mouth opened, then closed. Eventually he managed a muttered thanks. Talyn shot the prince a warning look—displaying such consideration for his human guard wasn't a smart idea—but he studiously ignored her.

"I also have a wedding gift for you." Cuinn turned back to Kiran, who passed him a square, flat package wrapped in paper.

"Your Highness, you didn't need to—"

Cuinn stepped closer, lowering his voice. "We both know I owe you a lot more than a wedding gift, Theac. Please, open it."

Talyn glanced over Theac's shoulder as he unwrapped the paper, curious to see what the gift would be.

"A painting." Theac cleared his throat. "I am honoured, thank you."

It was a skilful depiction of a small townhouse, red brick with white-painted windows and a delightfully colourful garden of flowers in the front.

"Oh, no." Cuinn's musical laugher rang out. "You can keep the painting, but its purpose is merely to show you what your new home looks like. It's rather too large a present to bring to you, unfortunately."

"I'm not sure I understand." Theac frowned.

"The house is in Dock City, in the Wall Quarter not far from Town Hall. It's in a quiet neighbourhood, a safe one for Errana's girls. Enough rooms for Halun's niece to continue living with you, too. And from the second story there's a view of Feather Bay." Cuinn paused. "It's yours, Theac. Tiercelin helped me organise it through his family —they already own so much in Dock City, they didn't notice us using their name to buy this."

As Talyn looked between Theac's stunned face and Cuinn's smile, something tight lodged in her chest. "I thought you only got a small allowance from your mother?" she asked.

Cuinn nodded. "I've just never spent any of it apart from what I needed for... you know. I still didn't have enough for even half, but

Tiercelin used his money for the rest—not sure if you've noticed the Stormflight family is even wealthier than mine."

"This is a wonderful gift, Your Highness." Theac was clearly overwhelmed. "I am deeply honoured. To you and Tiercelin both."

Cuinn nodded, turning brisk. "Good, well I hope Errana likes it too. Congratulations, Theac. I'd best be going."

He left without another word, wings furling as he passed through the door, Leta and Kiran following closely behind. She watched him go, struck by his and Tiercelin's gesture.

As the door closed behind them, Theac turned to stare at Talyn.

"Don't look at me." She shook her head. "I had no idea he was planning on doing that."

"But why? I don't understand."

"I suspect Tiercelin was listening the other night when you were talking about the fact you and Errana were trying to work out where to live, and that you weren't thrilled with the idea of them living here in the barracks with you. He and Cuinn must have come up with the wedding gift idea together."

"I feel truly honoured." Theac was so utterly taken aback it was almost amusing.

Talyn clapped him on the back. "Come on now, you need to go and get dressed."

THE LOOK on Errana's face when she entered the beautifully decorated Town Hall and saw the seats filled with friends and family—plus fifty off-duty Wolves—was worth all the work it had taken to put it together. Talyn's second looked uncomfortable in his finery, but the scowl on his face faded the moment his eyes landed on Errana.

Corrin beamed from ear to ear as he escorted his mother to Theac before going to stand with a straight backed and proud-looking Zamaril and Halun. Talyn watched from the front row of seats beside Andres and Evani, who were tasked with watching over Elsie and Janna.

Both girls behaved perfectly despite wriggling with excitement in their seats the whole way through, and so all three were free to focus on the couple as they spoke their marriage oaths before the mayor, who'd volunteered to officiate the wedding the moment he'd heard it was taking place.

The ceremony dragged on a little, and Talyn's gaze eventually wandered, running over the full-to-bursting hall. The winged Wolves stood out most, with their massive wings and beauty, but oddly enough, they didn't look out of place at all. They sat with their human comrades, and none of the Dock City residents had given them a second glance. Nor did they look strange sitting amongst a hall of humans. And it wasn't just Wolves. She spotted Ronisin Nightdrift at the back, a grin on his face as he leaned to the Wolf at his side to whisper something in his ear. The Falcons from his detail were there too.

The winged folk were accepted here as much as the human Wolves were. It made her sad that Tiercelin had to miss this. It also made her wonder... if this type of harmony could be achieved amongst a small number of winged folk, could it mean change in Mithranar was possible?

"I think it is. And I think you know it is."

"Not under the queen or Mithanis. Or even Azrilan."

"Under Cuinn it would be."

Talyn sighed. *"You know it's impossible for Cuinn to be king here. His mother, the nobles, they'll never name him heir. And even if someone drugged them all with mind-altering herbs and they did, Mithanis would kill him."*

"There are solutions to that."

"If you're about to suggest I start a coup in Mithranar, I'm going to suggest that you've gone loony living in my head," Talyn said with a huff.

A snort of indignation from Sari and then she was gone.

Soon after, the ceremony finished and Theac was a married man. Her second wore an expression on his face that was an amusing—and sweet—mix of stunned, awkward, and delighted.

The hall slowly cleared out, people making their way in small groups through the city and down to an inn in the Dock Quarter that had a lovely aspect over Feather Bay. Talyn strolled down with her talons, enjoying the warm late afternoon air and scent of flowers on the breeze.

By the time they arrived, celebrations had already begun. Laughing guests spilled out of the inn's garden and onto the sandy beach beyond, clutching glasses of ale and wine.

Talyn relaxed completely for the first time in months, drinking and dancing with her Wolves, allowing the atmosphere to evoke the good memories of her previous life, rather than the painful ones. The only blight on the day was that Tiercelin was not able to be there.

Later they all gathered, cheeping and whooping, as Theac and Errana left together in a waiting carriage. They'd be spending two weeks travelling in Mair-land to celebrate their wedding before Theac returned to duty. Evani stood with both girls to wave them off. The ex-slave had offered to watch them while Errana was away.

"What time is training tomorrow morning, Captain?" Andres asked as they returned to the party and ordered another round of drinks.

"Same as usual." She kept her face straight.

"You'll be the only one coming to training, in that case," Zamaril shot back.

"No, no training tomorrow." She laughed. "I think a day off is in order."

Talyn drained the rest of her ale, her attention catching on the odd sight of a Falcon in uniform wending his way through the guests towards her. He managed a surly nod when he reached her, and passed a sealed note with the queen's sigil on it.

He was gone before she could ask him what it was about.

"Something important?" Zamaril peered over her shoulder.

She frowned. "It must be from Ravinire. I hope nothing's wrong." She stood up. "I need some fresh air, anyway. Hold my seat."

He raised his glass at her then turned back to the conversation.

Talyn fought her way through the drunken revellers and out onto the beach. It was a lot emptier than it had been earlier—she hadn't realised how late it had gotten, though the air was still oppressively thick, the kind of humidity she remembered from the previous year in the days before monsoon season broke.

The sounds of the party faded behind her, to be replaced by the soft whisper of the waves breaking against the shore. With slightly unsteady fingers, she opened the note.

It was blank.

Her faintly inebriated mind was trying to process what that meant when the rustling sound of many wings came from the sky above. Falcons, at least twenty of them, dropping down onto the sand until she was completely encircled.

Two of them stepped forward. The first was Darian Strongswoop. One of the talons who'd travelled with them to Montagn. The other was Siran Brightwing.

Even though it was Brightwing who spoke, Talyn's heart was already sinking at the grave look on Strongswoop's face. "You need to come with us."

He hadn't addressed her by rank. That wasn't good.

"What's going on, sir?" she asked, fighting the urge to reach for her daggers.

"Prince Mithanis's orders. You're to come with us, or we have instructions to restrain you and bring you in forcibly," Brightwing said, surly and cold.

Shit. From what she knew about Mithanis, if she allowed them to take her, it might not end well. Yet she couldn't kill a group of Falcons on the beach in the Dock Quarter—if she did that, she'd be done in Mithranar. Dead, most likely, once they caught her.

"Dynan!" he snapped when she made no move.

"All right." She lifted her hands in the air. "I'm coming with you."

"I think you should run."

"Let's just see what's going on first."

"I have a bad feeling about this."

"Tell me about it," she muttered aloud.

CHAPTER 15

uinn sat at the table, a half-eaten plate of food in front of him. Lively music filled the air. Already, a few of the guests at Irial and Annae's party were up and dancing.

These dinners had once been fun, a chance to forget his despair and the difficulty of being the Shadowhawk, and disappear into his prince persona for a few hours. He'd drink, laugh as loudly as anyone else, and usually end up taking one of the winged women back to his room.

He hadn't taken a lover since ending his affair with Niya, and tonight was a perfect opportunity to bring another woman to his bed. It was exactly what he would have done only a few months earlier. But almost dying and the Wolves finding out who he was had changed everything irrevocably—he just hadn't realised how much until tonight.

Because he had no interest in bedding any woman at the party. And he had even less interest in being *at* the party.

The *only* thing he wanted was to be at Theac's wedding.

Worse, guilt curled uncomfortably through him at the fact that his Wolf detail couldn't be at the wedding either because they had to guard him. Especially Tiercelin. Those initial five talons thought of each other as brothers. His magic sensed the tight and profound bond between them anytime they were in a room together. And Tiercelin had to miss Theac's wedding because of him.

"Cheer up, Cuinn!" Irial tossed an olive at him as he sauntered over. "You're like a wet blanket this evening. What's with the long face?"

Cuinn sipped his wine and forced a smile. He couldn't afford Irial thinking anything was amiss. He'd report it straight to Mithanis, and his older brother was only now beginning to return to normal levels of anger after his return from Calumnia. "Just tired, I suppose."

"I could help you with that." The woman seated next to him leaned in with a slow smile—they'd been lovers on and off for years. Not from a particularly important family, Arini Softfeather was a casual option when he was between lovers and wanted the distraction.

Aware Irial was still watching, he smiled and turned to murmur in her ear. "I'm sure you could."

"Should we leave? Find somewhere more... private?"

Cuinn allowed his smile to widen. Arini was beautiful and could perhaps distract him for a few full-turns from the utter mess his life had become. He glanced up and saw Irial already walking away, going to join his wife in a dance, and instantly Cuinn's interest in Arini withered. He sat back, his expression changing to a wince. "Actually, I think I may have eaten something bad. I'm not feeling too well, maybe another time?"

"Shall I fetch a healer?" Arini asked in concern.

"No." Cuinn looked up and caught Tiercelin watching from one of the balconies above. When he gestured, Tiercelin nodded and flew away to gather the other Wolves. Turning back to Arini, he filled his voice was song magic, using it to convince her that he looked a little green. If Irial asked, she would sound sincere when telling him Cuinn was ill. "I think I'll just sleep it off. It might just be too much wine from dinner."

She smiled, her hand squeezing his thigh before she sat back. "Next time, then."

"I look forward to it."

Once outside, he decided to walk back to his tower. His limp was barely noticeable now, but he took the opportunity to build up the strength in his leg as often as he could. Walking also meant he didn't have to leave most of Tiercelin's detail behind. Tonight he needed the Wolves' silent presence around him, making him feel safe and protected.

They dispersed to surround the tower as soon as Tiercelin had checked the empty rooms to ensure there were no intruders or waiting assassins.

"I'm truly sorry you had to miss the wedding." Cuinn apologised to the talon on his way out.

"Don't be, Your Highness." Tiercelin smiled. "How's your leg feeling?"

"It feels great, stronger every day." Cuinn poured himself a glass of spirits. "Good night, Tiercelin."

"Goodnight, Your Highness." Tiercelin gave him that bow again, the one that made him uncomfortable and warm at the same time, and left to take up his guard position.

Jasper came padding over then, his green eyes suspicious as he tracked the winged man's departure. Once the door closed he wound his way around Cuinn's ankles before letting out a little yowl. It felt like the tawncat was asking him what was wrong.

"The old distractions aren't working anymore, buddy." He leaned down to rub the tawncat's ears until he purred in pleasure. "Probably a good thing, hey? If I tried bringing a new woman in here you'd probably eat her for dinner. It's not like I can keep you locked up anymore."

Jasper responded to that by curling up around his ankles and closing his eyes. Cuinn chuckled, needing a surprising amount of strength to shove the tawncat off his feet. "Not here. Up to bed."

CUINN WOKE SUDDENLY in the darkness of his bedroom. It was hard to know how late it was, but the sense he'd developed over endless nights on the streets of Dock City judged it was close to midnight. A shadow shifted outside the window nearest his bed—he rarely drew the curtains over at night, liking to sleep bathed in moonlight—and he started violently when Jasper suddenly hurled himself at the window. A blood-curdling snarl tore out of the tawncat's throat.

"Jasper, stop!" Cuinn hissed, not wanting to rouse his entire Wolf guard. Whatever was outside the window wasn't getting through the newly installed iron bars and he seriously doubted any real threat had gotten past his Wolves outside.

Jasper fell back, but kept pacing and snarling under the window as Cuinn cautiously approached it. A winged man hovered beyond the bars, shooting terrified glances at the tawncat. A man Cuinn recognised. He slid the window upwards, letting in a vaguely cool night breeze.

"Ronisin Nightdrift." The last person he expected to see at his window in the middle of the night was the talon of one of Azrilan's Falcon details. And he wasn't in uniform. In fact, he wore dark clothing, as if he didn't want to be seen. "What are you doing?"

"Your Highness, I'm so sorry to bother you like this." Ronisin was deathly pale, words spilling over themselves. Cuinn couldn't sort through Ronisin's terror and embarrassment at bothering him to work out what was actually wrong. In fact, the emotions were so strong Cuinn struggled to focus on what the man was saying. "Tirina said it was okay to come up and speak with you, though I think she's ready to shoot me full of arrows if I make one wrong move."

"Ronisin!" Cuinn hissed, trying to break through the torrent. "Why are you here?"

The Falcon swallowed. "I wasn't sure if you'd want to know or not, Your Highness, but I didn't want to just do nothing, and..." He took visible hold of himself. "Captain Dynan has been arrested."

Cuinn's heart stopped. He couldn't have heard right. "*What?* That's impossible. Theac was getting married tonight, she was at the wedding—"

"She was arrested by the Falcons just over a half-turn ago. I was at the wedding too, but we left early because I... anyway... I was in the barracks with some friends when Flight-Leader Brightwing came in with the orders." Ronisin was again talking too fast.

Cuinn's hand curled around one of the bars, white-knuckled. He shouldn't be showing how upset he was to Ronisin, but right now hiding was impossible. "Why?"

"I don't know. I just heard the orders."

"Shit." He swore unthinkingly, cold dread closing over his chest. "Do any of the Wolves know what happened?"

"The flight-leader took two details from Captain Strongswoop's wing down to Dock City. He told them to be discreet, that he wanted it done quietly. But that doesn't mean none of the other guests saw."

Shit. Shit. Shit.

"Why are you telling me this, Ronisin?"

Fear flared in the young man's eyes—he knew what coming to Cuinn could mean for him if the wrong people found out—but he spoke anyway. "She was good to us, treated us with respect. I didn't want to sit by and do nothing."

"Get out of here, and don't tell anyone what you've done. Am I clear?" Cuinn inflected his voice with enough song magic that Ronisin swooped instantly away from the window, winging off as quickly as he could.

Cuinn lurched from the window, dragging on breeches and shirt and hunting around in the dark for his boots. The whole time Jasper watched him, claws digging into the carpet, clearly understanding that something was wrong. Cuinn's thoughts raced as he moved, planning and discounting each plan as it came into his head. He had to move quickly or things were going to explode very fast.

And even now he didn't know if he'd be quick enough to stop it.

"Jasper, stay!" Taking one step out of his bedroom, he spread his wings and flew down to the main front door.

Tiercelin—on guard out front—was turning to him as he hauled it open. "With me, now."

"Where are we going?" the healer asked calmly. "Was Jasper—"

"The Wolves' barracks." He leapt into the air, forcing Tiercelin to follow suit. Behind him, the talon snapped an order to Tirina to follow and the rest of the Wolves to catch up as quickly as they could.

This mad rush to the barracks would look odd at best and suspicious at worst if a passing winged person saw and it got back to Mithanis... but if Cuinn wasn't quick enough, that would be the absolute least of his worries.

He landed an instant ahead of Tiercelin and Tirina in the dark drill yard and ran for the common room where the talons normally spent their off-duty time. If they weren't here, that meant they were probably still at the wedding, which meant they didn't know yet. Which was the best outcome he could hope for.

His heart sank when the door opened just as he reached it, Zamaril in the lead, sword at his hip, anger plastered all over his face. Cuinn hit him full stride, using his momentum and superior upper body strength to shove the slighter man back into the room before slamming the door shut the moment Tiercelin came inside.

Zamaril flew backwards, colliding with a couch and rolling over it and back to his feet with Callanan quickness and agility. His mouth opened, anger darkening his face—

"Stop, now!" Cuinn bellowed, using every inch of song magic he possessed to bolster his command and halt all four men in the room in their tracks. It took a second for its strength to fade and as Cuinn stood there, he was stunned by what he saw.

Zamaril's lip was curled back in a silent snarl, Corrin's green eyes gone dark with a predatory light. Halun's big shoulders were slightly hunched, expression a rictus of anger wanting to be let loose. Andres, the calmest of them all, had something on his face that spoke of hunting and death.

Wolves indeed.

What had she built?

"Your brother has her!" Corrin was the first to break free, lurching into movement. "We have to—"

"No!" Cuinn shoved him back. "You do *anything* right now and the Wolves will be dead to a man by morning. That will destroy her."

156

Fury sparked on Zamaril's face and his snarl ripped through the room. "You want us to sit here and do nothing?"

"What in skies is going on?" Tiercelin demanded, wings flinging wide in agitation and almost smacking Halun in the face. The big man was so worked up he shoved Tiercelin away. Tiercelin stared at him, eyes wide in shock.

"Captain Dynan has been arrested." Cuinn fought for calm. It was close to impossible with the same panic the Wolves were feeling churning in his own stomach. And then Tiercelin's response to his words hit in a fresh wave of terror, and he almost doubled over with the force of it. But for her sake... he had to be calm. Had to think clearly. Had to somehow save them all. "By Mithanis. I don't know why. But if any of you try to help her, they will assume the Wolves are also guilty of whatever they suspect her of and it will be the excuse they need to kill you all. Am I clear?"

"I don't think—"

"No!" Cuinn cut off Halun this time. "If any of you got hurt because of her, she would never forgive herself. You know that."

"What do we do then?" Andres demanded.

Cuinn took a breath. "You'll have to trust me."

"*Trust* you?" Zamaril had gone red in the face. "Trust a winged prince who doesn't give two coins for a human life, much less a foreign human?"

"Zamaril, you're being unfair," Tiercelin snapped. "We all know that's not how the prince thinks of humans."

Cuinn took a breath. "I'll find out where they're holding her, then we'll work out a plan. One step at a time. That's what she always says, right?"

Throwing Talyn's words at the talons seemed to calm them. Fractionally.

"Don't forget I have access to the Shadowhawk's resources." Those words, spoken to try and reassure, started a kernel of thought leaking through him. What if...

Tiercelin rounded on him. "You can't. They think you're dead."

"I don't much care about that right now. You saw what happened to the Ciantar and his entire family in the space of a single night." Cuinn spoke in a rush. "I won't let that happen to her or any of you. We'll find a way."

Tiercelin paled dramatically, his horror reaching out like a slap to the face. Before Cuinn could pursue what had caused that reaction, Corrin broke in. "What about us?"

"You stay in the barracks and do nothing. No speaking out against the arrest, no acting out either. You can't give them any excuse to arrest you too."

Halun spoke up. "The Shadowhawk can't be the one to break her out." A vein at his neck throbbed but his voice was quiet. "It will prove to your brother that she's been in league with him this whole time. It will make whatever they're charging her with worse."

"Agreed." Cuinn shook his head, trying to force his brain to think. "But that comes next. First we work out what's happened and where she is."

The door opened before any of them could protest further. It was Tirina, concern written all over her face. "Prince Azrilan just landed in the yard with a handful of his Falcons."

Panic swept the air of the room so fiercely Cuinn almost staggered from the force of it. "That's not helping." He clutched his head. "Mithanis isn't going to arrest me, at least not yet."

"You're just going to go out there?" Corrin had gone so pale his green eyes stood out starkly against his skin.

"I am. I'm going to figure out what's going on and then work out a plan." He began moving for the door—he didn't want Azrilan seeing the Wolves in this state. "You, *all* of you, do nothing. And you keep the Wolves in line. That's a direct order." His eyes ran over them. He wished Theac was here. The best thing for the Wolves right now was Parksin's steadiness.

Cuinn closed the door firmly behind him, took a deep breath and summoned hints of both song magic and glamour. Then, he strolled out to meet Azrilan and the Falcons with him, hands in pockets, idle expression firmly in place. "What's going on?" He projected the right blend of annoyed and snappish. "The Wolves are telling me some wild, panicked tale of Captain Dynan being arrested."

Azrilan reached out to lay a hand on his shoulder. "I'm sorry, Brother, it's serious. You'd better come with me."

He ignored the dread tightening his chest and huffed a long-suffering sigh. "Fine. Can we make it fast though? I have a warm bed to get back to."

Azrilan leapt into the air and Cuinn followed suit, the Falcons trailing behind. The prince of games led him over the buildings of the palace to their mother's reception room. More Falcons than usual stood guard outside the door, though they opened it without a word when Azrilan and Cuinn landed before them.

Inside the well-lit room, his mother paced back and forth, her expression difficult to interpret. Mithanis stood, arms crossed, face as dark as a storm. Opposite them was Talyn, hands tied behind her back, a Falcon at each shoulder.

The sight of her standing there, bound, was like a punch to Cuinn's stomach—the overwhelming flood of anger and terror was so strong he couldn't tell which was the primary emotion. Only years of practice allowed him to squelch that emotion before it took hold and became obvious to the song mages in the room.

Talyn glanced over at him as soon as he walked in, the warning in her expression unmistakable. But equally unmistakable were her emotions. She was leaving them open for him to read.

She didn't know why she was here.

She wasn't afraid either. Not yet.

"Did you know about this?" Mithanis snapped at him.

"Know about what?" Cuinn threw both hands up in the air and dropped onto the nearest sofa. "I was agreeably engaged *sleeping* when all this fuss disturbed me. Why have you arrested my captain?"

"Cuinn, please, show some maturity," his mother snapped.

He huffed a sigh, making a show of sitting up straight. "Maybe if someone would tell me what was going on, I could summon the appropriate level of gravity?"

"She's a Dumnorix," Mithanis said flatly.

A chill wrapped icy fingers around his heart, a response he buried as deeply as he possibly could. Instead, he chuckled. "Are you sure? How do you know?"

"I'm certain. I had some people travel to Calumnia to do a little digging on your human captain." Mithanis's voice was silky, edged with a note of triumph. "Did you know, Brother?"

"I certainly didn't," Azrilan interjected.

"No, I didn't," Cuinn said before Mithanis could turn his ire on Azrilan. "If you recall, I neither wanted nor asked for a human guard from the Twin Thrones. She and that wing are a constant pain in my rear. I'm not sure why you'd imagine for a second I'd bother enough to learn anything about her."

Talyn didn't dare look at him, but he sensed her approval across the room. Looking at her, he raised an eyebrow, trying to say, *they can feel that too*. "You might have mentioned at some point, Captain. Now look at the fuss you've caused."

"Oh, it's much, much worse than that." Mithanis's voice turned cold, and now their mother looked discomfited. The chill Cuinn had felt earlier turned into a bone-cold fear. Something else was happening here. Something worse than her being a Dumnorix.

"It's not what any of you think," Talyn spoke suddenly, cool and confident. "The Kingshield sent me here because you asked for one of us and I had Mithranan heritage. It wasn't because I'm Dumnorix. There was no ulterior motive."

"You lie well," Mithanis said, "and cleverly, threading your deceit with truth. My people asked about that too, when they were investigating you. They learned your father's name. Trys."

The queen's face tightened, and even Azrilan's expression had turned grim. The name echoed through Cuinn's thoughts before he realised... and then for a moment it was hard to breathe. Panic clawed at him, turning his muscles to jelly and his brain to fragments of chaotic thought.

If this was what he thought... she wasn't getting out of here alive.

She'd never told him her father's name. He'd never asked, he'd never *thought* to ask. If he had… he cursed himself for a fool. He could have prevented all this if he'd just—

"I don't understand." Talyn frowned. And it was clear she didn't. Cuinn desperately hoped Mithanis sensed that—it might save her.

The prince of night studied her, quiet menace oozing from every part of him. Cuinn watched, frozen, as he murmured. "Only one family in the history of the winged folk has ever had that sapphire colouring in their eyes… and wings. We never put it together because you're human. But you're not human, are you, Captain Dynan?"

Hesitation flitted across her face as she decided whether to be truthful. In the end she nodded. "I believe my father was winged folk, yes. But I don't know any more than that. He never told me anything more. He refused to."

"I think you're lying." Mithanis stepped up to her in a sudden, graceful movement. "Your father was Trystaan Ciantar, and I think you came here on some purpose for the Dumnorix king."

The room went deathly silent.

Trystaan Ciantar. A name that hadn't been spoken aloud for over two decades.

Talyn's father. Talyn was a Ciantar.

His mother's combined fear and guilt hit Cuinn like a slap, then vanished as quickly as it had come. Cuinn swallowed. He had to do something. Before Mithanis killed her on the spot. Or his mother did.

"Come on Mithanis, even for you that's absurd." Cuinn managed to recover his voice, though it sounded shaky rather than annoyed. "All Captain Dynan has done since coming here is train my Wolves. We're the ones that asked for a Kingshield."

"She's done a lot more than that and you know it," his mother snapped. "Cuinn, if it turns out you knew something of this…"

"Of course I didn't." He lifted himself to his feet, unable to sit still any longer. "And I don't know why you're making such a big deal of it. Even if the Ciantar was her grandfather, she had nothing to do with their activities."

"You're not as stupid as to think she—the daughter of Trystaan Ciantar and a Dumnorix princess—was sent here for no other purpose than to train our WingGuard? They knew who she was, it's why they sent her. I know it for a fact, actually. My spies are very, very good." Mithanis's voice was whisper-soft as he turned to Cuinn, more dangerous for how quiet it was.

Talyn's eyes were on him, willing him to protect himself, her focus on his safety rather than the shock of Mithanis's declaration.

"Oh all right." Cuinn sighed and threw himself back into the chair. "Fine. She came here with some dastardly plan in mind. And while enacting that plan—which was what, exactly?—she just happened to save my life from an assassination attempt at the same time. You do remember that, don't you?"

"We don't know what her plan is, not for certain," Mithanis mused. "But dead nobles and an increase in Shadowhawk activity? Humans being riled up? All since she arrived. None of it is a coincidence."

"I think you're reaching." Cuinn sighed, while inwardly his chest constricted. When painted in that light... things looked very bad. "What do you plan on doing with her?"

"She'll receive the same fate as the rest of her family," his mother said without hesitation.

Talyn was still, that mask she wore revealing nothing. Cuinn swallowed down his panic, his heart beginning to race in his chest. Death. Not an unsurprising pronouncement, but a fraught one, surely? There was a momentary silence while he realised nobody else in the room was going to disagree with his mother, then he laughed. "Not that I enjoy playing the role of sensible one, but you can't execute a Dumnorix princess out of hand. The Twin Thrones will crush us for it."

"He has a point," Azrilan said, leaning casually back against the wall.

Mithanis nodded. "We'll make it appear as an accident. Mother, you'll write a long and flowery condolence note thanking King Aethain for his niece's heroism in protecting you from another assassination attempt. She's already been hurt here once. It won't look odd for it to happen again."

The queen nodded tightly. "That can be arranged."

"What about the Wolves?" Azrilan asked. "We can't trust them, not after this."

"We'll disband them, send them fleeing back to the gutters they came from." Sarana waved a dismissive hand.

Talyn stiffened, hands flexing as if to work at her ropes.

"This is my protection wing we're talking about." Cuinn aimed for whining rather than outright protest, trying to draw their attention away from Talyn. He risked a brief look in her direction, hoping desperately she didn't try anything foolish. "You would really leave me unprotected?"

"Brightwing can assign you some Falcons. At least then you won't have to worry about daggers in the night." Mithanis looked at their mother. "It's what we should have done in the first place."

"And what if the Wolves talk?" Azrilan drawled.

Mithanis considered that while Talyn's shoulders sagged and Cuinn's heart plummeted into his stomach.

"They don't know anything. Once she's dead, we'll tell them the same thing we tell everyone else. That someone tried to kill the queen again and their beloved captain sacrificed herself." Mithanis shrugged. "They might guess we're lying, but will have no proof. And besides, they're human. What are they going to do?"

It was so casual, how horrifically they underestimated their own people. Cuinn would have laughed if he wasn't so terrified. The moment his brother killed Talyn, her talons would be on the next ship to Ryathl to tell the king exactly what had happened to his niece, if the two Callanan in the city didn't beat them to it.

At which point Aethain Dumnorix would unleash his full fury on Mithranar and its excuse for an army. He shuddered. Mithanis would seal their destruction and not even know he was doing it.

In that moment, Cuinn considered ending his charade, considered stepping forward and shedding his masks. Thought about arguing against killing her, against disbanding the Wolves, to try and convince them this could be their end.

But they would overrule him. And then he'd be exposed too. And he couldn't help Talyn that way. Or Mithranar.

Shit.

Azrilan shrugged. "We'll hold her here until we can organise a decent appearance of an assassination attempt. Shouldn't take more than a few days. We'll bribe the usual Patrolmen to loan us some expendable thugs from the Poor Quarter."

The constriction in Cuinn's chest eased fractionally. He had a few days to figure something out, but he'd need to act fast.

"And if any of the Wolves choose to protest her detention, we'll have grounds to arrest them too," Sarana said coolly. She didn't have to spell out that those Wolves could easily die as well in the fake assassination attempt Mithanis would cook up.

Mithanis nodded, calmer now that the problem was dealt with to his satisfaction. "Fine. Get her out of here."

Talyn didn't protest as they hustled her out. Her sapphire gaze met his briefly as she passed, conveying nothing but calm. He wondered what truly hid under that exterior. She would be planning already, no doubt, working out how to get herself out of this mess.

"Cuinn!" Mithanis's bark brought him back to the present. "You will let us handle this. Am I clear?"

He rose, performed a mocking bow. "I wouldn't dream otherwise, Brother."

CUINN WASN'T sure how he managed to get out of there without betraying his panic and terror, but finally he made it back to his tower. Tiercelin and his detail were waiting, their undercurrent of panic leaking out at him like needles jabbing painfully into his skin. He gritted his teeth, desperately holding on to his own focus.

"I'm fine. She's fine for the moment," he told Tiercelin in an undertone. "We've got a few days. Leave your detail with me and go and make sure the other Wolves are doing nothing. That is a direct order, Talon Stormflight."

Tiercelin saluted and leapt into the air.

Walking through the door to his bedroom, he stopped in surprise to find Ronisin standing in a corner, bayed up by a snarling Jasper.

Again, the tawncat's odd intelligence was notable. While he didn't like the intrusion of a stranger into his and Cuinn's territory, he clearly understood Ronisin was an ally, not an enemy.

"Tirina let you in this time?" Cuinn asked, making a sharp gesture at Jasper. The tawncat reluctantly moved away, allowing Ronisin to straighten up.

His cheeks coloured. "We're going to be betrothed. She trusts me."

Cuinn had a split-second decision to make. He needed help, and this young Falcon had come to him twice already tonight, risking his position and potentially his life to do so. If Cuinn was going to help Talyn, he couldn't do it alone. But he couldn't use the Wolves either.

"Mithanis sent spies to the Twin Thrones to learn more about Talyn," he said quietly. "He's learned that not only is she one of the Dumnorix family, her father was Trystaan Ciantar."

Ronisin took a step forward, violet wings rustling, dark eyes suddenly light. "Ciantar! Are you sure? I thought Trystaan was killed with the rest of his family."

"There were always rumours he'd escaped. I always assumed they were just that, but..." Cuinn hesitated. "For what it's worth, yes, I think she might be Trystaan's daughter."

"A Ciantar back in Mithranar," Ronisin murmured, then turned his gaze to Cuinn. "What are you going to do, Your Highness?"

Cuinn swallowed. He was about to risk himself, expose part of who he really was to a Falcon he barely knew. The very thought was terrifying. But this wasn't any Falcon. It was a man who'd spent time under Talyn's command. And knowing that, the terror faded.

"Why did you come back here tonight, Ronisin?"

He didn't hesitate. "To offer my help. If you're willing to use it."

A thick silence filled the room, then Cuinn decided to trust. "Can you find out where they're holding her?"

A startled look crossed Ronisin's face, and his mouth dropped open. Cuinn didn't blame him—it must have been the last thing he expected the prince of song to say. And even then, he'd still come.

"Ronisin!"

He closed his mouth, nodded. "I should be able to. But what then?

The moment she escapes, the Falcon will impound all the ships in the harbour. She won't be able to get out of Mithranar that way."

No, but... that lingering tease of an idea before. It would be a risk; he'd basically be transferring Talyn from one danger to another. But it was an opportunity they'd been looking for, one that might not come along again. And there was also... yes! Cuinn's head came up—Talyn's Callanan friends were still in the city.

"What?" Ronisin read the look on his face.

"I just need you to find out where she's being held. I'll take it from there."

Ronisin licked his lips, hesitated, firmed his shoulders. "I might... I might be able to do more than that, Your Highness."

He shook his head. "I can't have you risk your life for this. You know what will happen to you if you're caught."

"I do."

"Then why would you even think about doing more?" Cuinn frowned.

"Tirin Goldfeather and I grew up together, Your Highness. We've been best friends since we were babies." Dark eyes met Cuinn's. "He's told me about you coming to the council meetings, the things you've been saying. Tirina has told me a lot too. And Captain Dynan, well... if she is a Ciantar... it might be treason to say this, but she's broken no laws. She doesn't deserve to die. And she *is* going to die, isn't she?"

Cuinn nodded. "They'll make it look like an accident. But yes."

Ronisin took a deep breath, fear warring with resolve on his face. "Perhaps neither of you will ever get anywhere, with what you're trying to do here. But I'd like to help you try."

"What exactly are you proposing?"

"I can find out where she is and I can arrange it so that she can get out. But I won't be able to do much else. You'd have to find a way to get her out of Mithranar."

"Can you get her to the bottom of the wall? Where the waterfall cascades into the Rush. The eastern bank?"

A quick nod.

Cuinn hesitated, but even knowing the danger this would place

Ronisin in, he couldn't afford to hesitate. "Then do it. Someone will be waiting there to collect her."

"Your Highness." Ronisin bowed then, the same bow Tiercelin had been giving him since the day they'd returned from Calumnia. Cuinn's heart clenched with mingled terror and warmth.

"I will not forget this, Ronisin Nightdrift," he said, then his voice took on an edge, infused with magic. "And if you betray us, Jasper won't forget it either."

Ronisin swallowed, glancing at the tawncat. Then something seemed to occur to him and he looked back at Cuinn, wings flaring. "Actually, any chance I can borrow Jasper?"

CHAPTER 16

"*This isn't good.*"

"That's helpful, thank you," Talyn snarled aloud at her partner as she continued to pace. Prisoner! The stupid feathered bastards were holding her prisoner. And of course they couldn't manage a proper prison cell. No, instead they'd put her in a ridiculously plush room near the top of some tower on the southwestern edge of the palace. Although the two square windows were barred. Curious. It was the first time she'd seen bars anywhere in the citadel.

At least they'd untied her wrists.

A faint noise in the hall outside had her spinning, hands reaching uselessly for where her daggers were normally sheathed at her back. Those feathered morons calling themselves Falcons had relieved her of Sari's weapons before locking her in. But the door remained closed, and she breathed out, trying to force herself to relax and think.

"*Do you think they were right? About you being part of this Ciantar family?*"

She halted her pacing. "*Maybe. Da was hiding something from me, something that terrified him. If it was this, then no wonder he was so afraid of me being here.*" Talyn hesitated. "*And... it fits, Sari. The reaction Da had*

168

when I mentioned the Shadowhawk. And Cuinn said the Ciantar family were executed because of links to the old Shadowhawk."

"I don't like any of this."

Talyn brushed that aside. *"Do you think Mithanis was right, that the First Blade knew who my father was?"*

Sari was silent a moment as she mulled that over. *"It's possible. But she would never have knowingly sent you deliberately into such danger here —and if she knew who your father was then that's exactly what she was doing—without the approval of your uncle."* She paused. *"You need to get out, Tal, and soon. You and I both know Mithanis will make good on his threat to kill you."*

"Another superbly useful comment, thank you." Talyn took a breath. *"Sorry. I'm a little angry."*

Angry wasn't the word for it. Furious was better, but it still didn't encapsulate the blinding heat of what she felt. She'd never been held prisoner before. She didn't like it. At all.

"Forgiven. So, how are we going to get you out?"

Fighting her way out was one option—there was a good chance of success, but then she'd never be able to return to Mithranar, even if she could get offshore once she'd escaped. And if she left permanently, she would be leaving Cuinn unprotected. Leaving her Wolves behind forever. Not to mention leaving Vengeance to keep wreaking havoc on behalf of Montagn. No, she needed to get away cleanly and buy herself time to strategise a way out of this mess.

"Cuinn will be fine. He has your Wolves. They'll be fine too. It's time to think about yourself, Tal."

The Wolves.

Panic flooded her. *"What if they try something to get me out? Mithanis will kill them, all of them."*

Theac wasn't here. And Zamaril would be furious, Halun too, and she wasn't sure that Corrin or Tiercelin could or would try and stop them from doing anything. Andres maybe. But if even one of them tried to act on her behalf it would be the excuse Mithanis needed to have them all executed along with her.

"Talyn—"

Her breath came in short gasps and she fought to calm herself. Panic set off sparks throughout her muscles. Her heart raced and sweat slicked her palms. She dropped into a chair, hunching over, trying to gain control. If anything happened to the Wolves because of her... the panic descended again and it took several moments to fight it off.

"They wouldn't risk it, Talyn." Sari was trying to calm her, but didn't sound like she believed what she was saying. *"But either way, you need to get moving, before they have the opportunity to do anything. Dawn isn't far off, and daylight will make escape a lot more difficult."*

"I know that!" she snapped. "But I can't just fight my way out. I need a better idea."

A wave of disagreement from Sari, but then a little sigh. *"What then? You can't go through barred windows without using your Callanan magic—though I'm not sure even that would work, it's a shield, not an offensive force. Plus it would bring every Falcon in the area running."*

"The front door then."

"Sure." Sari was trying and failing not to sound exasperated. *"You could politely ask the Falcons out there to let you go so you don't have to kill them? And then what? Where would you go?"*

She opened her mouth to reply, but was cut off by a loud, blood-curdling snarl tearing through the night. The echoes of it hovered in the silence that followed, then another snarl ripped through the air again, closer this time.

There was a shout of fear from one of the Falcons outside the door, then the sound of booted footsteps and steel ringing.

"Was that Jasper?" Sari sounded thrilled.

"I think—"

The door to her room swung open, and Talyn stiffened at the sight of Darian Strongswoop standing there, hand on the hilt of his sword. He flicked a grim glance around the room. "You've got about two minutes before the guards are back. Go left out the door, take the first left after that and head all the way down the stairs to the bottom. It's a servant's stairwell so you shouldn't be seen." He spoke crisp and fast. "Someone will be waiting there to get you out of the palace."

She stared at him. "What are you doing?"

Impatience flickered on his face. "Isn't it obvious? I'm not willing to stick my neck out any further for you, Dynan, so if you don't walk out right now I'm leaving and won't be back."

It could be a trap. It probably was a trap—maybe if they killed her trying to escape Mithanis could claim it was accidental. Strongswoop had never liked her.

Another tawncat snarl ripped out, this one further away. Definitely Jasper.

Talyn didn't hesitate further. She ran past Strongswoop out the door, turned left, then turned left again. She kept her tread light even as she sprinted down the stairs he'd promised would be there, not running into anyone on the way. At the bottom, in the darkness between a pair of lamps, waited Ronisin Nightdrift, violet wings and dark hair looking black in the shadows.

He passed her a cloak and a bundle—her daggers. "Good to see you, Captain."

"The Wolves?" she asked, trying to keep the terror from her voice.

"Prince Cuinn ordered them to stand down." Ronisin's voice was calm, but his gaze darted all over the place. "He told them to stay in the barracks and do nothing to help you. We should go."

Relief flooded her so powerfully she had to pause for a moment and take a deep, shuddering breath. Once it passed, she was free to focus on Ronisin. "Why are you doing this?" she asked, shrugging the cloak on and pulling the hood well down over her head.

"No time for explanations. Let's just say I wanted to help."

She strapped the daggers on as they ran, instantly feeling better as their weight settled at the small of her back.

Ronisin led her through deserted areas of the palace and then down into the bowels where few winged folk ever went. Eventually he came to a halt at the end of a walkway that looked out over a hillside towards the top of the wall. The waterfall cascaded nearby, but they were well below the Falcon guards on the bridge and out of their direct line of sight.

"Time to fly." Ronisin looked at her. "You trust me, Captain?"

"Why is he helping you? He's a Falcon." Sari was wary.

"He's a Falcon I like," she said, then nodded at the young man. *"One I trust."*

Violet wings spreading wide, Ronisin stepped behind her and wrapped both arms around her waist. Then he leaned forward off the end of the walkway and dropped down, wings spread wide. Her stomach plummeted at the same time a sharp thrill went through her.

"I have to stay close to the treeline in case anyone is out flying nearby," he murmured in her ear.

He swooped down low towards the wall, his breath growing heavier as he navigated while carrying her entire weight. She kept as still as she could, trying to reduce the burden on him.

They swung in close by the northern side of the waterfall, cold spray dousing them, and then he was swooping over the top of the wall and dropping quickly to the eastern banks of the Rush. The moment they landed, hard, on the ground, he let go and stepped away.

"I should get back, show my face before they realise you're missing." He glanced around. "Or before anyone sees me down here."

"Ronisin, I don't know what to say." She truly didn't. What he'd just risked for her... what he and Strongswoop had both just risked. They'd be killed if Mithanis found out what they'd done.

"A better Mithranar, Captain." He smiled, then saluted sharply and leapt into the air.

Once he was gone, she glanced around. It had to be near dawn, but there were still a few people out and about. Hidden in the shadow cast by the wall and the spray of the waterfall, it didn't look like anyone had seen Ronisin drop out of the sky with her.

Now what?

Sari shivered inside her mind, but before she could offer her opinion, a small group of people stepped out of a nearby alley and came towards her. Talyn's eyes went straight to Cuinn, cloaked and hooded in his Shadowhawk guise. Relief and alarm fought within her at the sight of him. "What are you doing?" she demanded.

"Helping you," he observed. "You're welcome."

"Tal?" One of the others stepped forward, pushing back her cloak to reveal Leviana's concerned face. "You okay?"

"I'm fine." She accepted the hug, then smiled reassuringly at Cynia. Both Callanan were dressed simply, in attire that fit with their claim to be visiting merchants. No doubt there were several knives secreted around Leviana's body. Cynia wasn't carrying any obvious weapons, but when her bow wasn't accessible she was almost as good as her partner with a knife. "He brought you here?"

Cynia nodded. "And filled us in on what's happened."

Talyn looked at the fourth member of the group, a coldly-serious woman about her own age with black hair and brown skin. "Who are you?"

"The person who's going to get you out of the city," Cuinn said. "She's done it before for me, many times. You're in good hands. Saniya, this is Talyn Dynan."

Talyn's gaze shot to Cuinn's. He returned the look, a light glimmering there.

She turned back to Saniya, eying her up and down, noting Saniya was doing exactly the same thing to her. Talyn gave her a little nod of acknowledgement, then turned her attention back to Cuinn. "You shouldn't be out here doing this."

"How else were you going to get out of the city?" He raised an eyebrow.

"There's no time for chatter," Saniya interjected. "Lingering is foolish. Shadowhawk, you need to go."

"Right." Cuinn nodded, then stepped towards Talyn, awkwardly drawing her into a hug as if to say farewell. His mouth hovered near her ear as he murmured. "Here's your opportunity to get at Vengeance. I've said nothing to her about your friends apart from their names. Good luck, Captain."

She huffed, then turned her head into his neck, murmuring, "You're a genius."

He stilled. "Only if you survive. Please do that."

She hesitated, pulling back slightly. Leviana and Cynia were already following Saniya away into the nearest alley. She shifted back, wrapping her arms around Cuinn's neck, turning the pretend hug into a real one. "Thank you," she whispered against his warm skin, having to fight back the tears suddenly welling in her eyes. "Thank you for holding the Wolves back."

His arms closed around her, clutching her to him as if she were suddenly the only thing holding him upright. "I'd do anything for you, Talyn," he breathed. "Please be safe."

She nodded, closing her eyes and allowing herself to stay in his embrace for another couple of heartbeats before loosening her arms and stepping away. "Bye, Cuinn."

Whirling, she ran after her friends, not looking back.

THEY MOVED at a swift walk for over a quarter-turn. After three abrupt turns and a circled block it became clear Saniya was ensuring they weren't being tracked. Talyn followed without complaint—glad for the time to plan what to do next, not to mention figure out how to let Leviana and Cynia in on what Cuinn had orchestrated.

If they were right about Saniya's group being Vengeance, then he'd sent Talyn and two Callanan straight into the open arms of the group under a flawless pretence. The Shadowhawk had used Saniya's help getting people out of Dock City multiple times before, and the beauty of this plan was that Talyn genuinely needed to escape.

The courage that had taken... to essentially help her escape one danger and send her into another. Because he'd known this was what she would want. Known it was the opportunity she needed.

Not that there weren't risks. If Saniya was Vengeance, then she now knew the Shadowhawk wasn't dead. And even though this was something that he'd used her group to assist with many times before, Saniya might wonder why he'd reached out now, after months of absence.

Still, it was the best access they were ever likely to get.

Another four blocks deeper into the Poor Quarter, and closer to the looming shadow of the wall, Saniya led them into a dark house.

Talyn's hand slid to the hilt of her dagger, only moving away once Saniya lit a lamp—revealing the room was empty.

"What's the deal here?" Saniya's gaze roved between them before settling on Talyn. "I get why you're on the run—I'm surprised it took this long for the prince of night to decide you were more trouble than you're worth. Who are the other two?"

"If you've heard about me, I assume you know that I'm from the Twin Thrones?" If Saniya was Vengeance, she probably knew a lot more about Talyn than that. "Levs and Cynia are here visiting me from Ryathl, we're old friends." She took a frustrated breath, all for show. "It seems like Mithanis has had spies digging into me and my past."

Saniya turned her flat gaze on the Callanan. "You're merchants, I heard?"

"That's right," Cynia said. "It's part of the reason we came to visit Tal. Leviana's family business is looking to expand north."

"And why don't either of you look terrified at the prospect of being hunted down by the Falcons?"

Leviana laughed, joining Talyn's act without missing a beat. "If you had any idea the trouble Talyn has gotten us in before, you wouldn't ask that. Shall I tell you how we first met? Cynia and I were running one of my father's trade caravans across the Ayrlemyre mountains when Tal's Callanan group intercepted us, saying they'd heard brigands were looking to ambush us. Rather than turn around, she wanted us to act as bait so the Callanan could ambush them in turn. When we—"

"Enough." Saniya waved an impatient hand.

"What about you?" Cynia asked mildly. "How do we know we're not being led into a trap? You'll understand that some masked criminal showing up in our room a full-turn ago and telling us we might be in danger and that we needed to run has left us a little wary."

While Cynia held Saniya's attention, Talyn's fingers flickered briefly at her side, using basic Callanan code, knowing Leviana would be looking out for it.

"The Shadowhawk trusts me," Saniya said sharply. "So should you."

"No, he doesn't," Talyn said. There was a fine line to walk here. Saniya might start asking questions if Talyn capitulated too easily, but she couldn't challenge too hard either. "He doesn't trust anyone. He's not that stupid."

"I'm not sure that *we* trust the Shadowhawk. Merchants don't usually deal with criminals," Leviana said dubiously. Her fingers were flicking now too, this time for Cynia. The same code Talyn had communicated.

Have a plan. Pretend to trust.

"He asked me to help you, and he pays us well for our help," Saniya said flatly. "So either take it or leave it. In five seconds I'm walking out and never coming back."

Talyn shrugged. "I'm game."

Saniya gave her a long, considering look before turning abruptly and walking through to another room in the house. Surprise rippled through Talyn—she'd assumed this was a temporary location Saniya had used to test them before taking them to the real safehouse.

Instead they followed her through to a narrow back room. There, Saniya kicked aside a dirty rug, revealing a trapdoor in the floor beneath. Without a word, she reached down to open the trapdoor before standing aside and settling a challenging look on Talyn.

Talyn grinned.

And swung herself down onto the ladder.

For the moment she judged they were relatively safe. Saniya wasn't going to jump all three of them by herself. And if there was an ambush along the way, she was fairly confident she and two Callanan could handle it. Vengeance had no clue yet what Leviana and Cynia were—another clever move by Cuinn. Send her in with backup.

And there still remained the outside chance Saniya's network wasn't Vengeance. In which case their help would give Talyn the time she needed to work her way out of the mess she was in.

It was a long climb downwards, the complete darkness closing in like a tomb around them. Saniya came last, her lamp casting a faint light that didn't quite reach Talyn. Eventually her boots hit soft dirt and she stepped aside to make room for the others. Her right hand reached back to draw a dagger.

Just in case.

"You're in a good mood."

"I'm surrounded by danger."

A wistful sigh. *"I miss those times."*

A sudden, sharp ache ripped through her chest, gone as quickly as it had come, allowing her to breathe again. *"Me too, Sari."*

"Where does this lead?" Leviana was next down. She stepped close to Talyn, hands hovering close to where her knives must be hidden. Talyn had seen how fast Leviana could throw from that position, and she doubted there would be time to shout a warning before a blade lodged in her target's chest. Or before the second one landed. Maybe the third. Inwardly she grinned.

Saniya finally reached the bottom, hefting the lantern so they got a clear glimpse of her expressionless face as she answered Leviana. "You'll see."

"There better not be rats down here," Cynia grumbled. Leviana tossed a grin at her partner. Cynia's fingers flickered—acknowledgement of Talyn's message.

Talyn smiled. Now all three of them were playing the game.

"Not on this side there isn't." With that cryptic comment, Saniya led the way off down the narrow tunnel, lamp held high. She walked with fast, loose strides, and Talyn frowned. That agility was warrior-trained. This woman could fight. A swordswoman, if she judged correctly.

Sari spoke up. *"I feel like Cynia and Leviana are right to be worried."*

"I think the chances that this isn't Vengeance are decreasing," Talyn agreed.

"Out of the frying pan and into the fire, as they say." Sari said it with so much satisfaction, Talyn couldn't help but chuckle.

Leviana glanced back at her. "I see the old Talyn is making a reappearance. The one that enjoyed laughing in the face of dubious odds and reckless danger."

"I don't know if that's a good thing or a bad thing," Cynia heaved a sigh. "Next time you invite us to visit this miserably hot country, I'm going to politely decline. I was expecting warm ocean and sandy beaches, not being on the run from pretty winged men carrying swords."

"I'm not 'the old Talyn' anymore," Talyn said wistfully. "But there are bits of her still there inside me."

"Good," Leviana's voice drifted in the darkness. "Because I wouldn't want you to get too boring."

Saniya abruptly stopped ahead of them. "Would you like me to give the three of you some time to have your little heart-to-heart? Maybe find some comfy chairs for you, a pot of tea? Or can we keep walking and quit the chit chat?"

Leviana made a face as they increased their pace. "Where did you dig up this sourpuss, Tal?"

"The Shadowhawk did," she said lightly. "And he's a criminal. So let's not judge him too harshly on his associates."

"We don't usually make a habit of dealing with criminals or their associates. Even ones with cool names," Cynia said gloomily.

More banter. More chuckles. Each line designed to lull Saniya, to reinforce to her that Talyn and her friends had no idea what they were walking into.

Oh, this was fun!

THEY WALKED STEADILY DOWNWARDS for a long way, so long that Talyn grew increasingly suspicious. Almost a half-turn had passed. Where could they be going? She'd lost all sense of direction in the dark. Maybe Saniya's people had a hiding place under the bay—that could explain why the Shadowhawk had never been able to find their base of operations.

At one point, Cynia started shooting Talyn questioning looks, silently offering her view that they should consider turning back. Each time she did, Leviana shook her head, firmly siding with Talyn.

Saniya didn't say a word.

And then the tunnel floor levelled before starting to head upwards.

On they went for another quarter-turn and then they abruptly reached a dirt wall and the end of the tunnel. A ladder was wedged into the floor, illuminated by Saniya's lantern. And far above them, another trapdoor.

This time Saniya went up first. At the top, she rapped a coded knock into the wood. A moment later, it was opened from the outside. A faint thud drifted down from where the door landed.

Saniya scrambled up the ladder then turned to peer down at them. "You coming?"

Leviana went first, and Talyn didn't even try to stop Cynia following after her partner, so she went last. At the top, she scrambled quickly away from the ladder and followed the others out the door of a small hut, one hand on her dagger and ready to draw. She was so focused on being ready for any ambush that it took her a moment to realise where they were.

"Whoa..."

Thick forest surrounded them on all sides, the air even soupier than in Dock City and edged with the sweet scent of izerdia sap. Underfoot was rich, dark earth scattered with fallen leaves.

"Six thrices!" she swore aloud. "We're behind the flea-shitting wall."

"*I guess that explains why Cuinn could never find out where their hideout was.*"

Saniya looked far too satisfied with Talyn's shock for her comfort. "You're at our compound, so you're safe enough as long as you stay inside the walls. There will be other rules, too."

Talyn levelled a look at her. "It's not like you're going to let us waltz back out now we've seen your secret hideout, so why don't you explain the rules and tell us what to do next."

Saniya smiled. It held no warmth. "I heard you were no fool. Come on through, Talyn Dynan, and I'll do just that."

CHAPTER 17

*A*s soon as Talyn and her friends were out of sight, Cuinn shed his Shadowhawk persona and soared back up to the citadel. The sight of a large group of flying figures—Falcons—winging their way down towards the docks had him dropping out of sky and into the shadows of the treetops to avoid being seen.

Anxiety squeezed his chest. They knew she was gone. And as expected, Ravinire was sending Falcons down to impound the docks until she was found.

Night was creeping towards morning now, and weariness tugged at his body. Yet he was filled with an odd kind of elation too. She was out. She was with Vengeance, and she had friends to help her.

He moved as soon as the skies were clear, approaching his tower and making sure he was alone before wrapping himself in the remaining darkness of the night. He didn't want anyone seeing Prince Cuinn return to his tower at this hour and start asking questions about where he'd been.

Anticipating this, Tiercelin had removed the two usual Wolf guards from his front door, and Cuinn was able to slip quickly inside where the talon waited for him, anxiety emanating from him in a wave. He'd clearly been pacing, and his black curls were

180

rumpled, like he'd been running his hands through his hair over and over.

"She's out," Cuinn murmured, releasing his hold on the shadows and ignoring the flood of weariness that spread through him as he did.

Surprise and relief flared in the healer's grey eyes. "Where?"

"I asked Saniya for help, like I do whenever I need to get someone out of Dock City."

Tiercelin's mouth dropped open, the relief vanishing from his face. "You handed her over to the group she thinks is Vengeance?"

"It was the best option I could think of. Ravinire has already impounded the docks, and the City Patrol will be searching all the quarters at first light. Saniya has the ability to get Talyn clear and she has no idea that Talyn knows who she is. Plus I sent her two Callanan friends with her."

"I..." Tiercelin shook his head, none of the worry fading from his face. "A plan Captain Dynan would be delighted by."

"I need you to go to the barracks and tell the other talons that she's out. Make sure they know that drill needs to happen as usual this morning. The wall run, everything. Disciplined behaviour. No shows of temper," Cuinn said. "Clear?"

Tiercelin hesitated. "Prince Cuinn... they will want to know why Mithanis arrested her. Mithanis found out, didn't he?"

Cuinn went still. "Found out what?"

"That she's a Ciantar."

It took a moment to realise what Tiercelin was saying, and then fury swept through Cuinn. "You *knew*?"

Tiercelin flinched. "I guessed. I've been doing my best to keep it hidden. I thought it would be safest if I didn't say anything to anyone."

"Why didn't you warn her?" Cuinn was barely able to stop himself from roaring the words at his talon.

"Because she would have ignored my warning," Tiercelin said helplessly. "You know what she's like. Any danger to herself she disregards like it's nothing. And she's always said she'd never stay here forever, so I was hoping nobody would guess in the meantime."

"Well, somebody has. And they told Mithanis." Cuinn shook his head. Yelling at Tiercelin wasn't helping matters, and besides, he was right. Even so, his words were sharp with remaining anger when he spoke. "Get out of here. Make sure the Wolves are under control."

"Your Highness." Tiercelin bowed and left.

Alone in the silent darkness of his room, Cuinn's sluggish brain tried to figure out what to do next. First he had to work out what Mithanis planned to do about the Wolves now that Talyn had escaped. It should be clear that none of them had had anything to do with it if the talons were able to keep them under control.

But did Mithanis still intend to disband them? He might just decide to arrest them all anyway if he was angry enough about Talyn's escape. If he did, Cuinn would have to intervene somehow.

He couldn't go to Mithanis now, though, not when dawn hadn't even broken yet. It would be completely out of character. Besides, if he looked in any way desperate, his brother would seek to leverage that.

No. He needed to get some sleep, regain his energy. Then once morning came he could pay a visit to the prince of night.

Jasper let out an angry snarl when Cuinn dragged himself up to his bedroom, and didn't come over to have his head stroked, clearly upset Cuinn had left him behind to go to Dock City.

Sighing, he went to kneel by the tawncat, running a hand over his soft fur. "You were a massive help, you know? She wouldn't have got out without you."

After a moment, Jasper butted his head into Cuinn's hand in apparent forgiveness. Smiling, Cuinn rose and flopped face-first on the bed.

Time to rest. He was going to need it.

HE MANAGED JUST over a full-turn of sleep before a loud thumping at his tower door dragged him back to wakefulness. Jasper was a heavy weight on his legs, though his green eyes were blinking awake too, wariness gleaming in their depths.

The Wolf guards on his front door had already taken the message from Willir by the time Cuinn dressed and summoned a hint of glamour to hide the shadows under his eyes.

Ehdra waited below with the message. "Good morning, Your Highness."

"Thanks, Ehdra." Cuinn took the sealed note and ripped it open. Jasper busied himself weaving between his ankles while maintaining a warning glare in Ehdra's direction.

Mithanis wanted to see him.

Good. It meant he didn't have to manufacture a reason to go and see his brother. "You're in Corrin's detail, yes?" he asked as if he didn't already know.

"Yes, sir. Talon Dariel is just outside."

"Jasper, stay," Cuinn told the tawncat, adding, "And don't eat any of my Wolves."

Outside it was sunny, but grey clouds lined the southern horizon. The humidity was particularly oppressive too, like it always was before the rains broke. Corrin waited on the bridge, looking so serious that it added years to his youthful face.

"What is it?" Cuinn asked.

Corrin bowed. Hesitated. He was anxious, guilty, afraid, and a whole host of other things. It took everything Cuinn had not to shake him. Instead he forced himself to wait patiently for whatever Corrin had to say. "Without Theac here, I don't think the talons can hold the Wolves back," he said quietly.

Shit. Corrin's anxiousness began tugging in *his* gut now. Even if he sent a message to Theac, the man wouldn't get it until his and Errana's ship docked in Darmour. And then he'd have to get back. That would take days.

"What is it you're afraid they're going to do?" He'd hoped news she'd escaped might have calmed them.

"They want to help her, find where she is. Halun is talking about using his dock contacts to find a ship willing to smuggle her away and Zamaril says he can find her if he spends a few turns in the Poor Quarter. Tiercelin thinks he can convince some Falcons on the docks to turn a blind eye if Halun succeeds. Other Wolves are just angry, unsettled. I'm afraid they might start a fight with Falcons or do something equally dangerous."

The young talon's analysis was impressive, showing an instinctive understanding of his command that Cuinn had thought only Talyn and Theac possessed. But it also opened up a sinking pit in his stomach, one which he refused to let swallow him.

"Mithanis has demanded to see me. I can't afford to keep him waiting. Let me go and deal with that, then I'll come and talk to the Wolves," Cuinn said, keeping his voice calm despite his anxiousness. "Take the human Wolves in your detail and go back to the barracks. You need to hold them until then. All right?"

The Wolf's shoulders straightened. "I'll do everything I can, Your Highness. She told me that to be a leader I had to put you and my command first. No matter how terrified I am for her, how much I just want to... So I'll do it, whatever it takes."

Cuinn smiled. He couldn't help it. "You're doing the right thing, Corrin. And I'll be there soon. I'm your prince. I'll take care of it, I promise you."

Light flashed in Corrin's eyes and he saluted and walked away, emotions lighter than they had been when he arrived. Cuinn took a steadying breath, summoned Roalin and Nirini with a gesture, and leapt into the sky, determination settling into his bones.

I am their prince. I will take care of this.

THE PRINCE of night was predictably furious as he paced the lounge of his personal quarters. No Azrilan present. No Ravinire or their mother either. Cuinn wasn't sure whether that was a good or a bad thing.

"She's gone," Mithanis snarled at him.

"I gathered from the rage my song magic is currently being seared by," Cuinn said dryly. Mithanis wasn't even trying to hold it in. "How did she get out?"

"The guards on the door were distracted by a tawncat." Danger filled the room, prickling down his spine and shivering over his skin, as Mithanis stepped up to Cuinn. "Yours."

Cuinn was tired from the long night. Anxious and afraid too. Juggling so many balls he wasn't sure how much longer he could keep them all afloat.

But he'd been tired and anxious before, and always, *always* his magic had held steady. He knew how to push past that tiredness. And so he did it now, and for the first time ever, used his magic against Mithanis… not to hide from him or appear non-threatening, but to manipulate his brother into following the course of action Cuinn wanted. It was dangerous, but heady at the same time.

"Jasper slept at the foot of my bed last night, as he does every night." Cuinn threaded those words with truth, transparency. "I have to keep him in or he tends to attack my Wolf guards, or anyone else that happens to wander by."

"Then what was a tawncat doing prowling around here last night and coincidentally distracting the guards watching Dynan's door?"

"One got up here before, remember?" Cuinn said pointedly. "Twice, in fact. Do we have any missing nobles this morning? Maybe it's lucky you had guards on that door to hear the tawncat and chase it off before someone else had their intestines ripped out." This time he threaded belief in the words, making them sound like the most logical and sensible thing Mithanis had ever heard.

The prince of night's magic was strong, but he was too volatile to use it with finesse or subtlety. And he didn't notice now as Cuinn worked on him with every inch of skill he possessed. Some of the rigidity in Mithanis' shoulders softened and he stepped away, huffing out an angry breath.

"I fear having her loose, Brother. With Montagn breathing down our necks…"

Cuinn frowned. "What do you mean?"

"Nothing. Az has been working hard on our behalf with our uncle's family, we should be fine. But we've heard reports of their troop build-ups, and now the Twin Thrones have a spy amongst us." Mithanis appeared genuinely troubled. "We are such a small country, Cuinn."

"And your pretty WingGuard don't exactly strike fear into anyone, do they?" Cuinn remarked.

Surprisingly, Mithanis didn't tense at that. Instead, he nodded. "If any of your Wolves hear anything about where she has gone, you will tell me at once."

"Mithanis." Cuinn gentled his voice and stepped closer, threading sincerity into his words. "I told you I wanted to help more, and I meant it. I'm your brother. Of course I will tell you anything I hear."

Mithanis relaxed further. "At least if they're up here we can keep a closer eye on them. And once we catch her, maybe it would be best to arrest them all too."

Cuinn's mind turned over furiously. If Mithanis was contemplating arresting the Wolves, then it wouldn't be long before he thought executing them was the safest thing. All he would need was the tiniest excuse…

And then he had it. The perfect solution.

"Are you daydreaming?" Mithanis asked eventually. He sounded tired, annoyed, rather than angry. Cuinn's magic was working, making Mithanis believe his brother actually wanted to help for once. He fought back that triumph before Mithanis's song magic could sense it.

"No, I just had an idea." He let excitement tinge his voice. "I'll take a trip to Sparrow Island, just for a couple of days—the rains are about to break, so it will be good to have a change of scenery. I'll insist all my Wolves come. They won't be able to do anything to trouble you while stuck on the island. It will give you time to find her. And I can relax and enjoy myself without your angry presence marching about all over the place."

Plus, this way none of the Wolves would have a chance to go organising smugglers or tracking down Talyn or convincing Falcons to look away as she escaped and risking all their lives in the process.

Mithanis paused in his pacing. "That's actually not a terrible idea."

Cuinn beamed.

"Just a few days, mind. We should have her back by then and I don't want you disappearing on us again." Threat laced Mithanis's words, enough that Cuinn didn't have to fake his shiver.

"Not a problem." Cuinn managed a smile. "I'll bring Irial and Annae, and a few other friends. Some Falcons too, if that makes you feel better." The addition of Irial should relax Mithanis even more—Irial would report everything Cuinn did back to him.

Mithanis nodded. "Fine. Get out of here."

Cuinn bowed his head—filling it with the deference his brother craved—and left, Nirini and Roalin close behind him. As soon as they walked out into open air, he spread his wings and leapt into the sky.

He wanted to scream. To shout. To roar his triumph into the air.

He'd just faced down Mithanis, used magic *against* him instead of to hide from him, and succeeded.

Such a minor thing.

But it felt so good.

IT FELT like several days had passed, but it was still barely past dawn when Cuinn landed in the Wolves' drill yard. Those not on shift had just returned from the wall run and Corrin's voice rang through the morning, sharper and louder than usual.

Zamaril stood to the side, arms crossed. Halun was equally silent. Tiercelin and Andres kept glancing between Corrin and the other two, as if unsure which side they were on. Gathered all together, the anger and restlessness Corrin had described in the wing was a palpable presence to Cuinn's song magic. For a moment it had him angry, ready to hit someone, and then he took a deep breath, separating their emotions from his.

Focus.

All turned at Cuinn's arrival. He didn't bother with niceties or small talk. Neither was going to reach these men and women.

"I'm leaving for Sparrow Island this morning." He kept his voice a lazy drawl, exactly what they expected of him. "And given what happened on my previous trip there, I'll be taking the full wing with me. Every single one of you." He paused to let that sink in. "Be ready by midday down at the docks. A boat will be waiting for the human Wolves. Winged Wolves will fly with me. Go to it."

Corrin and Andres began issuing instructions to their details. Halun and Tiercelin followed suit, though the big man was clearly reluctant and kept shooting unhappy glances at Cuinn.

At the sight of Zamaril standing with his arms crossed, surly expression in place, Cuinn had had enough.

"You!" he snapped, striding over and gesturing for the thief to follow. "Halun, you too."

At least they followed, Halun silent as always, Zamaril looking even more surly. "Your Highness?" he asked.

"She was damned right to demote you, Zamaril," Cuinn said coldly. "What exactly is it you both think you're doing? You really think you're helping her with this attitude? You think it will help her to get all your comrades killed? Because my brother is already contemplating it!"

Halun froze. The thief opened his mouth, faltered. Looked away.

"Trust me to take care of this or not, but you need to think about the consequences of your actions, because neither of you are fools," Cuinn continued. "You will be on that boat at midday. If you're not, I will kick you out of the Wolves. Am I clear?"

Halun's shoulders straightened and he saluted. "I was wrong. I apologise, Your Highness."

Zamaril's jaw clenched but he nodded. "I'm sorry too."

"So you should be. Get out of my sight."

Cuinn let out a breath as they walked away, hoping he'd done enough. His gaze fell on Corrin, managing the more reluctant Wolves with a steadfast patience that had the tight ball of anxiety in his chest loosening.

It was going to be all right. He'd done everything he could.

He glanced up at the sky—the rain clouds were much closer now—

then leapt back into the air. Time to find Irial and Annae and tell them they were coming on a trip to Sparrow Island.

It was up to Talyn now.

If she wasn't back from Vengeance with some sort of plan before they returned from Sparrow Island, he wasn't sure what they were going to do.

CHAPTER 18

*R*ain streamed in steady rivulets down the windows and tapped noisily against the roof. Talyn stared out into the unending greenery of the forest, thinking. Move now, or be patient and wait Saniya out? She couldn't decide.

"I think he was lying, Tal." Leviana broke the silence, uttering this pronouncement with the gravity of a well thought out conclusion.

Talyn turned, lifting an eyebrow. Leviana and Cynia were sprawled on two of the hut's four narrow beds. So far, both had been enduring three unbearably long days of the 'stay indoors during the rains' policy of Saniya's people much more cheerfully than Talyn had.

All they'd seen so far was greenery and huts and a quick glimpse of a high wooden wall. And other humans, some with slave tattoos. No copper masks and no weapons. No hint of threat. No training warriors. There had been plenty to hear though, mainly the creatures outside the walls after night fell. Sometimes it sounded like a hundred Jaspers were prowling the darkness. It hadn't made for sound sleep for any of them.

Nobody had tried to take Talyn's weapons away. That was something.

But there hadn't been any direct conversation with anyone either.

Food had been delivered twice a day by a different person each time. When asked anything, the reply was the same—they weren't allowed to speak to the new arrivals.

Cynia glanced at her partner. "Who was lying about what?"

"Prince Mithanis. Cool nickname, by the way—the prince of night. Love it. Strikes fear at the hearts of all his enemies, no doubt."

A patient sigh from Cynia. "You were saying?"

"Oh, yes. I think he was lying about the First Blade knowing Talyn was a member of this Ciantar family before sending her here." Leviana sat up. "Think about it. What could your uncle possibly have to gain from putting you in that kind of danger, Talyn? They sent you because of your Callanan background, because they wanted you to investigate the Shadowhawk. You being part of this noble winged family only risks the mission."

"It's a good point." Cynia glanced at Talyn.

"It is." She began pacing. Again. Sitting still indoors was making her itch.

"So the question becomes…"

"…why did Mithanis want me to believe it?"

Both Callanan looked at Talyn oddly. "Everything okay?" Leviana asked.

"No. In case you hadn't noticed, we're stuck hiding out in a forest filled with vicious and bloodthirsty creatures—not to mention our hosts may or may not be a gang that's been hunting me for months and laying the groundwork for an invasion by Montagn. Yet this is the third day we've been here and we've learned absolutely nothing."

"My question is, how did Mithanis find out any of it?" Cynia ignored Talyn's rant.

"Right." Leviana picked up her partner's train of thought. "Callanan and Kingshield protect their own. Anyone asking questions about Talyn in Calumnia wouldn't have learned a thing. She wasn't raised at court, and never spent much time there. I challenge any regular person on the streets of Ryathl to know her father's name or even that she's Dumnorix."

Talyn dropped into a chair, rubbing a hand over her forehead.

"That's what's eating at me. Because you're absolutely right. The only thing I can come up with is the Armun... they can find out anything on anyone."

Both Callanan straightened abruptly. They knew as well as Talyn did the skills possessed by the elite Armun spies. They'd worked with them before on missions.

"The Armun Council would never spy on a Dumnorix then pass information to a foreign prince," Leviana said sceptically. "The Shadowlord would be hung if he approved something like that."

"But Vengeance has a mercenary Shadow working for them," Cynia said. "So maybe they have an Armun in their pocket too."

"Or their pet Shadow did the spying," Talyn mused.

Cuinn had said they might not come directly at her again. That they might use more clever means than that. What if they'd leaked the information on who she was to Mithanis, knowing how he'd react? But how had Vengeance gotten in Mithanis's ear?

"He pulls their strings—that's what your prisoner said."

"I still don't buy that."

"I'm unconvinced." Cynia echoed her thoughts. "If Vengeance truly worked for Mithanis, then why has he waited until now to move against you?"

Leviana sighed in agreement. "Nor does it make any sense that he'd be helping a criminal gang causing upheaval in a country that he's planning to be king of."

Impatience surged in Talyn. "Anyway, *how* Mithanis found out isn't important right now."

Leviana nodded. "Because we've managed to walk ourselves into the lair of a group you think is Vengeance and so far we've learned nothing."

"The fact they're essentially keeping us locked up in this hut is interesting," Cynia said. "We're behind the wall—there's no need to be worried about Patrolmen or Falcons seeing us, yet we're not allowed to roam the camp."

"That could just mean they have solid security practices and don't let outsiders see how things work here," Leviana pointed out. "For their own protection."

"But if they *are* Vengeance, why haven't they killed us already?" Cynia asked. "They want Talyn dead, don't they?"

"We need to do something." Talyn began pacing again, frustration edging her every movement. "I've been here too long. We need to confirm our suspicions or otherwise and then work out a way to convince Mithanis and the queen that I'm not here spying on them—"

"Even though you are," Leviana cut in.

"—and let me go back to being Wolf captain." She glowered at her friend. "I'm not here spying on them. I'm here to investigate and destroy Vengeance and protect Prince Cuinn."

"Tal, I don't understand why you keep focussing on Prince Cuinn's protection." Cynia gave her partner a warning glance as Leviana spoke. "You need to work out a way to get out of Mithranar and go home. Why would you risk staying here?"

"I am the captain of the Wolves, and I'm responsible for Prince Cuinn's safety." Talyn huffed an irritated breath as the Callanan exchanged another look. After the less than flattering things she'd told them about Cuinn, she wasn't going to be able to convince them that was important. So she changed tack. "I can't destroy Vengeance if I'm not in Mithranar, and that's our highest priority."

"Consider our position," Cynia said reasonably. "We're sworn Callanan and you're a Dumnorix family member. It's our job to make sure you're safe."

"You're not Kingshield," Talyn said irritably. "And I don't need you to keep me safe. I need you to help me figure this out."

That silenced them momentarily, and Talyn continued to pace, mind turning over furiously.

"Maybe you should tell them who Cuinn is. They might understand then," Sari suggested.

"No. If I told them, they'd be obliged to report it to the First Blade. And I don't..." Talyn halted her pacing. "That's it!"

"What's it?" Cynia asked warily.

"Mithanis was trying to make me feel betrayed and angry by

telling me the Callanan knew all about my parentage… it's what he does, he lives off the fear of others." Talyn smiled without warmth. "So I'll use it against him. I'll play up the reactions he wants. I'll tell Mithanis I'm not Kingshield or Callanan anymore and after what they've done to me, I'll happily work for Mithranar instead."

"You'll *what* now?" Leviana leapt off the bed, just avoiding her partner's restraining arm. "You're going to turn traitor?"

"Of course not." Talyn waved a hand impatiently. "I'll just tell him I will. You two will go back to the First Blade and tell her what's happened and what I'm doing. She can tell me what to feed Mithanis in terms of information."

Cynia baulked. "Talyn, this is a little extreme."

"The First Blade will not be happy," Leviana added.

"She's the one who's wanted me spying here all along," Talyn pointed out.

"She wanted you spying on the Shadowhawk and Vengeance, not the royal family. Your plan is dangerous, and for no good cause. You're not Armun." Leviana grew heated. "You said yourself how powerful this prince of night's magic is. He'll know you're lying the moment you open your mouth, and then he will have you killed."

Talyn shook her head. "No. With Cuinn's help I can make him believe me."

"With *Cuinn's* help? The spoiled prince who lost his spine somewhere around the age of three?" Leviana demanded. "Not to mention he's Mithranan too. What makes you think he'd work against his own brother?"

"You know nothing about him!" Talyn snapped, stung by that accusation, by how far from the truth it truly was.

Leviana reddened further, but Cynia intervened. "We know what you've told us about him."

"Yeah, and I haven't told you everything." Frustration was making her sharp, and not as controlled as she needed to be. And Cynia was right. They only had her account of Cuinn to go on. The false account that kept him safe. Shit. Talyn took a breath, trying to summon her cool calm.

"That's a theme with you ever since Sari died." Leviana's anger faded. She looked tired now, and sad. "We're your friends, and we've never wanted anything but to help and support you. But you've pushed us away and kept your distance and refused to even admit you had a problem until recently. And now you're being reckless and putting yourself at risk. What are we supposed to do?"

"You're supposed to trust me," Talyn said quietly.

Cynia and Leviana shared a look, silently communicating something. After a moment, they nodded slightly, and Cynia spoke. "Look, there's something else we should talk about. Levs and I have a theory, and we've debated whether to even tell you or not, because there's no proof and it's more an educated guess than anything, but before you decide to go through with this crazy plan, you should know."

Talyn stared at her. She'd never heard so many words come out of the usually brisk and steady Cynia before. "What are you talking about?"

"Tirigan told us that the arrow that killed Sari was probably from the same archer who killed your father," Leviana said carefully. "And it got us thinking."

"About?" She swallowed, glancing between them. Sari roused in her head, clearly intrigued.

"Everyone has assumed the two attacks—if linked—were directed at the Dumnorix, you and your mother, specifically," Cynia said.

Leviana shifted forward. "But what if we're looking at it from the wrong perspective? What if you *were* the link, but not the target?"

Talyn moved across the room to pick up a chair, then carried it over to place before the beds where her friends sat, using the time to calm her thudding heart. Then she sat, unsure she was going to be able to have this conversation while standing. "Explain."

The two Callanan glanced at each other. "Bear with us," Cynia said.

"Before Sari died, what were your plans, Tal? Long term, I mean," Leviana asked.

Talyn took a breath. She wanted to dismiss this conversation, push it away. Never wanted to talk about Sari or the plans she'd had ever again. But she trusted her friends and so she forced herself to speak. "I wanted to be a Callanan, working with Sari, for as long as my body held up. After that, probably go back to my parents' farm, or maybe retire in Port Lathilly if that's where Sari wanted to stay."

"And when she died, what happened? You went to Ryathl to join your family. To get their support?" Cynia said.

"Right."

"But rather than staying in Ryathl, staying with the court, you ended up in Mithranar." Leviana glanced at Cynia, then back at Talyn. "And it's becoming increasingly clear to us Mithranar is where you plan on staying, at least for now."

Talyn hesitated, took a breath, then nodded. "Yes."

"So what happened when your father died?" Cynia asked gently.

"I came back home…" Talyn's voice trailed off as she started to see where her friends were heading with this.

"And most people, including us—your closest friends—assumed that you would stay. That you would go back to Ryathl with your mother, both to help her through her grief but also to help hunt your father's killers. And even though we know it was your mother who was targeted, it's still the same outcome if she'd died instead of your father. You coming home and staying."

"So you think Sari and my father were killed to get me… what? Home? Joining the Dumnorix court?" Talyn asked, tone rich with disbelief.

"Something like that. I know how it sounds," Cynia said.

Leviana shifted forward, brown eyes intense. "Think about it. Instead of going to Ryathl after your father's death, you came back to Mithranar. And now look what's happened. Somebody has conveniently told Mithanis who you are, resulting in you getting kicked out of Mithranar and having no choice but to go home." Leviana threw the words at her, her voice vibrating with conviction.

Talyn shot to her feet. "You think someone is trying to get me out of Mithranar? That doesn't make sense. Sari was killed before I came here, *well* before."

"No." Cynia stood too, shaking her head. "I think someone is trying to get you to join the Dumnorix court."

"Six thrices, Tal, it's a compelling theory." Sari sounded startled.

"But who? And why?" Talyn demanded. "What difference does my being part of Aethain's court make to anything?"

"That's the part we're unsure about," Leviana muttered.

"Although I'll point out that nobody has yet come up with a strong theory as to who or why someone tried to assassinate your mother, either," Cynia said. "Our theory makes no less sense and fits the facts better."

"I—" Talyn opened her mouth to respond but was cut off as the door was suddenly wrenched open.

Saniya stood there, her eyebrows lifting as she presumably read the tension in the room. Talyn blinked at the sight of her, then belatedly realised that the rain had stopped.

"You're welcome to come and get something to eat. If you're hungry." Saniya glanced around the room.

Leviana scrambled off the bed. "I'm starved."

Cynia was close behind her partner and Talyn followed suit, anticipation kindling in her stomach. Finally, they were being let out.

This might be the opportunity she'd been waiting for.

"THIS PLACE IS VERY DAMP," Leviana grumbled as they walked along a muddy path, water dripping from the trees around them.

"Monsoon season just started," Saniya said. "It isn't any better in Dock City, trust me."

Talyn said nothing. She didn't know what to think about her friends' theory, and the frustration of having accomplished so little in three days wasn't helping her unsettled state of mind.

"You're worried about Cuinn."

"I'm the captain of his guard. I thought I'd have sorted this out by now, but the longer I'm away, the more danger he'll be in."

"Or maybe he's looking after himself just fine."

Talyn took a deep breath, allowing Sari's words to sink in. She was right. Cuinn was no fool. She knew that. And what he'd done in containing the Wolves and not only getting her out of the citadel but also delivering her to Saniya had showed impressive quick thinking.

"All right. I'll stop worrying so much."

Sari snorted, but said nothing.

Inside the smoky eating hut, Saniya ladled them a bowl each of a steaming, delicious-smelling stew, then served herself from the same pot. With a gesture, she invited them to sit with her.

Talyn opened her mouth to start a conversation, ask Saniya some innocuous questions to get her talking, but Leviana spoke before she could.

"We've been here three days and not a word from you," Leviana said grumpily. "What's the deal? When are we getting out of here?"

"I've been away from camp taking care of some things," Saniya explained as she ate. "We always give those we help the option to stay with us. But if you choose not to, we'll organise passage out of Mithranar for you once the fuss dies down. The streets of Dock City are thick with searching Patrolmen at the moment, even in the Poor Quarter."

"Stay with you?" Talyn asked. "And do what? What is this place exactly?"

"It's a community free of winged folk oppression," Saniya said. "It's a dangerous life—we've had to learn how to barricade out the tawn-cats, and they're always a danger when we go hunting. Not to mention the snakes that regularly manage to get through our walls, but at least here we're all free."

"So no winged folk down here then," Cynia remarked.

"None," Saniya said flatly.

There was nothing. Nothing in Saniya's demeanour or in their surroundings to help Talyn work out whether she was sitting in Vengeance's base or not. Except the clear disdain for winged folk... but all humans shared that.

"How do you defend yourselves from the animals?" Leviana tried another tack, keeping her voice light and conversational.

"We all learn how to defend ourselves before going out into the forest," Saniya said simply.

Helpful.

"If we joined your community, what would we have to do?" Talyn asked.

Saniya was silent a moment as she swiped a piece of bread over the remnants of her stew then chewed and swallowed. "You've heard the story about the Ciantar family?"

Talyn stilled, and had to fight not to look sideways at her friends. "One of my winged Wolves mentioned it once. Said they were all executed on the queen's order," she answered. "But nobody knows why."

"Lord Ciantar's heir, Trystaan, had an older half-brother. Before marrying and joining the Queencouncil, the Ciantar had an affair with a human woman, and the resulting child did not inherit his father's winged folk blood." Saniya's face tightened. Talyn tried to stop her mouth from dropping open. If Mithanis was right and Trystaan was her father, then that meant she had an uncle? "Because he was human, the child—Runye—went unacknowledged by all but Trystaan. As they grew older, Trystaan came to hate the way his brother was treated just because he was human, and Runye rebelled against it too."

Saniya fell silent, and they waited her out, trying not to look like they were hanging on every word. Leviana ate more stew. Cynia dug at a piece of lint on her sleeve.

Talyn kept her cool mask, but inside she felt completely at sea. The way Saniya described Talyn's father—loving his brother no matter what—made her feel warm and desperately sad at the same time.

"Runye was the first Shadowhawk, and this group was formed from his helpers." Saniya spoke so softly Talyn barely heard the words. "Trystaan knew what his brother was and helped him when he could. When the queen found out, she ordered the whole Ciantar family arrested. Runye sacrificed himself to warn Trystaan before he could be captured along with the rest of his family. I was a baby at the time, but I've heard the stories. We had to cut his wings out because he was never going to escape Mithranar unseen with them, not the colour they were. Now we work to avenge my father by breaking winged folk oppression."

"Your father?" Cynia managed. "Runye was your father?"

"Six thrices, she's your cousin!"

Saniya gave a single nod. Then she shifted her gaze to meet Talyn's eyes. And in that look was everything Talyn needed to know. Hatred. Anger. Resentment. A yearning for justice that hadn't been achieved.

Cynia's hand landed lightly on Talyn's leg, breaking her from the spell Saniya's words had cast. A sideways glance showed both Callanan had stiffened imperceptibly.

"Why did she just tell you all that?"

"Because she doesn't intend for us to leave." Talyn said.

This was Vengeance.

Because Saniya's group—Runye's group—had started out undertaking the peaceful activities of the Shadowhawk, but somehow, somewhere, that had changed. She'd heard it in the bitterness of Saniya's voice. A desire to help had turned into a desire for revenge.

Maybe someone had helped that along. Maybe it had happened naturally. But right now that didn't matter.

Talyn began surreptitiously looking for the exits, counting how many there were. Just one, the door they'd entered through, and there were at least fifteen others eating around them, though none of them looked like they were paying much attention.

They knew who she was. Why hadn't they killed her already?

"You're not just your group's contact with the Shadowhawk, are you?" Talyn asked with casual nonchalance. "You're their leader."

Another slow nod. Then a faint smile. "The Shadowhawk has never fully trusted me, and for good reason. I don't trust him for the same reasons. There was no need for him to know."

"Well, that was certainly an interesting story," Leviana said, pushing away her bowl and sitting back with a contented sigh. "Though I don't pretend to understand much of it."

"I suppose you wouldn't, given you're both Calumnian traders only here visiting." Saniya leaned forward slightly. "I am curious, though, why the Shadowhawk came to me for help. Why does he care so much about a WingGuard captain?"

"The Shadowhawk has an exaggerated sense of how much I've helped the human folk." Talyn shrugged.

Saniya smiled thinly. Talyn tried to wrap her head around the fact that this woman was probably her cousin, a blood relative, yet was very likely planning on killing her.

"You say your group works to avenge your father. What does that mean?" Talyn asked.

"We bring people here that are trying to escape the WingGuard or Patrolmen. Give them a safe place, time to recover if they've been hurt."

Instinct drummed at Talyn, nagging to get loose. "Not just humans from Dock City, is it?" she murmured, the pieces neatly falling together in her head. "You help slaves in Montagn too. You're the network that got Halun out."

Saniya nodded again. Talyn's blood thrilled.

There was the link to Montagn. Shit. She was sitting in a Vengeance camp.

Anticipation flared in her stomach.

"Certifiably insane." Sari sighed.

"As much as we appreciate your invitation, I'm afraid Levs and I are rather set on returning home." Cynia pushed aside her empty bowl. "Of course, we'll recompense you for getting us safely out of this pretty but rather dangerous country."

"And you?" Saniya's eyes moved to Talyn's.

Talyn gave a rueful smile. "I'm with my friends. I've overstayed my welcome in Mithranar, and it's probably time to go home. I do appreciate your help, though."

"Understood. Your departure will take some time to organise." Saniya rose to her feet. "A week at least, maybe more. You'll have to stay here in the meantime, and I'd prefer if you stayed inside your hut. The forest is dangerous, and I can't have you wandering around putting yourselves or any of my people in danger."

"That's the last thing we'd want," Cynia assured her.

"Good night, then."

Talyn looked at her two friends. And smiled.

CHAPTER 19

"*W*hy haven't they killed us yet?" Leviana muttered as they walked back through the darkness to their hut.

"Maybe we're being paranoid," Cynia suggested.

Leviana halted, giving her partner a look that suggested maybe Cynia had been smoking something. "That whole conversation back there didn't convince you we're sitting in the middle of Vengeance's headquarters?"

"It's more complicated than we thought, though." Talyn frowned. "The Shadowhawk has been working with Saniya for years—and her group have clearly been active since before Runye died—yet the murders, the assassination attempt, it all only started a year ago. Before that, they were helping slaves escape Montagn and presumably giving them a home here."

"Right. Judging by what Saniya said, they're all about getting revenge for injustices done to humans in Mithranar," Cynia said in a low voice. "That doesn't really fit with wanting to help prepare the way for a Montagni invasion."

Talyn agreed. Something wasn't clicking. "The Vengeance member I tortured said someone has been pulling Vengeance's strings. If we ignore his claim it was Mithanis, then presumably the string-puller is

Montagn... manipulating Saniya and her people into unwittingly acting on their behalf."

"Sure, but why Saniya's group? How did the Montagni know that Vengeance was the right gang to choose?" Leviana asked.

"The more immediate question is what Levs just raised—why haven't they killed us yet?" Talyn said. "Why hold us in a hut for three days then tell us all that?"

"Saniya seems like the patient, calculating type. She might be trying to work out exactly how much you know, how much the Shadowhawk knows, before she kills you."

"And where are the guards, the people watching us?" Cynia looked at the empty darkness around them.

"It's not like we can go anywhere," Talyn pointed out. "And I'll bet you a hundred gold pieces the entrance to the tunnel under the wall is bristling with guards. She's playing a game with us... almost as if she knows we know about her."

"That's not creepy at all," Leviana scowled. "What *are* we going to do? We've found Vengeance. Now what?"

"Now we figure out a way to destroy them." Before they could help Montagn take Mithranar.

"Three of us? Against a camp full of fighters?" Cynia asked pragmatically.

Leviana gave her a scathing look. Cynia rolled her eyes. "Fine. Say we take out this entire camp on our own. You haven't solved the problem until you find whoever their Montagni contact is. Otherwise they'll presumably just find some other nasty but capable Dock City gang to manipulate into doing their dirty work for them."

"Tal, your plan before, about convincing Mithanis that you're on his side," Sari said. *"I have an idea."*

Talyn stopped suddenly. The path they were on wound through the trees to their hut—the light they'd left burning inside was just visible in the distance. Around them was darkness, the area deserted as rain began falling lightly again. "Let's play Saniya's little game. I think it's time to explore the area."

Both Callanan followed without complaint as Talyn ducked off the path and began moving through the night. All three shifted into soundless pacing, each step careful and considered, sticking to the darkest patches of shadow and ignoring the rain beginning to soak through their clothing.

"You've got one of those crazy ideas of yours, haven't you?" Cynia murmured at her shoulder.

"I have a bad feeling about this," Leviana muttered.

"Let's test how far they'll let us get." Flashing them both a little smile, Talyn kept moving through the spaces between huts, heading to the outer perimeter of the compound, away from the lit areas. Eventually she reached a cluster of small huts in the northwest corner, no more than rough wooden walls and thatched rooves, all cast into deep shadow by the wall looming above.

Rain pattered on the leaves, hiding any sound they made as they approached the closest hut. Talyn stepped up to the windows while Leviana and Cynia went for the door. She squinted, trying to see through the narrow slits in the shutters, but it was too dark.

By then Leviana had the locked door unpicked and open. Talyn shouldered the Callanan aside and went in first. Once her eyes had adjusted to the darkness, she could make out several hessian sacks covering a small pile. A quick tug on the nearest sack revealed what was underneath.

Leviana gave a long, low whistle. "Six thrices, it *is* Vengeance."

"It's their masks, at least," Cynia said, always the pragmatic one.

"This is what she meant by 'fighting back any way we know how.'" Talyn tossed the sack back over the pile of copper masks. "Levs, you were right. We've been wondering where they got all their fighters from—enough for a thirty-strong assault on the queen? Enough to come after the Shadowhawk and me in the Darmour mines? Escaped Montagni slaves and ill-treated Dock City humans with motivation for revenge would be the perfect pool of recruits."

"But how did Montagn know all that in order to target Saniya's group?" Sari whispered.

Cynia turned to the door. "We need to see what else is here."

The three of them separated, spreading out to search the other huts. Talyn ran to the one on the far right, working at the lock with a hairpin for several seconds before breaking through. It was completely empty, nothing but patches of mould growing on the walls.

The next hut appeared just as empty at first, but then her sweeping gaze caught movement in the shadows in the far corner. Frowning, she edged closer. Another muffled sound.

Human. And gagged.

Sliding her right hand around the hilt of one of her daggers, she moved cautiously closer. The movement stilled, and then suddenly the shadows dispersed, revealing a hooded man lying on the floor. Days of growth stubbled his usually clean jaw, but she recognised him instantly nonetheless.

"Savin!" Astonishment filled her voice.

"Captain Dynan. You were not the person I expected to see coming through that door," he muttered as she knelt beside him. His ankles were shackled, the iron linked by thick chain bolted into the floor. "Can you get me out?"

"I can try." She knelt by the plate of iron attaching the shackles to the floor. Whoever had done it had reinforced the plate so that Savin couldn't just rip up the damp and rotting floor and free himself that way. Taking a deep breath, she sheathed her dagger, then hovered both palms over the metal plate. Her magic surged, and sapphire light flared with a hiss. Grunting with the effort, she fought to keep it contained to the small area around where the shackles were attached to the plate.

Despite that, blue light still flickered in the dark, and anxiety trickled through her. Anyone passing might spot the strange light and come to investigate. A sharp burning smell filled the room and slowly the metal began to melt. Her energy drained rapidly and she gritted her teeth, holding onto it until Savin gave a sharp tug and the chains around his ankle ripped free of the bolt holding them to the floor. She sank back, covered in sweat and gasping for air.

"How did you end up here?" she panted.

"Long story." He stood and stretched. "Suffice to say my snooping got me into trouble. You?"

"Essentially the same thing. Can you get out of here using the shadows to hide yourself—you'll have to use the tunnel?" she asked. "I won't be far behind."

He nodded. A moment later, all the shadows in the corners of the hut began coalescing around Savin. Within a few breaths he'd completely vanished from sight. Her mouth almost fell open—she'd never seen Shadow magic used so skilfully before.

And even though she tried, she didn't even see him leaving.

Outside, a short search found Cynia and Leviana breaking into the hut closest to the wall. Talyn followed them in. One wall was stacked high with sacks—grain, from a quick glance. No doubt from one of the Shadowhawk's hauls. In the opposite corner, sitting above the damp in a dry crate, was a small box—carved from Mair-land wood. The interior was lined with small ceramic casks of izerdia.

"Flea-bitten shit, Sari, they've got izerdia."

Leviana appeared at her shoulder, saw the same thing, and swore.

"Get it out of there," Sari counselled.

Cynia sighed as she too saw the box and recognised the contents. "So they are planning to kill us."

Talyn picked up the box, tucked it under her arm. "We need to go. Now."

"Slight hitch in that plan," Leviana said from the window. "They're waiting for us outside."

"I wondered how long it would take them." Talyn said, unsurprised.

Sari gave an impressive mental eye roll. *"You drew them out deliberately."*

"It was time to end this."

There was only one door to the hut, so no point trying to escape any other way. Talyn shared a glance with her two friends then walked out into the falling rain. She didn't have to look back to know the Callanan hovered at either shoulder. She hoped Savin had gotten clear of the huts. At least the distraction they were about to cause should help him get cleanly away.

She stopped several paces from where Saniya stood holding a torch hissing in the drizzle, then carefully placed the box of izerdia at her feet. At a gesture from Saniya, seven armed members of her community moved out of the darkness behind her. All wore copper masks.

"I was hoping you'd give me time to come up with a foolproof way of getting rid of you without the Shadowhawk realising you were dead. Now that we know he's still alive, I'd rather him not have any warning that we're coming for him," she said, not sounding at all disappointed.

"I'm not sure how you think any of this is following in your father's footsteps," Talyn replied. "Murdering innocent humans? Killing noble winged folk? Trying to kill a queen? You could have just stuck with helping the new Shadowhawk. Helping the Montagni slaves."

"That was getting us nowhere! The Shadowhawk is getting us nowhere. We need bigger change than that—we need to remove the winged folk rulers and their selfish, intolerant attitudes." The words were passionate, but she spoke so calmly. This woman was the most controlled person Talyn had ever met.

"*I'm thoroughly unsurprised you're cousins,*" Sari said.

"And you thought killing the queen would accomplish that?" Talyn lifted an eyebrow, taking a step forward. "Or what, making the human population so afraid from all the murders that they'd rise up against their rulers? Killing the Shadowhawk doesn't help that. Killing me and my Wolves doesn't help that."

"He betrayed us to you, a WingGuard captain, in a way that resulted in the death of my people," Saniya spat. "You and your Wolves slaughtered them."

"I hate to argue, but your people died because they tried to kill the man I was responsible for keeping safe." Talyn kept her voice cool, calm, with a hint of cockiness. This was her, this was how she'd always been. Never let them see you rattled, never allow them to shake you. Of course, she'd always had Sari at her side—Sari with her unshakable confidence in Talyn and reckless glee in the fight. But she was learning that this was still her, even without Sari.

And Sari wasn't gone.

"The prince of song is one of them." Cold anger filled Saniya's voice. "His mother murdered my father and his entire family. Cuinn and *his* family look down on us and treat us as inferior because we don't have wings. They don't care that their people are starving."

"You have no idea what you're talking about," Talyn said, voice as controlled as Saniya's. "You know what I think? I think someone is helping you, getting in your ear, whispering to you. Someone convinced you that violence was the answer. Who?"

Saniya froze. Only for the briefest of seconds. But enough to tell Talyn she'd hit a nerve. "We don't need help," she spat.

"So who gave you the niever-flyers and the Shadow?" Talyn took another step, pushing at that minor fracture in Saniya's calm.

"We did that on our own."

"A lie. But I can tell that logic and reason don't figure highly with you." Talyn glanced around. "We're going to leave now."

Saniya smiled tightly. "I think we've made it pretty clear you're not leaving this place alive."

"Yeah, we figured that out when you spilled all your secrets at dinner," Leviana piped up.

"Big mistake," Cynia added.

Talyn smiled slightly. "You saw what I did to your people on Sparrow Island. What I did to them in the mines under Darmour. You really think you can contain *three* Callanan?" Her smile widened as shock rippled briefly over the woman's face. "Oh wait, you really thought they were just merchants? You do like making mistakes, don't you, Saniya?"

She wasn't scared. Neither were the Callanan partners at her back. Exhilaration flooded her, the heady anticipation of a fight.

"I suppose we'll see."

Saniya must have made some sort of signal to her people because the hissing of arrows through the air was the first warning of attack.

Talyn stood where she was, lifted a hand, and summoned her Callanan magic.

Bright sapphire light leapt into the space between her and Saniya, crackling with energy and power. The arrows hit the shield and fried. The sharp scent of burned wood filled the clearing.

Talyn's eyes never left Saniya. When the colour of Talyn's Callanan shield—her *winged folk* magic—registered with the Vengeance leader, she paled, dark skin drawing tight over her cheekbones.

Meanwhile Cynia and Leviana were a blur of movement—leaping to Talyn's left and right to engage the fighters on the edge of the group behind Saniya. In seconds they'd disarmed and killed their first opponents.

Leviana shouted Cynia's name, then tossed her a bow and quiver of arrows. Talyn dropped her shield and threw herself at Saniya as Cynia began firing at the remaining Vengeance fighters.

Her cousin was a gritty, fierce fighter, handling her sword with consummate skill. Talyn parried her first two swipes, lunged for the woman's head, then stepped aside as Saniya countered with a quick thrust. When Saniya came at her again, Talyn sheathed one of her daggers, then ducked under the flashing sword and gripped the woman's wrist.

Twisting sharply, she forced Saniya to drop the sword, then threw her shoulder into the woman's chest. By the time Saniya had staggered back a few paces, hand scrambling to draw the knife in her belt, Talyn was launching herself forward.

They collided into the mud, Talyn's free hand pinning Saniya's knife arm to the ground, her left placing a dagger at her throat. "My father was Trystaan Ciantar. That makes us cousins, Saniya, so I'm not going to kill you this time," she said. "But you come after the Shadowhawk or my Wolves again, I'll spit you where you stand."

Not waiting for a response, she slammed the hilt of the dagger into Saniya's temple, ensured she was out cold, then rose to join the rest of the fight.

It was already done. Cynia and Leviana stood over multiple fallen bodies, weapons in hand, having barely broken a sweat.

"More will be coming." Talyn swooped to pick up a fallen quiver of fresh arrows and tossed it at Cynia. Then she went back to pick up the box of izerdia. "Cynia, cover our retreat. Let's go."

THEY GOT HALFWAY to the tunnel entrance before hitting another wave of armed fighters erupting from the surrounding trees. Either Saniya had already regained consciousness or some kind of silent alarm had passed through the community.

Shouts echoed through the night, and the number of flickering torches moving through the darkness had almost doubled. Rain continued to pour down, making the ground muddy and treacherous.

With Talyn in the lead, the three Callanan fought their way towards the tunnel entrance, doing their best not to stop and get caught up in the fighting. They had to assume there were hundreds of people in this compound—too many to fight if they allowed them time to gather themselves and form a proper attack.

Cynia and Leviana fought like two halves of a whole, back to back or side by side. Talyn, hampered by the box of izerdia, fought one-handed, ducking and weaving and taking any opening that presented itself to attack and kill.

Her breath came quickly, both sweat and rain slicking her skin, as they fought through to the hut sheltering the tunnel entrance. Leviana and Cynia slammed the door shut, dropped the bar into place, then took up positions guarding against anyone coming through while Talyn tugged the rug aside and opened up the trapdoor. Something heavy slammed into the door, rattling it on its hinges. Shouts reverberated outside.

"That bar isn't going to hold much longer," Leviana said.

Another thud against the door. One of the hinges ripped out. Glass shattered and a flaming arrow flew through the gap. It buried itself in the floor and the wood quickly caught alight. Smoke filled the small space.

Grabbing a burning torch from the wall, Talyn dropped it down into the inky blackness—the area at the base of the ladder looked empty. Wood splintered as the door caved halfway inwards. Flames licked up the eastern wall and the smoke was growing thicker.

"Let's go," she said, trying not to cough.

Leviana came last, closing the trapdoor behind them. They'd barely reached the bottom when it was opened again at the top, the sound of angry voices coming clearly down the shaft.

"Time to run," Cynia said, taking the lead.

They sprinted—again, tacitly agreeing it was better to keep ahead of their pursuers rather than be caught and held up fighting. Once they were back under the wall and up in Dock City, it would be easier to make a clean getaway.

There were two guards at the opposite end of the tunnel, but Cynia lifted her bow and fired two quick shots. Both guards were dead before they even realised what was happening. Cynia slung the bow over her back, leapt agilely over the fallen bodies and began scrambling up the ladder.

They emerged into the darkness of the Poor Quarter, the massive wall looming over the rooftops nearby.

"Where now?" Leviana asked, glancing at Talyn.

They couldn't go up to the citadel, and it was after midnight, so showing up at an inn was too risky. Too many questions, too high a chance someone would recognise her and consider passing that information on to the Patrol or Falcons for coin. They needed somewhere safe and hidden to go while they planned what to do next.

The answer came quickly.

"Follow me," she said.

Talyn led them through the tangle of grimy alleys and dark streets that made up the Poor Quarter until she was confident they were clear of any pursuers, then took them to the empty apartment that the Shadowhawk used.

They hovered in the darkness across the street until the area was empty before dashing over and slipping inside. The interior stairwell was dark and quiet, most inhabitants likely asleep. She'd picked this apartment's lock before, so it didn't take her long now. Talyn waved her friends inside and closed the door behind them.

"Nice place." Leviana made a face as she looked around, then touched her soaked clothing. "I don't suppose we're going to find a dry change of clothes in here?"

"At least we're out of the rain." Talyn went to ensure the sheet hanging over the window fully covered the glass, then placed the izerdia gently on the room's table. "And nobody but the Shadowhawk and I know about this place, so we're safe for the moment."

Cynia raised her eyebrows. "Only you and the Shadowhawk?"

"You're not like, sleeping with him or something, are you?" Leviana spluttered.

Talyn stared at them both. "What? No, of course I'm not sleeping with him. That's ridiculous." Completely ridiculous, no matter what her traitorous thoughts had recently been contemplating. It was much harder to maintain indifference to Cuinn's allure once she actually started *liking* the man. More than liking. Respecting. Admiring. And she was going to stop herself right there. She scowled when Sari started laughing in her head.

"He's kinda boring looking, Tal." Leviana made a face.

"And a criminal," Cynia said pointedly.

"I'm not sleeping with him!" she snapped, annoyed rather than amused by their teasing.

"Oh, but you want to."

"You shut up!"

Cynia and Leviana shared a look but said nothing further. Instead Cynia, practical as always, changed the subject. "What's next?"

Adrenalin swept through her—from the fight, and in anticipation of what came next. It was late, they'd been up for hours and fighting, but she didn't feel anywhere near tired. In fact, she couldn't sit still.

"You two will get on a ship to Ryathl first thing tomorrow, or as soon as the docks are no longer locked down. Tell the First Blade everything we learned tonight. Confirm who Vengeance is." Talyn hesitated. "Don't tell her I was arrested."

"So you're sticking with the crazy 'stay here and somehow convince Mithanis you're willing to be a spy for him' plan." Leviana sighed. "Cynia, I nominate you to explain that to the First Blade."

"Yeah, that won't be happening," Cynia muttered.

"It's not so crazy anymore." Talyn smiled. "Now I can offer Mithanis the location of Vengeance. This way I win his trust and ensure Vengeance is destroyed all at once. After all, they did go after the queen. Murdered a Queencouncil member, a senior healer, and a WingGuard flight-leader too."

Another shared glance. Talyn wondered if she and Sari had done the same thing, and if it had irritated other people as much as this was irritating her.

"Vengeance will be gone by morning. They're not stupid enough to stick around now that we've escaped," Cynia said.

"Not if I hurry. They won't have time to get everything out." Talyn pointed to the box. "Plus I've got the izerdia to give him, to prove my allegiance."

"If that's true, then once you do all that, your mission here will be complete," Cynia pointed out. "You've answered the First Blade's questions about the Shadowhawk and you've dealt with Vengeance. Why not come home with us?"

"You said it yourself—we still haven't found the Montagni link to Vengeance," Talyn argued. "Until I do that, they could find another gang to do their bidding. I need to stay."

Heavy silence filled the room.

"You know what? I think you *want* to stay," Leviana said. "It's been nagging at me, what the Shadowhawk said about you and your Wolves... how you've helped the humans here so much. You've been working with him, haven't you?"

"Shia tasked me with using him to infiltrate Vengeance." Talyn tried not to shift uncomfortably.

"So you're going to stop helping him now?"

Another silence.

"Talyn, you're a Callanan. You hunt criminals, you don't help them! What is it you're trying to achieve here?"

"I'm not a Callanan anymore. And I'm not a Kingshield either," Talyn snapped. "In fact, I'm half-Mithranan. I can do whatever I like.

And yes, you're right, I *do* want to be here. I don't want to go home. Are you happy now?"

"What about our theory?" Cynia said quietly. "What if someone is trying to get you back to court... what if they try something else?"

Talyn's jaw clenched, anger leaping white-hot in her chest. "That's unfair. There's no proof you're right, and even if you are, I can't live my life in fear of losing more people I love." Not anymore.

"Fine." Leviana lifted her hands in the air in capitulation.

Talyn let out a breath. "Tell the First Blade if she has further instructions for me, I'm happy to keep helping. From here."

Cynia echoed her partner's earlier sigh. "For the record, I still hate this plan."

"We can't lie to her, Tal," Leviana said soberly. "The Mithranan crown knowingly arrested and planned to kill a Dumnorix princess. If she found out we'd hidden that from her..."

"And found out I was still here despite the risks, I would be in a lot of trouble with my family," Talyn finished. "I won't ask you to lie, but if you could avoid telling her, I would appreciate it."

"We'll always have your back, but this whole situation makes me uncomfortable," Cynia said honestly. "I'm not convinced the First Blade and your uncle *shouldn't* know what Mithanis did."

"What if you tell them and my uncle decides retribution is required?" Talyn stepped forward, speaking earnestly. "I thought we were trying to stop a war. Mithanis and the queen are vicious and intolerant rulers, yes, but there are a lot of good people here. Isn't it better if my uncle focusses on the threat Montagn poses?"

The two of them shared a look, and after a moment they nodded slightly. Leviana reached out to squeeze Talyn's shoulder. "Your uncle isn't a fool, and I'm sure he's considered those things too, but we'll do it your way. We have faith in you."

"Thank you," she said, meaning it. "And thanks for helping me these past few days. It was good to have Callanan at my back once again."

"We're going to request the Montagni liaison post," Cynia said. "So we can be closer to you here. The First Blade might give it to us given our recent favour with the Horselord."

Talyn smiled. "Then I'll write to my uncle and ask a favour. And hopefully I'll see you both sooner than planned."

"We'll leave now," Cynia said. "Probably best if you wait a bit before leaving too. We'll wait for a message from you to confirm that your plan has worked and you're safe, then we'll be on the next ship out."

"You write to us at least once a week," Leviana said fiercely. "And don't think for a second we won't raise the alarm with your uncle if you miss a letter."

"I'll write, I promise." Talyn chuckled. "I'll be fine. You'll see."

"I'm glad you're confident."

Talyn grinned. *"Don't pretend like you're not too."*

CHAPTER 20

*H*e lasted three days on Sparrow Island before bringing the Wolves back. During those days he drank, lost himself in music when it was raining—which was most of the time—or soared the thermals with Irial, Annae and his friends when it wasn't.

And he hated every second of it.

Corrin and the other talons spent the time drilling the Wolves into exhaustion. Cuinn would fly past them running up and down the cliff path over and over again, before performing sword and *sabai* drills until they trailed into the mess each night, exhausted and sore.

For appearance's sake, he barely said a word to them the entire time, trusting to Corrin and the distance from the citadel to keep the Wolves in check. Their sullen mood, not entirely eclipsed by weariness, was obvious to both Annae and Irial, but fortunately Irial paid little attention to it.

Even Jasper was more on edge than usual, snarling and snapping at any winged folk that came close to Cuinn—so much so that he had to leave the tawncat locked up in his room most of the time.

And every minute of every day, controlled panic burned in his chest. There was no way to hear news out on Sparrow Island. If

Mithanis had caught Talyn he would have sent a message, but there was no way to know what was happening with Vengeance.

On the third afternoon he snapped, told Irial he was bored out of his mind by the constant rain, and informed the Wolves they were leaving.

"Thank the skies for that," Irial muttered. "I don't know how you ever thought it was going to be fun out here in the rain."

"Then why did you come?" Cuinn snapped, in no mood for questioning.

"Annae said it would be impolite to refuse."

"Your wife is a far nicer person than you are."

Irial grinned, his sour mood apparently forgotten. "On that we can both agree, my friend."

CUINN and his winged Wolves arrived at the citadel at dusk, the human Wolves much later than that. Mithanis wasn't waiting for him, and no message came from either Azrilan or his mother.

Talyn hadn't been caught, then.

He wrote a dutiful message to Mithanis to tell him he was back and would see him in the morning, and then went to bed.

Sleep was impossible—particularly with Jasper prowling the room and refusing to settle—and he eventually gave up at dawn, kicking off the blankets and sitting up. "Don't you need to sleep too?" He glared at the tawncat.

Jasper simply stared at him, green eyes unblinking.

"Are you seriously upset at me because I won't let you eat everyone standing between you and Talyn?" Cuinn scowled.

Jasper growled low in his throat, then snorted, as if Cuinn was the stupidest creature he'd ever encountered. After a moment he paced towards the bed and bumped his head against Cuinn's right leg, which hadn't stopped moving since he sat up.

"Oh. You're worried because I'm worried." A smile spread uncontrollably across Cuinn's face and he slid down to the floor so Jasper could lean against him. "Thanks, buddy."

The tawncat tossed his head then shifted away and prowled for the door. Cuinn grinned and followed.

TIERCELIN, in command of his guard detail, was closely supervising a servant delivering Cuinn's breakfast, his watchful demeanour suggesting the talon was worried the human man was intent on poisoning it.

"How are the Wolves?" Cuinn asked once the servant had left.

"Anxious, worried, afraid," Tiercelin said. "But the trip was a good idea. Enough time has passed that their panic has faded a little."

"The talons too?"

Tiercelin looked away. "I'm sorry about—"

"You should be," he said mildly. "You of all people are smart enough to understand the consequences of acting in support of her."

"I know, but I don't see how we avoid that no matter what we do. Even if Vengeance haven't harmed her in some way, she's still in danger from Mithanis."

Cuinn wasn't any less anxious, especially after a night of little sleep. He didn't know if he would see her again. He'd gotten her into Vengeance, but had no idea what she would do from there. It wasn't like she could come back to the Wolves while Mithanis was hunting for her. "We wait for her move, that's all we can do."

Tiercelin nodded, and his face cleared. "If anyone can see a way out of this, it will be her."

They both turned as the front door swung open, admitting a tense Zamaril, his gaze darting all over the place.

Fear gripped Cuinn's chest. "What is it?"

"Captain Dynan is back. She handed herself in to the Falcons at the palace bridge and demanded to see Prince Mithanis and the queen." Zamaril steadied himself. "She said you need to be there."

"She *what*? When did you talk to her?" Cuinn demanded.

He lowered his voice. "I didn't. She sent me a message through Petro."

"What else did she say?" Tiercelin asked.

"Just that Prince Cuinn should follow her lead. She said he has to trust her."

Cuinn didn't linger any longer. Tiercelin and Zamaril followed him out onto the bridge, Tiercelin's detail gathering at a sharp call from their talon.

"You stay back unless I order different," he warned them.

Tiercelin nodded. "But we'll be there if you need us, Your Highness."

Cuinn let out a breath, forcing his shoulders to relax. Excitement curled in his belly, making that hard. Talyn was back and she had a plan. "Good. Then let's go follow Captain Dynan's lead."

NONE of the Wolves were allowed into the room—it would have caused a straight up fight with the Falcons on the door to insist—but that didn't bother Cuinn overly much. Zamaril would have his ways of keeping an eye on what happened inside, and it was like Tiercelin had said.

If he needed his Wolves, they would be there.

His gaze went straight to Talyn, standing in the middle of the room, wrists tied behind her back, Ravinire hovering nearby. Her clothes were muddied and torn, wisps of hair escaping her braid in all directions, and there were patches of dried blood down her right arm from a wound that looked like it might still be bleeding. A wooden box sat at her feet.

His heartbeat kicked up a notch.

It took all he had to look away from her—she was fine—and switch his attention to Mithanis. "You found her. Well done."

"Actually, I came back of my own accord." Talyn spoke clearly, confidently. "I have some things to say that might change your mind about executing me, Your Grace."

This was directed at the queen, who sat in a chair, watching the proceedings with expressionless features. Mithanis stood in the corner, arms folded across his chest. Cuinn tentatively used a touch of magic to read the room. His mother was annoyed and afraid, making him frown—what was it that scared her so much about Talyn? Mithanis was surprised at Talyn's bold move, intrigued enough by it to listen to her, confident in the knowledge he could kill her anytime he wanted. Ravinire was a jumble of conflicting emotions that would need a much greater use of magic to untangle.

Talyn was confident. Almost aglow with it.

Of course she was. He fought the smile that wanted to spread over his face.

"Go on then, spit it out," Mithanis said, waving a hand at her.

Cuinn heaved a sigh, leaning against the wall in a pose of affected boredom. "And make it quick. I've an alleya game to be at."

"If you're convinced that my father was the son of the previous Ciantar, then I'm not going to argue with you," she said. "But my father never spoke about his past here in Mithranar, and I didn't even know he was one of the winged folk until very recently. It seems that before he fled here, he cut off his wings."

They all flinched, even Mithanis. The idea of cutting out one's own wings was abhorrent, utterly unthinkable. As bad, if not worse, than cutting out an eye, or chopping off a limb.

In that brief moment of distraction, Talyn glanced at Cuinn. And in that look was, *I'm going to need your help here.*

She was glancing away before anyone in the room but him noticed, continuing on with, "You also tell me that my uncle knew who I was before he sent me here. That he deliberately placed me in danger without telling me what I was facing. I've had a few days to reflect on that, and well, it makes me pretty damn angry. I'm not Callanan or Kingshield anymore, Your Grace, Prince Mithanis. I'm Mithranan. And I'm WingGuard."

Another quick glance at him, then a slight shift of her eyes towards Mithanis.

Whose face was already scowling in suspicion.

All at once he knew what she needed from him. Cuinn glanced discreetly around—all of the room's occupants were focused on Talyn, not him. Ensuring his posture remained lazy and bored, he took a deep breath and drew on his magic.

He'd done this before a thousand times, to make sure his brothers thought he was a fool, to confirm everyone's low expectations of him before they could notice anything different, to hide that he was the Shadowhawk. But now, for the second time in a handful of days, he used it to manipulate and mould instead, to change *their* emotion. This wasn't passive use of his magic, it was direct and deliberate and risky.

"What are you saying?" Mithanis snapped.

"I'm not loyal to the Twin Thrones, and I'm not here to spy on you for them," Talyn said firmly.

Cuinn surrounded Mithanis with his magic, ever so subtly erasing his doubt, soothing the edges of his suspicion. Such fine work, to move so softly that another song mage wouldn't know what was happening. It was the hardest thing he'd ever done.

"You expect us to believe you because you say it?" his mother asked.

"No. I came back with a way to prove my loyalty. A gift of sorts." Talyn shrugged. "And no doubt your magic can sense my sincerity."

Already Mithanis' shoulders were relaxing, his crossed arms dropping to his sides. Sweat beaded on Cuinn's forehead, and he worked even harder to hide the effect this was having on him. A hint of glamour to smooth his features and maintain the bored look.

"What sort of gift?" Mithanis asked.

"The location of Vengeance, the criminals who murdered Counsellor Goldfeather, Flight-Leader Iceflight, and Healer Flightbreeze, and tried to kill Prince Cuinn. Their leader is named Saniya, and they've been living beyond the wall all this time. In the forest."

Cuinn froze, his hold on Mithanis slipping momentarily in shock. Beyond the wall? He'd had no idea.

She said to follow her lead. And trust her. Zamaril's message floated back to him. He squeezed his eyes shut, taking a deep breath before opening them again.

Trust her.

He refocused his magic, surrounded Mithanis and his mother. He checked that Ravinire wasn't overly suspicious either.

"Nobody lives in the forest," Mithanis said scathingly.

"I was there. I've seen their community." Talyn pointed to her bloodied arm. "I got this escaping to bring the information here. For you. Not for my uncle or the Callanan. I stole their izerdia too, so it couldn't be used against you."

Everyone's gaze dropped to the box at Talyn's feet. Cuinn worked harder, sucking away Mithanis' suspicion, and then his mother's, before turning suspicion into the beginnings of trust. Then he added more magic, bolstering their interest in wanting to believe Talyn. She glanced at him again, and there was a light in her eyes he'd never seen before.

She lived for this.

"You tell a wild tale of people living in the forest being behind the murders of our people and expect us to believe you." Mithanis scoffed, but Cuinn's magic told him he wasn't as sceptical as he sounded.

"I infiltrated their compound and allowed them to catch me. Saniya, their leader, told me to my face that they were behind the murders." Talyn was succinct, clear. "They hate you with a passion and she took great joy in bragging to me."

Cuinn worked harder, feeding Mithanis's desire to believe Talyn—he and their mother had been so worried about not finding those responsible for the murders. This was the answer they needed. He pushed at that while simultaneously smoothing away their suspicion and wariness.

A silence lingered, but eventually Mithanis glanced at Sarana. She nodded.

"You'll give us the location." Mithanis's voice dropped to a purr as he stepped closer to her. "And when I take a flight of Falcons there, we'll find a base of criminals."

"I'll tell you right now," she said without flinching. "And in return you let me go and allow me to return to my position as captain in the WingGuard. I suggest you decide on my offer quickly. They know I escaped, and I'm sure they're in the midst of fleeing right now."

Mithanis glanced over at the queen again, then back at Talyn, clearly considering. Cuinn didn't trust him, not for a second, but he did trust how badly his brother wanted Vengeance.

"I'll agree to your bargain, Captain Dynan, on one more condition."

"Name it," she said.

"You allow one of our healers to cut out your wing buds."

Cuinn wasn't sure who the horrified gasp had come from, but he thought it might have been Ravinire. Nausea flooded him so powerfully it was an effort to regain control of his magic, keeping it pressing in on his brother and mother.

Believe her. Believe her. Believe her.

"They'll do it cleanly and painlessly," Mithanis assured her. "But no matter where your loyalties lie, you're a threat to us as long as you're winged folk. I can't have that. You allow us to remove your wing buds and you never use the name Ciantar again. You will always be Talyn Dynan, and you will never rise above the rank of captain."

"Deal," she said without hesitation.

The two of them locked eyes, a little smile on both their faces. Cold for Mithanis, triumphant for Talyn.

"Captain, no!" Cuinn couldn't help himself. He stepped forward, wings rustling with agitation. "You don't know what he's asking of you. You cannot agree to this."

"She can make her own decisions, Brother." Mithanis rounded on him, snarling.

"I can," Talyn said. "It's all right, Prince Cuinn. I have no interest in growing wings."

But you'll be more powerful with them, he wanted to say. You'll be a rallying cry for the humans and the winged folk will follow you. As a human they never will.

Mithanis offered his hand. "Then we're agreed."

Talyn shook without hesitation.

Cuinn sagged against the wall, exhausted from his magic use. It had worked. But any victory was tarnished by the deal Talyn had made.

"Tell us the location," his mother said crisply, rising to her feet.

"Ravinire, you'll take care of the criminals. Captain Dynan will remain here until we can be assured she's telling the truth."

Cuinn swallowed, then yawned. "I'm not expected to sit here and wait, am I?"

Mithanis barked a laugh of contempt. "No, go off to your fun. We'll let you know what the final outcome of all this is."

Cuinn didn't know how he did it, but he managed to force himself to walk out of that room and leave Talyn behind.

Trust me, she'd said.

So he would.

CHAPTER 21

*V*engeance was even more efficient than she'd given them credit for. They were gone by the time Mithanis and Ravinire landed at the compound with a full wing of Falcons, but there was enough evidence left behind, including the pile of copper masks and what had to be a significant portion of their weapons stockpile—not to mention proof that a large number of people had been living there—that convinced them Talyn had been telling the truth.

She was released at nightfall, Mithanis warning her she had a week to go to the healers and get her wing buds cut out, or he'd have her re-arrested. That was fine. Wings weren't something she wanted—after years of training her body to be a finely turned weapon, the last thing she wanted to do was mess that up by adding a pair of heavy and awkward wings. And even if she had, they were worth giving up in order to be able to remain in Mithranar.

Cuinn was keeping up appearances at an alleya game, so it was easy enough to leave a note in his room, then go back to her quarters at the barracks.

The Wolves training out in the yard called relieved greetings to her when she entered through the gate.

They looked tired, their mood low, so she lingered a while, reassuring them everything was fine, before going to speak with her talons privately and explain everything in more detail. Theac, fortunately, was still away in Mair-land with his new wife, so wouldn't know anything of this until he returned.

"Thank you," she told them. "For doing what Prince Cuinn ordered."

For a moment they all stared at each other. None of them looked happy, and for the first time ever she sensed a hint of discord between them. Concern stirred in her chest. "What is it?"

"He took us to Sparrow Island, Captain," Corrin eventually said, almost defiantly. "To ensure we stayed quiet."

"I see." She glanced between them, reading their expressions. So they hadn't been confident in keeping the Wolves contained. Or, more specifically, from the dark glances thrown his way, Corrin hadn't. And he'd gone to Cuinn.

"It was the right thing to do," she said firmly.

Another thick silence. They didn't agree.

"There's something else you should know, about who my father is," she began.

"We already do," Zamaril snapped, shooting a dark glance at Tiercelin this time. "Tiercelin told us."

She stared at the healer. "You knew?"

"I guessed," he said uncomfortably. "And since there was no way to know for certain, I thought it safer to simply stay quiet."

"Can you explain why you thought that was necessary?" She lifted her eyebrows. "Why did Mithanis want to murder me the second he found out? Was it just because the old Shadowhawk was my father's half-brother?"

They all goggled at her, even Tiercelin. "You didn't know?" she asked in surprise.

"When the queen executed the Ciantar family, she gave no reason for it apart from saying they'd committed treason. Nobody knows what they did." Shock rippled over Tiercelin's face. "You're saying the Ciantar family was linked to the Shadowhawk?"

Talyn nodded, relaying what Saniya had told her. "What can you tell me about my father's family?"

Tiercelin glanced at the others—they'd fallen utterly silent, the same shock on their faces—then turned back to her. "They were once the right hand of the Acondors. They always had sapphire wings and eyes, and always had warrior magic. The Ciantar commanded our army."

"You're not just Twin Thrones royalty, Captain," Corrin said eagerly. "You're Mithranan royalty too."

Sari's laughter pealed in her head as Talyn scowled. "That explains why Mithanis was so keen to have me killed."

"It's why he forced you to agree to have your wing buds removed," Halun said softly. "Without wings, you can never be a threat to his power."

Talyn sat back in her chair, lifting one hand to rub at her forehead. Some of the weariness she'd been holding back began seeping through. "I didn't realise how dangerous it was, coming here. My father tried to warn me, but I didn't believe him."

"It's all worked out for the best," Halun grumbled. "But we don't like that you made us stand down, Captain."

"You've trained us to be warriors yet you refuse to let us fight," Zamaril added.

"Your fear is holding us back," Andres said quietly.

"I was afraid for you, yes. But you know as well as I do that if you had acted in support of me, Mithanis would have killed you all." She met each of their eyes in turn until they acknowledged this too. "Don't forget you are leaders now. Would you truly have those under your command killed because you made a choice to help me?"

More exchanged looks, then a resigned sigh from Tiercelin. "No."

"You're not *my* army," she added softly. "I am your captain, but I, like you, am part of the Mithranan WingGuard."

"*Actually no, you could be head of the WingGuard, if you didn't have your wing buds cut out,*" Sari said.

"*Are we back to starting a coup in Mithranar? Because I thought I made it clear that was never going to happen.*"

227

"No matter how sensible and logical your words, Captain, we're heading for a choice." Zamaril rose to his feet. "You know it and we know it. One day we Wolves will have to decide where to fight, and when that happens, our choice will be you."

"Your choice should be Cuinn," she said softly.

Halun shook his head. "You still don't understand, Captain."

They left then, filing out one by one, each in a sombre mood. She didn't like leaving things unsettled with them, but that was part of being a leader. Giving orders that they didn't like and ensuring they followed them.

"Maybe it would be easier for everyone here if I did leave. Go home," she said, troubled.

"That's not what you want, though, is it?"

"No, it's not."

SHE'D INITIALLY PLANNED on getting a full-turn or two of sleep before heading out, but found herself too wired.

Her crazy plan had worked.

Cuinn had known what she'd needed and he'd stepped in exactly when she needed him to. And without Mithanis noticing. His magical skill was a marvel indeed.

So she washed and changed, then headed out of the palace, through the citadel and down into Dock City. Assuming Mithanis would be keeping an eye on her, she made sure she left her quarters discreetly, leaving lamps lit to make it appear as if she were still inside.

She'd only just come through the window of the Shadowhawk's apartment, gaze scanning the place to make sure it was safe, when the door jiggled and he entered. Once the door was closed and locked, he dropped the glamour, revealing Prince Cuinn.

She grinned at him.

He stared at her incredulously, as if astonished she was *grinning*, then a slow smile began to spread across his face as well. It blinded her for a moment.

"We did it." Triumph and relief filled her voice.

"We fooled Mithanis." He said it like he couldn't believe it, voice full of wonder. "And we got Vengeance."

"We did. And now I'm back as your captain and I don't have to escape to Calumnia." She stepped closer to him. "You trusted me. Right from the beginning."

His smile spread wider. "I never imagined you could turn getting inside Vengeance into such a victory, though. Have Mithanis destroy them for us and win his fledging trust at the same time."

"I couldn't have done it without your magic in that room."

Sadness flickered over his face. "Saniya... her people... they really are Vengeance, huh?"

It must seem like such a betrayal to him, and her voice softened despite herself. "She admitted it—she hates your family, and she has reason to. That's probably a story for another time."

"And she really told you they committed the murders?"

"Not in so many words." Talyn shook her head. "But who else could it have been?"

He took a breath. "Sending you to her... I knew it would be what you wanted. But I was terrified for you. Part of me just wanted to get you out of Mithranar as soon as possible, get you home safe. And the Wolves... the whole time, all that emotion beating at me. They were about to lose it, Talyn, and I had to—"

"You made all the right decisions." She took another step towards him. "You got me out and away from Mithanis. You made sure I had two Callanan with me. And if you hadn't sent me to her, I wouldn't have had anything to bring back to Mithanis to bargain with."

He took a shuddering breath, then raised his green eyes to hers, one hand lifting to gently touch her cheek. The touch burned through her, her reaction to it so strong she almost didn't hear his words. "You should have left, gone home where you are safe, where you belong."

"No." She shook her head. If anything had finally become clear to her these past months, it was this. "I belong here, with you and the Wolves. Your fight has become mine. It's time I admitted that."

His eyes turned dark, and she read his intention to kiss her, but couldn't find it within herself to stop him. She was still wired, recklessness and excitement weaving through her in equal measure, burying the nagging voice that this wasn't the smartest idea. As he leaned towards her, she moved up to meet him, wrapping an arm around his neck as their lips met. There was no hesitation or awkwardness, and no gentleness either.

Cuinn's emotions flooded her as his magic flared and she felt everything he felt: the guilt and shame that was always there, his relief she was alive and safe, and overpowering all of that, his reaction to the intensity of the kiss and his overwhelming desire not just for her body, but for her.

She buried her hands in his hair as his arms pulled her tightly against him. They were moving, stumbling, and then her back hit the rough wood of the wall. His mouth was hungry on hers, tongues tangling as if neither could get enough. She tried to slide her arm around his back to pull him closer, her hand hitting soft feathers instead. He chuckled at her groan of frustration and pushed closer. Every inch of him was pressed against her, and it felt good. Really, really good.

Her heart was racing by the time they pulled apart, gasping, skin flushed. She could barely think, so strong was his magic and the emotion surging through her.

Cuinn gave a half-disbelieving, half-wondering laugh. "You kissed me back. I was waiting for a punch in the jaw."

She grinned, then reached up and tugged him down, bringing his mouth back to hers. His hands slid under her shirt and over the bare skin of her back, tugging her closer and closer. How she wanted him.

That thought had her eyes flying open.

He sensed her response immediately and pulled back, swallowing. "Sorry, I didn't mean to—"

"No, don't apologise." She took a breath, trying to calm her racing heart and heated body. She shouldn't have done that. She *really* shouldn't have done that. "But I've been keeping something from you, and while I very much enjoyed... well, that... this is a really bad idea on a number of fronts."

He stepped away, one hand running through his rumpled hair.

That wash of loneliness she sometimes felt from him hit her hard, though he quickly quenched it.

What he'd done these past days. Turning her arrest into an opportunity. Managing the Wolves and Mithanis to keep everyone alive and increase Mithanis's trust in him. Following her lead without question earlier to save them all.

Cuinn was clever, and quick thinking, and he had a natural instinct for all of this. And he had no idea. He had nobody to tell him.

"*I'm going to tell him, Sari.*"

Sadness sank through her mind, then, "*I think you should.*"

"You trusted me today," she said quietly, making a decision that was beyond momentous but also one of the easiest she'd ever made. "And it's time for me to trust you in the same way."

Some of the sadness in his expression faded. "I would like that."

She took a deep breath. "Sit down. We need to talk. Properly."

He dragged the room's only wooden chair over to the ratty sofa on the opposite wall. Talyn took one look at it and shook her head. "I'm not sitting on that."

Amusement flashed over his face—such a stunning face when it was alight with humour—and he moved to sit on the couch. She drew the chair up to sit opposite him, their knees just touching.

No point beating around the bush.

"You are a Dumnorix, Cuinn. That's why I was sent here. King-shield only protect those of Dumnorix blood."

He blinked in confusion, shook his head a little. "How...?"

She took his hand, entwined their fingers. Then she told him everything she knew, about Rianna, about his father, the reason his bloodline had been kept so secret, all of it. By the time she'd finished his green eyes had gone dark, and the intensity that had always been there with the Shadowhawk blazed from him like a furnace.

"So I'm..." He swallowed, arched an eyebrow at her. "We're related?"

A smile tugged at her mouth. "Very distantly. We share great-grandparents."

He huffed out a breath. "That's why your uncle and mother and every other Dumnorix came traipsing out to poor Ceannar's home while I was there."

"They wanted to meet you." She hesitated. "There's more. It can't go beyond these walls, not to the Wolves, not to your family, not anyone."

"If it's so secret, why tell me?" he breathed.

"Because I trust you." She swallowed. "And I want to share it with you."

"Then tell me."

"The Callanan have an informant who says that Montagn is planning to invade Mithranar. Apparently they're using Vengeance to create instability. Only a handful of people are aware of the informant's existence, and if their information got out, their life would be over."

"And you'd lose your access to information on the ahara's intentions," Cuinn finished quietly, voice filled with worry. "Mithanis and Mother have been worried, but I had no idea we were in such danger."

She hesitated. "Do you forgive me for not telling you?"

"You never hid the fact there were secrets, Talyn," he murmured. "And I understand why you had to keep these ones. The fact you're telling me now... what you're trusting me with..." His voice trailed off, his eyes molten as they met hers. Abruptly she realised how close they'd become, how much she wanted to be closer, to touch him again. That kiss had been... electrifying.

"Now you see why this is all such a terrible idea." She forced herself to lean back and let go of his hand. "I'm the captain of your guard, and if Mithanis got any hint that you and I were... if my uncle got any hint..."

"Big problems." Cuinn matched her almost-whisper.

"Very big."

He took a deep, steadying breath, then rose to his feet and put some distance between them. "We have to lay low for a while anyway. Mithanis will be watching you closely—we have to ensure he continues to believe you're no threat."

"I agree."

His mouth tightened then. "Talyn, you can't agree to have your wing buds cut out. You have no idea what you're giving up by agreeing to that. I'm sure we can find another way to prove to Mithanis—"

"Stop." She raised her hand. "I don't want or need wings. It's a small price to pay for being able to stay here."

Pain rippled over his face, his magic no doubt telling him how serious she was. "I can tell there's nothing I can say to make you change your mind, but I really wish you'd reconsider."

She stood too. "The Wolves will notice you're gone sooner rather than later, and whatever spies Mithanis has watching my room can't notice I'm gone either."

"We'll talk soon, once things have calmed a little," he agreed, then hesitated at the door. "I... I'm getting stronger, Talyn. Working out how to do this."

She allowed the smile to spread over her face. "I couldn't agree more."

Once he was gone, glamour firmly back in place, door clicking shut behind him, Talyn let out a breath, sagging back against the table, the previous day and a half finally crashing over her.

As right as it had felt, she'd just done something expressly against her uncle—her king's—orders. And that kiss. How could she have allowed herself to fall into that?

Because she'd wanted it. Had been wanting it for some time but ignoring the desire because of how impossible it all was.

She had to forget about it.

And trust that Cuinn would keep her secrets.

CHAPTER 22

The evening following her return, Talyn arrived at her room after dinner in a still subdued mess to find the tin cup on her windowsill had been turned upside down. She sighed. It was late, and she was exhausted after having relatively no sleep for the past week.

Still, she was eager to talk to Savin. Pushing her weariness away, she climbed up to her rooftop garden. Rain pattered on the leaves of the plants and dripped onto the paved stone. She huddled under a thick tree branch, peering into the blackness of the night.

He materialised a moment later, his ability to hide not at all affected by the fact his cloak and hood were dripping wet.

"Everything all right?" she asked. Though he hadn't seemed hurt at the time she'd rescued him, she'd worried that he might not have been able to get out of Vengeance's compound unscathed.

"I'm fine, thanks to you," he said, a faint note of gratitude flickering in his voice before its usual businesslike tone resumed. "I made it out before you did—you and your Callanan friends provided quite the nice distraction."

"How long did they have you?" She frowned.

His face tightened. "Several weeks. Not long after the Acondor family returned to Dock City, I started hearing snippets from my sources about a Vengeance ambush on the Shadowhawk in the Darmour mines. The rumours indicated he'd been killed. None of it was clear, but one of my informants seemed to think the Wolves were caught up in the attack. Given you weren't here to ask about it, I got a little overzealous with trying to access Vengeance."

She nodded, keeping her expression bland as she tried to figure out how much to tell Savin. "Prince Cuinn got drunk and bored and decided he wanted to travel. It suited my purposes to go along with him because your source was right, the Wolves and I were caught up in an ambush, and I thought it best to get away from Mithranar for a while."

Confusion flitted over the Shadow's face. "Why would they go to the effort of coming after your Wolves?"

"Apparently they didn't take kindly to the fact we foiled their assassination attempt last year and took out a serious chunk of their manpower at the same time."

"Hmm." He didn't sound convinced. "But what does the Shadowhawk have to do with any of it?"

She took a breath, hesitated. "He was the source that warned me about the planned assassination. Somehow Vengeance found out. They were the cause of the avalanche in Darmour, knowing it would likely draw in both us and the Shadowhawk to help. It was well planned."

"You're running the Shadowhawk as an informant?" Savin was shocked, though it was always difficult to tell with him whether the slip of emotion was natural or deliberate.

"Not exactly. I tracked him down because I thought he might be able to help with what the Callanan have me working on here." Not a lie. "It was a dead end." Definitely a lie.

"And the Shadowhawk? Did they really kill him?"

"I never saw him in Darmour," she lied smoothly.

Suspicion leaked from Savin in a tangible cloud. "How did Vengeance know he would be there?"

"I believe the Shadowhawk has worked with Vengeance members

in the past." Again she was skirting perilously close to the truth, but to this she didn't have a good answer. It was one of the many things that had gnawed at her since the ambush. "My guess is they have mutual contacts, and learned ahead of time that he planned to travel to Darmour."

Savin was silent for a long time, and when he finally spoke, his voice was calm, deliberate. "You're leaving things out. How did you and two Callanan end up in Vengeance's camp the other night?"

"There was an incident with Mithanis. He learned that I'm a Dumnorix and of course immediately suspected I was here as a spy." She scrambled for another convincing lie. "He had me arrested, but I managed to escape. While you were missing I identified a Vengeance contact—so after my escape I went to her and requested their help in getting out of the city. The rest you know. As soon as we got out of the camp, I offered Vengeance up to Mithanis in return for allowing me to stay."

"And the other two Callanan?"

"Sent here undercover as merchants to help with my assignment. Which you know I can't tell you about any more than you can tell me about your tasking."

The silence between them turned icy. "Does your uncle know that an Acondor prince was going to have you killed? And don't try and pretend that wasn't exactly what Mithanis intended when he learned who you were."

She met his stare with a slight smile. "He doesn't know, and you're not going to tell him. That's not your job, Savin."

Savin let out a breath. "I owe you one. Is there anything I can do to help?"

"Yes, actually," she said, glad he was letting it go. "I've forced Vengeance to abandon their camp and flee, but I want them completely wiped out. Will you let me know if you hear anything about where they've scattered to? I assume they'll disperse to safe houses across the city."

"Why so interested in destroying Vengeance?"

"They tried to kill me, and my Wolves. Isn't that reason enough?"

"Yes," he said. "But I know there's something else going on here that you're not telling me."

"He's a Shadow, Tal, he might be able to do more than just track down where they're hiding."

Anticipation leapt inside Talyn's chest. *"You're right. I can't tell Savin about the Montagni planning an invasion, but that doesn't mean he can't help us identify the person connecting the Montagni to Vengeance. Then Queen Sarana can be warned of the potential invasion while the informant stays safe in the Montagni court."*

"Exactly."

She looked at Savin. "I have a theory that *someone* is behind Vengeance, giving them resources, access to mercenaries. Someone playing a bigger game."

There was a moment's silence, then a dubious, "Why would someone be doing that?"

"I have a feeling if we learn the answer to that, we'll be able to destroy Vengeance from the roots." When he still looked reluctant, she pushed. "You asked what you could do to help, Savin, and this is it." Talyn was certain the First Blade would support her tasking him with this.

He swept into a mocking bow. "Your wish is my command, Captain Dynan."

TALYN CONCENTRATED FIERCELY, palm held out in front of her. Magic ran through her veins, and sweat broke out on her forehead as she fought to focus it. Sapphire light glimmered around her outstretched hand, and with a massive effort, she forced it outwards. A bright sapphire bolt of energy leapt from her palm, flew through the dim hall and past the target she'd set up, and slammed into the stone wall behind.

"Damn," she muttered.

"Not bad," Tiercelin said approvingly. "How does your back feel?"

She shot him an irritated look in lieu of an answer. It was the sixth time he'd asked her that in the space of a full-turn. To prove her sincerity to Mithanis and the queen and reinforce their fledgling trust, she'd had her wing buds removed two days after they'd come to their agreement. It had been painless, as promised, but until the neatly stitched wounds on her back healed, she was prevented from undertaking her normal training routine.

Tiercelin—who still looked horrified at any mention of her wing buds—had offered to help teach her how to use her winged folk magic. Finding out her father's identity had changed something in her attitude towards her winged folk blood. She didn't need or want wings, but her warrior magic had always lain dormant inside her, released only in the quick bursts of a Callanan shield. If Tiercelin was to be believed, she was capable of a lot more.

So she'd come down to the lower level training hall where Zamaril and Corrin—and now Ehdra and Dansia—practiced their Callanan shields. Every now and then a green or blue glow flashed from the opposite end of the hall.

"Try again," Tiercelin said patiently.

She relaxed her stance and held out her hand again. This time her determination was so great that when she loosed her magic, it flew meters wide of the target and hit the wall hard enough to gouge out a huge chunk of stone.

A spattering of applause sounded from where the human Wolves were training. Zamaril added a whistle. She shook her head, a chuckle escaping her. So much for being good at everything. She'd yet to get anywhere near the target.

"Do you think they could do this too?" she asked Tiercelin.

"I suspect so, though they'd find it much harder and their power wouldn't be as strong," he said, looking grim.

"Captain!"

Talyn dropped her hand and spun around, ignoring the twin tugs of pain in her upper back from the sudden movement. Corrin's tall form strode through the hall. "Corrin, what is it?"

He stifled a smile as he glanced at the gouges in the opposite wall. "I was just down in Dock City visiting my sisters."

"Theac's back?" She perked up.

"He is, and raring to return to duty, even though he's not on shift until tomorrow." Corrin's smile widened a little. "He and Mam both look happy though."

"You didn't fill him in on what happened while he was away, I take it?" she asked drily. Theac certainly wouldn't be looking happy if Corrin had.

Corrin's smile faded a little. "I didn't know how to even begin explaining it without Talon Parksin ripping my head off. I thought explanations were best left to you."

Talyn frowned. "I'll go and see him tonight, but I'm in the middle—"

"Sorry, that's not why I interrupted." He cut her off, worry replacing the smile on his face. "Petro found me on my way back here. He said there was an attack in a house in the Market Quarter last night."

"What sort of attack?" she asked, dread uncurling. It had only been two weeks since Falcons had chased Vengeance from their base beyond the wall. Surely they couldn't have gathered themselves so quickly?

"He said it was an animal attack. The City Patrol is investigating, of course, but Petro asked if we could take a look." Corrin hesitated. "He didn't say much—we were in public and he didn't want to linger —but I got the impression that the family might have been linked to the Shadowhawk's network."

A shiver went through her. "We'll go. But not all of us. And we make it an off-duty thing. No uniforms." The last thing she needed was Mithanis hearing the Wolves were acting outside their remit by investigating crimes in Dock City.

"Halun's on shift, so Andres and I will run afternoon training," Tiercelin offered. "That way you can take Corrin and Zamaril with you."

Zamaril was already coming over, Corrin's entrance having drawn him from where he'd been teaching Ehdra and Dansia. "Something wrong?"

"An attack in Dock City last night," she said grimly.

"You don't think—"

"Let's just go and take a look."

TALYN WAS THOROUGHLY unsurprised to find Theac waiting for them at the bottom of the wall walk, glower firmly in place. Fortunately he too was out of uniform.

"It's good to see you," she said, a rush of delight sweeping through her at having her dependable second back. "I take it someone came to you about the attack as well?"

"The mayor." He nodded, scowling when Zamaril added his own warm greetings. "Yes, yes, hello. I wasn't gone that long. Only three weeks."

"Oh, a *lot* can happen in three weeks," Zamaril said slyly, shooting a pointed look in Talyn's direction.

"What happened?" Theac snapped.

"A story for later," she said firmly. "Right now there are more pressing concerns."

"The mayor is aware of how it might look to have Wolves poking around, but he's asked for some advice. The Patrol haven't experienced anything like this before," Theac explained.

"Petro gave me directions." Corrin set off through the streets.

The city was as bustling as always around them, several people calling out greetings or lifting a hand to wave when they recognised the Wolf captain and her talons. They returned the greetings, but each was preoccupied with their own thoughts.

Her talons were still unhappy, and it wasn't just over making them stand down when she was arrested. Though none of them had said anything, it was clear they were just as upset that she'd so willingly agreed to have her wing buds cut out. She was temporarily at a loss, not sure what else she could say to them, and was left hoping that their dismay would blow over with time.

Theac, no fool, picked up on the tension and kept shooting her questioning looks. She ignored them.

Petro's news was more worrying. She hadn't forgotten the grisly murders of Goldfeather and Iceflight, and the clear evidence it had been a tawncat attack linked to an Armun Shadow. They'd thought Vengeance had been behind those killings.

But Vengeance were scattered, on the run.

Unease spilled through her, tainting some of the good mood she'd been in since successfully dealing with Mithanis and the Vengeance situation. If they were active already, after their base had been taken from them, after they'd been forced to flee in a hurry... maybe Montagn was an even stronger supporter of them than she'd realised. Maybe they were already making their move.

"This isn't going to be good, is it?"

"Oh, you're back," Talyn grumbled.

"Don't give me that tone. I can't help it that you've been so caught up recently that there's no space for me in your head."

A chill wrapped around her heart. *"What do you mean?"*

"Oh relax, it's not a bad thing." Sari hesitated. *"Truly it's not."*

She stopped walking, trying to halt the panic spreading through her veins. *"Are you trying to tell me you're leaving? Sari, please don't—"*

"No!" Genuine reassurance filled Sari's mental voice. *"Your healer Wolf had it right. I'm a part of you, Tal, and barring a winged folk healer taking me away, I'm here for always."*

"Captain?"

The Wolves had stopped, looking back at her in concern. She summoned a smile and kept walking. "Sorry, I was just thinking something through."

"So what are you trying to say?" Talyn pushed.

There was a silence so lengthy she began to think Sari had gone again, but then she let out a little sigh. *"Nothing. I'm not trying to say anything. Carry on."*

Talyn wanted to pursue the obvious evasion of truth, but Sari was gone from her mind before she could even think the words. Shaking her head, she returned her focus to Corrin, who was leading them steadily away from the noisy streets to one of the quieter housing areas in Dock City—not far from where Errana had lived with her girls before marrying Theac.

Eventually they turned a corner into a wide street lined with neat houses, most with flowering gardens out the front. The mayor stood outside one of the homes, pacing up and down and chewing on his bottom lip, an odd look for such a bear of a man. His face cleared when he saw the Wolves, eyes going straight to Talyn.

"Ciantar!" he exclaimed.

A flare of irritation combined with fear and a hint of pride flashed through her. Word of Talyn's true identity had inevitably spread after Brightwing made the mistake of discussing the reason for her arrest in front of a handful of Falcons in their mess. According to Cuinn, the news had spread through the palace like wildfire, although everybody was too afraid to say anything too loudly.

And once word spread from the Falcons to the Wolves—a matter of half a day given how close some of them had become—it was inevitable the information would leak out to Dock City. And now, the genuine delight in the mayor's face was dangerous.

"Mayor," she greeted. "Please just refer to me as Captain. I think we both know it could be dangerous to do otherwise. Now—"

"Excuse me!" Theac barked. "What the hell are you both talking about?"

"Turns out the captain's father was Trystaan Ciantar," Zamaril said idly. "Prince Mithanis found out while you were away."

Talyn shot a glare at Zamaril, who was starting to seriously piss her off, then turned to Theac. "I will explain all this later, I promise. In private."

He looked angry—absolutely furious, in fact—but gave a terse nod. "As soon as we're done here."

"As soon as," she said, then addressed the mayor, who was politely pretending not to listen to their conversation. "Theac said you asked for some help, that there's been an animal attack. What can you tell me about it?"

"Not much, I'm sorry. The City Patrol arrived earlier this morning after the neighbours raised the alarm. The entire family has been killed." The mayor's jaw clenched. "It's a terrible sight."

Talyn reached up to lay a reassuring hand on the mayor's arm, then motioned her Wolves a short distance away. "Theac, can you speak with the Patrolmen? Let them know we're not here to take over, just to help."

"I'll find out what I can." He strode off.

"Zamaril, find out how access was gained to the house by whoever or whatever did this. Corrin, speak to the neighbours. They look upset, so be gentle. I want to know what they know—anything they saw or heard could be important."

The Wolves dispersed, and Talyn walked into the house. Immediately the warmth of the sun on her back faded, a chill descending around her. She stopped dead for a second, hit by a lingering miasma of dread.

"Talyn!" Even Sari felt it somehow.

She walked further inside, following the unmistakable hint of darkness. At the back of the house they came to what must have been the parents' bedroom. The sharp tang of drying blood filled the air, and she could taste it on her tongue. The Patrolman on the door looked pale and sick.

"Captain." His eyes widened in hope and surprise when he saw her. "Do you know what happened here?"

"Not yet, but I'm going to do my best to find out. Are you all right to stand guard a little longer?"

His shoulders firmed. "I'll be fine."

Talyn entered the room, closing the door behind her. She didn't want the horror to be open for everyone to see.

The parents were laid out on the bed, throats torn open. Dried blood drenched their bodies, the bed covers, and had dripped into pools on the floor around the bed. Two small children had been dragged out from under the bed, and lay in a heart-wrenching pile, their eyes sightless with death.

"What happened here?" Sari's mental voice was stark with horror.

Talyn swallowed, fighting hard to maintain her composure. She'd never seen anything like this before, not once, even during the most violent parts of her Callanan days. The sight of the small children lying there, having been killed so horrifically, tore at her heart. She closed her eyes and took a deep breath, not knowing which emotion she felt strongest, anger or grief.

"I'm going to find out, so I can destroy whatever did this." Ice filled and wrapped her words, an iron-clad promise of vengeance. It didn't matter how it looked to Mithanis or anyone else bothering to pay attention.

A knocking sound came from the open window, and she looked up to see Zamaril clamber inside. The thief's face blanched at the sight before him.

"Take a breath, Zamaril," Talyn said. "We're going to find out who did this."

He nodded and closed his eyes for a long moment. His jaw worked. "Whatever it was came through the window as I just did." His voice caught and he stopped for a moment, continuing once he had control of himself. "It was left open, and there are scratch marks on the wooden frame. The front and side doors haven't been tampered with, and neither has any other window."

"Scratches?" she asked. "As in, made by something with claws? Another tawncat?"

"That would be my guess."

"Captain!" Corrin pushed the door open. As soon as he took in the scene, he gulped in a breath and his eyes filled with tears.

"What is it, Corrin?"

"I spoke with the neighbours. They heard faint hissing and snarling in the early hours of the morning. It went on for a half-turn or so. They thought about investigating, but said the sounds made them unusually afraid."

Talyn went to lean over one of the parent's bodies, needing all her self-control to study it closely without emptying her stomach. "I saw these same wounds on Goldfeather's and Iceflight's bodies." She straightened and backed away.

"That would mean a tawncat somehow got over the wall to come here and kill this family," Zamaril said. "How? And why?"

"We know why." Corrin's scanning gaze caught on something clutched in the mother's dead hands. He gently tugged it away. It was a bloodied piece of paper, the word on it mostly obscured, but she recognised it instantly when he passed it to her. "Vengeance want retribution. And the how is easy. They came under the wall."

"If they wanted retribution, why kill an innocent family?" Zamaril asked.

Talyn crushed the paper in her hand, having to take a deep breath through the sudden tightness in her chest. "Corrin, you said Petro thought the father might be part of the Shadowhawk's network."

Silence fell over the room.

"Tal, I'm not convinced."

"Me either," she murmured. When the three talons turned to look at her, she explained, "I'm not convinced it's Vengeance. The Wing-Guard only just routed their base, and this doesn't feel like them."

"Which part? The murder or the killing with a tawncat?" Zamaril asked. "They've done both before."

"The Vengeance murders of humans were all men, men who took bribes from the winged folk in a way that harmed the human population. Those are children lying there." Talyn's voice broke as she glanced at them. Could her cousin, her father's niece, be capable of this sort of senseless violence?

"They came after the Shadowhawk. And this family helped him," Zamaril said.

"There's still the question of how the tawncat was directed to attack." Corrin broke the silence. "I know it's been said before, but the creatures in the forest are wild, untameable. It's the reason the citadel was built above the forest."

Theac entered the room, obviously having caught the last part of the conversation. "What about someone with winged folk magic? Could they use their power to bind these creatures to their will? Isn't that exactly what Prince Cuinn has done with Jasper?"

Corrin frowned. "For all the prince's formidable skill, I wouldn't say that he's bound Jasper to him... more that he's won him over. And that tawncat doesn't do anything at the prince's command apart from not kill us."

"It's true. He can't even keep Jasper in his tower when he wants to get out," Talyn said, frowning. "And I can see a winged person orchestrating a murder of a Queencouncil member for political reasons. But this human family? What would be the motivation?"

A knock on the door interrupted them, and the Patrolman appeared. "Captain, the undertaker has arrived to take the bodies for burial."

"Thank you." She glanced around one final time. "I think we're done here. Allow them through."

"Captain?" The mayor was waiting for them outside the house as the Wolves emerged. "May I have a moment?"

She nodded and they moved away from the front of the house, out of hearing distance of those moving around it.

"We met only briefly on the night of the floods," he said. "So you may think this an imposition, and if so, I apologise."

"You let us stay in your home afterwards, I think that makes us friends." She smiled. "What is it, Mayor Doran?"

"I knew your father, Captain," he said gently.

She swallowed. She hadn't expected that, or the rush of emotion his words caused. "You did?"

"We knew each other as boys. We met through his half-brother, Runye—Trys would often escape from the citadel and come down to Dock City to play with us. He never cared that we were human and he was winged."

Talyn smiled at the thought of her father as a youth, running about Dock City with other boys his own age. "That doesn't surprise me."

"As we grew older, our friendship remained strong. All three of us wanted to make things better in Mithranar. I got my education and started working for the Dock City council. Runye began working as the Shadowhawk, and Trys used his wealth to help him. I was one of the few people who knew the identity of the Shadowhawk."

"You knew?" Talyn glanced around before drawing the mayor over to a more isolated part of the street. "How did you escape being killed?"

"As we grew out of boyhood, your father was always very careful to hide his human friendships, especially once Runye started acting as the Shadowhawk." An expression of unutterable sadness filled his face. "When he was caught, Runye sacrificed himself so that I would have enough time to warn Trys to get out of the citadel—I got to him just as the Falcons were about to arrest his family. I don't know what happened after that. Runye's people took your father and got him away. I never saw him again."

"He missed you," Talyn managed through the lump in her throat. "I never knew why he was so sad sometimes, but I always sensed that he yearned for something."

"I had no idea you were his daughter," Doran said. "But you are just like him. Having Trystaan Ciantar's daughter in Mithranar is a wonderful thing."

"It's also a dangerous thing," she warned. "You knew my father, so you know better than anyone that my position is precarious, and Prince Mithanis cannot think that I have ambitions above being captain of Prince Cuinn's guard. If the human folk start parading me around as their Ciantar, not only will Prince Cuinn be in greater danger, but I will be as well."

His face turned grave. "I haven't forgotten what it was like before. I will pass the word around, Captain. Be sure we will not put you in any more danger than necessary."

"Thank you, Mayor," Talyn said, then hesitated. "Did you know that Runye had a daughter?"

"She was a baby when he died. I never saw her again. His people withdrew completely into hiding and I haven't spoken to any of them since." Sadness crossed the big man's face.

"But as far as you know she's alive?" Talyn waited for his nod before continuing. "So why such a fuss over the revelation of my parentage when there's already a surviving Ciantar in Mithranar?"

"Runye's daughter was born as human as he was. No wing buds, no magic. She's not a Ciantar, not by winged folk standards."

"I see. Thanks, Mayor."

He took a breath. "Can you tell me anything about what happened to that poor family?"

"Killed by a tawncat is my guess," Talyn said softly.

He blanched. "Why?"

"I'm told the parents may have been part of the Shadowhawk's network," she said carefully.

"But the Shadowhawk has been gone for months." Doran looked confused.

Talyn almost smiled. Clearly the mayor kept himself apprised of the new Shadowhawk's activities. "I'll tell you at once if I learn anything more. Would you do the same, Mayor?"

"Of course," he said. Unease filled his face. "Keep safe, Captain."

THEY WALKED BACK to the citadel in silence, all shocked to the core by what they'd seen in that house. Despite her angry words promising revenge, Talyn dreaded being asked by one of her talons what they were going to do next—she truly had no idea. Ravinire was continuing to hunt Vengeance, combing through everything left behind at the abandoned compound beyond the wall, but hadn't yet had any luck.

She worried too. Worried that by leaving Saniya alive she'd made a huge error.

And what if she was right about this not being Vengeance? If something else entirely was behind this... she had no idea where to even start with that.

"Do you think we should get Prince Cuinn away from here for a while?" Zamaril said suddenly.

"Why?" Theac asked.

"Because of that." Zamaril gestured in the direction they'd come from. "And because Vengeance now know the Shadowhawk is still alive."

Talyn cut in before Theac could ask when that had happened. "They still don't know who he is, and never will, and the Shadowhawk activities have stopped." But not for much longer. Cuinn had been more patient than she'd expected with his recovery, but he was back to full health now, and if this family *had* been among his helpers... he wasn't going to stay on the sidelines any longer.

"Nor do we have a good enough excuse to suddenly remove the prince from Mithranar again," Corrin added. "He and the captain are being watched closely enough as it is right now. We can't afford to do anything suspicious."

Talyn ignored Theac's scowl, cutting him off before he could start demanding answers again. "And we don't talk about this aloud, remember? Not ever."

The Wolves nodded, none of them saying anything more. They were still out of sorts with her, and the day's events hadn't helped their sour mood. Once at the barracks, they left with muttered good-byes, Corrin to take over Halun's shift with his detail and Zamaril to training.

Theac cleared his throat pointedly.

"Yes, all right." She sighed. "Let's go up to my rooftop garden. We'll have privacy there."

THE SUN WAS HOT, the air humid and sticky, as they clambered up the narrow ladder. Talyn led Theac over to the cooling shade of a weeping tree, squared her shoulders, and came straight out with it. "About a half-turn after you and Errana left your wedding party, Prince Mithanis sent Falcons to arrest me."

A thick silence, then, "You'd best explain it all, Captain. And quick-ly," Theac barked.

She did, only leaving out the part about how she'd met with Cuinn once it was all over and told him who he was and what Vengeance was truly doing. Once she'd finished, a silence settled over them. Theac reached up to rub his face, then let his hand drop back to his side.

"Why didn't you send word?"

"You'd just gotten married," she said lightly. "I didn't want to ruin your trip with Errana. None of us did."

"That's not acceptable," he said with quiet dignity, and her heart lurched in her chest. "I am your second, and you were perilously close to being executed. I should have known. I should have been given the opportunity to help."

"You couldn't help," she said, trying to make him understand. "The Wolves couldn't do a thing or Mithanis would have killed them too. Surely you see that?"

"Of course I do," he barked. "Which is why I needed to know. So that I could hold them back, make them stand down. That was my *job*."

"They did stand down," she said quietly. "Cuinn ordered them to."

"Putting himself at risk to do so. What if Mithanis found out Cuinn was so concerned about his Wolves, so concerned about *you*, that the first thing he did on learning you'd been arrested was order the Wolves to back down? It doesn't exactly fit with the spoiled princeling act, does it?"

"He was smarter than that," she countered. "He took them away, to Sparrow Island, made it look like he was helping Mithanis. He did well."

Theac merely stared her down. "He would not have needed to take them away if I'd been here. I could have held them back and you know it."

"Theac, I… I don't know what to say." She let out a breath. "You were gone. We chose to let you have some happiness."

"You chose wrong."

"Would Errana agree with that?" she challenged.

His face flushed. "That's unfair."

"Yes, well so is you pushing back so hard on me. I am your flea-shitting captain." The anger burst out of her, part frustration, part guilt, part the horror of what she'd seen earlier and her fear of what it meant. "Choosing not to tell you was my call. *My* call. You live with it."

"You don't get it," he muttered. "Even after all this time, you don't understand."

"You all keep saying that, and it's getting old," she snapped. "I have no idea what you're talking about."

"You came here, Captain." He threw the words at her in a steady, unflinching way, daring her to dispute them. "You came here, and you keep calling yourself a born warrior, a Kingshield, a Callanan, a Wolf. Born to fight and win. Well, that's not true."

Her chest heaved. "What?"

"You're a gods-damned born *leader*. That's what you don't seem to understand. You came here and you won us, and you won him too, heart and soul and everything in between. We would fight for you, and we would die for you, and we would do it without hesitation. A winged folk lordling and one of the saltiest Falcons I've ever met literally risked their lives for you... all after spending a matter of weeks under your command."

"Theac—"

"You are no follower, no soldier. You are a leader," he bellowed at her, then stopped, voice gentling. "It's time you understood that and accepted what it means."

Her mouth opened, but there were no words to say. Nothing came. Theac shook his head, and then he turned and left.

Talyn stared after him, and continued staring once he'd vanished from sight.

CHAPTER 23

Talyn's coded message was waiting for Cuinn when he returned from a game of alleya, sending a jolt of relief through him. Despite the physical exercise, he remained restless, agitated.

Before, it had been easy to don Cuinn's indolent prince mask, easy to lose himself and his worries in parties and sport and women. But it had been growing increasingly difficult for a long time, and now... it just made him feel sick, like he was wasting time when he could be doing something more important.

He'd bested Mithanis. Twice. The first time had been small, but the second... hope that had shrivelled and died inside him years ago was reawakening. It brought with it new shoots of confidence, of wondering whether there might be a way. To do more. To be better. To throw aside this mask and not die.

And since he'd kissed Talyn... well, it was impossible to even pretend interest in any other woman. He hadn't so much as touched one in weeks, and soon questions would be asked.

She'd kissed him back. She'd *wanted* to. He'd felt it. Giddiness expanded in his chest.

And he was behaving like a lovesick fool. Crumpling the note, he went out to speak with Corrin. "Captain Dynan needs to see me. You'll make sure it looks like I'm in here?"

"I will." The young man nodded. His eyes were shadowed.

"So it's bad then?"

"It's not good," Corrin said. "Liadin will shadow you there to make sure you're alright."

Cuinn took a breath, spread his wings, and lifted into the sky.

TALYN'S BALCONY door was open, a clear invitation, so leaving Liadin outside, he swooped in. Talyn leaned against the wall by her bedroom door, a small frown on her face.

She was upset.

But she wasn't hiding it from him. She was sharing, knowing he'd pick it up. He carefully closed the balcony door and waited for her to speak first.

"Thank you for coming."

Cuinn swallowed, panic and worry unfurling inside him. "What is it? What's happened?"

"A family in the Market Quarter was killed overnight," she said, remaining at her spot by the door. "It looks like another tawncat attack. Probably Vengeance."

He frowned, confused. "I don't understand. If this is retribution, why an innocent family?"

Talyn closed her eyes, her reluctance to give him the answer clear as day. He tensed. "Petro thinks the father was a member of the Shadowhawk's network," she said.

Cuinn's face twisted and it took a moment to control his thundering emotions so that he wouldn't drown her with them. "I see."

"This isn't your fault," Talyn said quickly, sensing his distress anyway. "It's mine. I was cocky and thought I could manipulate Mithanis. I didn't consider what Vengeance might do next."

"No," Cuinn said heavily. Guilt burned in his chest. "I put all of these people in danger when I started my activities as the Shadowhawk." He frowned. "You said *probably* Vengeance?"

"It looks like them, down to the use of a tawncat." She hesitated. "But the victims—killing *children* to get back at you? It doesn't feel right. And how did they organise themselves so quickly? They should be on the run, desperately trying to stay hidden from the Falcons and Patrol searching every inch of Dock City for them."

Her words pounded through him, his mind following along with hers. She was so quick, so incisive. It thrilled him. "Who else could it be?"

Talyn threw her hands up. "A random murder? They happen often enough in Dock City."

"Not with a tawncat. Not children. Not without some obvious motive."

"Nothing was stolen from the house," she murmured, answering his next question before he could ask it. "And the family had no criminal links that the Patrol knew about."

"We need to do something about this." Cuinn shifted, wings half raised in anger. Someone needed to do *something*.

Silence met his words. His frustration was hers too, twining around and through the both of them. He'd been trying to help, but instead he'd only caused more problems. There had to be another way. He looked at her. "I want you to find out who is behind the attacks by these creatures. Confirm whether it is Vengeance or not."

She nodded. "We still need to find the Montagni link to Vengeance too. Until we do, they're free to find some other gang to bribe into doing the same things Vengeance did."

Her voice—cool and confident—soothed him, even though it shouldn't. "None of this feels like Montagn trying to invade Mithranar."

"I agree." She sounded troubled. "But at the same time, it makes logical sense. All this disturbance, making people uneasy, instilling distrust in the WingGuard. A way to weaken you before invasion?"

Silence fell. She remained leaning against the wall by the door, gaze distant.

"Something else happened," Cuinn said, unable to leave without addressing it. "You're unsettled."

"I had a fight with Theac," she said tiredly. "The Wolves are still unhappy with me over being made to stand down."

He'd been aware of it. Though it had been his words that made them stand by and do nothing while their beloved captain was arrested and almost killed, he'd done it for her, and they knew it. They knew what held them back. Just as well, he understood her fear—after losing one partner she couldn't conceive of losing more comrades she cared about, especially because of another decision she'd made.

"Do you want to talk about it?" he asked.

"No, it's nothing. You should go."

"Before I do." He hesitated, digging his boot into the carpet. Something had crystallised in his mind since Talyn had broken the news of the murders, something that had been brewing there for weeks, ever since coming back home. "I can't sit this out any longer. The humans need the Shadowhawk."

Her eyes whipped to his, bright and sapphire. "They need the Shadowhawk to be alive, which you certainly won't be if you're caught."

"I managed not to get caught for a long time before you even came to Mithranar," he said, a thread of irritation in his voice. "And you don't seriously expect me to sit here and do nothing while someone is out there murdering people associated with me?"

"I don't," she said quietly. "I understand what drives you better than anyone—it's the Dumnorix part of us. But I'm responsible for your safety, and you know what my advice is. It's too dangerous."

"I respect your advice, Talyn, and I always will." He took a breath, met her gaze unflinchingly. "But I plan to return to my activities as the Shadowhawk. If Ravinire and the WingGuard can't, I will stop Vengeance."

There was a moment of silence, then a little smile curled at her mouth. "When I was arrested, you didn't try to protect me. With your contacts, you could have gotten me out of Mithranar before the WingGuard shut down the docks. But instead you handed me over to Vengeance, because you knew that's what I would choose. Because you had faith in me and my ability to succeed."

"Yes," he said simply. It hadn't been a question, despite how afraid he'd been for her, despite the danger.

Talyn pushed off the wall, coming to stand in front of him. "And I will do the same for you. I have faith in your abilities as Shadowhawk."

His shoulders sagged in relief. "Thank you."

"One thing though." Her smile widened slightly. "You're not doing it alone this time."

He loved her. It punched through him in a wave of certainty and emotion that was so fierce it took his breath away. She was everything. Beauty and fierceness and joy all bleeding through him. His eyes slid closed as he fought to keep what he was feeling from leaping out and reaching her.

She was still healing. The last thing she needed was the pressure of knowing how deeply he felt. So he took a deep breath and kept everything but gratitude from his expression.

"Together," he agreed, eyes sliding open to meet hers.

CHAPTER 24

"I've got a question for you, Tiercelin." Andres took a swig from his ale and placed it on the table before leaning back in his chair.

"Yes?" Tiercelin looked up from the thick book lying in his lap. He had his feet up on the table, his great wings taking up the remaining space on the sofa he was reclining on. The others—bar Halun who was on Cuinn's guard shift—were spread around the common room.

Talyn hunched over a pile of administration forms Ravinire wanted completed by the next day, allowing the idle chatter of the talons to relax her. While their annoyance with her hadn't subsided entirely, the camaraderie between them seemed to have returned to normal levels, and she was glad to be back on even footing with them.

"I was wondering about Prince Cuinn's recovery," Andres said. "Specifically, if his injuries had affected his ability to... ah... entertain women?"

Talyn glanced up, astonished at such a question coming from her most professional talon. A little frown creased Andres' eyebrows, indicating his interest stemmed from genuine concern, not an attempt to gossip.

"Watch it." Theac growled. "The prince's private life is none of our business. I'm sure the captain doesn't need to hear about it either."

"I'm not a delicate flower." Talyn scowled at Theac, irritated. "I *have* actually experienced what you're talking about. On multiple occasions."

All except Tiercelin stared at her for a moment, gape-mouthed. Andres and Corrin had gone a deep shade of red. Zamaril looked down, a little smile at the corner of his mouth. Theac's glower deepened.

She rolled her eyes. "It's not all that shocking to you, surely."

"No." Andres coughed. "Just...you're the Captain, so it's..."

"What? Odd for me to—what did you call it—'be entertained?'" Talyn was having fun now. Sari's laughter tinkled in her head.

Tiercelin grinned. "I'm with the captain. It's a perfectly natural and enjoyable thing to do. You humans get so uptight about it for absolutely no reason I can think of."

Theac rustled his papers loudly. "That's about enough of that conversation. Let's talk about something else."

"This book is really quite fascinating," Tiercelin gamely took up Theac's request. "It's about tawncats, the only book I could find in the library—"

"Why did you ask, Andres?" Corrin interrupted. "Is there something you think we should be concerned about?"

"I'm not sure. The prince hasn't taken a woman to his bed in weeks. It's such an abrupt change from his previous behaviour that I wondered if maybe his accident had something to do with it," Andres said, none of the redness fading from his light brown skin. "It made me question if his health is really okay, that's all."

"The winged folk have noticed the same thing." Tiercelin grinned. "But the answer to your question is no. He's fully recovered."

"This is NOT any of our business!" Theac snapped.

"Maybe he's lost interest," Zamaril offered, looking as serious as Andres. Talyn sighed inwardly. At least she had two talons who could manage to talk about sex without cringing with embarrassment.

"Being so close to dying, it might have changed him. What do you think, Captain? You're a woman."

"Thanks for noticing," she said dryly. She knew from firsthand experience that Cuinn had certainly not lost interest or ability, but she was hardly about to admit that to them. "If Tiercelin says he's okay, then we shouldn't worry."

"Exactly, can we change the subject?" Theac asked.

"Maybe he's got a secret love nest," Tiercelin speculated. The book lay forgotten on his lap as he warmed to the task of needling Theac.

Talyn shot him a look, pretending seriousness, but happily joining the game. "Prince Cuinn isn't stupid enough to go off to a secret love nest without protection."

"Maybe he's following Azrilan's lead and expanding his interests to include men?" Tiercelin waggled his eyebrows.

"In that case, maybe our Zamaril is in with a chance. He is very pretty." Andres smirked.

Theac's face reddened further.

Corrin shot Zamaril a sideways look, stifled his smile. "I don't think winged princes are Zamaril's type."

"Tiercelin's pretty too," Zamaril commented, deliberately not looking at Theac. "I think I even heard Prince Cuinn call him that once."

"Right, that's it," Theac barked, slamming his ale glass on the table. "I'm off home where I can have a sensible conversation."

They waited until the door closed behind him before bursting into raucous laughter.

"Did you really find something interesting in that book of yours?" Andres asked once the laughter died down.

"According to this, tawncats are pack animals, but without a hierarchy." Tiercelin's face lit up as it always did when he was fascinated by a topic. "This author thinks family groupings have not only a physical but mental bond that allows them to keep track of each other when hunting, and also sense when one of them is in danger."

"That could explain how Jasper found Prince Cuinn in the mines," Zamaril said.

"It doesn't explain how Vengeance is using one of them to murder people." Corrin made a face.

"Is the author still alive?" Talyn gestured to the book.

"Long dead, I'm afraid." Tiercelin sighed. "He lived not long after winged folk first settled in Mithranar, so tawncats and other creatures of the forest were at the forefront of their minds. Nothing new has been written on them in decades."

Talyn stood, gathering her papers. "I'd best get these to Ravinire before he gets too grumpy. I'll see you all in the morning."

"Captain?" Zamaril's voice stopped her at the door, a note of warning in it that had her immediately on edge. "Halun was down in Dock City this afternoon, as we discussed."

Since Cuinn had stated his intention to go back to being the Shadowhawk, she'd employed her talons as the go-between to check for messages from the Shadowhawk's contacts. The first time one of them had gone down, there hadn't been much, with most people presumably thinking the Shadowhawk's long absence meant he was gone or dead. But Zamaril had left new markings and Halun had gone earlier in the day to see if there had been any responses.

"And?"

"He wasn't specific." They never were. Never out loud. And never in the citadel. "But he said there was something waiting."

Code for one of the contacts leaving a message for the Shadowhawk... a message Halun would no doubt be passing to Cuinn during his current shift. "Thanks, Zamaril. We'd best be prepared."

They all nodded.

A SHARP TAPPING on the glass of her balcony door woke Talyn instantly. She rolled out of bed and padded over to the door, unsurprised to see the Shadowhawk outside, heavily cloaked and masked.

The material was plastered to his skin from the rain, and Cuinn's glamour wasn't hiding the deep shadows under his eyes—he was under stress.

"Come in," she said, concerned. "You're soaked."

"No." His hand gripped her wrist and pulled her outside. "I don't want to risk being seen in case they're watching your quarters. In this spot I can hide us in the shadows."

She searched his face. "Is something wrong?"

"A ship docked in the harbour this afternoon. The bulk of its cargo is grain," Cuinn said. "Halun collected the message from my Dock Quarter contact."

"And you want to go and steal it?" she asked.

"You were at the council meeting yesterday. The increased taxes in Dock City are already having a detrimental impact on the human folk." He took a breath. "The grain is scheduled to be unloaded tomorrow morning. If we can get it off the ship tonight, my network can distribute it throughout Dock City. It won't be as easy, but we can do it without the help of Saniya's group."

She considered that. "You've been quiet for months, so the WingGuard won't be expecting you to hit this ship. But Vengeance could be a problem. If they really have been able to re-establish themselves so quickly, they might see the grain arrival as an opportunity to ambush you. Saniya knows what targets you go for, not to mention they'll be desperate for supplies too."

His smile flashed. "Exactly. Which is why this ship is such a good opportunity. If Vengeance come for us, we spring their ambush—depleting their manpower even further. Maybe we could even capture one of them, find out who their Montagni contact is. What do you say, Captain?"

She hesitated. "Where is your Wolf guard?"

"Surrounding my tower. Tiercelin just took over the night shift, and I told him what I was planning. He wasn't happy about it, but he helped me sneak out when I promised I wouldn't do anything without talking to you first."

Talyn let out a breath. It was risky—it hadn't been that long since she'd struck her deal with Mithanis, and sparking an open battle with Vengeance in the streets of Dock City could just lead to escalating violence.

And the consequences if they were caught, particularly for Cuinn, were unimaginable.

But she'd promised to trust him. And she'd meant it.

"I know what you fear," he said softly. "But this was my life before you came. It's all I know to do to protect my people."

"*This was why you came back,*" Sari whispered.

"I never thought I'd say this, but you're as bad as every other Dumnorix I know," she muttered, conceding.

A thick silence fell suddenly, the only sound the rain falling around them. He shifted his weight uneasily, like she'd touched a nerve. "I haven't... since you told me I've not thought about it much. It all seems so... unreal. My whole life I ignored my father, his identity, who his family was. All of it. And even now there's so much else going on that needs my attention."

She touched his arm. "I understand. It's a lot to take in. Whenever you want to talk, I'm here."

"Another time." He firmed his shoulders. "Tonight there's grain to be reappropriated."

"I meant it when I promised you I'd help," she said. "But I want more protection for you than just me, so I'm going to bring some of the talons. I assume you have a way to sneak out of the citadel?"

He nodded. "Gather the others and I'll meet you by the back entrance to the barracks' kitchens, it's not far from there."

TALYN DRESSED in dark breeches and shirt and a black oilskin cloak, and pinned her hair in a braid at the base of her neck. Finally, she shoved a black mask into her pocket and slid a sheathed knife into the small of her back.

Sari's daggers she left behind—they were far too distinctive if spotted by a Falcon or Vengeance member, or anyone else out and about on this rainy night.

Her talons had individual rooms on the floor below hers, and it didn't take long to wake them all and let them know what was happening.

"We're going to help the Shadowhawk?" Halun didn't seem to understand.

She hesitated. "You wanted me to let you fight, Halun. This is me letting you loose."

"Finally," Zamaril breathed, then ducked back into his room to dress. Corrin's face shone with the same delight when she woke him.

She went to Andres last—he was still awake, reading by lamplight. "I'm leaving you here to keep watch. If anything goes wrong or someone comes looking for me, you send a Wolf to come and warn us as fast as you can. Okay?" she said.

He considered that a moment. "As long as I get to come next time and one of the other talons stays behind."

"Agreed."

Theac was going to murder her when she informed him of all this tomorrow. But if the worst happened and Ravinire came storming to the Wolves' barracks asking questions while they were gone, Theac would honestly be able to say he knew nothing—given he now lived down in Dock City with his family—and any song mage would read that. At least they would be protected.

The four of them, all dressed in black and carrying masks, met the waiting Shadowhawk at the back entrance to the kitchens.

"Before we go." Talyn looked each of her talons in the eyes. "You know the consequences if we're caught. Not just for you, but for all the Wolves. Not to mention that you could be hurt or killed if Vengeance try an ambush. Are you absolutely sure you want to come?"

"The captain is right," Cuinn interjected as they all opened their mouths to insist that yes, they wanted to come. "You are not just risking yourselves. You have to remember that. If you get exposed, the Wolves in your details will be affected by the consequences."

She flashed him a grateful glance as it became obvious he'd used a touch of magic in his voice. All three talons sank into thoughtful silence.

"I want to come," Corrin said eventually. "But I won't forget I have other lives in my hands. If I need to make the choice between with-drawing or risking capture or exposure, I'll withdraw."

"As will I," Halun said gravely.

Zamaril simply nodded.

"What's the plan?" Corrin asked.

"A merchant ship docked this afternoon carrying grain," Talyn said. "Now that Vengeance knows the Shadowhawk is alive, they might be planning an ambush. If that's the case, we'll spring the trap, then get the supplies off the ship."

"My Dock Quarter contacts will be helping with that part of it. They're ready to go," Cuinn added.

Halun nodded. "Good."

"Let's do this." Zamaril pulled his mask snugly down over his features.

Tonight there would be five Shadowhawks.

DOCK CITY WAS MOSTLY DESERTED GIVEN the late hour and the drenching rain, and Cuinn and the Wolves were mere shadows flitting along the streets. They easily evaded two Patrolmen making their rounds near the docks and came in over the roof of a warehouse across from the main wharves. Their target, *The Black Hand,* was anchored a short distance out.

"Looks deserted," Corrin observed.

"It won't be," Halun rumbled. "Not if there's grain for the winged folk on board."

Cuinn nodded. "There's usually a Falcon detail guarding these ships. They'll be stationed inside in this weather."

"Zamaril, how would you get onboard without being detected?" Corrin asked.

"From the water," he said. "And make sure to climb the side of the ship in shadow. There's not much moonlight under that rain cloud, but you never know if that will clear unexpectedly. So, I'd go up the port side. That section of the deck should be pretty dark too."

Talyn glanced at Cuinn. "The question is, are Vengeance here? And if so, are they already on board, or waiting here somewhere, watching for us to move?"

At her side, Cuinn stiffened suddenly, pointing down. Petro had just walked into sight, another man with him. "Vengeance won't wait for us on the ship. They'd know Falcons will be there too."

"True," Talyn murmured. "Zamaril, go down and get into position near Petro. If Vengeance spring anything, show yourself and tell Petro and his people to get out of here."

"And what do we do?" he asked.

"Put them down," she said coldly. The time for arrests and saving lives was gone. She'd given Saniya her single chance. If they were now sending tawncats to murder children in their beds… she didn't want those types of killers left alive. "We'll have your back."

Cuinn glanced her way, something unreadable flashing over his glamoured human face. She didn't soften—while she understood his aversion to violence, in this instance they couldn't afford to show any weakness.

Zamaril rose lithely to his feet while Talyn shifted and continued giving orders.

"Halun, shadow him. If things go awry, you get in there and help. Shadowhawk and I will circle around from behind Petro, spring the trap if it's there. Corrin, you stay here with an overview of the situation. If we get in trouble we'll herd them in this direction so you can throw those knives of yours."

Halun followed Zamaril into the night while Corrin settled into position. Cuinn rose too, determination in his face. The sight gave her a sudden, sharp worry for his safety. She pushed it away, telling herself to stop being a fool.

"Be careful." She couldn't help herself.

"You too, Captain."

MOVING SWIFTLY, Talyn and Cuinn came out the back of the ware-house and circled the block. Talyn led the way, one hand on the knife at her back, eyes scanning the way ahead for any movement. The streets were dark and empty, her sight limited by the curtain of falling rain soaking through her clothes and hair.

They circled the dark streets surrounding the warehouse, seeing nothing out of place. Talyn made sure to scan what she could see of the rooftops too, but apart from the rain, nothing moved around them.

Eventually Cuinn glanced at her, questioning.

"I think we're clear," she murmured.

They came up behind Petro and his associate, catching the murmur of their soft conversation. At the sight of them, Zamaril and Halun emerged from where he'd been waiting in a nearby alley.

Petro looked taken aback by the number of people with the Shadowhawk, his gaze lingering curiously on their masks. "I was surprised to hear from you, Shadowhawk. We were worried that something had happened."

"I got hurt on that last job," Cuinn replied. "Took me a while to get back on my feet, but I'm good to go now."

"Glad to hear it." Relief ringed Petro's voice, but he glanced warily at Talyn and the others. "You brought help."

"Thought we might need it," Cuinn said. "Don't worry, they can be trusted. I hope you're being careful, Petro."

His eyes darkened in concern. "Do you really think it was Vengeance behind those murders like the Wolves do?"

Cuinn shook his head. "I don't know, but either way, we all need to be careful."

"Is there any chance there's an ambush waiting for us on the ship?" Talyn muffled her voice as best she could. "We didn't spot anything on our way here."

Petro shook his head. "We've had our eye on it since before dusk. Nobody has rowed out there apart from crew. Plus six Falcons have been on board since it arrived. They changed shift at dusk."

She looked at Cuinn, matched his frown. Where were they? It was odd that Vengeance wouldn't take a prime opportunity like this to come after them again.

"*Or they weren't behind the recent murders, and like you assumed, are too busy trying to keep together what's left of their gang while Falcons and Patrol are hunting them all over the city,"* Sari murmured.

Talyn nodded slightly. *"Then who murdered the family?"*

"We should move." Petro glanced up at the sky. "We've got some boats ready to row out—a friend organised that for us earlier today. The rain will provide good cover."

"Good. Row for the port side." Talyn glanced at Zamaril.

Petro nodded and headed off. Talyn caught Corrin's gaze from the roof above and made a few signals telling him to stay where he was to watch for an ambush at their rear before following along behind.

Talyn, Halun, Zamaril and Cuinn clambered into one long rowboat, while Petro and his friends took another, and three other men materialised to row a third. A tense quarter-turn followed in which Talyn kept glancing between the sky and the docks, hoping nobody would appear to notice the boats rowing out. The rain and darkness helped hide them, though, and they reached the port side of *The Black Hand* without incident.

She sent Zamaril in to scout while they bobbed on the water below. He climbed up the anchor chain and slipped over the railing, disappearing into the shadows. Several long moments later, he leaned over the railing above and gave the all clear signal.

Cuinn tossed a rope to the Wolf, who secured it and waved them up. Talyn went first, Cuinn next, Halun remaining behind. The occupants of the other boats followed suit, leaving a rower in each to move them around closer to the ship's cargo hold.

The deck was empty of Falcons and crew when she swung herself over the side.

"There's only a skeleton crew on board and they're all asleep belowdecks," Zamaril murmured. "Three Falcons are guarding the hold, and two more are stationed at the top of the stairs leading down to the passageway where the hold entrance is."

"This is my part," Cuinn said, moving forward before she could stop him. Talyn and Zamaril followed close behind.

Cuinn didn't even try to hide their presence from the two Falcons at the top of a narrow stairwell leading down into the dark bowels of the ship. Both winged men straightened at the appearance of three masked and hooded figures, drawing steel with a loud ring.

"Don't." Cuinn's voice rang out, but it sounded nothing like Cuinn. It was all Shadowhawk, and it carried a potent mix of imperious order and fear. Talyn almost took a step back in reaction. "Drop those swords and back into that cabin to your left, and you get to live. We're not interested in hurting you if you don't get in our way."

The Falcons looked at each other, then shifted their gaze to Cuinn, Talyn and Zamaril. She stood still, poised, ready to fight in an instant.

And then the Falcons were dropping their swords with a clatter onto the deck and backing into the narrow room, closing the door behind them. Cuinn immediately stepped forward and latched the door. "That'll hold them for a bit," he said with satisfaction.

"That magic of his is impressive," Sari piped up.

"You don't say."

The three Falcons below were dealt with in the same way, and then they had free access to the hold. Zamaril ran back up to fetch Petro and the others, while Talyn and Cuinn dropped into the hold and set about opening the exterior door.

The Shadowhawk's people had done this plenty of times before, and the cargo was swiftly and efficiently unloaded into the waiting boats. Halun switched places with Zamaril, leaving the thief to manage the boat while he put his considerable strength into hauling cargo out of the hold. Talyn didn't miss Petro shooting several glances Halun's way. Despite the mask and cloak, it wouldn't be hard to guess his identity given his obvious bulk and strength. She could only hope if Petro guessed anything about who was helping the Shadowhawk tonight he would keep it to himself.

Within a full-turn they were rowing the heavily listing boats away from the ship and towards the deserted beach of the western head-land. Three more of Petro's people waited to transfer the crates into several waiting carts.

In another full-turn they'd packed the carts full and their drivers were clambering up, calling soft instructions to the horses to start moving.

"I'm a proper criminal now, Sari," Talyn said with a touch of glee.

"I never thought I'd see the day," came the gloomy response. *"You don't feel even a little bit guilty, do you?"*

"I really don't." That surprised her. It went against everything she'd been for most of her life. But this was her new life. And it felt right.

"We'll use a few warehouses in the Dock Quarter to keep them hidden for now," Petro said as the carts trundled away. "It might take some time to distribute it safely without Saniya's help though."

"Do your best," Cuinn told Petro. "And thanks for your help tonight."

Petro hesitated, gaze flicking uncertainly to Talyn and the other Wolves. "Where was Saniya tonight?"

Cuinn stiffened. "Saniya's group is Vengeance, Petro."

Petro's face whitened with shock. "You're sure?"

"Yes. Our work with her is over. Never again."

Petro nodded slowly, taking a steadying breath. "It's never easy is it? What we do, trying to work out what's right and wrong. Her people helped us so much, but..."

"I know."

"I'll see you around, Shadowhawk." Petro managed a faint smile, then turned and ran off into the darkness. His helpers followed suit and soon all of them had been swallowed up by the night.

DAWN WAS ONLY three or four full-turns away by the time they reached the back entrance of the barracks' kitchens and split up to return to their rooms.

Instead of returning to his tower, Cuinn followed Talyn back to her quarters. Soaked to the skin, she tugged off her mask and cloak and went straight upstairs to strip off the rest of her dripping clothes and leave them in a wet pile on the floor. Pulling on a robe, she hunted around for a towel and blanket, then tossed them down to Cuinn.

By the time she came back downstairs, he was pacing back and forth, glamour gone, rubbing his soaked hair with the towel, wings dripping all over the floor by her unlit fireplace. A frown creased his face. "Where were they?"

"Vengeance? I don't know." She thought about starting a fire to help them dry off, then discarded it. If anyone out there was watching, or even passing by, the light would make it clear Prince Cuinn was in her private quarters in the early hours of the morning. Damn the winged folk and their insistence on pretty glass everywhere.

"They should have been there."

"But they weren't." She pushed damp hair back from her face. "I'm not entirely surprised. The WingGuard and Patrol is still actively searching for them throughout the city and they don't have access to any of the weapons or supplies they had at their base. They probably didn't have enough to come at us tonight."

He stopped pacing suddenly, a shiver racking his frame. "I wanted them to be there, Talyn. I can't stop them from killing more of my people if they're not there."

"You're wet and cold." She picked up the blanket and towel he'd discarded on the floor and handed them to him. "Dry off before you make yourself sick."

He nodded absently and began rubbing the towel over his hair and face. Eventually he gave up, dropping the towel before wrapping the blanket around his shoulders and dropping onto her couch.

A sigh escaped her. He really needed to go. Ignoring her common sense, she went to sit beside him. "Are you all right?"

His eyes were firmly on the floor, but he reached out to touch the back of her hand where it rested on her knee. Talyn's breath hitched.

"I am. What we did tonight, it was good. It will help. I just wish... I wish I could do more," he breathed. "I need to *be* more, especially if your Callanan are right about what's coming."

"Does it help if I tell you that need is part of being a Dumnorix?" she asked, shifting to face him. "We don't do well when we're kept apart from those of our blood, and you've had that your entire life. This drive you have, to do more, to do better, that's part of it too."

"Tonight, when you told Zamaril to kill if Vengeance attacked..."

I've never told you why the Shadowhawk doesn't use violence," he said softly.

She looked at him, surprised by the odd note in his voice. "After I learned who you were, I figured it was because while you were trying to help the human folk, you didn't want to hurt Falcons in the process, because the winged folk are your people too."

"That's part of it." He swallowed. "It's the reason I insisted on my network never using violence either. But for me... I'm a song mage, Talyn. If I hurt someone, I *feel* that... their pain, and despair. It's not in me to willingly inflict that on someone. And to deliberately kill a person... what I would feel... I think it could break me."

Her heart thudded. She hadn't thought, hadn't considered what that would be like.

"Do you think that makes me a coward?" His voice was barely audible.

"Not for a second." She framed his cheek with her hand, turning his head to force him to meet her eyes. "You are one of the bravest people I know. The courage you have... all those years alone, to keep fighting as the Shadowhawk, without anyone to help or to trust. And then in your recovery. To keep fighting so hard despite the pain you must have been in. Cuinn, you are no coward."

He sucked in a breath, eyes shining with tears. "You really mean that," he murmured.

"I can't lie around you, remember?" She smiled a little, trying to lighten his mood.

His hand curled around hers, their fingers tangling. Abruptly she realised how close they'd gotten, unconsciously leaning towards each other on the couch until she could feel his warm breath on her face.

Talyn hesitated on that clifftop for only a moment before closing the distance and kissing him like she'd wanted to ever since that moment in the Shadowhawk's apartment. The instant they touched, fire burned through her. Cuinn's hands slid to her hips, helping as she shifted forward into his lap, her fingers going straight to the buttons on his soaking shirt.

The kiss was fierce, demanding, bodies pressing together as close as they could get. He had her robe untied and off in a matter of seconds, prompting a laughing, breathless, "Don't remind me how many times you've done this before."

"You seem pretty expert yourself, Captain," he half-breathed, half-groaned a moment later when her mouth found his neck and began trailing kisses towards his collarbone.

There was a glorious tangle of limbs and mouths, and then, "How do you do this with wings?" she complained, utterly failing to get his shirt off his shoulders.

He laughed, warm and rumbling in her ear, then he guided her hands to the other buttons along his hipbone and ribs, slipping them undone with a soft murmur, "See, it's easy."

Then there was warm skin under her palms and she just wanted more, more, more....

A tiny voice in the back of her mind tried to speak up, to say this couldn't happen, that she was complicating things a hundredfold, but she shoved it away.

This was the reckless Talyn coming out and being allowed full rein, and with it all the delight of wrapping her body around Cuinn's and bringing them together heedless of the consequences. And when his emotions hit her, when he could no longer hold back what he was feeling, any doubt that might have remained was swept away as if it had never been.

She wanted him. He wanted her. And it was breathtaking.

It was full morning when Talyn awoke, sunlight shining through the glass and into her eyes. She was alone on the sofa, half buried under the blankets and towels they'd used to dry off. Cuinn's scent was still on her skin, but he was gone.

Judging by the light, she'd been sound asleep for several full-turns and the Wolves would be returning from their morning wall run and starting breakfast. Theac was not going to be impressed with her.

She made a face—if only he knew what she'd been doing.

A sharp rapping at the door startled her from a tumultuous

descent into a tangle of conflicting emotions about what she'd allowed to happen the previous night. "Who is it?" she called, rolling hurriedly off the couch, muttering at herself when she got halfway to the door before realising she was naked.

"It's me." Ravinire's impatient voice rapped out.

Talyn cursed under her breath and returned to the couch, picking up the towels and shoving them under the cushions. Once she was satisfied that they were hidden from casual observance, she tied on her robe and went to the door. The Falcon's eyebrows lifted at finding her still in her quarters and barely dressed.

"Good morning." She greeted him before he could say anything, then winced internally at how ridiculously chirpy she'd sounded. Shit. She had to get it together. "What can I do for you?"

Sari coughed. *"That was even worse."*

"There was an incident down at the docks overnight. I'd appreciate it if you could turn out your Wolves onto the drill yard. They'll need to be questioned."

His words instantly sent discomfort and awkwardness flying and replaced them with fear and dread. "Questioned about what?" She squared her shoulders, trying to behave as if she had no idea why he was asking this.

"It's not for you to question my orders, Captain. Do as I ask, and make it quick." Ravinire turned and strode away, wings held stiffly behind him.

Talyn shut the door and ran upstairs to dress.

273

CHAPTER 25

*Q*uinn paced his bedroom. It was already too hot from the bright sunshine slanting through the windows, but he didn't notice. He couldn't sit still. He could barely restrain himself from spreading his wings and flying as high as it was possible to go.

Energy filled him, bright and infectious and seemingly endless.

She'd been sleeping when he woke, her breath soft against his chest, her arms wrapped loosely around him, their legs tangled together. And somehow, in that moment of deep, untainted happiness, the fear that had been his constant companion since Raya's death was gone.

Things were a hundred times more complicated now. But they were also a hundred times simpler. He wasn't going to hide. He didn't need to hide. Not completely. Not anymore. Because Talyn wasn't Raya. She was strong and capable and could take care of herself better than anyone else he knew.

And *he* had changed. The terrible injuries, being unmasked before his Wolves... he'd grown stronger from that. Had begun to realise he was capable too, more than he'd imagined he could be. And with her and the Wolves behind him...

The banging on his front door sent him leaping into the air in startlement. From where he was curled up in a patch of sunlight under the window, Jasper let out an undignified huffing sound.

"Are you laughing at me?" Cuinn stared at him.

Jasper cocked his head, blinked innocently.

Shooting a scowl at the tawncat, Cuinn left the room and spread his wings to swoop down to the ground floor entrance. His mood didn't even sour at the sight of Brightwing standing there.

"What brings you by, Flight-Leader?"

"I'm assigning some Falcons to your detail for a full-turn or so. The Falcon wants the full wing of Wolves turned out for an inspection."

The fear returned then, but only out of habit, and it kept itself a faint hint at the back of his mind. Anger unfurled in its place. "Why?"

"He didn't say why, Your Highness." Brightwing maintained a thin veneer of politeness but his contempt for Cuinn was obvious. "I've already sent your detail back to their barracks."

"Leave your Falcons here. I don't want them." Cuinn shoved past him, walked out the door and leapt into the sky.

THE WOLVES WERE LINED up neatly on the parade ground, Ravinire and his lackey Grasswing there too. Grasswing looked like he was counting while Talyn stood off to the side with Ravinire, Theac hovering nearby. The day remained hot, but stormy grey clouds on the eastern horizon presaged rain sooner rather than later.

None of them noticed Cuinn landing—a strong sign of how unsettled they were—so he lingered, wanting to get a read on the situation before intervening. He was angry enough that Ravinire had summoned his wing without telling him, but if it was worse than that...

"What's this about, sir?" Talyn's voice was clear, confident. "The wing is all here, you don't need to go and count them."

"There was an incident at the docks late last night." Ravinire's voice was hard as stone. "Cargo belonging to the royal family was stolen from a ship by the Shadowhawk."

Cuinn checked the urge to reveal his presence as shock rippled through him. The Shadowhawk had been active the entire time the Wolves had been in existence and they'd never been called out like this before. Why now?

If Talyn was worried, she didn't sound it. Only annoyance edged her not-quite-polite-enough tone. "I don't like the insinuation that my wing had anything to do with that," she said evenly. "I would know if any of them were involved with the Shadowhawk."

"I agree." Ravinire's voice had gone ice cold.

"Then why turn them all out like this? I expect you to trust my word when I tell you they're all here, sir."

"And I am your superior officer," Ravinire snapped. "I shouldn't have to point out that you are not a princess in this country, Captain Dynan. It is not your job to involve yourself in the struggles of the human population."

"I'm aware of that. We've had this conversation before."

"Yes, we have," he said coldly. "And I thought we understood each other."

"Sir, I'm confused. Do you actually have any evidence that members of my wing are involved in the Shadowhawk's activities?"

"That's irrelevant. If I see fit to question you, or do a head count of your wing, I will."

She was angry. It leapt clear across the intervening space to Cuinn, and probably the song mages amongst the Wolves, if they were paying attention.

Ravinire seemed to pick up on it too. "If I were you, I wouldn't forget what happened to your grandparents. The protection of Prince Cuinn is your only job here in Mithranar," he said tightly. "I suggest you focus on that."

Cuinn's own temper sparked then, and he'd abruptly had enough of standing in the background. But Talyn's fury was increasing, and she was already retorting as Cuinn began walking towards them.

"I'm trying to protect him, sir," she said stiffly. "But I wonder exactly how far you'd like me to go in protecting him, for example, from his eldest brother, who would be more than happy if Prince Cuinn ended up dead."

Theac was the first to notice Cuinn approaching, and he straightened, looking momentarily worried. Cuinn sent him a touch of reassurance with his magic.

"You go too far," Ravinire snapped, fury radiating from his rigid stance. "Your position can be terminated at any time, Captain Dynan. Talon Parksin could quite easily replace you. Press any further, and you will be expelled from this country today."

At those words, Cuinn's simmering anger broke into white-hot fury and he quickened his strides, simultaneously gathering his magic. "Ravinire!" he snapped.

Talyn and Ravinire both turned to stare at him in astonishment, both having been too focused on their argument to have noticed him.

"Your Highness." Ravinire bowed his head politely.

"Talyn Dynan is captain of my protective wing," Cuinn said coldly, keeping the words measured, controlled, lacing them with magic. "If you threaten her with dismissal again without seeking permission from me, I will have you summarily removed from your position and expelled from the WingGuard. Are we clear?"

Ravinire performed a visible double-take at Cuinn's sudden assertiveness. Satisfaction curled through him. A second later the Falcon's temper sparked, burning against his magic—no doubt at being spoken to like that by someone he'd always regarded as a weak-willed fool. "Your Highness, I am the Falcon. It is my responsibility to manage the dismissal of WingGuard officers."

Cuinn's lip curled. And then he threw his gathered magic at the man, not even needing to use his voice as he cowed Ravinire until the winged man took a full step back, shaken, shoulders hunched. Cuinn was so angry he barely registered Ravinire's emotions—he was throwing so much magic at the Falcon there was hardly any room for them to leak out.

When the man dropped to his knees, Cuinn let go. Talyn stared between them, stunned, as Ravinire slowly came back to his feet, looking more shaken than Cuinn had ever seen him.

"You forget which of us is the Falcon and which is the Acondor prince here, Ravinire," Cuinn said. "Don't you dare challenge me."

"Your Highness." Ravinire swallowed. "I apologise for my words."

"So you should," Cuinn said. "Captain Dynan's performance since arriving here has been beyond reproach. As has the performance of the Wolves. Next time you feel the urge to turn them all out and accuse them of something they haven't done, discuss it with me first."

"Yes, Your Highness," Ravinire gritted out.

"Get out and take Grasswing with you."

Ravinire had been thoroughly defeated by Cuinn's display of strength, but he was not a stupid man, and Cuinn had made a mistake by dropping his soft façade in his defence of the Wolves. Sickening realisation crossed the Falcon's face as he glanced between Talyn and Cuinn. His wings sagged, skin turning grey.

"It's you, isn't it?" he whispered in horror. "You're all involved?"

"No, we're not," Talyn said flatly. Her cool mask was back, calm and controlled. "And you have no evidence of anything."

He swallowed, straightened his shoulders. "I have to report you."

"You do that, and we'll all be dead within a week," Cuinn said softly. Once again he wrapped his magic around Ravinire, sure and strong. "Think about that, Falcon. Think about the kind of Mithranar you want to live in, and whether the death of Captain Dynan, myself, and all my Wolves will get you that world."

Ravinire's eyes flicked between them again, expression pale and sick. Without saying anything further, he turned and left.

"Captain?" Cuinn caught her attention from where she stared after Ravinire's retreating figure. "I'll make sure this doesn't happen again."

Worry flickered in her eyes. "He knows."

"He guesses. But he doesn't have any proof."

She stepped closer, and he almost smiled at her conflicting emotions—she wasn't sure whether to be furious or impressed with him. "What possessed you to do that? I had the situation under control."

"It's time to stop hiding and pretending," he said simply. "Do you know what I realised this morning, lying there with you curled up asleep in my arms? I don't fear anything as much as I fear going back to the pretence of weak, playboy Prince Cuinn. So it's time to shed the glamour. If Mithanis comes for me... well, I have sixty highly trained warriors to keep me safe."

Something in his face and voice, his determination, or maybe the lack of the debilitating fear that had always been there, seemed to register with her. She nodded slowly. "And a Ciantar, Prince Cuinn."

His smile was blinding. "And a Ciantar."

There was a cleared throat, then bootsteps as Theac came over. "Everything okay?"

Cuinn glanced at Talyn.

Theac read their expressions, his own turning grim. "The Falcon knows, doesn't he?"

"He guesses." Talyn let out a breath. "Cuinn interrupted him trying to fire me and lost his temper, rather spectacularly. It's safe to say Ravinire is starting to question the foolish prince façade."

Both of their worry hit Cuinn and he winced. "We're going to be fine. I'm not going to waltz into Mithanis's chambers and demand a duel. I'm just going to start acting more like myself... the real me. It's long past time."

"Your Highness." Theac bowed, then gestured to the Wolves, still gathered and pretending not to stare. "I doubt they heard much of that, but it will have been pretty clear what was going on."

"The song mages will have read a lot too," Cuinn murmured. He'd probably just revealed himself to more than just Ravinire.

Which gave him an idea. A *really* good idea.

"What?" Talyn read his change in expression and gave him a suspicious look.

He grinned at her. "It's time for Queencouncil, that's all. Who's on my detail this morning?"

"Corrin's unit," Theac said. "I'll get them." He strode off.

"We'll be fine, Captain," Cuinn murmured. Her worry hadn't faded much.

She took a deep breath and the emotion vanished, buried beneath her mask. "We should probably talk about—"

"Your Highness!" Corrin bowed, his detail only a few steps behind him. "Talon Parksin says we're going to Queencouncil?"

"That's right. Let's walk there. It's a lovely morning for it." Cuinn smiled, then winked at Talyn. "We'll talk soon, Captain."

His heart thudded a little as he walked away, Wolves surrounding him.

Brave words aside, they'd just entered extremely dangerous territory.

CUINN PUSHED OPEN the doors to the Queencouncil chamber, Corrin at his left shoulder, his Wolf detail immediately deploying around the room. Rain cascaded in a curtain down the side of the room with no wall—they'd barely made it under cover before the downpour had started.

"Keep a close eye out," he told the young Wolf in an undertone.

"Always do," Corrin assured him, green gaze already scanning the room in such a perfect imitation of Talyn that Cuinn almost smiled, despite the gravity of what he was doing. She'd made warriors of these humans, and he truly believed that none of the winged folk, Ravinire included, understood that.

Good.

The table in the centre of the room held the usual attendees. Ravinire was there, sickly pale, refusing to look at Cuinn. Who knew what the song mages in the room made of the Falcon's demeanour. His mother gave Cuinn a pointed look, communicating clearly she had no patience for any antics today. Azrilan smirked. Mithanis heaved an annoyed sigh as Cuinn slid into a chair at the table. "You're late."

"Sorry, but there's a reason for it. I'm here with a request."

"And that would be?" Mithanis asked.

"I want you to give me responsibility for hunting down what's left of Vengeance." Cuinn spoke as if he were commenting on the weather, leaving a beat once he finished for them to process what he'd said.

His mother sighed in irritation. "Cuinn, what foolishness is this?"

"I'm serious," he said. "I told you I wanted to do more to help, to pull my weight. I'd like you to give me this responsibility."

The councillors goggled. Cuinn, his brothers, and their mother ignored them, their attention only on each other.

"And what makes you think for a second you're capable of hunting down a criminal gang?" Genuine disbelief coloured Mithanis' voice.

"Any more than the WingGuard, who have failed miserably at it so far?" Cuinn shot a contempt-filled look at Ravinire—at whom he was still furious, how *dare* he threaten Talyn—then looked back to his brother. "To cover for his inadequacy, Ravinire called my Wolves out this morning to do a headcount, suspecting them of having something to do with what happened last night merely because some of them are human." Cuinn paused. "It gave me an idea. I think they're better suited to hunting a human criminal gang than Falcons."

Mithanis' shoulders relaxed slightly. "Ah, so you intend to outsource your rabble of a guard."

"Your Highness, I really don't think this is a good idea." Ravinire spoke out, still avoiding Cuinn's eyes. "We can't be sure members of the Wolves aren't connected to this criminal gang."

"Because they're human?" Cuinn asked, an edge to his voice. "I've already made it clear I don't appreciate you seeking to blame my Wolves because you and your Falcons have so far failed to find a single gang member since they escaped their compound."

"The Falcon has been protecting this country since you were a child, Cuinn. While you've been doing what?" His mother's voice was cool and sharp. To be expected. After all, Ravinire was her man— probably the one person she could count on whose loyalty was to her and not her powerful eldest son. Especially since Anrun Windsong had been dispatched back to the icy north.

A moment's fear took hold—what would she do if Ravinire told her what he suspected, that her own son was the Shadowhawk? Would he meet the same fate as Talyn's family? Or would she find some less permanent means of dealing with him? Cuinn wasn't sure... and the fact he couldn't be sure of his own mother hurt, more than he cared to admit. But he wasn't letting that fear back in. So he pushed it away and continued.

"Point taken." He inclined his head. "But who protected me when Vengeance came for you, Mother? My Wolves. So give me this job. Allow me to start sharing my load of the responsibility."

His mother's gaze sought his, searching, clearly seeking to see whether this was just another game of his. He allowed his magic to seep out, showing her his sincerity and the depth of his determination. It surprised her, unsettled her too. She glanced briefly at Mithanis, then back to him. "All right, Cuinn."

"You have a month," Mithanis interjected. "To demonstrate you're taking this seriously and come up with some results. Otherwise the responsibility goes back to the Falcon."

Their mother's face tightened—she didn't like Mithanis usurping her authority in making the unilateral decision—but she said nothing. Cuinn merely smiled. "Fair enough."

Across the table, he caught Azrilan's eye. His brother gave him a little nod—he wasn't sure whether it was condescension or genuine approval. Either way, he acknowledged Azrilan with a wink.

His brother winked back.

CHAPTER 26

*O*nce drill was over—an air of unease hanging over the Wolves like a pall following Ravinire's inspection—Talyn gathered with her talons in the common room. The queen was holding a formal dinner for the Queencouncil families that evening, and they needed to discuss the logistics of Cuinn's detail.

Heavy rainfall hammered on the roof as they talked. Talyn was half-focused on the conversation, half trying to juggle the multitude of worries on her mind. Not the least of which was the potential implications of what had happened between her and Cuinn the previous night, including the fact that despite all of those implications, she wanted it to happen again. Wanted *him.*

That then led to a plummeting sensation in her chest that she was pretty sure was terror. Untangling that was too difficult to contemplate, so she then forced her thoughts back to what to do now that Cuinn had essentially outed himself to the Falcon.

"Captain?" Halun's deep voice broke her reverie.

"I'm sorry." She shook her head, dragging herself back to the present. "What were you saying?"

"Theac was proposing a double guard for the dinner tonight, and we agree. My detail has the next two days off, so I'm happy for us to join Tiercelin's detail tonight."

"I agree." She nodded. "Do it."

Theac looked at her. "And you and I will be there as guests too."

"Since when are we going as guests?" She frowned.

Her second gave her a frustrated glance. "As I said earlier, all WingGuard captains from the protection flight have been invited— that's normal for an event like this, the queen likes to go all out for her most powerful lords. Some talons have been included too."

Tiercelin gave her a strange look. "Captain, is there something on your mind?"

"Nothing more than the obvious." She managed a smile. "I apologise for being distracted. The plan for tonight sounds solid. Well done, all of you."

The door to the outside suddenly pushed open. Corrin appeared, Cuinn just behind him. Both had rain-dampened hair and clothes, despite the cloaks they held over their heads. Talyn's gaze went straight to Corrin, whose green eyes were alight, his lean form trembling with energy.

"Dare I ask?" she said, rising to her feet.

Cuinn flashed her a smile before turning to Corrin. "The rest of the detail aren't out in the rain, are they?"

"Liadin is, because it's his job to watch from above," Corrin said without guilt. "We don't compromise for weather, Your Highness."

Talyn gave Corrin an approving look as Theac cleared his throat. "Can we help you with something, Prince Cuinn?"

"I've just come from Queencouncil," he said, all business. "I requested that we be given responsibility for hunting down what remains of Vengeance. My mother and Mithanis gave their approval."

A beat of silence. Talyn and Theac glanced at each other.

"We?" Talyn asked.

"The Wolves," he clarified. "The WingGuard has been useless so far, and I thought if we got royal approval, we have carte blanche to go after them any way we see fit. As long as we get results, my brother won't care how we do it."

She stared at him. "You're looking to establish cover for the Wolves operating down in Dock City. Because if we're down there instead of the WingGuard..."

"The Shadowhawk network is protected," Halun finished for her. "And we don't have to hide the fact we're going after Vengeance."

"Exactly." Cuinn beamed in satisfaction. His eyes flicked briefly to hers, communicating the same thing she was thinking. He'd done more than that. He'd found a way to devote significant resources to hunting and destroying a group that potentially threatened Mithranar, without exposing the Callanan informant's information.

After a moment's shocked silence, Theac cleared his throat. "We can do that, Your Highness."

"We get through tonight's dinner first," Talyn said to her talons. "And then tomorrow, we'll start planning."

The atmosphere in the room became charged, excited. Cuinn was letting the Wolves loose for the first time and they couldn't wait. She tried to keep the fear buried because she knew she couldn't hold them back forever.

"I'd like a moment with Captain Dynan if you don't mind?" Cuinn said. "And then I've got to get to lunch with Irial."

"We'll be waiting outside, Your Highness," Corrin said, and disappeared through the outside door. The others saluted with far more vigour than usual, then left via the internal door through to the kitchens, no doubt intent on lunch before the afternoon's training.

Once they were gone, a thick silence descended. Talyn was trying to work out what to say when he beat her to it.

"I won't stay long," he said. "But I wanted to talk to you, to make things clear. When I woke this morning, you were sleeping. You looked so peaceful I didn't have the heart to wake you. I didn't leave because what happened between us was some brief interlude I'll promptly forget about."

"Oh." She swallowed. She hadn't thought that—it was impossible to think that after what had happened between them. His magic had made it abundantly clearly how much what was happening meant to him during every moment of their encounter, and she doubted she'd been hiding much either—it hadn't been possible to hold back. But that he'd thought to reassure her…

"I also wanted to make it clear that what happened last night was very… precious to me, Talyn." He held her gaze. "I know that it's different for you, because of everything you've been through, because of who you are. I also know that there are many important reasons that a relationship between us can't happen. But we agreed we would be honest with each other and so there it is."

She let out a breath, gaze dropping to the floor. "You're making this very easy on me. I'm not sure I deserve that."

He was there suddenly, one hand framing her cheek. "You deserve everything," he whispered. He pressed a warm kiss to her forehead, lingering there as if he couldn't bear to move away. She fought the urge to reach out and draw him closer.

"It meant something to me too," she whispered, swallowing. "But if we keep going down that path, it will only end in heartache for both of us. Because of who we are, there's no future in it." Even if she might be starting to wish there was.

"I would never want to cause you pain. Not after…" He took a deep, shaky breath, then stepped away from her. "As for what I said earlier, about not hiding anymore. I don't intend to be reckless or foolish about it. For as long as I can, I'll work to keep Mithanis from seeing me as a threat. But the playboy prince is gone."

Talyn cleared her throat, tried to return to some semblance of rational thought. "I'm glad for you, that you've reached a place where you feel strong enough to do this. And you know we're here to keep you safe."

"No protest," he murmured. "You trust me to do this."

"Without hesitation." Their gazes met, held.

Again, it was Cuinn turning away, this time heading for the door. "I'll see you at dinner tonight, Captain?"

She tried to smile, failed. "I'll be there."

As the door closed behind him, she found herself frozen there. "*Sari?*"

"*Tal?*"

"*I wish you were here.*"

"*This isn't something you need me for. It's something you need to work through for yourself.*"

"*I know that. But I always felt stronger, clearer, when you were around.*"

"*I still am,*" Sari whispered. "*And the truth is... it breaks my non-existent heart to think you'd never have met him, known him, if I had lived.*"

That was too much. Too soon. Too painful.

She fled her thoughts and went to join the training Wolves.

THE DINNER WAS stuffy and overwhelmingly boring. Talyn was glad that Theac was beside her to talk to, or she was afraid she might have fallen asleep somewhere in the midst of it. It brought back memories of some of the court events she'd had to attend during her time in Ryathl—and this time she didn't have Leviana or Ariar around for entertainment.

Instead they were seated at a table with other WingGuard captains. Astonishingly, three of the winged men had offered a polite nod to Theac and Talyn when they'd first sat down—Strongswoop being one of them. And when Theac had commented on the rich flavour of the fish served as an earlier course, one of the captains had asked whether Theac fished much, and if he could offer his thoughts on the best locations to fish in Feather Bay.

Cuinn was at a table with his mother and brothers and Queen-council lords. It was quite a distance away, but Theac and Talyn had made sure to seat themselves where they had a direct and clear view to the prince.

When a gaggle of winged women descended on the prince of song, Talyn rolled her eyes and turned her attention to the food before her. It was well-made and flavourful, but she wasn't overly hungry. Too much had happened. Too many thoughts careening through her head for something so mundane as hunger to make an appearance.

"I can't decide whether to be impressed or worried by his sudden change in behaviour," Theac murmured at her side.

She glanced up, surprised. The women were leaving Cuinn's table, expressions of disappointment and annoyance on their faces. She couldn't help the twinge of relief she felt, even though she was horrified at herself for even *thinking* about being jealous.

"Do you think we have to worry about Ravinire tonight?" Theac asked.

"No." She considered. "If Ravinire was going to go straight to the queen, he would have done it and we'd all be dead or arrested by now. No, he's weighing his choice. We have to worry about what that choice will be, and when he will make it, but it won't be tonight."

"I feel the same," he grumbled. "Which means I'd much rather be in my warm bed right now."

"With your beautiful wife, of course," Talyn teased, laughing when Theac scowled. "Married life seems to suit you, Theac."

His face softened. "Maybe Prince Cuinn should consider it. If he chose a bride from a powerful family, it would be support for him against his brothers."

He'd tried that. Mithanis had killed Raya. Talyn shuddered, imagining the pain Cuinn must have felt. Knowing it all too well.

"I don't see Prince Cuinn settling down with one woman," she said lightly, ignoring how the idea of Cuinn with any woman but her made her insides squeeze. Ugh. She rolled her eyes at herself.

Theac glanced at her. "Now he's even got you buying his act, Captain."

She sighed sheepishly. "All right. Fine. Although neither the queen nor Mithanis would approve Cuinn marrying anyone from a powerful family. Never going to happen." She didn't mention what Cuinn had told her about his mother planning a match for him with the Montagni princess. It had been clear that wasn't for any ears but hers.

"When do you think the betrothal will happen?" Sari roused. *"It's been well over a month since he told you about it."*

"What if he did it without their approval?" Theac asked at the same time.

Ignoring Sari so she could give Theac her full attention, Talyn put her fork down, frowning. "What are you getting at?"

"With the right support, Cuinn has a shot at—"

"Stop!" She cut over him before he could say the words. "And remember where we are."

The conversation around them was loud, and Theac had been practically whispering, but even so those words were far too dangerous to be spoken aloud.

He scowled, but nodded. "Sometimes I forget you have another home to go back to," he said, turning to his food. "I wonder if you ever consider what it would mean to Mithranar to have a better person sitting its throne."

She made no reply to that, attacking her food with a vengeance.

CHAPTER 27

The Wolves patrolled Dock City every night for the next two weeks. Talyn didn't think it would be as easy as Vengeance showing themselves to the patrols, but for a start she wanted a visible presence on the streets. Her hope was that it might deter any further murders, or at the very least make them difficult to undertake without being caught.

And while they patrolled, the Wolves spoke to those they passed on the streets, seeking information about unusual behaviour or people in the city. Again, they didn't get much—Vengeance were too smart to betray themselves to anyone that would talk to the Wolves— but the patrols were a cover for where they were getting their *real* information.

The Shadowhawk.

Talyn went out with Cuinn as the Shadowhawk every night. Slowly, steadily, with messages moving back and forth through his network, added to the occasional bit of info Talyn received from Savin, they began to unravel what remained of Vengeance in Dock City.

Within days, based on a snippet Cuinn obtained from an information broker he used named Navis, they had their first arrests—two

Vengeance members, escaped slaves from Montagn, hiding out in an abandoned building in the Poor Quarter. Talyn, along with several Falcons sent by Ravinire and Mithanis, tried to interrogate them, but they refused to say anything.

Two nights later, thanks to Petro, they found a supply stash of masks and weapons hidden under floorboards in another safehouse, and cleared it all out.

The following morning, Cuinn took the lot to Queencouncil, dumping it on the table before the astonished stares of his family and the council members. For her part, Talyn dutifully reported to Ravinire each morning, outlining in detail their activities of the night before, and attributing all their information to the patrolling Wolves.

After a week, following more information from Navis, they arrested three men and a woman hiding out in an empty warehouse in the Dock Quarter.

The prince of night had no idea the Shadowhawk was the one finding all the information that allowed them to have these small wins against Vengeance. But it was inarguable that the Wolves were having far more success than the WingGuard.

"If we're not careful, he'll send us after the Shadowhawk next." Theac scowled one night.

She chuckled, but it made her think. Maybe they should slow their progress.

But there had been no more tawncat murders. And the next night they cleared a safehouse and sent seven Vengeance members to the City Patrol jail.

Talyn walked into the Patrol headquarters the following afternoon to find two Falcons beating one of the prisoners with fists and boots. The man was curled up on the floor, blood pouring from his nose, both eyes swollen and closed. Her attempts to intervene fell on deaf ears and a later summons from Ravinire warned her to cease obstructing the WingGuard attempts to interrogate the prisoners.

"This isn't why we arrested them," she said in frustration as she and Cuinn walked the streets of the Poor Quarter that night. "Torture doesn't work. Worse, it makes us as bad as they are. If the walls hadn't been caving in around us during the ambush I wouldn't have even considered torturing that man—and even though I did, half the information he gave us made no sense."

"The ironic thing is, we know a group that could help the mistreated prisoners escape Dock City," Cuinn said with a little smile, but it faded quickly. "I'm glad I wasn't there."

"Yeah, your song magic," she said softly. "I feel responsible."

"We both should. But what other option is there? Let Vengeance continue to run free and murder innocent families?"

"*If* they were behind that murder. There haven't been any others since."

"Even if they weren't, they aren't going to stop coming after us," he said quietly. "I can't believe I'm the one saying this, but they put themselves in this position."

"I know. It's just that…"

"Back home your Callanan would treat these prisoners with fairness and respect, no matter what they'd done." Cuinn glanced at her. "You find it hard being here."

"I do," she admitted.

The words lay uneasily between them. They turned into a particularly narrow and pungent alleyway, and Cuinn stiffened suddenly.

"What is it?"

"This is where Saniya would always leave messages." He pointed to a chalk mark on the wall. It looked fresh. "She wants to meet."

Talyn looked at Cuinn, smiled grimly. "Then we'll meet. And we'll bring fifty Wolves with us."

A SERIES of messages went back and forth, setting the meeting for two nights later. Talyn didn't tell Ravinire, and Cuinn didn't mention it to Mithanis either. Both wanted to see what Saniya had to say first.

If there was a chance they could learn more about the planned Montagni invasion through meeting with the Vengeance leader, Talyn wanted to take that opportunity before Ravinire or Mithanis insisted she be arrested or killed. And she judged the risk to herself and Cuinn small—even if Saniya brought reinforcements, Talyn intended on bringing every Wolf not on guard duty. Petro's people would keep an eye on the area the day before the meeting, making sure nobody planned an ambush.

The night before the meeting found Talyn sitting in companionable silence with her talons in their common room, the door open to let in a vaguely cool evening breeze. A steaming cup of half-drunk tea sat beside the shift schedules Theac had prepared before leaving for the day to go home to his wife and family.

Footsteps sounded as someone approached from the drill yard and Zamaril appeared in the door, carrying what looked like a letter.

"You got the mail?" Corrin asked.

"Just one for the captain." Zamaril tossed it to her. She took it, recognised her mother's handwriting, and tucked it away. The second she'd received since coming back to Mithranar, it no doubt held more subtle nudges that perhaps it was time to come home. She'd read it later.

Andres rose soon after—his detail was about to go on shift—and on impulse, Talyn decided to join him. Tonight Cuinn was attending a dinner party, and she was keen to read the mood of the room for herself, check whether anyone looked unduly concerned about the prince of song's recent change in behaviour.

"Captain, a second?" Tiercelin followed her out the door.

She waved Andres on and looked at her talon curiously. "Something wrong?"

"Not at all. I just wanted to give you these." He passed her a small jar of crushed plant-like material. "This combination of herbs works much better than the stuff you've been drinking. Tastes better too."

"What are you talking about?" She frowned.

He gave her a look. "I'm a healer, Captain, and you expect me not to notice when you're drinking a contraceptive tea?"

"Oh." She tucked the packet in her pocket, doing her best to not look awkward. "Thanks."

"Anytime." He smiled. "I prepare it for other Wolves too. You know you can ask me about things like this? I *am* the wing's healer, after all."

"You're absolutely right." She smiled, forcing away her discomfort. It wasn't that Tiercelin knew she was sleeping with someone that made her uncomfortable, only the fear he might guess who it had been. She didn't even know why she was still drinking the stuff. It had been more than a fortnight since she had been with Cuinn. "And I appreciate it. I'll start using these from now on."

"At least once a day, or it won't work," he said, then saluted. "Night, Captain."

She jogged after Andres, catching up to him just as he and his detail arrived at the sprawling Swiftwing quarters on the western corner of the palace. They spread out in various directions while she and Andres took up positions by the door of the lounge where the guests were gathered.

The party had already started, and the Wolves previously on duty filed out past Talyn, wishing her and Andres a good night. Halun punched the much smaller man good-naturedly in the shoulder, sending him almost careening into the wall. Talyn hid her smile.

When Cuinn caught sight of her, he came straight over. Andres moved discreetly away to take up position out of hearing distance.

"I didn't know you were on duty, Captain. Is something wrong?" Cuinn asked.

"No, just checking in, keeping sharp," she said, then asked hopefully, "You going to sing tonight?"

His smile matched hers. "For you, anything. Besides, it'll help me avoid Irial. He won't stop asking questions about what's going on with me, and while I'm not going to get drunk and ogle all the women in the room like usual, if I sing it should allay at least some of his curiosity."

"You should spend time with Annae instead, she's the nicer one." Talyn's mouth quirked.

"She's not the one reporting to Mithanis on me," Cuinn said. "Best to keep Irial close."

Talyn's mouth opened in surprise, but Cuinn was already gone, weaving back through the room toward the harpsichord in the corner.

Andres came over, his voice a murmur. "The winged folk have noticed the change in him. He's different. Still non-threatening. But different. Irial's not the only one asking questions."

"That's why I wanted to join you tonight. See for myself." She'd heard similar from the other talons as well.

"What's the endgame, Captain?"

Talyn glanced at Andres. His gaze was on the room, watching Cuinn carefully, but his voice was serious, almost grim. "What do you mean?"

"He's decided to drop the mask. That's fine. But then what? He still can't effect change here, not unless he outright challenges Mithanis. Not unless he—"

"Never aloud," she cut him off.

"You know what I'm asking," Andres persisted.

"I don't have an answer for you. What you're suggesting is impossible," she said. "And he has his own way of helping, as you know."

"How long do you think he'll be content with that?"

Talyn just shook her head. She had no answer for that either. Fortunately, Cuinn began singing then, saving her from more difficult questions.

She and Andres stood there, half their attention on the area around Cuinn, the rest delighting in his beautiful music.

THEAC APPROACHED Talyn after the wall run the next day. They'd set the morning aside for paperwork and a discussion about how the individual details were running.

"Thought we could talk a moment before we get started on the work, Captain," he said gruffly as they took seats in the common room.

"About tonight? I think we're pretty well sorted, unless something worries you?" she asked. They'd already had a long conversation with the talons to plan for the meeting with Saniya. "I'd rather not talk about it too much up here."

He cleared his throat. "No, it's not that. I just wanted to make sure everything is all right with you. Zamaril told me you received an important-looking letter last night."

A rush of affection for the grizzled old warrior swept through her. He was worried about her. "I'm fine, thanks, Theac."

"Are you sure?" he asked. "I remember what happened last time you received a letter from home."

Her heart clenched at the same memory—the news of her father's impending death. She swallowed and pushed that memory away. "It was a letter from my mother," she explained. "She was asking after me, giving me news from home, and dropping in a few not-so-subtle hints that it might be time to return. Which I will ignore when I write back." She nudged him teasingly. "Were you worried?"

"I think you belong here, Captain, pardon my saying," Theac burst out. "Despite all the troubles, you're loved here. Loved and respected. This is your home as much as the Twin Thrones is."

Talyn stilled in astonishment at his heartfelt words.

"I didn't mean any offence." He cleared his throat. "Figured I'd say my piece, maybe you'd consider my advice."

Tears pricked at Talyn's eyes. "I don't know what to say to that, except that, well... you, the Wolves, you're why I want to stay."

"Just want to make sure you're happy, Captain."

She smiled and punched him lightly in the arm. "Now you're getting all mushy on me."

He glowered at her and fell silent. She couldn't wipe the smile from her face.

"THIRD DOOR ON THE LEFT." Cuinn—cloaked and masked as the Shadowhawk—stepped out of the shadows on the corner of the alley as Talyn approached. She had her daggers out, one in each hand, spinning them idly as an outlet for her anticipatory restlessness.

"You snuck out okay?" she asked quietly.

"No problems. Corrin's detail is making it look like I'm in the tower."

"Then let's do this."

A bright moon was out, casting the alley in a silvery glow. The air was thick and dank, the damp scent of the earlier downpour still in the air. The shadows were still and watchful.

She'd spoken with Petro on the way in—his people reported no unusual movement around the meeting site. Despite that, Wolves surrounded the area. In the sky above. In each and every alley leading to this small house. On the roof across the street. If Vengeance tried anything, they were going to be very, very surprised. And over-matched.

Cuinn was solid at her side, not a trace of fear showing, and she glanced up with a smile before pushing open the door and walking through.

Saniya stood in the opposite corner of the empty room. A single lit lantern hung from the roof between them, casting a warm glow on the interior. A steady drip from a hole in the roof was the only sound. Her eyes widened slightly when she saw Talyn. "Hello, Cousin."

"Saniya." Talyn kept her voice even, ignoring the twinge she felt at the moniker. It was hard to reconcile that this woman was both her father's niece, *family*, yet also a woman who'd been the cause of so much violence and damage.

Saniya's cool gaze flicked between Talyn and Cuinn. "I was curious about why the Shadowhawk asked me to help you, the captain of a WingGuard wing. And now it appears you're working with him. How interesting."

"The queen ordered Prince Cuinn's wing to assist in hunting you down—she thought given most of the Wolves are human, they might have better luck than the Falcons," Talyn said. "I asked the Shadowhawk for help, since he knows these streets better than any of us."

A soft laugh. "Well, sending your Wolves after us is the first halfway clever idea our Acondor queen has ever had."

Cuinn shifted, voice faintly bored as he spoke. "Why did you ask to meet?"

"I want to call truce," she said flatly.

Talyn scoffed. "You tried to kill us. You murdered innocent people. And now you want a truce? Unless you've got something more interesting to say, we're seconds away from arresting you and taking you to the Falcon."

Saniya's face tightened, anger flashing in her dark blue Ciantar eyes. "You're so cocky, Talyn Dynan. You think you know everything."

"Why a truce?" Cuinn asked quietly.

A beat of thick silence. Then, something slipped from those rigid shoulders. Saniya's voice sagged with defeat when she finally spoke. "You have us, okay? You win. Now all I want is for what's left of my people, my work, to make it out of this."

Anger swept through Talyn. "If you think I'm going to give up now, and let you live to thrive and come at us again—"

"We won't." Saniya cut her off. "Agree to the truce and we'll leave you alone. You have my word."

"What about my network?" Cuinn asked.

"That wasn't us." Saniya's gaze shifted from Cuinn to Talyn and back. "We don't murder innocent children."

"You really expect us to believe that?" Cuinn shook his head.

"You can believe me or not, I don't care." Saniya turned to Talyn. "But someone sure was keen to make you extra motivated to come after us, weren't they? Killing an innocent family was a stroke of genius when you think about it from that perspective."

"You're saying you were framed?" Scepticism filled Talyn's voice. Not all of it was genuine. She'd never been sure Vengeance were behind the recent murders, and Saniya's words made a chilling amount of sense.

Saniya's expression hardened. "You've been getting help these past two weeks, haven't you? Little bits of critical information that all happen to be accurate, forcing me into this corner."

Talyn shared a look with Cuinn.

Shit.

Saniya's shoulders firmed. "You leave us alone, we leave you, your Wolves, the Shadowhawk, and your precious prince alone. Deal?"

"I want more than that." Talyn shook her head. "I want to know who's helping you, where you got that izerdia from and who your contacts in Montagn are."

Saniya's eyes flashed. "I'm not exposing the rest of my network to be hunted down by you or the Falcons."

"Then no deal," Talyn said simply. "You give me what I want, or we arrest you now and take you to the Falcon. I'm sure you've heard what the Falcon interrogation methods are like—you'll spill that information to someone. I'd prefer it was me."

Another long moment of silence. Talyn wondered if Cuinn was using his song magic to influence Saniya to talk, but it was impossible to tell, his Shadowhawk glamour firmly in place.

Saniya eventually let out a bitter laugh. "I'm proud, but I'm not stupid. I know when I'm beaten. I'll give you the identity of the man that's been... in our ear, helping, encouraging, giving us resources. I give you that, and swear to leave you alone, and we have a deal."

"And what makes you think Captain Dynan is going to let you walk out of here in exchange for one name, after everything you've done?" the Shadowhawk drawled.

"Because she's my cousin." Saniya looked directly at her. "And I ask it of you on behalf of both our fathers."

"I've already saved your life once on that score," Talyn said quietly. But Runye had sacrificed his life for Trystaan, and in her bones, Talyn knew what her father would want her to do here. So... "Ask it of me again, and there will be no more reprieves."

"I know that."

Talyn looked at Cuinn. She couldn't make this decision without his approval. It had been him Saniya had come after, Saniya he'd worked with all these years not knowing who and what she was.

"Your call, Captain," he said softly. "She's your family."

"This is what you've been after, Tal. With this name, you'll have the Montagni link—from there you can work to unravel the whole thing and use that to warn Queen Sarana."

And then Mithranar would at least be able to prepare to defend itself.

"Give me the name, tell me everything I want to know about him, and I'll let you walk away," she said softly. "Kill one more person, even *try* to harm one more person in Dock City, and the deal is off. I will kill you without hesitation."

Saniya's gaze shifted from Talyn to Cuinn. "He found us through you, Shadowhawk."

"Who?" Cuinn's voice turned to granite.

"The information peddler. Navis. He came to us just over a year ago, said he could give us a way to properly fight back. He helped us with the break-in at the palace and told us where the izerdia would be. He said it would be a test run, for going after the queen. When we were spotted so quickly, we changed our plans and decided to wait for her to travel to Sparrow Island." Saniya's gaze shifted to Talyn. "And he made it clear you were to be left alone."

"Where is he now?" Talyn snapped.

"In the wind. Our relationship... broke down. We weren't his puppets, and when he realised that, he decided we were no longer any use to him."

"Who does he work for?" Talyn asked.

"Don't know."

"Not Prince Mithanis?" Cuinn probed.

Saniya shot him a look like that was the stupidest thing she'd ever heard. "Not as far as I know."

"Why did he want to protect Captain Dynan?"

"Not a clue." Saniya smiled without warmth. "But us going after you in Darmour was one of the key reasons for the relationship ending, Cousin. He was severely unhappy about it. But like I said, we don't work for him."

Cuinn sucked a breath in, glanced at Talyn. In that look was everything she needed to know. Cuinn believed she was telling the truth.

Talyn turned back to Saniya. "Go."

Saniya moved for the door, hesitating when neither of them made a move to stop her. "One more thing, Talyn, because of our fathers. We're desperate, on the run, and we certainly don't have access to a tame tawncat. If I were you, I'd think about who might want you to think we murdered that family. And why."

"And the murders of Goldfeather, Iceflight and Flightbreeze?" Talyn asked.

Saniya gave a bitter laugh. "You saw how we came at you. Front on. We don't mess around with tawncats and poison."

She was out the door without another word.

Talyn let out a breath, trying to relax the rigidity in her shoulders. "I wish she hadn't been... I would have liked to know her. She's the only family I have here."

"The Saniya I knew before all this... you would have liked her a lot," Cuinn murmured. "I did."

"Was she telling the truth?" Talyn changed the subject, turning to business.

"Hard to tell for certain," he said, guilt and regret rippling across his face. "But if I had to say, then yes. She hides her emotions well, but she's a pretty direct person. She doesn't play games or manipulate."

"What can you tell me about Navis?"

"I started working with him about a year before you came here. I approached him after researching the information peddlers in Dock City. He seemed to have the best access to the things I needed to know."

"If Saniya was telling the truth, he used you to get access to her group."

He nodded, jaw rigid. "That's two links to Vengeance I had absolutely no clue about."

"Captain?" Halun ducked his head in. "Everything okay?"

"Yes. I let her go—it's a long story. Tell the Wolves to stand down for tonight. We'll need to discuss this later. Will you let the other talons know that all is well?"

He nodded and withdrew.

"I should go. Give Corrin and his detail a break from pretending I'm in my tower." Cuinn offered her a smile, but it didn't quite reach his eyes. "Will you have the talon on my next detail pass on whatever you discuss tonight?"

"I will." She wished she could do it. Wanted to see him again. But she couldn't. Not with Mithanis and the rest of the winged folk's watchful gaze always there. "You doing all right?"

"I'm tired," he admitted. "But doing this, I feel better than I have in a long time."

He missed her too. It was in the emotion laden in his words, even though it cut off so suddenly it was obvious he was trying to keep it from her.

"Do we really let Saniya go?" he asked before she could say anything. "After everything?"

"My father would want me to," she said softly. "And I wouldn't even be here if it weren't for Runye's sacrifice. But it has to be your decision too."

"If I believe anything of what she just said, if my magic is right, then she truly feels beaten," Cuinn said. "And not just by us. I think she's questioning a lot right now."

"I worry that if we give them an inch of breathing space, it might be a mistake we regret bitterly," Talyn said.

"We have Mithanis to consider too. He would never agree to letting up, he wants them all wiped out."

She was tired. They both were. As satisfying as their success had been, the past weeks had seen little sleep for any of them. "If Saniya stands by her word, then it's going to appear as if Vengeance *is* gone. So we claim the victory and let it lie. But let's sleep on it and consider with clearer minds. I'll talk with the talons, get their thoughts. We'll go from there."

A hint of a smile. "Sounds like a plan, Captain Dynan."

CHAPTER 28

*A*fter sneaking back from Dock City and checking in with Corrin, Cuinn sank into bed, his thoughts awhirl with the meeting they'd just had.

Navis. He'd never trusted the man. But he'd never suspected this either. Guilt and bitterness were corrosive in his chest, making it hard to think clearly. At least now they knew. If he'd been the one grooming Vengeance, then he must be the agent in Dock City acting on behalf of Montagn.

They had their link. Now they just had to work out how to use it to warn his mother.

Jasper had been pacing the room—he never liked it when Cuinn went out as the Shadowhawk, as if he sensed his friend was in danger —but came to settle on the bed once it was clear Cuinn wasn't leaving again. The tawncat at his feet helped him settle, as it always did, and despite the business of his thoughts he sank into a deep sleep.

He didn't wake until sunlight streamed through his windows.

Tiercelin's detail had taken over the guard shift and the talon was waiting for him downstairs, having already ordered breakfast from one of the palace's servants. Cuinn gestured for Tiercelin to join him

—he always protested, and Cuinn always insisted—and then began buttering some toast.

"How are you feeling?" Tiercelin asked the same question he always did.

"My back and leg feel absolutely fine, and I managed a few hours of decent sleep, so I'm good," Cuinn answered. "You've spoken with Captain Dynan and the other talons?"

"Not until a bit later. She wanted us to get some rest."

A knock came at the door. Renasa appeared from somewhere—Cuinn hadn't even noticed the human Wolf standing guard nearby—and crossed to answer it.

He shook his head. It was fortunate taking Talyn as his lover had turned out to be an impossible affair—there would have been no way for them to ever manage a moment alone without the Wolves knowing all about it. An ache rippled through him. He ignored it. It was enough. Enough just to have her there at his side, leading his Wolves, offering her advice and help, keeping him safe.

Renasa opened his door, relaxing as he saw who it was, then stood back to wave Willir in.

"Your Highness." The boy straightened his shoulders. "Your mother would like to see you."

THE QUEEN of Mithranar was waiting for him in her sitting room, staring out a window drenched with water droplets, even though the rain had stopped earlier. Mithanis was there too, frowning over a parchment unrolled in his hands.

"I was summoned?" Cuinn asked. There was no languid sigh or annoyed rolling of the eyes, not anymore. Now it was just a polite and deferential tone.

Mithanis's eyes snapped towards him. The prince of night had noticed, of course he had. But so far he had seemed more confused than threatened, as if he were still trying to work out what was going on with Cuinn.

His mother turned towards him. "Thank you for coming so promptly."

"I aim to please." His smile was there, but not as flippant as it had once been. "What is it?"

"You've been doing well," Mithanis said grudgingly. "The Vengeance gang is on its heels and from what I understand, the Wolves have broken the back of their strength. The council is pleased."

Mithanis's gaze was dark on his, wondering. As had become more and more frequent, Cuinn sensed Mithanis's power searching him out, trying to ascertain Cuinn's true thoughts and feelings. Well-practiced, he employed his own magic to deflect Mithanis's away.

"Thank you," Cuinn said, wondering if this was the first time in his life he'd actually pleased his elder brother. It was an odd feeling. He liked it, but didn't want to. "Judging from the Wolves' most recent patrol, the gang is all but gone. We'll monitor for continued activity, of course, but we may have seen the last of Vengeance."

"The prisoners you've captured will be executed within the week," Mithanis said, an air of satisfaction coming from him. "We'll do it down in Dock City, outside Town Hall. Making an example of them should deter anyone else thinking to follow in their footsteps."

Cuinn winced internally. It's not like he hadn't known this was where the arrests would lead, and an argument could be made the Vengeance members deserved their fate. But they were still his people, and they deserved better from him.

"Now that this is almost done I expect you to keep those Wolves to heel," Mithanis added. "I don't want them getting false ideas about their own importance."

Cuinn's mouth quirked. "I will ensure they continue to be sensible of the fact they are mere humans, far inferior to their winged rulers."

Mithanis scowled, but their mother waved a hand before he could respond to Cuinn's snide comment. "I received a letter from Ahara Venador yesterday," she said. "He has formally agreed to the betrothal we proposed and has invited you to Arataire to meet his daughter."

His heart sank. Cuinn had half-hoped his mother had forgotten about the whole thing, or that maybe the ahara had turned her down. Maybe he could get Mithanis to do that. He frowned, looking at his elder brother. "Are you really in agreement with this plan to marry me off? You can't be comfortable with the idea of me marrying a Montagni princess."

"I'm more than comfortable with you carrying greater responsibilities." Mithanis met his gaze, jaw tensing slightly. "You've shown progress, and I'd like that to continue."

For a moment Cuinn wasn't sure what to say. His magic read sincerity from his brother... but a hint of something else too. Impatience? No, not quite. Anticipation? Before he could work it out, his mother spoke.

"As would I," Sarana said coolly. "I will be writing back to the ahara today to accept his invitation. You'll leave this week. Once you return, a wedding date can be set."

Despair surged, and not only because he had absolutely no desire to marry someone he'd never met. If his mother packed him off to Arataire now, that meant his Wolves would have to come, which meant they wouldn't be able to track down Navis and his ties to whoever was pulling the strings in Montagn. "Mother, I really can't—"

"You will do as I say, Cuinn," she said, anger rippling unexpectedly over her face. A little curl of his magic ran over her—she wasn't angry at him. Not exactly. She was angry at his resistance. She wanted this for him. "I am queen, and my word is law. Mithranar needs this alliance, and you are otherwise useless to me."

That hurt, even though he understood why she thought it. He let the wince ripple over his face. "I'm warmed you think so highly of me."

"Kaeri Venador is beautiful, Az tells me," Mithanis said. "So you should have no problem there."

"I would prefer to choose my own bride," he muttered.

His mother met his eyes unflinchingly. "You are a prince, you don't get to choose anything. You will go to Montagn and court Princess Kaeri. Am I clear?"

"Why aren't we marrying Mithanis off?" Cuinn tried to avoid sounding petulant. "He's the one that has to provide heirs, no?"

"Mithanis is not the subject of this conversation." Warning entering his mother's voice.

Their song magic wrapped Cuinn in their intent, loud and clear. The consequences would not be pleasant if he didn't do this. He considered flat out refusing, making a stand here and now and to hell with the consequences. But then what? No, if he was going to make a stand he needed to do it with a clear plan in mind.

Besides... going to Montagn might not be the worst thing in the world. It would give Talyn a chance to do her Callanan thing and investigate. Maybe she and Zamaril might be able to work together to get a read on how close the Montagni invasion was.

Not to mention it would give him time to work out a way of escaping this marriage without negative repercussions.

So he sighed in capitulation. "Very clear. If there's nothing else?"

"There is, actually." His mother's mouth tightened, and she flicked an unreadable glance Mithanis's way. "After we announce your betrothal, I will formally state my intention to name my heir, and invite the court to the SkyReach to initiate the process."

Cuinn sucked in a breath. "I see."

"It's long past time we all stopped pretending it will be anyone other than me," Mithanis said. "Queencouncil support is a foregone conclusion."

"I agree." Cuinn spoke politely but without his pretence of boredom. This shouldn't shock him—it had always been inevitable.

Mithanis's dark eyes roved over Cuinn's face, then he gave a little nod. "Have fun in Montagn, little brother. Take your friends with you. I'm sure Irial and his wife would enjoy another trip away."

Cuinn smiled, stepped away. "I'll speak to them this afternoon."

TIERCELIN WAITED OUTSIDE, wings rustling in agitation, clearly anxious about the fact Cuinn had been in close proximity with Mithanis. The sight irritated Cuinn for no particular reason that he could pin down. "I'm fine, Tiercelin. My mother was in there. Mithanis is hardly going to assassinate me in front of her."

"You hope," Tiercelin said darkly.

He ignored that. "Tell Captain Dynan we'll be leaving for the SkyReach in a few days. All the Wolves will come."

Tiercelin hesitated, frowning. "Is something wrong?"

"Direct orders from my mother. I'm to visit Arataire at the ahara's invitation. Pass the message on, please."

A rustle of wings sounded as Azrilan dropped out of the sky, cutting Tiercelin off before he could ask anything else. Instead the talon bowed his head and stepped away, leaving the brothers their privacy.

Azrilan slung a companionable arm around Cuinn's shoulders. "Congratulations on your betrothal, little brother."

"I'm not betrothed yet," Cuinn muttered. "She might refuse."

Musical laughter pealed out. "No woman would refuse after taking a single look at your pretty face." Azrilan let him go. "Sorry I can't come with you. I asked, but Mithanis refused."

Cuinn smiled at Azrilan's apologetic glance. "Of course he did."

"Can't have his two younger brothers plotting nefarious things together in Arataire." Azrilan winked.

"As if." Cuinn snorted.

"Don't look so glum," Azrilan counselled. "You never know, marriage might suit you."

"She'd better be pretty, that's all I can say," Cuinn said out of habit, then abruptly felt guilty. Whether this princess was pretty or not, he didn't want her. "Why is Mithanis so supportive of this anyway? It's clearly all Mother's idea."

Azrilan stopped walking. "I don't know for certain, but if I had to guess? He's gambling on the fact you'll have human children... something that takes them out of contention for the throne. And you too, quite effectively."

Cuinn groaned. "I don't *want* the throne. When's he going to get that through his thick head?"

"Here's the thing about ambitious, paranoid people like our dearest brother." Azrilan leaned closer. "They think everyone around them is as ambitious and paranoid as they are, no matter what they say."

"Even so, there are plenty of other human options to marry me off to other than the ahara's only daughter," Cuinn pointed out. "And what if one or more of our children *are* winged folk? Seriously, Az, what's in this for Mithanis?"

Azrilan shrugged, leaning back against the railing.

"You know something," Cuinn accused. A chill brushed over him. Mithanis *was* planning something. It was all over Azrilan's face. "What is it?"

Azrilan let out a breath. "You know how dangerous Mithanis is just as well as I do. Be careful not to assume he's fine with Talyn Dynan being the daughter of Trystaan Ciantar."

"She had her wing buds cut out." Cuinn gritted his teeth at the horror of that idea. Azrilan winced. "She's no threat."

"Paranoid and ambitious, remember?"

"You would tell me, if you knew he was up to something?" Cuinn asked uncertainly. He'd never truly known the answer to this question. Azrilan hadn't warned him about Raya. But maybe he hadn't known.

"You'll be fine." Azrilan ignored the question. "Talk to my uncle if you run into any trouble in Arataire, Brother. He'll look out for you."

Cuinn huffed an incredulous breath. "Thura Manunin thinks I'm a useless fool."

"But is he right?" Azrilan frowned a little. "I do wonder sometimes."

"Is Thura Manunin going to help when Mithanis comes after me?" Cuinn snapped. "Quit with your vague warnings, Az. If you know something, tell me."

An easy smile crossed his brother's face, dispelling the grim look he'd worn as if it had never been. "I'm simply endeavouring to make sure that you are just as afraid of Mithanis as I am. If you are, you'll be sensible. I'll see you when you're back. Have fun in Arataire."

Cuinn watched him fly away. Melancholy and exhaustion rose up, threatening to swallow him whole. They'd been doing so well...

hunting Vengeance, finding the link to Montagn. He'd pulled back the foolish prince act. It had felt like things were getting better, like he'd finally been able to stop hiding and be himself. But that had only been an illusion. His mother and brother ruled his life and would always do so.

He was still trapped.

CHAPTER 29

The order to go to Montagn was sudden but not entirely unexpected. She'd been wondering when the queen would progress with her plans to marry Cuinn off. And Talyn couldn't think of any other reason why Cuinn was suddenly being dispatched to Arataire.

Andres reported in late that night after his detail had finished shift, telling her and the other talons that Cuinn had been quiet and uncommunicative all day.

"It's the worst possible timing." Theac scowled. "Right when we've got a solid lead on Vengeance's string-puller we have to drag ourselves all the way to bloody Arataire."

"What if we ask Petro to do some discreet digging while we're gone?" Andres suggested. "His people could ask around, see what they can find out about Navis."

"No." Talyn shook her head. "I don't want Petro or his people to risk themselves like that. They're not warriors and Navis is a dangerous individual. We'll have to wait until we return."

She wasn't as disappointed about this sudden trip as the Wolves were. It was a perfect opportunity to get a firsthand look at Montagn. No doubt they'd be watched closely the whole time they were there, but even so, if the ahara was planning invasion, surely there would be some sign of it. Even better, Leviana and Cynia should have arrived in Arataire by now—she'd received the coded message from the First Blade informing Talyn of their posting through Savin.

"I'll stay in Dock City and track Navis," Halun offered. "I can't come with you to Montagn anyway."

Talyn hesitated. She didn't like the idea of Halun going after Navis alone and without support. At the look he was giving her, silently asking for her trust, she nodded. "All right. See if you can locate him. But you don't do anything until we get back. Clear?"

"Agreed, Captain."

"We should give Halun some time off, Captain," Theac suggested. "He can stay with Errana and the girls, keep an eye on them while I'm away, and be much more discreet moving around Dock City than if he were in uniform."

"Done." She also liked the idea of Halun being away from the citadel and winged folk while they were gone. Down in Dock City he'd be out of their immediate reach. "We'll have to leave Jasper with him too."

"Just as long as he doesn't eat my family," Theac said sourly.

"I'm sure he'll behave himself." She grinned.

Tiercelin rose, stretched. "I'm off to bed. Tomorrow's going to be a big day if we need to organise moving the full wing to Arataire."

"Before you go." Her sharp voice had them all unconsciously standing to attention halfway to the door. Once she was certain of their unwavering focus, she spoke. "We will not be experiencing a repeat of what happened last time. The Wolves will accept the presence of slaves in Arataire without complaint. Any that don't will face serious consequences. As talons, you are responsible for managing the behaviour of your details."

"Captain—" Tiercelin began, but she cut him off.

"I don't want to hear it," she said. "Prince Cuinn's safety is our priority. Do I make myself clear?"

They all glanced at Zamaril, the prime example of the consequences for going against her wishes. He bore their scrutiny with calm dignity.

"They'll stay in line," Theac said. "I'll make sure of it."

"He won't need to, Captain. My detail will do as you ask," Corrin said.

"Good," she said, meeting his look. "Because you'll be responsible for Halun's detail as well as your own for the duration of the trip." Cuinn had spoken to her of the exemplary leadership Corrin had displayed after her arrest, and she hadn't forgotten it.

He straightened, saluted. The sidelong glances switched from Zamaril to Corrin, but nobody complained.

Talyn sank back into her chair, thoughts occupied, as the talons filed out to find their beds. She wanted to go and see Cuinn, but ignored the urge. It was best they limited any private interaction. Still, she wanted to find out what had made him so subdued all day.

"It's about the marriage, Tal. You know it." Sari came to life.

She let out a long breath. *"Yeah."*

"Marriage to the ahara's daughter will help protect him from Mithanis."

"I know. So why is Mithanis agreeing to it?" The question nagged at her. Marrying his younger brother to the favourite child of the Montagni ahara was a strange move for someone so paranoid about other potential claimants for the throne.

"There must be something in it for him. Maybe he just hopes Cuinn will have human children."

"That's a hell of a gamble, and even though Mithanis has Montagni blood running through his veins, I've never picked him as a gambler."

Sari hesitated. *"What are you going to do?"*

"Use the opportunity to see if I can corroborate the Callanan informant's claims. Hopefully even get an idea of how imminent the invasion is."

"That is so not what I meant."

Talyn rose from the chair, heading in the same direction as the others. *"I need to leave a cup out for Savin. He can get a message to the First Blade to let her know I'm off to Montagn. Then, I should get some sleep. Tiercelin was right, it's going to be a big day tomorrow."*

· · ·

THE FOLLOWING MORNING, Talyn was unsurprised to be summoned to Ravinire's presence.

"I've been apprised of the prince's trip to Arataire." The Falcon spoke before the door had even closed behind her.

"We're beginning preparations now, sir."

"Good. I've sent messages ahead to Darmour—Prince Cuinn will stay a single night there before taking the coastal road north to the Causeway. Inns will be booked ahead of your arrival, and the horses that you used last time will be prepared."

"Can I ask why the prince isn't staying up in the Summer Palace?" A flicker of irritation went through her that Cuinn hadn't told her this himself. "Are the tunnels still closed after the cave-ins?"

"Some tunnels remain closed, but I understand workers are making steady progress through the cave-ins," Ravinire explained. "Prince Cuinn simply thought it would be easier for his party to depart directly from Darmour along the coastal road, rather than the human Wolves hiking all the way up to the palace and back down for a single night."

Of course. Cuinn was being thoughtful. Her irritation abruptly subsided.

"Yes, sir," she said, then hesitated. "May I ask a question?"

He nodded.

"Prince Cuinn mentioned the planned betrothal to me. Am I correct in assuming that it was the queen's idea, sir? How does Prince Mithanis feel about it?"

Ravinire's gaze narrowed. "He is fully supportive."

The question hung between them. *Why?*

Ravinire broke the heavy silence. "I don't like the fact that you'll be out of my sight and supervision on this trip, Captain," he said bluntly.

"Sir, I don't—"

"Save it." He waved a hand to cut her off. "You will escort the prince to Arataire, protect him while he is there, and return him safely after the agreed period of time. You will do *nothing* else. Do I make myself clear, Captain?"

"Perfectly." She saluted.

He sat down without another word, his attention turning to the parchment on his desk.

Talyn left.

THE AWE-INSPIRING SKYREACH mountains seemed even more stark and unforgiving than the previous time Talyn visited, when it had been summer. Now winter was almost upon them, and the air was bitterly cold, especially as afternoon faded into dusk. The damage from the avalanche was still devastatingly obvious—that area of the town remained mostly rubble—but otherwise the place was bustling as she remembered.

The Wolves rose early the following morning. By a full-turn past dawn, the main street outside the inn where Cuinn and his entourage had spent the night was packed solid with Wolves and horses. Conversation, neighing and hoof-stomping broke the silence of softly falling snow that had draped the town.

Once her wing seemed well on their way to sorting themselves with horses and transferring their belongings to saddlebags, Talyn left Theac in charge and sought Cuinn out. He wasn't in the main room of the inn where Irial and his friends were devouring breakfast, but Corrin waved her to the back door.

"Give us a moment?" she asked him, and he nodded.

Cuinn stood on the porch out the back, staring up at the mountains looming over the town. Nobody else was outside with him, and the two Wolves that had been watching slipped back inside at Corrin's quiet order.

"What is it, Captain?" His musical voice was leeched of colour, worn down, and without thinking she went straight to him, reaching up to touch his jaw and gently turn his face towards her.

"What's wrong?"

He stilled, but didn't move away from her touch. "What do you mean?"

"Talk to me," she murmured, searching his face.

"The ahara has agreed to the betrothal," he said eventually.

315

Talyn dropped her hand, shifting back a little. "I figured. When you first spoke of this, you said it was your mother's idea?"

He nodded. "She tells me that Mithranar needs the alliance, and since I am otherwise useless, I must marry this princess. The plan is for us to formally meet in Arataire, so that when I return, they can set a marriage date." He hesitated. "After which, Mother will begin the process to formally name Mithanis heir."

Silence fell. The news wasn't surprising, but that didn't make it any easier to hear. She tried to ignore her discomfort. "Why didn't you tell me?" she asked softly.

"We haven't spoken since our meeting with Saniya."

"And you didn't think to mention it to one of the talons to pass on to me?" She lifted an eyebrow.

He stiffened slightly. "This is my problem to solve, Captain, not yours."

"Is it a problem?" she asked. "The betrothal, I mean?"

Hurt flashed over his face and she cursed herself. "I'm sorry, I'm not trying to be cruel. I just meant, marrying a Montagni princess could be protection for you. Mithanis is less likely to come after you if he risks incurring the wrath of the ahara. I'm guessing that's why your mother is insisting upon it?"

"Partially, yes." Cuinn swallowed. "But Mithanis approves of the match too."

"Which is odd," she murmured.

"Very. And Azrilan hinted that there's something more to it, but refused to tell me what." Cuinn let out a frustrated breath. "I can't escape the feeling that there's something else going on that I'm missing."

Talyn let out a breath, not knowing what to say. "Whatever it is, we'll figure it out."

"*We* will?" Hope flashed in his eyes.

She shrugged. "Together, right?"

A smile curled at the corner of his mouth. "Together."

"I'll come and see you once we're in Montagn. We should talk about our options, how you can use your magic to try and work out what the ahara is up to. Until then, I get the distinct impression Irial is keeping a close eye on you, so I'll keep my distance."

Cuinn nodded. "My change in behaviour has unsettled Mithanis. He's not worried yet, my magic has ensured that, I think, but he'll be looking for any sign that he needs to worry, especially now he's about to be named heir."

"We'll be on our best behaviour," she promised.

His eyes flashed. "I'm not sure that's possible for you, Captain Dynan," he murmured.

A grin teased her lips. "For you, I might be able to manage it."

They'd shifted so close that she could see the deeper emerald flecks in his green eyes, the silver highlights in the blonde strands falling over the right side of his face. She'd just decided to throw all her sensible talk out the window and kiss him when the back door opened.

"Captain, you out here?"

They flew apart so quickly at Theac's shout that Talyn almost tripped over an uneven board in the deck. Heat flooded her face, and she was still straightening when her second walked out.

"I'm here," she said, clearing her throat.

He gave them both an odd look. "We're all saddled up, ready to go. Lord Swiftwing is looking for you, Your Highness."

Cuinn was grinning, no doubt able to feel her discomfort. "I'll find him, thanks, Theac."

The prince disappeared without a backwards glance at her, and Talyn crossed to Theac. "Let's go. No time for dawdling."

THE TRIP north passed without incident. The human Wolves moved much faster now they were more accustomed to horseback riding, and Cuinn and the winged Wolves spent the days in the air, wheeling through the thermals above.

The Montagni escort wasn't led by Thura Manunin this time, but instead by a nephew of the ahara's, and it was much smaller. These cavalrymen wore a different sigil on their chests than the one she remembered on the uniforms of Azrilan's uncle and soldiers. Talyn presumed it was that of the Venador House.

In a week they were riding into Arataire, the massive city no different than she remembered. This time, though, she rode into the place aware that the mighty military resources she'd witnessed on the journey might soon be levelled against Mithranar, if not the Twin Thrones.

It was a sobering thought. Her determination to figure out what was going on in time to stop it increased.

The ahara assigned the Wolves the same barracks they'd used last time—in the draughtiest, dampest corner of his castle fortress. Insult aside, she preferred it this way. It kept the Wolves well away from the busier parts of the fortress where slaves frequented.

As soon as she'd seen the Wolves settled, Talyn washed off the dust and sweat from travel, then dressed in a clean uniform. Outside their barracks, she flagged down a passing servant—one of the few castle servants not a slave. His eyes ran over her uniform and he hesitated, as if not knowing the best way to address her. In the end he settled with an inquiring eyebrow and, "My lady?"

"Can you tell me where I can find the quarters assigned to the Callanan representatives from the Twin Thrones?"

Last time, she'd steered clear of the Callanan in Arataire, not wanting to make her Callanan links obvious to anyone. Now, Mithanis knew she was Dumnorix and Ciantar. There was no need to hide anything.

Puzzlement crept over the servant's face as if he was trying to work out why she would want to know that. But ingrained politeness won, and he simply said, "Of course. I will show you at once."

She hadn't meant that. "Oh no, you can just tell me the way. I'll find it."

The young man looked horrified. Presumably he was under firm instructions that the visitors were not to be left wandering the hallways unescorted. "But you might get lost. It is better if I show you."

"All right." She capitulated reluctantly.

He led her on a long walk through the castle—the guards positioned in every main corridor watching her carefully until she left their sight—before finally coming to the end of a lavishly appointed corridor. Her guide stopped outside the door at the end.

"The Callanan quarters are inside," he said. "All the offices in this wing belong to the ahara's senior military officers."

"Thank you." Talyn waited with a smile while he lingered, awkward, clearly unsure how to insist that he stay. Eventually he cleared his throat and left. Her smile widened.

Once he'd vanished, Talyn pushed the door open and found herself in an empty lounge area. A short hall led away from the lounge to her left and she followed it. As she approached its end, familiar voices floated to her.

"Anyone home?" she called out as she stepped into a smaller room that held two desks and a view of an empty drill yard. A high wall bounded the yard, but these rooms were on the fourth floor, high enough to see out over the lake and forest lining the western shore.

"Talyn?" Cynia looked up from her desk in astonishment.

Leviana leapt up, mouth falling open. A moment later she was lunging forward to envelop Talyn in an excited hug. "What are you doing here?"

Talyn laughed at their exuberance, inexplicably cheered by it. She'd not realised how much she missed her friends. "I'm here with Prince Cuinn, actually."

Leviana's eyes widened.

"He's here to court the ahara's daughter," Talyn explained. "His mother has decided it's time for him to marry."

"So your plan worked, I take it?" Cynia asked. "Given you're not locked up or dead."

"It worked. Cuinn helped, and Mithanis bought everything I told him," Talyn assured them. She decided against mentioning her wing buds being cut out. "He still doesn't trust me completely, but he allowed me to stay."

"Glad to hear it. It was a crazy plan," Leviana declared.

She grinned. "Those are the best kind of plans."

"How exactly did Cuinn help you?" Cynia asked curiously. "And how is it you trust him not to betray you to his brother?"

"That is a very long story to be told over several ales," Talyn hedged.

Fortunately it worked. Cynia frowned and glanced at her partner, before changing the subject. "Prince Cuinn marrying a Montagni princess could have implications for the Twin Thrones. We'll have to let the First Blade know."

Talyn winced. That would mean her uncle finding out. She wasn't sure how he would take Cuinn marrying into the Venador family.

"Any more details for us?" Leviana was already pulling parchment from a drawer.

"That's all I know," Talyn said. "Though I have even better news for you. Vengeance are all but wiped out. I've already passed the information to the First Blade via the Shadow in Dock City."

Cynia's eyes widened. "How did you manage that so quickly?"

"You thought it would take me longer?" Talyn huffed with mock offence.

"You said *almost* wiped out?" Leviana asked.

"They got out of their base before the WingGuard descended on it, but we've been pushing hard after them ever since," Talyn explained. "Saniya even called for a meeting with the Shadowhawk."

"What did she want?"

"A truce. She conceded she'd lost, and wanted to salvage whatever was left of her network." Talyn lowered her voice even further. "In return for the truce, she gave us the Montagni link. Unfortunately Queen Sarana dispatched Cuinn here before I could track that lead down."

"It sounds like even if Vengeance aren't gone completely, they're not going to be much help to Montagn in the short term." Cynia dropped her own voice so it was barely audible.

Talyn nodded, stepping closer. "Have you learned anything?"

"Absolutely nothing," Leviana grumbled. "Our hosts are very strict about what we see and what we have access to."

"Case in point, they gave us a view of their soldiers training every morning." Cynia waved a hand at the windows. "To make sure we understand how powerful they are."

"We haven't dared try and talk to anyone unofficially, let alone recruit informants, not yet." Leviana glanced at her partner. "They follow us whenever we're out of the castle."

"It will take time. You knew that going in," Talyn reassured them. "You just have to be patient."

"Not Levs' strong suit." Cynia sighed.

"*Or mine*," Sari said cheerfully.

It had been so long since she'd heard Sari's voice in her head, Talyn did a mental double-take. "*Welcome back.*"

"*You're cheerful.*"

"*So are you.*"

"Talyn?" Cynia was staring at her.

"Just thinking, sorry. I'll see what I can do while I'm here, too." Talyn rolled her eyes. "Though they've even got the poor servants watching my every move. The ahara's people will know by now that we're meeting."

"How long will Prince Cuinn be here wooing?"

Talyn shrugged. "No idea."

Leviana leapt up suddenly. "Cynia and I have some free time, let's hit the city. We can show you around."

"I'd love to, but I need to make sure my Wolves are settling in without mortally offending someone over the idea of slavery, and then ensure we have a solid detail around Prince Cuinn." She headed for the door. "As soon as I get a free moment, I'll take you both up on your offer though. I've missed you."

"We've missed you too." Leviana hugged her again. "Don't keep us waiting too long."

DESPITE TALYN'S WORRIES, the Wolves were more settled this visit. Zamaril seemed calm too, and Talyn suspected Halun had had a word with him before they'd left. It remained clear that none of them liked the situation, but they focused on their duties and their training, and held their heads high.

Talyn was proud of them.

The ahara received them graciously, entertaining Cuinn and his retinue for three days before formally introducing the Acondor prince to his daughter.

"He's making the prince wait, even though the betrothal has already been agreed to," Theac muttered the night before the first official meeting between the pair.

"The ahara does like to demonstrate his superiority," she murmured agreement. "I haven't seen his general about though, Manunin. Have you?"

Theac shook his head. "I overheard some nobles talking about it on shift today. The princess's mother is from the same House as the ahara—the Venadors. They've always competed for power with the Manunin House, who apparently don't like this match at all."

"So the queen is allying her son to a different Montagni House than the one Mithanis and Azrilan are linked to." She considered that. "Clever."

"Trying to protect him, you think?" Theac grunted.

"I do think. The question is, why is Mithanis happy with the match?"

Theac glowered at the thought of anything that pleased Mithanis. "We'll keep an extra close eye on things tomorrow, just in case the internal politics here cause some trouble."

"I'll join your detail." She told herself it was to ensure Cuinn was safe, like Theac had said, and not because she wanted to see him.

It was a lie.

Princess Kaeri Venador, the ahara's youngest daughter, was a tall, slim woman with chestnut hair that curled down her shoulders and a pale green gaze that revealed nothing of what she was thinking. She carried herself with an air of aloofness not unlike Saniya's, and Talyn got the distinct impression there was steel underneath that beautiful exterior.

While Kaeri and Cuinn greeted each other politely enough, neither seemed particularly overwhelmed by the other.

"She's not as beautiful as you."

Talyn stifled a laugh. *"Back again so soon. You must miss me."*

"I'm just saying."

"I'm flattered. I never knew you thought of me that way."

"Keep making jokes. I know you're just deflecting."

"Seriously." Talyn hesitated. *"You've been gone a lot recently."*

"I'm here when you need me."

"I hope you're not suggesting I don't need you anymore."

"Would that be such a bad thing?"

Talyn lifted a hand to her face, squeezing the bridge of her nose. *"You're my partner."*

"I know," Sari said gently. *"But all this has been about you learning to live again, Talyn. Don't stop that process because you're afraid of me leaving. I'll always be here—but it's okay if that's not as often as it used to be."*

Before Talyn could think of an answer to that, Sari was gone again.

CHAPTER 30

"$\mathcal{D}$o they really think we haven't noticed them?" Leviana asked.

"Who? The two soldiers who've been following us since we left the palace?" Cynia asked. "I doubt it."

Talyn glanced around them. The tea shop they'd found was cosy and warm, an escape from the bitterly cold wind sweeping through the Arataire streets. "Think we should wave to them?"

Leviana chuckled, reaching for her pot of tea. To Talyn's disappointment, there'd been no kahvi shops in Arataire, at least none her friends knew about. Instead they were sharing freshly buttered pasties and steaming herbal tea. Their table was in the corner of the half-empty store, out of hearing distance of the other patrons.

"What have you got?" Talyn kept her posture relaxed for the benefit of anyone watching, a smile on her face as if she were making a joke.

Cynia sighed. "As far as we can tell, there's no change in the behaviour of the generals or the military. No visible troop increase, no flurry of meetings between the ahara and his generals. In fact, General Manunin—the ahara's overall commander—is away from the city spending time at his family estates."

"I seriously doubt the ahara is planning a war without him," Leviana added.

"Obviously the Montagni aren't going to let us see anything if they were secretly planning invasion," Cynia said before Talyn could point it out. "But there are little things you can't hide."

"More than that." Leviana leaned forward, using filling her cup as a pretence. "The Callanan have sent Armun in and out of Acleu and Darinoue, crewing on merchant ships. They report nil change at the large military bases outside both those towns. No increase in troops barracked there, no extra training activity, nothing."

Talyn frowned. "Maybe we need to consider that the First Blade's informant is making this all up."

"*Why?*" Sari asked.

"For what possible reason?" Leviana echoed Talyn's partner.

"The First Blade talked us through all the details when she briefed us," Cynia said. "She and Master Ranar verified other information the informant provided us. There's no reason to think he or she is lying about this."

"Which leaves us with the ahara and his generals being far better at concealing their planning than we expected," Talyn reasoned. "Any preparation must be happening outside the capital and away from easily accessible areas like the main ports—maybe in the interior of the country, or even in the mountain region. A troubling thought."

"But not surprising." Cynia sounded uneasy, though she kept a smile on her face for the benefit of the soldiers watching. "Given the informant says knowledge of the ahara's plans is being held inside a trusted circle of associates."

Talyn's hand curled around her teacup, and she fought to keep frustration from her face. "We have to do something more than just sit around waiting for the invasion to happen." Now that Vengeance was done, she needed something more to do. Something to make sure they all stayed safe.

Leviana shrugged. "The informant will keep us apprised, surely."

Cynia shot a look at her partner. Leviana made a face.

"What?" Talyn snapped.

"We communicate with Master Ranar via coded messages," Leviana said. "We send a lot of official letters that I'm sure the Montagni read before they leave the capital, and that gives us nice cover for the more discreet messages. We can't afford to do it often, but we just got one yesterday."

"Ranar wanted to know if anything out of the ordinary had happened here. The informant missed his last scheduled contact."

Talyn hid the chill those words sent through her. "There are a million different reasons why that might have happened."

"Agreed," Leviana said. "And nothing out of the usual has occurred here. No nobles suddenly going missing or anything like that."

"*I don't like it, Talyn.*"

"*Me either.*" Talyn ran her gaze past the shop windows. The two soldiers were still across the street, awkwardly pretending to loiter in conversation. "We should go. I don't want them getting suspicious about how long we've been in here."

"*And if the ahara is clever enough to hide his plans so well, he's clever enough to have you followed without you realising.*"

The Callanan caught the tone in Talyn's voice and complied without complaint. Leviana swallowed the remainder of her tea, and the three of them made their way to the door.

"How would you like to come and meet my Wolves?" she asked loudly as they emerged onto the street.

"Sounds great!" Cynia said cheerfully.

THE WOLVES not on duty were taking part in a mock scrimmage as Talyn and the two Callanan came through the gate.

"Wow, the ahara thinks highly of Prince Cuinn, doesn't he?" Cynia noted when it became clear how far away the barracks were from the main areas of the palace.

"I think that applies to the whole family apart from Azrilan," Talyn said.

The talons were supervising, but came over when Talyn appeared, as always pleased to see her. She wondered if she would ever get used to the warmth that spread through her at that. Neither Callanan missed it either, but she ignored their sidelong glances.

"Leviana, Cynia, my Wolves." Talyn made introductions. "You've met Corrin and Zamaril. Theac is my second, and the pretty one is Tiercelin. Andres is my fifth talon, but he's commanding Prince Cuinn's detail right now."

Talyn waited while the Wolves and Callanan exchanged greetings. Her talons looked pleased to be meeting friends of Talyn's, and the two Callanan were fascinated, their glances frequently shifting to where the Wolves trained in the yard—particularly the winged folk.

"How long have you been in Arataire?" Corrin asked them.

"Just over a month," Cynia explained. "It's an interesting place."

"Do we have visitors?" a musical voice interrupted.

Both Leviana and Cynia's eyes widened as Cuinn dropped out of the sky, silver-white wings catching the afternoon sun as he landed gracefully then furled them behind his back. Liadin and Kiran were with him, keeping a closer eye on their charge until the rest of the detail could catch up. The three standing together were a stunning sight for one not accustomed to winged folk beauty.

"Prince Cuinn." Talyn turned, her smile widening at his arrival. "Meet Leviana and Cynia. They're the Callanan pair currently filling the Twin Thrones' liaison post in Montagn. They also happen to be two of my oldest friends."

Cuinn's eyes shifted to hers, reassuring her without words that he remembered he wasn't supposed to know them, then he beamed at both Callanan. "Captain Dynan has told me about you. It's lovely to meet you."

"She's spoken of you too." Cynia was the first to recover from Cuinn's beauty and charm, though Leviana was still gaping like a fish. Talyn nudged her discreetly.

Cuinn laughed. "I can only imagine the awful things she's told you."

"Are you here for a good reason?" Talyn interjected, raising her eyebrows at him.

"Is needing to escape the cloying attentions of the ahara's nobles a good reason?" He made a face. "I thought coming back here for the shift change would give me some breathing space."

Talyn smothered a smile. "Tiercelin and his detail are ready to go."

"Good." His smile was all for Talyn, lingering a moment before turning to the Callanan. "Leviana, Cynia, it's been a pleasure. Will I see you again before we leave?"

Leviana had recovered, and returned the prince's smile. "We've been invited to attend the ball being held in honour of you and Lady Kaeri tomorrow night, Prince Cuinn. And as we have it on good authority that the Montagni rarely indulge in anything as frivolous as a ball, we're extremely excited about it."

"Good. I look forward to it." Cuinn turned to go, but then hesitated, a frown on his face. "You are old friends of Talyn's. Does that mean... did you know Sari?"

Both Callanan stilled, and Cuinn flinched at the grief that must have emanated from both of them. "I didn't mean to bring up old wounds," he apologised. "From what Talyn has told me, she was a great friend and warrior."

Theac shot a warning glance in Cuinn's direction, but cleared his throat. "We talons feel the same way. If Captain Dynan had never known Sari, I doubt any of us would be here today."

Talyn couldn't look at either of them. Both Callanan murmured a genuine thanks, then Cuinn was gone, Tiercelin and his detail falling in around him. Clearing her throat, Talyn turned and gave Leviana a playful shove. "You gaped."

Neither of them laughed.

"He knows about Sari, Tal?" Cynia asked, puzzlement in her voice.

"My talons do. I spoke to them about it. What of it?"

"Well, we just..." Cynia's voice trailed off and she glanced at her partner. Leviana shrugged. "Nothing."

"In that case, how would you like to train with us this afternoon?" Talyn changed the subject. "I'd love to see one of you try and beat Zamaril and his sword in a sparring match."

"Hells, yes!" Leviana agreed with enthusiasm. "Let me at him."

She lost. So did Cynia.

. . .

BOTH TALYN and Theac were expected to attend the ball, news which Theac took with a look of distaste so intense Talyn burst out laughing. Although she and Theac would be required to attend in dress uniform, Talyn joined Leviana and Cynia to keep them company as they prepared themselves beforehand.

"I certainly don't hate this part of being a formal liaison of the Twin Thrones." Leviana sighed in pleasure as she began applying eye makeup. "It's been too long since I've enjoyed a ball."

"This is why I joined the Callanan." Talyn shot her friend an affectionate glance. "Smaller chance of having to dress up like that."

"I'm with her." Cynia jerked a thumb at Talyn.

Leviana gave them both dirty looks.

"How many knives have you got hidden in there?" Talyn asked once Leviana had satisfied herself that she looked perfect—which she absolutely did. She was a stunning sight.

"Guess?"

Cynia groaned. "Can we not play that game? I don't want to be late."

They approached the enormous ballroom from above. Pausing there, they leaned over the railing to observe the event unfolding below them. The ahara and all his attendants were dressed richly, and many had their wives with them. All were liberally draped with gold and jewels. It was a sight that made Talyn inherently uncomfortable— she'd never enjoyed the formality and glamour that came with being part of court—and she reached back to slide a hand over the hilt of one of her daggers for reassurance. She was a warrior. Nothing more.

For such a grim castle, the room below was full of light, courtesy of the lamps lit on what appeared to be every available surface. Slave girls moved in and out of the throng delivering drinks and plates of food, and attending whenever one of the guests wanted something.

"It's quite the affair," Cynia murmured in wonderment.

"I miss these," Leviana said mournfully.

Cynia squeezed her partner's arm in quiet sympathy.

"It would be lovely if it weren't for the slaves," Talyn muttered.

"And there's our dear Dumnorix friend." Leviana sighed.

The women shared a smile.

Cuinn and his retinue arrived a few moments later. They looked magnificent as winged folk always did, but Talyn couldn't tear her eyes from Cuinn. He wore a sky-blue silk jacket over white breeches and boots, and wore an amused smile as he spoke to Jenseno and Annae.

Talyn's heart clenched. What *was* this she was feeling? It was unexpected and unfamiliar and made her as uncomfortable as staring down at the finery of the ball did.

"You could have any one of them that you wanted tonight, Tal," Leviana said mischievously.

"What?" She tore her eyes away.

"Uniform aside, you've got those stunning Dumnorix eyes. Perhaps you should think about taking a handsome Montagni lord to your bed?" Cynia teased. "Your uncle would certainly be impressed if you snagged a powerful one to take home. Especially since you've ditched Tarcos."

Talyn smiled at her, chuckling. "I'm sure he would. Shall we go down?"

Talyn followed a step behind as the two Callanan made their way down the stairs and spent the next full-turn moving about the room with her friends, engaging in small talk with members of the ahara's nobility.

Part of Leviana and Cynia's job that night was not only to network and build on the relationship between Ryathl and Arataire, but also seek to identify anyone that might be willing to give them information, someone susceptible to extra coin or other inducements. After a while she left them to it, not wanting to interfere.

Even though part of her ached to go back to the time when that had been her and Sari.

Sari roused. *"It's been a while since you've felt that."*

"It has."

And she left it at that.

Cynia had been right—multiple Montagni lords invited her for a private walk in the gardens outside, or had something to show her in a private room a short distance away. Each of these invitations she refused as politely as she could, before sharing a laugh and smile with Leviana and Cynia whenever they passed.

Theac glowered from the corner and refused all but one of her attempts to engage him in conversation. "Bloody rabble," he muttered on the one occasion he did speak. "All these pretty clothes and expensive food, for what?"

"It's diplomacy, Theac. We're witnessing a prince and princess courting."

His scowl deepened. "She's not a princess."

Talyn's eyebrows lifted. "You don't like her."

"I don't know her. But I don't want some Montagni marrying Prince Cuinn."

She chuckled. "You sound like an over-protective father. Who would be okay for him to marry?"

Theac glanced at her, then away. "You don't want to hear my thoughts on that."

"All right, Theac." She left him to it.

Eventually the servants finished delivering the food and drinks, and the ahara called for a start to the dancing. Leviana was led off by a handsome general and Cynia fell into conversation with another commander—a white haired man who seemed interested in her take on Montagni weaponry. Talyn stood sipping at a glass of wine and watching the dancing.

Corrin's detail was on duty, and they had the room guarded from every angle she herself would have chosen, so there was little for her to do. When Cuinn and the ahara strolled in her direction, Talyn straightened and discreetly put aside her glass.

"Your Majesty." She bowed politely.

"It is sad to see such a beautiful woman not dancing at my ball," the ahara said. "It is remiss of your prince not to remedy that."

"I prefer not to dance. I am more warrior than courtier, Your Majesty."

"My captain is polite, Your Majesty, but I believe she is making the point that it would be more appropriate for me to dance with one of my own retinue," Cuinn said smoothly.

"Ah yes." Distaste flickered over the ahara's face. "Winged folk attitudes towards your human people are most puzzling."

"Not to us." Cuinn smiled to take the sting from his words. "Perhaps your daughter would agree to another dance with me, if you permit it?"

"I am sure she would." The ahara dismissed Talyn without a look and the two made their way across the ballroom.

Talyn's eyes closed briefly in relief. Irial would have reported any dancing between her and Cuinn back to Mithanis. Not to mention being so close to him would only bring the memories of their night together flooding back, how it had felt to touch him, press against him, the sensation of his mouth, his hands... She forced such thoughts from her head and lifted her wine glass, draining it in one swallow. How many had she drunk?

"Three," Sari offered promptly. *"Aren't you on duty?"*

Maybe she'd go and do another check on the Wolves.

Cynia caught at her arm as she moved away from the dance floor, giving her a start. She hadn't even noticed her friend approach. "What is going on with you, Tal?"

"What do you mean?" she asked, puzzled.

"Talyn..." Cynia guided her over to a quiet corner. "He's been staring at you all night."

She frowned. "Who, the ahara?"

"No." Cynia's voice gentled. "Prince Cuinn. Talyn, you told him about Sari?"

She rolled her eyes, huffing out a breath. "I don't understand why that's such a big deal."

"Then you're being deliberately obtuse," Cynia said pointedly. "I'm your friend. You can talk to me. What's going on?"

"There's nothing—"

"I saw you earlier, when Prince Cuinn was dancing with Lady Kaeri. You looked sick," she said.

"I did nothing of the sort." Discomfort was turning to an aching need to stop talking about this. "Listen to you—does that sound like me at all?"

"Talyn, stop!" Cynia shook her slightly. "Stop thinking you have to keep everything hidden and buried inside you just because Sari is gone. We are your friends too. You can lean on us."

"Cynia…" Talyn lifted a hand to rub her forehead, suddenly tired. "There are things you don't know, about Cuinn, about me, and I can't tell you what they are. Not because I don't trust you, but because they're not my secrets to tell."

"Then I won't pretend to understand why, but…" Cynia's gaze searched her face. "You have feelings for him?"

Talyn gave a sharp nod, the words coming out in a rush. "It's not like you think. It's impossible, and I know it."

"Why's it impossible?"

"You know the answer to that," Talyn said sharply, resentful that she was being forced to say it out loud. "I'm a Dumnorix. He's an Acondor prince. We don't get choices about things like this."

Cynia's eyes widened. "Yeah, but that wasn't a consideration when you took Tarcos as a lover. You had lovers before him too. Why would it matter now, unless you wanted more than…"

"What?" Talyn frowned.

"Your mother made her own choice, Tal."

"This is different."

"Right." Cynia sighed. "More secrets. Do what's best for you, that's my advice. "

Talyn leaned over and hugged her. "Thanks for being my non-judgemental friend."

"Any time." Cynia smirked. "He is very pretty."

She managed a chuckle.

"*Talyn—*"

"*Not you too.*" Talyn cut Sari off.

"*Why, for once, can't you do what you want, rather than what everyone else expects?*"

She needed more wine.

333

. . .

SHE WENT in through his bedroom window. Fortunately Cuinn's quarters were on the ground floor of the guest wing. Even so, she'd almost been spotted by Wolves on guard on three different occasions, and it took standing still as a statue in the shadows by the window for almost a quarter-turn before she had an opportunity to slip inside unseen.

She'd changed out of her formal uniform after the ball, not wanting to try sneaking around in such easily marked attire, instead donning shirt and breeches and bare feet for silence.

The reckless Talyn was back—spurred on by too many glasses of spiced wine, having to stand and watch Cuinn dance with another princess, and the admission she'd made to Cynia that had left her aching and unable to stay away.

He was awake in the darkness, gaze distant as he stared up at his ceiling, clearly thinking rather than trying to sleep. Those luminous green eyes shot to hers, surprised, as she reached the bed and slid under the covers, shifting over him before leaning down to capture his mouth in a long, heated kiss. He didn't hesitate, didn't object, simply wrapped his arms around her and kissed her back as if he were dying of thirst and she was the only water left in the world.

"Don't marry her," she whispered, kissing him again. "Don't marry her."

He kissed her back, hard, then slid his mouth along her jaw, down her neck, turning them in the bed until he was above her. His hands slid to the hem of her shirt, tugging it up and over her head. "I'll never marry her," he whispered in her ear, then brought his mouth back to hers. "Never."

They were slower this time, an exploration of heat and touch and shuddering breath. It hadn't been like this before, not with Tarcos, not with anyone else, and she craved more of it, of the magic and sensation and feeling of utter safety.

Eventually, panting softly, skin slicked with sweat, they lay entangled, Cuinn's wings shrouding them like a silver blanket.

"I'm glad you came." He pressed a kiss to her forehead.

She closed her eyes, nestled closer against him. Everything inside her felt calm. Content. "Me too."

Cuinn shifted back so he could capture her gaze. "Not that I want to ruin the moment," he said. "But this is the first chance we've had to speak privately since we got here. Have you found anything?"

"Frustratingly little," she said, and filled him in on what she'd learned from Leviana and Cynia. "What about you?"

His eyes narrowed thoughtfully. "Disturbingly consistent with your Callanan, I'm afraid. I've been using every inch of song magic I possess, and there's nothing. No hint of secrecy, or of something being hidden from us. I've never felt aggression from the ahara, or any malevolent intent."

"I don't like it," Talyn said. "The Callanan have their informant and will be well-warned before anything happens to the Twin Thrones. But Mithranar doesn't have that luxury."

"What are you suggesting?" He turned to face her, his wing curling closer around her body, the silky touch of feathers a delight on her bare skin.

She hesitated. "I don't want to keep sitting back and waiting for more information from the First Blade. As soon as we're home, we go after Navis with everything we have. And if that doesn't get us anywhere, then we work out some other way of warning your mother and the Falcon."

"Then that's what we'll do." He pressed his forehead against hers.

"I can't stay," she whispered.

"I know," he breathed. "Together?"

His eyes were watching her, unblinking, and she leaned across the incremental distance to press her mouth to his. "Always together."

It wasn't long after midnight when Talyn snuck out of Cuinn's rooms and turned to head back to the barracks.

"Captain?" Tiercelin's surprised voice rang out.

Shit.

335

Talking a breath, she did a quick check to make sure all her clothes were in place, then turned with a smile. "Tiercelin. You're on shift?"

He nodded. "But my detail has everything in hand. What brings you here?"

"You know me." She shrugged. "Just doing an extra check before I turn in."

He stopped, hands clasped before him, head cocked slightly. "So you weren't just sneaking out of Prince Cuinn's bedroom?"

"I—"

"You were the one that trained us, Captain. If I didn't know who was in there at all times, I'd hardly be doing my job, no?"

She cleared her throat. "I had to talk to him about something." It was technically true.

"You'll need to tell me how you got past my guards. That's a vulnerability I want to patch quickly."

Heat flooded her cheeks at the twinkle of amusement in his hazel eyes. "You're having fun with this, aren't you?"

"To be honest, I don't know what to think."

"Then how about we just leave it at that."

"Fair enough." He chuckled. "Except to say that I hope you're drinking that tea I gave you, because if you—"

"I understand the consequences better than anyone, Tiercelin." She cut him off sharply.

"Good. Then can I walk you to the barracks? This fortress is a bit of a rabbit warren and it's a long walk." He paused, glancing back. "That is, of course, unless you'd like to sneak back in there?"

"What I'd like is to put you and your detail on barracks-cleaning duty for a month if you don't stop there," she warned.

He straightened. "Yes, Captain. I'll walk you back quietly."

They fell in together, not saying anything, just comfortable in each other's presence. After a while, it became obvious they were in a section of the castle she hadn't been to before. She halted. "Where are we?"

Tiercelin looked around. "I have no idea," he said sheepishly.

"So much for escorting me back." She scowled. "You've gotten us lost."

Footsteps sounded behind them, approaching from around the corner. Her Callanan training automatically assessed them—two men, talking softly. Tiercelin put his finger to his lips and drew her into an alcove.

"What are you doing?" she hissed.

"Who knows what section of the castle we're in?" he said. "I don't want to get arrested for accidentally stumbling into the ahara's personal quarters or something."

She thought he was being a little paranoid, but by then the men had drawn close enough that it was going to look suspicious to be seen emerging from a hidden alcove in the corridor. With a sigh and rolled eyes in Tiercelin's direction, they huddled further into the shadows.

The voices grew clearer as the bootsteps rounded the corner and stopped outside a doorway almost directly across from them. She craned her neck, trying to see. Their backs were to her, but she could hear them talk.

"You shouldn't hesitate, General. Everything is in place." Eagerness threaded the man's voice. He sounded young, around Corrin's age.

Tiercelin started in surprise, and she touched his shoulder to still him. If this was the mysteriously absent general of the ahara's armies, they definitely did not want to get caught eavesdropping.

"I'm not hesitating, I'm waiting for the right moment. That's a difference you'd do well to learn, Asyan."

"I understand."

"The repercussions if we failed could be... and I don't trust..." Manunin's voice quietened even further, making his next words unclear.

"House Neserin have promised an alliance against..." Again the voices dropped too low to make out. Eventually the door opened with a soft creak, Asyan stepping back deferentially to allow Manunin to enter first. Voices from within welcomed them as they entered, and then the door closed, leaving the corridor empty.

Talyn took a breath. "What was that all about?"

"Sounds like internal Montagni politics to me," Tiercelin said. "Neserin is another of the powerful families. From what I understand, the Houses are constantly jockeying for power and influence with the ahara."

She sighed. "We'd better get out of here before someone sees us. The last thing we need is someone accusing us of spying."

As they walked off, Talyn made a mental note to let Leviana and Cynia know what she'd overheard. They might be able to make better sense of it than her.

"*Are we going to discuss the fact you just snuck into Cuinn's bed?*" Sari asked.

"*Nope.*"

"*Excellent. What about the fact you essentially just promised him that you would breach the First Blade's trust and warn Mithranar about impending invasion?*"

"*I'm not going to breach her trust. I'm going to find another way.*"

"*And if Montagn invades Mithranar. What are you going to do?*"

Talyn smiled grimly. "*I'm going to fight.*"

CHAPTER 31

Theac's detail was just beginning its shift when Cuinn awoke the next morning, and he sent the grizzled talon off with a request for an audience with the ahara before settling down to breakfast. As usual, Irial and Jenseno came to join him once they were awake.

Irial looked surprised when Theac returned to say that the ahara had agreed to see Cuinn in a half-turn in his personal quarters. "I thought you were trying to avoid as much of the official stuff as possible?"

"I am." Cuinn pushed away his plate. "But this should be quick."

Before either of his friends could say anything, he left them to go and dress, choosing a simple outfit of dark blue jacket and breeches over a sky-blue shirt.

He hummed a light melody as he dressed, unable to keep the smile from his face. He should be anxious, worried. But instead he was... happy. It had been so long since he'd felt it, it took him a moment to recognise the emotion.

All he'd needed her to do was ask.

It still bowled him over that she had.

Theac cleared his throat from the doorway, interrupting the humming. "How concerned do I need to be about this meeting?"

"I'm not entirely certain." The ahara wasn't going to be happy... probably. It had been difficult to determine how the man truly felt about Cuinn marrying his daughter. But like he'd told Talyn the previous night, his song magic hadn't picked up an inch of malice or aggression from the ahara where Cuinn was concerned—all he'd sensed was the usual politely-concealed contempt he received from all the Montagni nobles. "Though Mithanis is going to be very upset with me when we get back. Probably."

It continued to make him uncomfortable that he didn't understand why Mithanis was supportive of the proposed marriage. At least by refusing the betrothal, he didn't have to worry anymore what Mithanis's motives were.

"Perhaps you'd like to tell me what this meeting is about, then, Your Highness?" Theac asked.

"You'll see soon enough." He glanced over. "Come on, let's go!"

Theac's glower deepened, but Cuinn was sweeping out of the room before he could demand more answers.

IRIAL INSISTED on coming with him, which was expected. His friend couldn't report back to Mithanis if he wasn't there to hear everything that was said during Cuinn's meetings with the ahara. Sometimes Cuinn wondered if Irial knew how obvious it all was. He probably didn't care. After all, Cuinn was no threat to Irial. Mithanis was.

Theac and his detail followed dutifully, eyes studying their surroundings as carefully inside this fortress as they would anywhere else. The guards outside the ahara's personal quarters—two hulking Berserkers with massive broadswords strapped to their backs—stepped aside silently at Cuinn's appearance.

Theac gave both Berserkers a polite nod, then stepped forward and opened the double doors. When no danger lunged out, Theac moved aside so that Cuinn and Irial could enter. Irial smirked at this display of protectiveness. Cuinn gave Theac a wink.

Seated at a table beyond the doors, dressed far less formally than usual and sipping at a glass of water, the ahara remained an intimidating man. He seemed in an amiable mood though, rising to greet Cuinn with a polite bow of his head.

Behind them, Theac closed the doors and stood at attention. Irial, at Cuinn's side, bowed respectfully.

"Is there something wrong, Prince Cuinn?" the ahara asked. "I had not expected to see you until our scheduled lunch with my daughter this afternoon."

"Nothing is wrong, and I apologise for interrupting your morning. I understand how busy you are," Cuinn said respectfully. "I won't take much of your time."

"Then how can I help you?" The ahara remained standing, seeming to sense that this wasn't going to be a conversation for sitting comfortably around his breakfast table.

"I came to speak to you in regard to your daughter." Cuinn used hints of magic to infuse his voice with respect, sincerity and a dash of apology. "Princess Kaeri is beautiful, accomplished and a credit to you, Your Majesty. It is because of this I must decline your offer of marriage. She deserves better than a life as a human in Mithranar."

Understanding and something like shock rippled over the ahara's face. He frowned. "I don't understand. Your mother and I have agreed to this match."

"I think you do," Cuinn said gently.

Irial had stiffened at Cuinn's side, and he was sending sharp jolts of emotion Cuinn's way—a warning to stop and think about what he was doing. Cuinn didn't dare say more with Irial standing right there, but the ahara knew exactly what Cuinn was getting at. The man was too smart, too well informed, not to understand what life would be like for his human daughter in Mithranar.

"You are the third, unnecessary prince," the ahara said crisply, ignoring Irial as clearly as Cuinn was. "You would be welcome to live here, with my daughter and her family."

"A generous offer, but one I could not accept. Unnecessary prince or not, my home is Mithranar, Your Majesty," Cuinn said.

There was a long moment of silence as the ahara stared at him and Irial continued being furious at his side. Shonin Venador was a powerful man. He could take this as an insult, as the excuse he needed to start a war, but Cuinn's magic told him this was unlikely. The ahara was a hard man. Ruthless. But he cared about his daughter, loved her even. And while he'd agreed to this match because he was a king and his children were strategic tools, Cuinn was offering him a graceful out.

"My daughter will be disappointed, I think," the ahara said eventually. "But like you, she loves her home, and I think it will cheer her that she won't have to leave it."

Everything in Cuinn relaxed. "I am glad, Your Majesty."

"Prince Cuinn, can I have a moment to—" Irial interjected as politely as he could, his song magic pummelling Cuinn with his anger and insistence.

Cuinn didn't take his gaze off the ahara as he threw his own song magic back at Irial, stifling him completely. Irial flinched and took a half step back.

"I appreciate you coming to speak honestly with me, Prince Cuinn." Was that a hint of respect in the ahara's eyes? "And I accept your decision. Does this mean you'll be returning to Mithranar earlier than planned?"

"We will leave tomorrow, Your Majesty. I think that's best." Cuinn offered a smile. "But I look forward to seeing you in summer when my brother Azrilan and I come for our usual visit."

The ahara offered his hand. "Until then, Prince Cuinn."

Cuinn took it, shook firmly. Irial was a stewing mess of frustration and anger at his side, but he remained firmly quelled.

Leaving the ahara to his breakfast, Cuinn turned to leave. Theac's expression was impassive as he opened the doors for Cuinn and Irial to walk through.

"What do you think you're doing?" Irial hissed as they walked away, Wolves silently falling in around them.

"Isn't that obvious?" Cuinn asked.

"You've lost your mind. Why didn't you discuss it with me before speaking with the ahara?" Irial's fists clenched tightly at his side.

"Because it has nothing to do with you," Cuinn said mildly. "It's *my* potential marriage."

"Your mother and brother arranged the match. You can't just blow it off."

"And yet I just did."

Irial stopped walking, forcing Cuinn to stop too. "I'm your friend, Cuinn, and this is a mistake."

"Why?"

"Because you know what happens when people go against Prince Mithanis."

Silence fell, Irial's words echoing down the corridor while the Wolves pretended not to listen. It was the first time Irial had ever spoken so bluntly aloud.

"I'm not going against him," Cuinn said quietly. "I will never do that. He is my brother and our future king and I will help him when and where I can. I just don't want to marry this woman."

Irial's jaw clenched. "I think we should stay like we planned to. Give it some more time. I can speak to the ahara's people today, tell him you were temporarily having doubts. If you spend more time with Lady Kaeri, you might—"

Cuinn smiled. "I don't need more time. She's nice enough, but I don't want a wife. You know me."

"I did." Irial's eyes roved his, not fooled. "But you haven't taken a lover in months, so this can't be about your predilection for bedding every pretty woman in sight."

"And exactly how closely have you been paying attention, Irial?" Cuinn stepped closer, an edge to his voice. The man's constant pushing was beginning to grate.

An edge of hurt lined Irial's voice. "I'm your best friend. I know when you have a lover."

You're Mithanis's informant. He wanted to throw those words at Irial, but it wouldn't be smart to reveal how much he knew. "Exactly.

So I don't know why it surprises you so much that I don't want to marry." Cuinn threw his hands in the air in exasperation.

"I just think we should stay longer," he said stubbornly.

He caught it then. The flash over Irial's face. The hint of desperation in his emotions. Irial was a skilled song mage, and he hid himself well, but Cuinn was better. Irial didn't want them going home earlier than planned.

Fear thudded through him as sickening realisation took hold.

Had Mithanis just wanted him out of Mithranar for a time? Was *that* the reason he'd supported their mother's insistence on sending him here—not because he supported the marriage, but because he wanted Cuinn far away?

"Why, Irial?"

"Your brother wants you to be here, courting the princess." Irial had recovered his poise. "This match will help our country. You should be doing as they ask."

Cuinn hesitated. He was seconds away from throwing every bit of song magic he had at Irial and forcing him to tell the truth, to reveal what Mithanis was up to. But if his guess was wrong, he'd be revealing himself and the depth of his power to Irial, who would tell Mithanis the moment they returned.

So he took a step back, mastered himself. "We're going home tomorrow. First thing. Make sure you and the rest are up and ready to leave at dawn. If you're not we'll leave you behind."

"Cuinn, I think—"

"Enough, Irial," he said, then strode away. Anxiousness churned in his gut. Something was wrong... he could feel it. Why would Mithanis want him out of Mithranar? Was that what Azrilan had been trying to warn him about?

Theac caught up to him as he reached the door to his quarters. "Your Highness?"

"Tell Captain Dynan we leave at first light. I want to get back to Mithranar."

"Something wrong?"

Cuinn swallowed. "I just want to get back to the citadel as soon as possible."

Theac's gaze searched his. "Then we will, Your Highness."

He hoped he was being paranoid. Imagining problems where there were none.

And if not… well, then he hoped with everything he had that they got back in time.

CHAPTER 32

alyn went to see Cynia and Leviana after dawn drill, wanting to relay the conversation she and Tiercelin had overheard the night before. Sipping tea, the three of them puzzled over what it might mean.

"Internal politics, I'd say," Cynia said, agreeing with Tiercelin. "A lot of it goes on here, the Houses vying with each other for more power and influence."

"It doesn't help that the next ahara won't necessarily be the current one's child." Leviana sighed.

"Right." Talyn frowned, reaching back to her old Callanan lessons. "When an ahara dies, the most powerful Houses argue over who replaces him? The strongest candidate wins."

"Yes. So what you heard is probably a bit of pre-positioning," Cynia said. "Even though the ahara isn't that old, and he's a healthy man."

"It nags at me though." Talyn lowered her voice and leaned forward. "The general has been strangely absent from all the gatherings since we arrived, yet he's clearly here in the city."

"He might be hiding from your winged song mages," Leviana said. "He would be the one preparing an invasion, after all."

346

"That is a really good point."

Talyn smiled a little. "Sari says you're smart."

Distracted, she'd spoken without thinking, but Cynia only chuckled. "She sends you messages from beyond the grave?"

Talyn opened her mouth to laugh it off, but something stopped her. Leviana and Cynia were her closest friends in the world. Cuinn hadn't treated her like she was crazy after she told him. Maybe she should have more faith in them. So she took a breath, then... "Actually no, she's still with me. In my head."

Talyn braced herself for the sudden furious attention of both Callanan, unsurprised to see puzzlement, concern and awkwardness there. "Before you start becoming seriously worried that I've lost my mind, I haven't. It's a result of my winged folk magic."

"Explain," Leviana instructed.

So she did.

And to her everlasting relief, they believed her.

Cynia frowned. "This whole winged folk magic business totally confuses me."

"It shouldn't. I'm pretty sure our Callanan shields are a remnant of winged folk magic. It's just stronger in me because my father was winged." She hesitated. "It's part of the reason I struggled so much when she died—my magic was injured, torn apart."

"That actually makes a lot of sense," Leviana said quietly. "She's still really here?"

"Part of her, yeah." Talyn nodded. "It's not the same, but it's—"

A knock came at the door. Both Callanan started, the shroud of sadness and still-there grief that had fallen over them broken by the sharp noise. Leviana bellowed for whoever it was to come in.

Talyn's eyebrows lifted in surprise to see Theac pushing the door open. "Is something wrong?"

"Not exactly, Captain." He glanced at the two Callanan. "Prince Cuinn asked me to inform you we'll be leaving tomorrow. First thing."

"Why so soon?" Leviana frowned. "Weren't you scheduled to be here another week or so?"

Theac cleared his throat. "He went to visit the ahara this morning, to tell him he wouldn't be marrying Lady Kaeri."

Talyn slowly put down her mug of tea and studiously ignored the burning stares from her two friends. Her heart had started thudding so loudly she was surprised the others couldn't hear it. Even though she'd asked Cuinn to turn the princess down, she didn't realise he'd take it so seriously, that he'd go straight to the ahara. Emotion churned in too confusing a tangle to understand.

"Did he say why?" Cynia asked.

"He just said that the lady deserved better than life as a human in Mithranar." Theac turned serious. "Lord Swiftwing was furious. And I think something about their exchange worried the prince."

Talyn cleared her throat. "Thanks, Theac. I'll come and find you in a bit and we'll get everything sorted for departure."

He saluted and left, closing the door behind him.

Talyn turned to face her friends, bracing herself for the inevitable questions, when another sharp knock came at the door. This one was a slave, holding a message for the Callanan.

Leviana tore the seal open, frown creasing her forehead as she read its contents then passed it silently to Cynia to read. Her dark eyes lifted to meet Talyn's. "It's from the First Blade. She wants us home immediately."

Talyn's heart thudded again, this time from shock. "Why? You've only been here a month."

"It doesn't say," Cynia murmured, reading the contents again. "Just that we're to leave immediately and come to Ryathl."

"Won't the ahara ask questions?"

"The king has already written to him apparently, providing an excuse for our departure."

Her unease deepened. "Why would she demand you back so precipitously?"

"The only thing I can think is that she's gotten something from the informant that prompted this." Leviana's face was worried as she looked at her partner.

Cynia nodded. "Or maybe he still hasn't made contact. We'd better get moving."

"I should too." Talyn stepped closer, wrapped an arm around each of them and drew them into a tight hug. "I'm so glad I got to see you. Be safe."

SHE WENT to see Cuinn that night once she'd satisfied herself that the Wolves were packed up and ready for a dawn departure. Anticipation and unease rippled through them, a feeling she'd had difficulty dispelling. Those who'd been on duty with Theac that morning had relayed news of Cuinn's fight with Irial to the rest of the wing. And Lyra, on afternoon duty with Halun's detail under Corrin, reported that Irial was seething with well-hidden anger and fear.

The ahara hosted Cuinn for a farewell dinner. Kaeri was not present, yet it was the most relaxed and friendly Talyn had ever seen the ahara with winged folk.

Cuinn's anxiousness was apparent though, despite how well he hid it. So she went openly to his quarters after the dinner, ostensibly to discuss the following morning's departure. He was standing before his fire, entire frame tense, his friends dispensed with for the night. At her appearance, he turned, relief flashing over his face.

The minute Andres closed the door behind them, she spoke. "Tell me what happened."

"Irial was predictably upset at my decision to spurn the match." Cuinn's eyes darkened as they met hers. "But I pushed him on it, and I think he was more worried that we were leaving early than anything else. I got the distinct impression he was afraid of what would happen if we went home too soon."

"*Oh no, Talyn.*"

She leapt to the same conclusion as Sari. "You think Mithanis wanted us out of Mithranar for some reason?"

Cuinn swallowed. "We've been trying to figure out why he supported this match. What if he just wanted a good reason to get me out of Mithranar for a while?"

"But why?" She frowned. "If he wanted to move against you, then why would he hesitate about doing it openly?"

"I don't know. Maybe I'm overreacting." He ran a hand through his hair.

"And maybe you're not," she said quietly, trying to come up with some other possibilities. "You've been more active in the Queen-council recently—maybe there were some things he wanted to introduce, like more taxes, and didn't want to have to deal with you protesting it."

He shook his head doubtfully, and she found herself agreeing. That didn't feel right. Mithanis didn't need to worry about Cuinn's protests in the council. Still...

"What if Ravinire said something?" Cuinn addressed the elephant in the room.

She let out a breath. An axe was hovering over their heads. She'd been hoping that the more time that passed without the Falcon doing anything about his suspicions, the more likely it was he never would. After all, he was the queen's man through and through. And the queen didn't want Cuinn dead.

"You can't rely on that."

"I know. But I don't see any other options." And it wasn't just that.

"If Ravinire said something, Mithanis would have had you arrested and killed straight away. He wouldn't have concocted a reason to get you out of Mithranar."

"But...?" Cuinn picked up on what she wasn't saying.

"I worry," she admitted. "You've been wonderful, the way you've used magic to deflect Mithanis's suspicions and keep from being seen as a threat. But the way he found out about me being a Ciantar—we still don't know how he got that information. What if he finds out about you?"

Cuinn's glimmering green gaze shifted to her, a question in them. "Finds out what?"

"Who your father is? If his spies found out who I am, when *I* didn't even know, then it's possible they could learn about you too."

He frowned. "But from what you've told me, the fact I'm Dumnorix is a tightly held secret. Only a handful of people know."

But that wasn't the only dangerous truth. She hadn't mentioned it to him, mainly because it hadn't occurred to her at the time or since. She'd been focused on telling him he was Dumnorix, and that Mithranar was under threat from Montagn. "I should have told you this too, but if Mithanis investigates your father... Cuinn, he wasn't just from the Dumnorix line. He was descended from the Acondor royal line too. You have Mithranan royal blood from both your parents."

Surprise flared over his face. "You're saying I technically have the strongest claim to both the Twin Thrones and the Mithranan throne?"

"Yes," she said firmly. "And if Mithanis learned that..."

Cuinn shook his head in amusement. "I couldn't think of a less worthy candidate to be heir to such power."

"Actually." Talyn couldn't hold his gaze. "I couldn't think of a better one."

There was a long, stunned, silence, then, "Talyn..."

"Enough." She straightened her shoulders. "All this speculating isn't helpful. Let's just get back home as quickly as we can and deal with whatever is waiting for us. Hopefully it's nothing, and we can turn our attention to Navis."

"It's not nothing." Cuinn said it with such certainty she shivered.

"I know."

"Go and get some sleep, Talyn."

"I..." She hesitated. "You didn't have to do what you did. Turn down Princess Kaeri, I mean. I shouldn't have asked."

"I'm glad you did," he said simply.

She opened her mouth, but had no idea what to say, so she just gave him a small smile and left. Andres saluted as she opened the door and left Cuinn's rooms. She managed a nod in his direction, then walked away, long strides carrying her quickly back towards the barracks.

"Talyn, be careful."

"*I know. I was just... I didn't even know I was going to say that about him being worthy of both crowns.*"

"*For what it's worth, I don't disagree.*"

"*I'm making it worse, the danger he's in. I should never have even contemplated those words, let alone said them out loud.*"

Sari hesitated. "*I don't disagree there either.*"

Talyn pressed a hand to her forehead in an attempt to forestall the headache brewing there. What was she doing?

CHAPTER 33

heir ship docked at the jetties of Feather Bay in the late morning almost two weeks later. Weariness tugged at Cuinn's muscles, clouded his thoughts. The trip home had been filled with nothing but growing anxiety about what might be awaiting them. He'd barely slept, and it hadn't helped that his worry had spread through the Wolves too.

On the surface, nothing appeared different from when they'd left. His shoulders relaxed at the familiar, bustling sight of Dock City. It was a warm day, but a faint breeze ruffled pleasantly through his hair and feathers, taking the edge off the heat.

Irial, Annae and his other friends had taken flight the moment the ship had entered the headlands of the bay. Cuinn had lingered on board. He shouldn't have—it was another thing for Irial to remark upon to Mithanis—but he'd wanted to get a proper look at the city before going in.

"I'm going to send two details up with you, just in case." Talyn appeared at his side, her eyes studying the city as well. She hadn't doubted his concern for a second, but that only made him more afraid. Her instincts were rarely wrong. "I'll settle the Wolves and go straight to see Ravinire to check in. If anything has happened, he'll tell me."

He nodded. "You'll pass any concerns through your talons?"

"I will. And you'll do the same?" Her voice was cool, professional.

They hadn't talked properly about it. About the second night they'd spent together, him refusing to marry Kaeri because she'd asked him to, none of it. He understood why. She hadn't been wrong when she'd said they'd only be chasing heartache if they kept going with their affair.

And she wasn't going to be here forever. He felt it in his bones. Eventually the Dumnorix would insist she come home. And she would answer her family's call.

Even then, he couldn't bring himself to regret what had happened between them. It didn't matter that she would leave. Whether he had her for a single night or a year or a moment. The joy of it... anything was worth that.

"Be careful, Captain," he couldn't help saying.

Her smile flashed. "I'm always careful."

SHE SENT Corrin's two details with him. He flew to the top of the wall with the winged Wolves, but there he hesitated, dropping lightly to the marble surface rather than continuing on. Everything *seemed* fine. The city bustled below him with its usual level of noise and chaos and heat.

But there was something.

He couldn't quite grasp it. A dissonant note echoing against his song magic.

Whatever it was, he wanted as many Wolves as possible at his back before he headed deeper into the citadel, so he waited for the human Wolves to catch up.

He wasn't waiting long before they were fanning out around him, Corrin just a step behind, not questioning why he'd waited, the talon's steadiness a comforting warmth to his magic.

The two Falcons on guard at the bridge over the Rush straightened in surprise at Cuinn's appearance. They stared for a moment, seem-ingly unsure what to say or do. Was it just that he was on foot instead of flying, that he was back earlier than expected? No. There was something else in their empty expressions.

Eventually one cleared his throat and stepped to the side. The other quickly followed suit. "Your Highness."

Cuinn studied them as he walked by. Both were pale. One was trembling slightly, as if he felt sick, or nervous. Or both.

"Lyra. Roalin?" he called quietly to the two song mages when they reached the other side of the bridge. Both alighted beside him a moment later, hands hovering near their weapons.

"Did you sense that?" he asked them.

"What is it?" Corrin's voice asked sharply.

"I felt fear," Lyra said.

"Shock, too, I think," Roalin added.

Cuinn nodded. "Something was wrong with those Falcons."

It wasn't just the Falcons. The sense he'd felt from them—fear and shock and something more—grew stronger the deeper they walked into the palace. The skies were quiet, too quiet, only a handful of winged folk out flying despite the sunny afternoon and cool breeze.

Dread crawled with icy fingers up his spine. His magic roused, warning him, worried.

"Corrin, was Halun at the docks waiting for you when you disem-barked?" he asked quietly.

"No, Your Highness. But he wouldn't have known we were returning so early."

He hoped that was all it was. Swallowing, and trying to keep the fear from his face so as not to alarm the Wolves, he began following the source of the emotions that had settled over the palace like a cloud. Behind him, Corrin called out a quiet order and the Wolves closed in protectively.

Cuinn's magic led him towards the Falcon barracks near the royal quarters. The air grew progressively quieter the closer they came, as if the afternoon were holding its breath. He began sensing the Wolves then—their growing trepidation, Corrin's increased focus, their preparation to fight if needed.

Lyra and Roalin dropped back out of the sky, both pale, the skin around their eyes drawn tight—typical signs of a song mage under emotional stress. At the sight of them, Corrin called another order, sending Dorsan to the Wolf barracks to fetch Talyn. Cuinn barely heard his reply. His magic was swirling through him now, the emotions beating at him like a drum. Fear. Grief. Shock.

What had happened?

They rounded a corner, the barracks housing the protective wing of the WingGuard laid out before them. Cuinn took half a step and froze, wings furling rigidly at his sides. Corrin drew steel, moving quicker than thought to stand in front of him, as if to block him from what was ahead. Several Wolves let out cries of horror and distress.

Eleven Falcons hung from the archway that formed the entrance to the barracks.

Dead. Days dead, by the look and smell of it.

Cuinn pushed Corrin aside, made himself walk forward, close enough so that he could see their faces. His throat closed over and tears pushed at the back of his eyes.

Ronisin Nightdrift and his entire detail.

A trembling hand rose to his mouth.

"Prince Cuinn!" Corrin's voice was sharp, a wiry arm tugging at his sleeve. "Prince Cuinn, look who it is."

He nodded, swallowed, tore his gaze away from the Falcons to look at his talon. "I know. I know."

"Ehdra, go down to Dock City. Find Halun." Corrin's voice was carefully controlled panic.

Ronisin had helped Talyn escape. He and his detail been friendly with the Wolves. If they'd killed him because of that, because of…

His entire body went cold.

Talyn. The Wolves.

Cuinn turned and leapt into flight.

CHAPTER 34

Talyn chuckled half-heartedly as Tiercelin made a joke, part of her attention on him, the rest taken up with worrying about what Mithanis might have done in their absence. The Wolves filed into the drill yard after her and the talons.

"Tiercelin, take a group inside to make sure everything is in order. Theac, Andres, get the rest cleaning the yard. A full-turn of that, then give them the rest of the afternoon off." She handed out orders quickly, wanting to be away, to see Ravinire, to work out whether everything was okay or not.

"Your wish is my command, Captain." Tiercelin bowed low and gracefully, knowing how it would irritate her, knowing that it would also distract her from her worry.

She gave him a smile, rolled her eyes like he was aiming for. "Get away with you."

But as soon as he walked away, her lighter mood vanished. Her instincts warned that they weren't okay. That something was off.

"Talyn, look at the sky." The same unease filled Sari's mental voice.

She glanced up, saw what she'd missed but her partner hadn't. It was a bright day, the sky above a cloudless blue, the thermals no doubt warm. Yet there were hardly any winged folk in the sky.

"Captain?" Liadin approached her, a worried look dispelling his usual cheerful expression. "My song magic... something's not right. I feel uneasy, on edge."

"Theac." She called him back. "Where are the winged folk?"

His face turned grim as he caught on to her meaning. "It's early afternoon. Maybe they're still eating or—"

"Captain!"

Talyn spun at the sound of running feet. It was Dorsan, face grim. "What?" she snapped.

"Talon Dariel wants you right away. Something's not right at the palace."

If Cuinn thought something was wrong, then... Talyn turned back towards the barracks, where Tiercelin was good-naturedly waving a few members of his detail inside. "Tiercelin!"

But they were out of earshot.

She started running, trying to catch them, dread filling every inch of space in her chest, warning her that something was wrong, instinct telling her to get them out. "Tiercelin!"

He turned, ducking back out the door, a questioning look on his face.

The sudden explosion tore away her words as she screamed her talon's name again.

A shockwave hit her a heartbeat before the roar of the blast did. The force of it lifted her off the ground and sent her flying through the air. Something slammed into her leg. She landed heavily, the back of her head smacking into the ground.

Blackness filled her vision.

TALYN'S MIND groped towards consciousness. Her eyes flickered open only to be blinded by the afternoon sun directly above. She blinked, coughing, as the acrid tang of smoke hit her lungs.

Pain ripped through her head when she tried to move. Nausea roiled in her gut. Clutching her forehead, she tried to understand what was happening, where she was, but coherent thought was failing.

"Talyn?"

She was lying on her back. That wasn't right. She shouldn't be lying down. Why was she lying down? Ignoring the stabbing pain in her skull, she forced herself up into a half-sitting position.

It took a few moments for her blurry vision to focus, but when it did, her mind almost reverted to blackness.

"Talyn?"

A chunk of the upper floors at the front of the barracks had been torn away, and flames licked around the edges of the destruction. Debris lay scattered across the parade ground. Wolves were on the ground too, some bloody and unmoving. Others were stumbling out of the building, most wounded and supporting comrades.

The sweet scent of izerdia hovered on the afternoon air.

"No," Talyn whispered to herself, her mind unable to comprehend what had happened.

"Talyn, are you okay?"

"Sari?" She looked around, desperate for her partner. She needed to be here, needed to help Talyn stand, to make sense of what was happening.

But Sari was gone.

She tried to get to her feet. When her left leg collapsed under her, forcing her to her knees, she looked down to find blood soaking her breeches from a ragged gash along her calf.

"Talyn, you're hurt. You're really hurt. You need to find help." Sari's voice was panicked, but she barely heard it.

"No, I..." Glancing frantically around, her eyes fell on a figure lying nearby. It was Dahl, his dark eyes glazed over in death, a piece of shattered glass embedded in his chest. Talyn stared for a moment, uncomprehending. Her brain was slow to start, slow to process and understand. Her leg was slick with blood but the pain was a distant throbbing.

Tiercelin.

He'd been turning towards her, half through the doorway when the explosion... she started crawling, ignoring the pain in her leg, desperate to find him.

And then she did.

He must have gotten halfway in the air before being caught in the blast, because he lay a distance away from the entrance, mostly buried by crumbled stone. His eyes were closed, skin covered in dust.

"Tiercelin?"

His eyes slid open, but they were unfocused, and his breathing rattled in his chest. She knew the sound of that rattle, had heard it before. It made her go cold with dread. He coughed. "Can't feel…"

"You're going to be fine." She stopped beside him, frantically scanning the rubble, working out how to get him clear. They needed Halun. Where was Halun? Her thoughts were scrambled, unclear, and an odd weakness was spreading through her. "I'm here, Tiercelin. I'm here. I won't leave."

She grabbed his hand, not knowing what else to do. His eyes slid closed, and he took a shallow, gasping breath. "Worth every moment… Captain."

And then he stopped breathing. She bit down on her lip so hard it broke skin, and the lump in her throat was so large she couldn't breathe.

"Tiercelin?" she begged, squeezing his hand. "Please don't…"

Grogginess flooded her and she swayed. She blinked, but couldn't clear her vision.

"*Talyn, find Theac!*" Sari's voice thundered through her mind, centring her thoughts and giving her temporary focus. "*You need his help.*"

"Theac," she whispered, then the full horror of what had happened began welling up in her chest. Tiercelin's hand had gone limp in hers. "THEAC?" she screamed. Her mind stumbled over the possibilities. Theac had been with her, Zamaril also outside.

She tried again to get up, but her leg wouldn't hold her. Desperate, she crawled across the ground, sobbing with relief when she found Theac close by. A cut above his left eye bled sluggishly, but he was moving, eyes flickering as he returned to consciousness.

"Theac?" She slapped his cheek. "Come on Theac, you need to wake up!"

He groaned and opened his eyes, one hand lifting to his head. "What?" Wincing, he slowly moved into a sitting position, his face turning to stone when he saw the carnage. "Oh, no… not this."

"Theac, you have to go and get help. Find Ravinire." She forced firmness into her voice, but it still came out shaky. Her brain still wasn't working, and weakness trembled through her, either from shock or blood loss or both.

He shook his head a little and looked at her. "What about you?"

"I can't walk. Bleeding," she said, struggling to find the right words. "You'll have to go. Hurry! Please!"

Theac stood and stumbled off, clearly groggy too.

"Staunch the wound. You're bleeding too much. Come on, Tal, you know how to do this."

But she was too tired, too dizzy, too heartsick. She pressed her hand half-heartedly against her leg, hissing at the pain that broke through her numbness and seared her entire body.

She sank back, still looking all around, as if that would change anything. Winged figures were landing in the yard—they'd either been flying above or heard the explosion, she figured. Wolves were getting to their feet, stumbling towards fallen comrades.

Not again.

"Talyn, stay awake. You need to stop the bleeding."

"I don't know how," she whispered, then let the blackness claim her.

CHAPTER 35

Cuinn flew like he'd never flown before. The Wolves. Talyn. If his brother had gone after Ronisin… maybe he knew. Knew what had happened, how she'd escaped. And Azrilan had warned him, about Talyn, about how threatened Mithanis felt. Yet he'd done nothing.

The winged Wolves followed him, barely able to keep pace. He didn't care. He just had to get there before—

"Prince Cuinn!" Lyra was the closest behind him, her shout warning and plea both. To slow down, to let them catch up.

A muffled roar tore through the afternoon air.

He craned his head back. "I don't—" His ability to speak was stifled by the sudden rush of terror and pain that slammed into him. He spiralled out of the air, unable to fly, to think, as the flood of emotion rocked through his body, closing his chest in a vice. A strangled gasp escaped him.

He righted himself barely in time, crashing into a pillar before sliding to the floor of an empty balcony.

"Prince Cuinn!" Nirini dropped down after him, Lyra and Roalin right behind. "What's wrong?"

As the wave of emotion ebbed, Cuinn was able to stand, though it took another moment before he could form words. "The Wolves," he gasped. "Something terribly wrong…"

Roalin let out a cry then, grief filling his voice. Lyra gasped and swayed where she stood. Cuinn doubled over, wave after wave of grief and pain hitting him.

"What is it?" Nirini stared between them, her green warrior magic sparking in her palms uselessly. "What's happened?"

Cuinn staggered to his feet, spread his wings. "The Wolves."

Numerous Falcons were visible in the distance, massing in the sky above the main barracks. The sight sent his stomach plummeting, and he redoubled his efforts to fly faster.

What he saw as he landed in the Wolves' drill yard almost destroyed him.

Destruction. Smoke. Fallen bodies clad in grey and white. Others trying to get up, or to help fallen comrades. Someone was groaning in unimaginable pain. His fists clenched at his side so hard his nails dug into the skin of his palms, drawing blood. Roalin's horrified gasp echoed through the stillness.

"Oh no." Tears were sheeting down Nirini's face, and she lunged forward, as if to go and help, then remembered her duty was Cuinn, and stopped herself with an effort.

"Go!" Cuinn snapped at her, voice ragged. Nirini had healing magic as well as warrior ability. "Go and help them. All of you."

Talyn.

Terror ripped through him so powerfully he thought he might vomit. He fought it back, refusing to succumb. He would find her. No matter what. It took precious seconds, minutes, but he fought down his panic, fought back the grief and pain hitting him from those in the yard, fought until his mind was clear.

He was moving towards the fallen Wolves when Ravinire's voice barked behind him. "Prince Cuinn, you shouldn't be here."

Cuinn took a single, steadying breath, then turned on the Falcon. "I want an ordered search of the yard. Injured Wolves will be tagged in order of severity. Have two of your Falcons fly to fetch the healers. You will ensure every single able-bodied winged healer comes here at once, without exception. If any refuse, your Falcons will drag them here. Organise another group to comb through the wreckage of the building and look for survivors. Have more set up a room close by for the healers to treat the most severely injured."

"Your Highness." Ravinire saluted, turned, and began rapping out orders.

Cuinn left him, walking through the carnage, fighting a constant battle to keep the panic and grief from shutting down his brain. He made himself look at each and every one of the injured or dead Wolves, his heart beating a steady, barely-under-control rhythm in his chest. Each time he stopped, checked the man or woman's breathing, then waved over a Falcon to make sure they got treatment.

The panic grew the longer it took to find what he was looking for.

Then he spotted her.

She was unconscious, blood seeping into a pool on the ground from an awful-looking gash in her leg. Her skin was pale as death, and he had to use every single bit of will he possessed to force himself to kneel down and press his fingers against her pulse.

She was breathing.

His shoulders crumpled in relief and for a moment he couldn't do anything but bite down hard on his lip to stop the racking sobs that wanted to escape.

"Ravinire!" he bellowed.

To his credit, the man arrived in seconds. He paled at the sight of Talyn lying there.

"Get a healer here now." Cuinn rose to his feet. "She's still alive."

Now that he knew Talyn was alive, now that the initial flood of grief had washed through him, a bright hot anger was taking hold in his chest, dispelling the fear. He pointed a shaking hand at Ravinire's chest. "I find out you had *anything* to do with this, and I will end you."

It didn't matter that he would feel it. His Wolves were injured and dying. Talyn was badly hurt. He would rip those responsible apart. The fury literally burned through his veins.

"I didn't," Ravinire said simply. He looked tired and beaten, but his words were honest.

"Yeah, well, I know who did," Cuinn snarled, and leapt into the air.

MITHANIS WAS in their mother's informal meeting parlour. Azrilan wasn't there, but Sarana was, along with two Queencouncil lords.

Cuinn saw nobody but Mithanis as he burst into the room. They all turned towards him, astonished. Maybe Irial hadn't told them he was back yet. Or maybe it was a reaction to the emotions bleeding from him. The fury inside was white-hot, fuelled by grief, desperate to escape, to find its target.

"Did you do this?" he screamed at his brother.

Mithanis looked genuinely taken aback. "What in the skies—"

"I'll kill you." And Cuinn launched himself across the room, wings spread wide, hurtling into Mithanis with as much force as he could muster.

They flew backwards into the opposite wall, Cuinn slamming Mithanis's body into it, forearm at his brother's throat. "How could you!"

"Cuinn, what is going on!" His mother's voice was sharp, but he ignored it.

Mithanis ignored her too. He braced himself, then slammed his knee into Cuinn's stomach, giving himself enough momentum to break free of the hold. Cuinn staggered back, ignoring how the blow had sent the air rushing from his lungs.

"How dare you come in here and attack me?" Mithanis roared.

"I'm not attacking you. I'm going to kill you." Cuinn threw a fist into his brother's face, hard, savouring the impact in his knuckles and the blood flying from Mithanis' nose. Fury darkened his brother's face and then he was fighting back, landing punches to Cuinn's face and stomach.

He barely felt the hits, or the blood or the pain—either Mithanis's or his own. His fury and grief were too powerful to let anything else in. Screaming his anger, throwing the emotion at Mithanis, he punched and kicked and wrestled. Mithanis's own fury tangled with Cuinn's, and their magic battled as wildly as the physical fight. Cuinn used none of the nuanced skill with which he had kept himself safe and hidden all these years, too upset for the focus it required. They hit the room's table. Cuinn was momentarily above Mithanis, until with a single sweep of black wings the prince of night sent Cuinn flying to the floor.

"We both know I'm the superior fighter." Mithanis spat blood. "You can't beat me."

"I don't care." Cuinn panted, scrambling to his feet. "You killed Raya and now you've killed my Wolves. I'm going to put you down."

When he launched himself at Mithanis again, a fist slammed into his face, then a boot into his stomach. Shouting in pain and fury combined, he managed to bury his fist in Mithanis' ribs, but then his brother moved too quickly for him to counter, wrapping an arm around Cuinn's neck and tightening the hold until Cuinn couldn't breathe.

Stars spotted his vision, his lungs desperately choking for air. He continued to fight the hold, refusing to give in, buffeting Mithanis with his magic. But Mithanis was merciless, stronger and taller and, yes, a much better fighter.

"Mithanis, enough!" The queen's voice rang through the room, more commanding than Cuinn had ever heard it.

Mithanis squeezed tighter for a brief moment, then let go and shoved Cuinn away. "I though you felt only contempt for your protective detail, little brother." He sneered. "I feel now that you love them. What more have you been hiding from us?"

"They saved my *life*. Unlike any of you, they care about keeping me safe!" Gasping, choking, still incandescent with an anger only fuelled by Mithanis's fury beating at him, Cuinn went straight back at the prince of night, ignoring his mother's commands to stop. Then a fresh pair of arms wrapped around his chest from behind, holding him back.

"Let go!" he shouted. "Let me go!"

"Enough, Cuinn." Azrilan spoke, his voice in Cuinn's ear somehow both gentle and commanding. His song magic wrapped him in calm. "He'll kill you if you keep going."

"I don't care. Do you know what he did?" Cuinn lunged again, unsuccessfully trying to dislodge Azrilan's hold. He was too upset to focus his magic properly to fight Azrilan's soothing hum and he found some of his rage fading.

"I did nothing," Mithanis said as he straightened his clothing and wiped blood from his face. "I didn't kill Raya, though I know you've always thought that. I'm not going to kill you either. You're my brother, Cuinn."

"Enough!" His mother spoke again, moving into Cuinn's line of sight. Her magic and Azrilan's combined were a match for Cuinn in this state and his white-hot fury continued to fade under their onslaught of calm. "Cuinn, get out of here and don't come back until you've calmed down."

"He just orchestrated an attack on my Wolves." Cuinn struggled with less vigour now. "He killed them. And all because he's afraid of me."

Mithanis' laugh was loud. "Afraid of you? You have got to be kidding me. There is *nothing* about you to be scared of."

The queen glanced between them. "Cuinn, if there was an attack, it wasn't your brother. Is Ravinire informed? We need to learn who was behind it, immediately—there could be more coming."

"I know where it came from," Cuinn said, finally sagging in Azrilan's hold. "And so do you, Mother. You just won't admit it."

Her eyes shifted to Azrilan. "Get him out of here. Then find Ravinire and tell him he'd better get here and tell us what is going on *immediately*."

Cuinn didn't fight Azrilan as his brother hustled him out of the room. Once the door closed behind them, Azrilan let him go, holding out a wary hand. "Are you done yet?"

"I'm done." He spat blood onto the floor. He was shaking, numb to the bruises Mithanis had inflicted on him. "Did he kill Ronisin and his Falcons too?"

"They committed treason. It had to be done."

Cuinn stared at his brother. "What treason?"

Azrilan shrugged. "I warned you. Your captain has been cultivating support amongst the WingGuard. Ronisin and others had become loyal to her. Mithanis couldn't let that lie."

The anger leapt up inside him again. "He's a murdering cold-hearted bastard. They were innocent men."

"No they weren't," Azrilan said firmly, grabbing him by the shoulders. "Go, Cuinn. Get out of here. And I'd recommend you not show your face around Mithanis for a little while."

Cuinn huffed out a bitter laugh, reaching up to touch his bruised face. "I'm not scared of Mithanis." Not anymore. He was too angry and grief-stricken for fear. Too determined to make this right somehow to let anything like fear of his brother stand in his way.

"Then you're a fool."

"No. He's the fool. For not fearing me." Empty words, maybe. But for the first time ever, Cuinn wanted to make them true.

"Cuinn?" Azrilan's voice stopped him.

He turned, snarling, "What?"

"You know that it won't be long now before he moves against her," Azrilan said quietly.

Cuinn turned and walked away.

CHAPTER 36

*T*alyn drifted back to consciousness to find a winged healer crouched over her leg, putting the finishing touches on a bandage. Her eyes flickered open, and though her head throbbed dully, her thoughts were clear. Devastation flooded her so powerfully for a moment she couldn't do anything but ride it out and suck in a gasping breath, fingers curling against the warm stone beneath her.

"I've cleaned and stitched the wound," the winged woman said when she noticed Talyn was awake. "But you should try to keep your weight off it. Use this." She proffered a wooden crutch.

Talyn grimaced in pain as she dragged herself to her feet. "Anything else?"

"You've got a mild concussion, but I treated that, so you should be fine apart from some headaches over the next few days." The woman glanced around. "If you're good, there are others for me to see to."

"Go, please," Talyn rasped, swallowing around her dry throat.

Looking around, she spotted Theac talking to a winged healer who was working on an injured Ehdra, and limped over to him, trying to ignore the pain stabbing through her leg. His uniform and skin were covered with dirt and patches of dried blood, a mirror of hers. Deep lines were furrowed into his brow.

"You're okay?" he asked, emotion leaking into his usually gruff voice.

She blinked tears away. Tried to summon an even voice. Failed. "A scratch. The healers stitched me up. You?"

"Just this." He waved at his head. "It's minor."

A thick silence fell between them, and Talyn had to take a deep, steadying breath before she could manage the words that had to come next. "What can you tell me?"

Theac flinched, and he lifted a hand to rub the bridge of his nose. His fingers trembled. "The lower floors of the east corner of the barracks are almost completely destroyed. They must have packed a lot of izerdia in there while we were gone. Everything else, including the indoor halls, the kitchen, the common room and the mess, is untouched."

She swallowed. "How many dead?"

"Seven. Many were hurt in some way but will recover. Prince Cuinn got the winged healers here quickly enough to save those most badly hurt, but there are still a few who might not survive." Theac hesitated, his shoulders sagging, and Talyn tried desperately to think of a way to stop him saying the words that were coming next.

A way to make it all not true.

"I sent Tiercelin inside before it blew. I know he's..." she whispered, but couldn't finish.

"He took Vanton and Renasa with him. Jessra and Rojen were inside too." Theac's face worked with emotion. "They didn't make it out. Ash and Dahl were killed by flying debris."

She was stricken, a lump closing up her throat. She placed a hand over her mouth to stifle the scream rising unbidden. Silent tears welled and poured down her cheeks. When she tried to speak, her voice broke, failing her.

Theac looked like he wanted to say something, but couldn't get the words out. She couldn't imagine a world without Tiercelin. Without Ash's humour and Vanton's steadiness.

She had to focus on something else. Otherwise she couldn't... Not again, not again, not again. The words kept looping through her thoughts, unstoppable.

"Captain." Theac's hand settled on her shoulder.

"Cuinn, his detail, he…" She scrambled to grasp what she should do, where she should go next, but it kept escaping her. As hard as she tried, she couldn't put the fractured pieces of her thoughts together.

"Prince Cuinn was here earlier. I don't know where he is now. But Corrin, he would have made sure that…" Theac stuttered to a halt.

"And Halun. Has anyone seen him?"

"Tirina flew down to Dock City and found him. He didn't know we were back, didn't know that…" Theac shook his head. "I don't know where he went."

"I need to…" She looked around. "I know I have to do something… I just don't know what."

"Me either." The veteran soldier's face crumpled, and the sight of it sent her flying back into the vortex of grief and guilt. She stepped away from him. "There's nothing you can do here. Go and be with your wife and Corrin's sisters. Make sure they're okay."

Theac merely nodded and walked away without protest, leaving Talyn standing there. With nowhere else to go, and still reeling with shock and grief, she limped over to join the Falcons that had obviously been given orders to help clear the debris from the yard.

For the next full-turn she worked, helping to move the injured onto stretchers to be carried to the healer's wing in the palace, then lifting debris, sweeping up and cleaning away the blood. She made herself focus on the physical work, knowing if she stopped, if she allowed herself to think about what happened…

Not again.

So, she worked. She worked until her shoulders ached and her hands were raw. Her leg was an agony of pain, and the dull throbbing in her head returned.

In the end Ravinire appeared. He took one look at her and told her to stop and leave to get some rest.

"I need to help, sir."

"You'll hurt yourself even more if you keep going, Captain," he said firmly. "Go. That's an order."

But she couldn't face returning to her empty quarters. How could she go into that building after it had exploded right in front of her, taking Tiercelin and her Wolves with it?

"Talyn, listen to me."

"What?" she asked dully.

"You always listened to me, right? That's what we do. We're partners, and we help each other."

"But you're gone." A sob welled in her throat.

"I'm not. I'm here. I'm here to tell you that you know where you need to be right now. You don't need to get through this alone. Not this time. Listen to me, Tal. Please."

She closed her eyes, letting the warm tears run down her face. *"Okay."*

SOMEONE HAD HAD the presence of mind to ensure a detail of Wolves was guarding Cuinn, though the two standing guard at the tower door —Liadin and Lyra—were shaky and grief-stricken, and the entire area was utterly silent. Even so, they saluted at Talyn's limping approach.

That simple act of courage and respect almost broke her.

"We've made sure enough healthy Wolves are surrounding the tower, Captain," Liadin said quietly. "We'll be here as long as is needed."

She nodded at them both, but that was all she had in her to give them. She opened the door to Cuinn's tower without knocking, then closed it behind her, letting her eyes adjust to the dim interior.

For a moment she frowned at the sight of shredded cushions scattered across the floor along with deep gouge marks in one section of the carpet. Jasper padded out of the darkness a moment later, a low snarl rumbling in his throat.

"He showed up just before you," Cuinn spoke. "Upset and bent on destroying my furniture. I suspect he knew something was wrong and feels he got here too late." He was standing by the window, and a shocked gasp escaped her when he turned and she saw his bruised eye and split cheek.

"It's nothing." He waved a hand at his face. "Just a little altercation with Mithanis after I..." His voice broke, and he shook his head, unable to continue.

She should be worried about that. Afraid of the implications if Cuinn had openly challenged his brother. But there was nothing in her but grief. She bit her lip, the tears beginning to spill down her cheeks again. "I need your help, Cuinn, because I don't think I can..." She trailed off. "Is that okay?"

He was across the room in a second, pulling her to him and wrapping her in his arms and wings. "It's okay," he whispered. "It's more than okay. Thank everything you're all right."

The grief broke through then. She began to cry in huge, gulping sobs. Cuinn wordlessly guided her over to the couch. There, he wrapped an arm around her shoulders and drew her against his chest before cocooning them with his wings.

Then he began to sing softly, a wordless tune, his magic not taking away her grief, but soothing it, making it something she could bear, something that hurt like she'd only ever once been hurt before, but a hurt she could live with.

His voice broke occasionally, when his grief cracked through, and each time she clung more tightly to him, trying to offer her own comfort. After a time, her grief ran its course, her sobs fading away. Across the room, Jasper continued to prowl protectively, green eyes glancing towards them every few moments.

"I'm sorry," she mumbled, her voice hoarse. Sorry for dumping all this on him when he was grieving too.

His only response was to draw her tighter against him. She rested her head against his neck and clenched her fingers into his shirt, eyes closed against his skin, needing the strength he was giving her.

"Don't let go," she whispered.

"Never," he promised.

CHAPTER 37

*T*alyn blinked as her groggy mind rose from sleep. Cuinn was moving, his arms unwinding themselves from around her waist. Her leg ached with a painful throbbing, her emotions were bruised, battered and sore, and grief made her close to tears, but she was alive.

"Sari, I'm all right."

A shiver of a smile through her thoughts. *"I'm glad to hear it. Thank him for me, will you?"*

"Dawn broke a little while ago," he murmured. "I figured you'd want me to wake you."

Was it morning already? She'd slept far longer than she'd realised. She grimaced down at her bloodied, torn uniform. "Thanks."

"You're beautiful," Cuinn said quietly, a hand reaching out to touch her cheek. "How's the leg?"

"Painful," she admitted, wincing as she tried to get to her feet. The rest of her body was tight and sore too. She wouldn't be fighting anytime soon, a worry that flared strongly for a moment before she tucked it away as a problem to deal with later.

One thing at a time.

"I have to go." She looked up at Cuinn. "I have no idea what state the Wolves are in—I shouldn't have abandoned them last night."

"You did what you needed to so that you can be the captain they need today," Cuinn said gently, but firmly.

Her mouth quirked. "You sound like Sari."

"I'll organise the funerals," he said quietly. "I want to make sure they're properly honoured, and nobody else up here will do that."

She shook her head. "I don't know if we're safe. Where the attack came from, if—"

"For today, we honour our dead," he said firmly. "I will keep a double detail with me at all times, I promise, and after tonight we will decide what comes next." He paused. "Talyn, we'll have to move quickly. Mithanis is no longer under any illusions about how I feel about the Wolves and I..."

"What is it?" More dread filled her at the desperate sadness in his gaze.

"It wasn't just the Wolves. Mithanis had Ronisin Nightdrift and his entire detail hanged."

She swayed on her feet, fresh grief rising and threatening to flood her.

Cuinn held her tightly. "It was because of their loyalty to you. They loved you like the Wolves do and Mithanis won't stand for it."

Ronisin. His quick smile and good heart. He'd risked his life for her and it had cost him everything. And Cuinn was right. If Mithanis had executed Ronisin it wouldn't be long before he came for her.

One step at a time. She took a breath. "Thank you, for everything."

"There's nothing to thank me for." His hand lifted to cup her cheek. "Together, remember?"

She hadn't really meant anything by those words the first time she'd spoken them; it had just been an attempt to help him understand that he had her and the Wolves at his side. But each time she'd said it since, it had meant more, and now she allowed herself to acknowledge and accept what it truly signified. Not a partnership—she'd never have another partner after Sari—but something just as powerful.

There was fear with that acceptance. It would be impossible for there to be no fear, but there was a sense of relief too. And rightness.

"Together." She reached up to cover his hand.

She moved away and opened the door, knowing that if she didn't go then, she wouldn't be able to. Halun stood outside, silent and sad. Relief swamped her. He was okay—she should have made sure of it the previous night. Guilt sank through her chest.

Talyn glanced back at Cuinn. "Can you come to the drill yard in a quarter-turn? I need to speak to all the Wolves at once."

He bowed his head. "We'll be there."

She walked over to Halun. "You're all right?"

Halun, who knew better than most how what happened would have affected her, simply reached out and settled his hand on her shoulder. She almost burst into tears.

"I'm okay," she reassured him. "I'll see you in a quarter-turn."

FIRST SHE WENT to the infirmary that had been set up to treat the most severely injured Wolves. It looked busy, two winged healers moving between beds and checking on the status of the patients. But it was the man at the door that caught Talyn's attention.

Corrin.

Standing straight backed, drawn knife in his hand. Nobody could get to any of the Wolves without going through him.

"You've been here all night?" she asked him softly.

He turned bloodshot eyes towards her. "Yes, Captain."

A passing healer paused, glancing between them. "They took heart from your presence, Talon Dariel. We could feel it in our magic... a most unusual thing."

Talyn lifted her hand to Corrin's shoulder, squeezed in gratitude. "Thank you."

"What happens next?" he asked.

"I want to speak to all the Wolves. I think they'll be safe here with the healers for a short time. Come to the drill yard in a quarter-turn."

"I'll be there," he said, then turned his attention back to watching over the injured.

TALYN THREW OPEN the doors to the main dormitory—she wasn't sure what to make of the fact that the blast had spared the main living areas of the barracks. Luck? A deliberate calculation? Or maybe they'd returned too early, before everything was in place—with enough force to send them thumping loudly against the stone walls on either side. Some of the Wolves were still asleep in their bunks, while others sat listlessly in various stages of dress.

"Up!"

Those who hadn't been awakened by the doors either awoke at her shout, or were shaken awake by their comrades.

"If all of you aren't fully dressed and out in the drill yard in a quarter-turn, you'll be washing dishes for the next six months," she bellowed. "MOVE IT!"

Not waiting for them to react, she turned on her heel and strode upstairs to where the talons' private rooms were. She went first to Theac's old room, hoping he'd spent the night down in Dock City with his family, but doubting it.

Outside, she hesitated before going in, part of her terrified about what state she might find him in. She had never forgotten his drinking problem—it was always in the back of her mind, the fear that he might relapse. Not that she'd blame him if he had. If it hadn't been for Cuinn the previous night, she wasn't sure what state she'd be in herself.

And even with that, grief still weighed so heavily on her it was a struggle to breathe properly, to walk strong and tall. She wasn't sure if her newfound strength could cope with—

You did what you needed so you could be the captain they need today.

Right.

"I'm with you. Every step of the way," Sari whispered.

Taking a deep breath, she gathered herself and opened the door. Instantly her eyes teared up. Theac sat at the foot of his bed staring into space. He was unshaven and hadn't changed out of his previous day's bloodied and torn uniform. A bottle of spirits sat on a small table directly across from him, unopened and untouched.

"I've been staring at it all night," his voice rasped, and he clambered stiffly to his feet. "But I'm stronger than that, Captain. You taught me to be."

Talyn half-sobbed and stepped forward to hug him fiercely. He stood shocked for a moment, then returned her embrace with the same fierceness.

"Thank you," she whispered, her voice full of feeling. "Thank you so much."

He patted her awkwardly on the back. "It's all right."

She sniffed and stood back. "It's a half-turn past dawn and the Wolves are still in the dormitory."

Theac didn't look surprised. "I didn't know."

"Where are Andres and Zamaril? Halun is on Cuinn's shift," she said.

"I'll help you find them." He fell into step with her, looking down in discomfort. "I haven't seen them since... I'm sorry, Captain. I should have done better."

"No, it's my fault." She sighed. "I let you all down. What happened... it was... I didn't do well last time this happened to me. But things will be different this time. I'm stronger than I was."

Theac laid a hand on her forearm. "I can't tell you how relieved I am to hear it. We need you now more than ever, Captain."

She straightened her shoulders. "I won't fail you or them again."

They arrived at the door to Zamaril's room, next to Andres'. Tiercelin's was on the opposite side of the hall, empty now. Talyn couldn't even look at it without a sharp tug of pain in her chest that made it a struggle to breathe.

Theac opened the door without knocking. Andres was passed out on the bed inside, with Zamaril slouched asleep in a nearby chair. Both were unshaven and rumpled, and empty ale bottles littered the floor.

Talyn turned straight back around, walked down the hall to their shared bathing area, filled a jug with water, and marched back. Without preamble, she dumped the water all over their faces.

"Drill yard," she snapped as they groaned loudly, rousing to groggy wakefulness. "Be there or you're both out."

Theac picked up Andres by the scruff of the neck and hauled him bodily into a half-standing position, then kicked Zamaril's chair over so that he was forced to either scramble to his feet or hit the ground.

Leaving them to it, Talyn and Theac headed straight back downstairs.

"Liadin and Lyra took responsibility for Prince Cuinn's guard last night. They rounded up those that weren't hurt and stood guard until Halun got there. They've been watching his tower all night," Talyn said.

Silence fell between them for a few seconds. He knew what she was suggesting without her having to say it.

"They'll do," Theac said. "You don't think it's a problem to have two winged talons?"

"Talons earn their position on merit. I don't care whether they're winged, human or pink with purple spots." As achingly painful as it was, the Wolves needed leadership, which meant Tiercelin's empty spot needed filling. It was time to do something about Zamaril's too.

And she was their leader, so it was on her to do what was necessary.

"Fair enough, but what about Zamaril?"

Talyn jerked her thumb back in the direction of where they'd found him and Andres. "Andres has a pass for today because of how close they all were, but Zamaril hasn't done a thing since I demoted him to demonstrate he learned his lesson."

Theac nodded in reluctant agreement. "What are we going to do with him?"

"A problem for another day."

Theac sighed and his shoulders sagged a little in relief. "I've lost men under my command before, but not men that were like my own family. To see you so destroyed by their deaths only made it worse.

Whatever it is that has helped you to come back to us, I'll be forever grateful."

"I'll never leave you," she promised quietly.

Another silence, then, "What do we do next? That explosion was a direct attack on us, Captain."

"I know." She looked away. "And we can't be sure of where it came from or what's next. But let's get through today—as Cuinn said, today we honour our fallen. Tiercelin, the other Wolves that died... they deserve our respect and honour."

Theac nodded, his eyes full of unshed tears.

To THEIR CREDIT, all the Wolves were dressed and out in the yard by the time she and Theac arrived. It took them a little longer to organise themselves into neat rows, but she forgave them that. Andres and Zamaril, clean shaven but bleary-eyed and haggard, emerged by the time they were all in neat rows. Cuinn stood off in the distance, watching quietly.

Talyn stood before them, shoulders straight, hands loosely clasped behind her back. The weight of their attention was unbearably heavy.

But she had the strength to carry the load. She was their captain.

"*Sari?*"

"*I'm here.*"

Talyn held on to that, and then she spoke.

"What happened yesterday, the deaths of our friends, our comrades, our *family,* it was heartbreaking." Talyn swallowed. "You don't recover from that kind of loss, but you do keep living. If I can give you any advice, it's that you should hold on to those you've lost. Keep them in your heart. Use their memory to make you strong. To make you true. To honour them every day for the rest of your life. That's what I'll be doing."

She paused for a moment. The Wolves stood in their neat rows, every gaze watching her, unblinking. Tears streamed down many of their faces.

"You all know that we are a part of something special here in

Mithranar. We are here to do things the right way—to respect each other and watch out for each other. And you all know by now that Prince Cuinn is part of that too." She looked over at the prince of song, and as she did, so did the Wolves. His eyes flashed. Then he bowed his head.

She paused again.

"We are Wolves. And we will keep training and fighting and we will keep him safe, because that's our job, it's how we'll make things better. And it's how we'll honour the comrades we lost yesterday."

A moment's silence, then Liadin threw back his head and howled. Lyra joined a moment later, the other winged Wolves adding their musical voices until the haunting howls of a wolf pack reverberated through the morning air.

Once the echoes had faded into silence, each and every one of them drew themselves up and saluted sharply.

Talyn waited a moment, rocked to her core by the solidarity of this wing she'd built. "Good," she said in satisfaction. "Liadin Skywing, Lyra Songdrift, step forward please."

Shooting a quick, curious glance at each other, the two Wolves stepped forward.

"We're short two talons," Talyn said briskly, pitching her voice so that all could hear. "You will fill the posts. We've lost brothers and sisters, so details will be short-handed. I am confident you can make it work until we recruit new Wolves."

They looked stunned, but recovered quickly.

"Aye, Captain." Liadin saluted crisply, and walked over to stand beside Corrin.

Lyra was right behind him. "Thank you, Captain."

Talyn turned her gaze back to the assembled Wolves. "Corrin, Halun, your details will stay on Prince Cuinn today. The rest of you, time for the morning wall run."

Cuinn lifted into the sky, the winged Wolves on shift following. The rest of the Wolves began moving off at a jog towards the exit. She was watching them go, allowing the sight of them to give her strength, when an unfamiliar musical voice called out. "Captain Dynan?"

A winged man stood a short distance off. Even if she hadn't met him before—as the senior healer who'd undertaken the removal of her wing buds—she would instantly have known him as Tiercelin's eldest brother, Jystar. His brown skin, grey wings and hazel eyes ... he looked like a slightly older, more serious version of her Wolf talon. Her heart clenched, and she swallowed, trying to keep her voice even. "Lord Stormflight, can I help you?"

He bowed his head with a touch of winged folk arrogance. "Our family never approved of Tiercelin being a Wolf, but..." He swallowed, clearly struggling with emotion. "I would like to honour his memory by enlisting with the Wolves. I am a healer, as my brother was, and I am willing to do what it takes to learn to fight."

"You want to join the Wolves?" Talyn asked warily. "Even though you hated the fact your brother was one of us?"

"No matter what I thought of my brother's choices, I loved him, Captain." Jystar's voice was taut with emotion. "And for him to die like that... it tears me apart to think that's the end for him. I want to continue what he started."

"How can I trust you?" she demanded. "I'll be blunt, I know your family is a close ally of Prince Mithanis, and I'm not convinced he wasn't behind what happened yesterday."

Jystar flinched. "I don't believe he was, but if so then... it doesn't change what I want. As for trust..." He stepped closer to her in a single, graceful movement, head lowering, voice dropping. "I never removed your wing buds, Captain Dynan."

Her head jerked back in shock. "What?"

"Tiercelin asked me not to, as a personal favour, because I am his brother," Jystar said. "So I made the incisions, but never removed your wing buds. If Mithanis found out, I would be dead."

She studied him for a moment. "I'll think on it. Await word from me. It won't be long."

SHE CAUGHT up with the Wolves as they reached the top of the wall, glad to see Andres bringing up the rear.

"How are you holding up?" she asked him, falling into step with him as they began their descent.

He wouldn't look at her. "I'm fine, Captain."

"You weren't fine this morning," she said. "Drinking doesn't fix problems, it only makes them worse. You know that better than anyone."

He turned red, his mouth tightening. "It won't happen again."

"I understand what you're feeling, because I feel it too. If you need to talk, I'm here, Theac is here, and so are your wing mates."

"I'm going to be okay, Captain," he said quietly.

Talyn looked at him, saw the quiet determination she'd always seen in Andres' face, and was reassured. "I think I am, too."

As the Wolves reached the bottom of the wall, their pace slowed, and then stumbled to a halt entirely. Talyn said nothing. Her eyes were on the thousands of flowers laid out at the base of the wall, covering the area where the Wolves always came down for their morning run.

All colours and sizes. Some with bright ribbons holding them together. Others a single stem. And more were coming. On their own, with their families, in small groups, the residents of Dock City were walking over to the wall to place flowers amongst the others.

"Wolves, form up." Theac spoke before Talyn could, and Corrin was already moving, echoing Theac's order. In moments the Wolves were lined up before the offering of flowers. Talyn stood with them, back straight, head bowed.

"Salute," Theac called.

Boots stamped and wings rustled as the Wolves saluted sharply.

And there they stood.

CHAPTER 38

*T*alyn called an early end to morning training, then joined the Wolves in their mess for lunch. Conversation was scarce, the atmosphere heavy with grief and the ache of loss. She felt for them—she knew firsthand how sorely wounded they'd been by the horrific attack, and it was going to take time for them to recover. She was their leader, and they needed to see her with them, but while she ate, her mind was working furiously.

"*Any thoughts?*" she asked Sari.

"*You're in a bad spot, Tal. Yesterday was a direct attack on you and the Wolves. It could have been Mithanis, it could have been Vengeance—*"

Pain and guilt seared her. "*If I caused this because I let Saniya go...*"

"*You can't think like that. Your guilt almost destroyed you before, don't let that happen again.*" Sari's voice was firm, insistent. "*You will make mistakes, Talyn. That is life.*"

Her hand clenched around the spoon she held, painfully so, but she nodded. "*I have to move quickly. I won't sit idly by while another attack could come at any moment. And Cuinn was right, Mithanis is likely to come for me next. Not to mention Cuinn attacking his brother yesterday has put him in more danger. But I don't want to assume the izerdia blast was him—if he wanted Wolves dead he could have just executed them like Ronisin's detail."*

Sari's relief at Talyn's acceptance seeped through her mind. *"Go back to our old strategy lessons. The answer is there."*

"Strategic retreat," Talyn murmured aloud.

"Exactly. Withdraw. Somewhere safe, where you can recover, work out what's going on, and make a plan to strike back."

Sari's fierceness filled Talyn, and her grip on the spoon tightened again, a silent snarl curling at her mouth.

And she had the answer.

Nearby, Theac saw her change in expression, and he rose, making a gesture to Andres, Liadin and Lyra. She waited for them to come, to sit close around her. Something like relief and anticipation lit up her second's face.

"Light training this afternoon, enough to maintain appearances, but at the same time, I want them packing up and preparing to leave. Not a word to anyone." Once, she would have been worried that one of the Wolves might talk, but not anymore, not after what she'd seen from them earlier. "We're leaving tomorrow, all of us, on the dawn tide. I'll speak to Halun shortly, ask him to arrange a ship."

Theac stared at her. "To go where?"

"Port Lachley, it's where my uncle is right now," she said. "They came after us directly, Mithanis or Vengeance, or both, or someone else entirely. Without knowing, without understanding where the next attack might be coming from, we can't protect ourselves or Cuinn. We're getting him out to somewhere safe and then we're going to plan what to do next."

Andres looked at her. "So we're not leaving permanently?"

Talyn smiled coldly. "Oh no. We're coming back. And when we do, things are going to be different."

"Does Prince Cuinn know about this?" Liadin asked.

"I'll talk to him." She looked at each of them in turn. "I want every single Wolf, even the injured ones, on board that ship at dawn. Nobody sees us preparing, am I clear? We're gone before anyone realises what's going on."

Lyra gave her a wolfish grin. "We can do that, Captain."

All of them looked up when a handful of Wolves from Corrin's detail entered the mess, Mikah coming over to Talyn. "The prince would like a word with you all. He and the other talons are waiting in the common room."

Talyn's gaze went straight to Cuinn as she stepped into the common room, but he looked fine, if not slightly drawn with shadows like bruises under his eyes. Corrin and Halun were equally calm, so she relaxed.

Liadin came through last, closing the door behind them for privacy.

"I heard about the flowers down by the wall," Cuinn said quietly. "So I've arranged for the funeral to be held up at the citadel this evening. If the humans of Dock City turn out in force for a funeral down there... I can't be certain Mithanis won't feel threatened and retaliate."

"Thank you, Your Highness," Theac said gruffly. "For everything you've done to—"

"Don't, Theac." Cuinn cut him off. "Your Wolves train to give their lives for mine, and that's what happened yesterday. I owe them this. I owe them so much more than this."

"Will you attend?" Theac asked.

Cuinn's head lifted, an intoxicating mix of determination, resolve and fire on his face. "There's not a thing in this world that could stop me singing for them."

"Then we'll make sure you're safe, Your Highness," Corrin said with quiet confidence.

"I know you will," Cuinn said simply. "Now I should go. I don't want to intrude on you any further."

"A moment before you do? There's something we need to discuss." Talyn spoke, glancing at her talons. "Do you mind?"

Theac bowed to the prince and the talons shuffled out.

"How are you?" She moved closer to him as soon as the door closed.

"I've spent most of this morning veering between grief so painful it made me close to tears and anger so intense I wanted to punch a wall," he said, huffing out a rueful breath.

"I know what you mean." She smiled sadly and pressed her forehead against his chest for a moment, welcoming the comfort his nearness provided. His fingers slid into her hair, gently combing through the strands. The edge of her pain faded as she allowed him to soothe it away.

After a moment, his hand cupped her neck and drew her up to meet his eyes. There was a steely determination in those green depths that bolstered her. "What you did this morning, rallying the Wolves the way you did, making them strong even though their hearts are breaking... I can't be any less strong, Talyn. I refuse to be."

"What are you saying?"

"Ronisin Nightdrift said something to me when I asked him why he was helping you escape. He told me he wanted a different Mithranar, the one he saw you trying to build, saw me—somehow—trying to build. Tiercelin wanted the same thing. As do your Wolves." Cuinn's mouth tightened. "I won't let their sacrifice be wasted. I'm going to build that world. And for that to happen, Mithanis cannot be named heir."

She didn't look away from his gaze. "To build that world, *you* need to be named heir."

He nodded. No doubt. No hesitation. "I want to be king, Talyn."

"Burn bright and true," she murmured.

His eyes blazed. "Burn bright and true."

"So we make you heir," she said firmly. "But not from a position of vulnerability and weakness."

His gaze searched hers. "Tell me what to do, Ciantar."

She smiled. "We're leaving tomorrow."

His eyebrows shot upwards, the expression of surprise making her chuckle. "And where might we be going?"

"I can't protect us properly here. We need to get away temporarily. Recover and plan what comes next."

"A strategic retreat," he said, then smiled. "You're taking me home."

"Port Lachley, actually. That's where the family is at the moment."

She turned serious. "It's time we claimed you as our own, Cuinn. Not only will that offer you greater protection, it will give us safe harbour while we plan."

He was as serious as she was, green eyes fixed unflinchingly on hers. "Plan to come back and deal with Mithanis once and for all."

A little thrill went through her. "Exactly. And when we come back, we do it with the full might of the Dumnorix at our back."

He sucked in a breath, eyes brightening. "That's quite the plan. You don't think we risk Mother naming Mithanis heir in my absence?"

"I know that was her intention, but I doubt she'll do it soon. I think Mithanis might have erred in going after Ronisin and the Falcons like he did—the lords will surely be wary of confirming a man who just executed an entire detail out of hand." Talyn frowned. "And even if she does, then we'll figure something out."

"All right." He smiled, his hands tracing their way down her back, and she leaned up to kiss him, unable to help herself.

"As much as I'd love to stay." He pulled away reluctantly. "I should go before Corrin or Halun get impatient and someone walks in."

She sighed. Kissed him again. "We leave tomorrow at dawn."

He got halfway to the door before he hesitated, as if deciding whether to do or say something. His wings rustled in agitation.

"Tell me," she said softly.

He firmed his shoulders. "Talyn, I love you."

She knew. Had felt it when they'd been together, the depth of his feelings for her unmistakable. And the terrifying thing was... it didn't terrify her. It made her happy.

"I ask for nothing in return," he continued. "I just needed to say it, because I almost lost the chance in that explosion."

She took a breath. Reason tried to assert itself, to tell her that she was betraying her family, that what they had was impossible and would inevitably have to end, but she ignored it. Because she wanted to hold on to that little bit of happiness amidst the grief and pain. "Whenever we can manage this, time together, I want it. I want you."

"Despite the complications?"

"I won't pretend they don't exist," she said. "But let's just take it one step at a time. Together."

He smiled, eyes alight. "I'll see you tomorrow at dawn."

"I'll be waiting."

THE BRIEF MOMENTS with Cuinn had restored any strength she'd lost from a morning spent doing everything she could to help her Wolves, and so after ensuring the talons had afternoon drill and preparations for departure under control, Talyn went to see Ravinire.

Retreat was all well and good, but she wanted to know as much as possible before they left. At the very least she wanted a stronger indication of who had been behind the explosion. Given the timing of Ronisin and his detail's murder, it seemed more likely the attack originated from Mithanis, rather than Vengeance, but then why hadn't he just publicly executed the Wolves and Talyn too?

Ignoring the pain from her leg, she put as much weight on it as she could manage, not willing to betray an ounce of weakness to anyone who might be watching. There probably weren't many. The palace had grown even quieter than the day before, if that was possible. The execution of Ronisin and his men, followed by the attack on the Wolves, had presumably left many winged folk uneasy.

She wondered what they thought of what had happened. While she'd been distracted by her grief and guilt and her focus on the Wolves, she'd seen no visible attempts by either Mithanis or his mother to reassure anyone or publicly explain what had happened.

Surely the winged folk, not to mention the Queencouncil, were asking questions?

The Falcon on duty outside Ravinire's office took one look at the expression on Talyn's face and waved her straight through.

Ravinire stilled at the sight of her entering his office.

"Did you tell him?" she said flatly.

He shifted, eyes sliding away. "Captain, I don't think this is the appropriate time to—"

Cold anger took her over, and she didn't try to hide it. "People *died*, Ravinire. Good people. *My* people. Is that what you wanted?"

Ravinire flinched. "I didn't tell Prince Mithanis."

Talyn leaned over the table in a move so quick he had no time to react and grabbed his tunic, forcing him to meet her eyes. "Are you trying to tell me that yesterday's explosion was a coincidence?" she asked, her voice dropping to a deadly whisper.

"Captain—"

"Tell ME!"

"I told the queen," he admitted, tearing himself from her grip and sagging back in his chair. "It was my duty—she is my queen."

She wanted to rip him limb from limb. The hunger for vengeance, to take action against the person who had killed her Wolves, roped through her. And she could do it. Ravinire, winged or not, was no match for her.

But while Talyn was sometimes reckless, she'd never, ever, allowed the heat of her emotion to dictate her strategy. And killing Ravinire wasn't the solution to this.

She stepped back from the desk, contempt dripping from her voice. "Are you happy with the results of that little confession?"

"She wouldn't have told him." Ravinire shook his head stubbornly. "She loves Prince Cuinn and she knows the consequences if she told Mithanis."

"Then how else do you explain what happened?" Scorn filled her voice. "Ronisin murdered and my Wolves killed within the space of days."

A ripple of anger crossed Ravinire's face then. "You don't know the two things are connected. Ronisin Nightdrift had nothing to do with your little secret. He and his detail were executed for treason."

She lifted an eyebrow. "And tell me, Ravinire, what was their treason?"

His mouth tightened. "You."

She stiffened. Cuinn had implied as much, but... "What?"

"They were loyal to you!" Ravinire snapped. "It wasn't just Ronisin and his detail, Captain Dynan. Mithanis expelled thirty other Falcons from the WingGuard. Stripped them of their titles and their position and tossed them out."

She stared in shock. "That doesn't make any sense."

"You haven't noticed the Falcons playing alleya with your Wolves? Haven't noticed the evenings they spend together in the barracks playing cards and music?" Ravinire threw the words at her as if he were furious, not at her, but at the situation. "Well Prince Mithanis did. *He* noticed the little upswell of support for the heir to the Ciantar name and he didn't like it. So he bided his time, waited until he knew the full extent of the problem, and he acted."

"I never acted against Mithanis. I gave him Vengeance, I had my wings cut out, I did everything he asked."

"That's flea-biting bullshit and you know it! You've pushed him every chance you've had since you first stepped foot in this country, and you dragged Prince Cuinn along for the ride," Ravinire roared, then abruptly the fight went out of him, and he sagged. "I didn't know that Prince Mithanis was capable of this."

"Yes you did." Scorn filled her voice. "You're not a stupid man. You've always known what he's capable of."

"My duty is to my queen," he said simply.

"If one more thing happens to hurt either Cuinn or my Wolves because of your betrayal... I will kill you. That's not an idle threat."

He flinched. "I am your superior officer."

She laughed without mirth, backing away towards the door. "No, you're not. I am Ciantar, remember?" She glanced around his office, finally settling her gaze back on his. "Maybe it's time I claim my rightful position. Yours."

He said nothing as she left, slamming the door behind her.

CHAPTER 39

hey gathered at dusk. The funeral biers for the dead Wolves lined the barracks yard, with Tiercelin's at the centre. Lit torches surrounded them, the flames flickering in the evening breeze. Wolves slowly filed in.

Cuinn drifted out of the sky, landing and furling his wings. His gaze searched for Corrin, who stood with Lyra and Liadin on the other side of the yard. By the time he crossed to join them, the Wolves had finished arriving.

Talyn and Theac were the last to enter. They stood together, both stiff and clearly holding back strong emotion. Aching grief and loss filled the open space, pressing down on him, threatening to smother him.

He would be strong.

He took a deep, freeing breath, then glanced at Corrin. The talon stepped forward, his flute cradled in his hands. He lifted it to his mouth and began to play. Mithranan funeral music drifted across the yard, haunting and ethereal.

Cuinn opened his mouth to begin singing, but stopped, stunned, as winged figures appeared above, dropping out of the sky to stand amongst the Wolves. There were at least twenty of them, if not more. Others remained hovering in the sky above. All wore teal and scarlet.

Falcons. Come to honour the fallen Wolves.

His gaze shot to Talyn, and he found her looking back at him, torn between unease and gratitude.

Another deep breath, and he began to sing a wordless melody.

His magic spread through him, strong and pure, wrapping his music in gratitude—for the fallen Wolves, for what they'd sacrificed for him. For Ronisin and his men too. He sang of their bravery and their honour.

Slowly, Talyn and her talons stepped forward, each picking up a torch and lighting the biers. Bright orange flame leapt up into the sky, highlighting the tears on the faces of the watching Wolves.

Liadin and Lyra added their voices to Cuinn's.

And then, from the sky above and from the Falcons standing with the Wolves, more musical voices rose, joining with Cuinn's until the yard reverberated with music. At a silent cue, they turned the farewell melody into song, Cuinn leading, pouring everything he had into singing the words of Mithranar. Of farewell.

We remember all those we lost

Feathers bright they will not be forgot

Our citadel shines golden and true.

For all time for all time for all time.

Cuinn allowed the magic of others to entwine with his, soaring through the night sky. Music and song magic filled the air, wrapping the fallen Wolves in love and respect and trust.

As one, dear heart, as one.

We fly as one.

The wind will guide us home

To glory under the sun.

All glory under the sun.

And then, slowly, he stopped, his voice fading into the night. At his side, the flute stopped too, Corrin's head bowed as tears poured down his face.

"Wolves!" Talyn's voice, loud and clear through the night.

As one, the Wolves bowed low to their fallen comrades.

CUINN LEFT the Wolves to their mourning as the flames began to burn low, moving on foot so that his full detail could remain with him. Grief tugged unbearably at his chest, not helped by the emotion washing over him from everyone nearby. He was glad they were leaving at dawn the next day—he wasn't sure he'd sleep tonight or anytime soon.

The halls in the area of the palace assigned to Queencouncil members were oddly empty, and no Falcon guards stood outside the residence Cuinn stopped at. He knocked anyway, but there was no response.

He changed course, leaving the palace and heading out over the Rush, covering the relatively short distance to where the most powerful families had their homes in the most exclusive and wealthy area of the citadel.

The human servant who answered the door of the Nightdrift home, while clearly astonished to see the prince of song standing there, let him in without a word.

"Stay out here," Cuinn murmured to Andres. "I'll be fine."

The servant bowed low. "Prince Cuinn. How can I help you?"

"Lord Nightdrift wasn't at his quarters in the palace. Is he here?"

"I am afraid Lord Nightdrift is currently indisposed. Perhaps you could come back tomorrow?"

"I will see him now," Cuinn said, edging his voice with a hint of command. "Take me to him if he's not feeling well."

The servant nodded, reluctantly showing him through to what looked like a study. At a look from Cuinn, he left without a word.

Charl Nightdrift sat in a chair by the window, clutching a glass of spirits in his hand, wearing rumpled shirt and breeches. He was unshaven, his skin pale, the feathers of his scarlet wings unkempt and hanging lifelessly at his sides. The room was mostly dark. A single lamp flickered where it sat on a desk on the other side of the room.

"Lord Nightdrift." Cuinn spoke when it became obvious the man had no idea he was there.

He shifted, turned to Cuinn. His eyes were desolate. His pain and grief thumped into Cuinn like a punch, even though he'd prepared himself for it as best he could. He breathed through the emotion, not allowing the pain to become his.

"I am truly sorry about the loss of your son, Lord Nightdrift," he said. "Ronisin was a man I liked and respected very much."

Charl barked out a bitter laugh. "What do I care what you thought of my son?" Clearly he was far enough gone in his grief he'd stopped caring about offending princes.

"I didn't say it for you," Cuinn said simply. "I said it for Ronisin, who deserves to be honoured."

"He was a traitor."

"He wasn't. And you and I both know it."

Silence fell, heavy and thick. Charl rubbed a weary hand over his face—Cuinn thought he might be scrubbing away tears. "My son..." he began hoarsely, then trailed off.

"Your son wanted a better Mithranar," Cuinn said softly. "And that is why he died."

"He was a traitor." But there was no feeling in the words, just a sense of hopelessness.

Cuinn moved, crossing the room to crouch before the man's chair, forcing Charl to meet his gaze. "I would never have done to your son and his detail what Mithanis did." His words shook with the force of his resolve. "Never. I want you to remember that, when it's time for me to claim what's mine."

Nightdrift blinked, and Cuinn rose to his feet. "I'll see you soon, Lord Nightdrift."

He left quickly, re-joining his Wolves outside. It was getting late, and he had ten other families to visit tonight.

CHAPTER 40

Talyn stood at the prow of the ship, staring out at the light drizzle drifting down to the ocean's surface. Now that they were safely away from Mithranar, there was little to distract her from how much she missed Tiercelin and the other Wolves that had died. Or the guilt she felt over Ronisin and his detail and the other Falcons who had been expelled from the WingGuard. Or her worry over the injured Wolves on board with only Jystar to monitor them. What if one of them got worse? What if leaving was a mistake?

"They'll be safer with you than anywhere else," Sari said firmly.

"Captain." Theac appeared at her side. "Are you okay?"

"No." She gave him a sad smile. "I just wanted to stand and stare at the ocean for a while."

"I've been doing the same," her second confessed. "I know Corrin has too. Zamaril can't bear to mention any of their names. Andres keeps everything inside, but his eyes have gone so bleak. And the winged folk… they won't stop singing."

She huffed a laugh. It was true. Music filled the ship almost constantly, the winged Wolves' way of dealing with their grief.

Theac cleared his throat, changed the subject. "Did you mention this little trip to the Falcon, by any chance?"

Talyn looked away. "I almost killed him, Theac."

"I see," he said heavily. "He betrayed Prince Cuinn to Mithanis then?"

"He betrayed Cuinn to the queen." She hesitated. "Although he insists she wouldn't have told Mithanis."

"I can't see how else this would have happened." Theac rubbed his jaw. "Vengeance... we did a lot of damage to them, and we seized their izerdia supply. They couldn't have organised an attack on that scale, surely?"

"I think you're right. We had them on their heels." She hesitated again. "Ravinire claimed Mithanis acted against Ronisin and the other Falcons because of me... because he saw their loyalty to me as a threat. But how could I know, Theac?" The words tore out of her, raw and painful. "I didn't *know*."

Theac was silent a long moment. "I tried to tell you, lass. They looked up to you, wanted to follow someone like you. That doesn't make you responsible for their deaths."

"He's right."

"I'm going to make it right," she said determinedly. That was clear to her more than anything else. With Cuinn, she was going to make it right. And she was going to make Mithanis pay.

Theac nodded, accepting that, and changed the subject. "Have you told Prince Cuinn that Ravinire told his mother?"

Talyn looked at her second helplessly. "How do I tell him that his own mother probably betrayed him to his brother?"

"You don't need to." Cuinn dropped out of the sky, startling them both. "I already worked it out for myself."

"Your Highness." Theac straightened in surprise. "I am sorry. Your mother... well, lad, I'd just like to say in my view she doesn't deserve you."

Cuinn's smile was bright as he rested a hand on Theac's shoulder. "Thank you, Talon Parksin."

All three turned as Jasper prowled towards them across the deck. The tawncat could rarely be found far from Cuinn's side since the explosion.

"Has he eaten any sailors yet?" Talyn changed the subject, sensing the pain under Cuinn's smile and not wanting to prolong it.

"You're hilarious." Cuinn gave her a look.

"How are you going to explain that vicious beast to your family, Captain?" Theac asked.

"He'll have to stay contained." She looked at Cuinn. "We can't afford to have him attacking people in the castle fortress because he thinks you're threatened."

Cuinn knelt to stroke the tawncat's silky head—he remained the only one allowed to touch Jasper. "I think he's smart enough to know I'll be safe there. And we'll leave him with Halun. Jasper likes him most."

"After the captain, you mean." Theac scowled.

"After Talyn, yes." Cuinn smiled. "How are the injured Wolves doing?"

"Jystar is confident they're all going to pull through," she said. She'd decided to accept the healer's request to enlist with the Wolves. His entreaties had resonated with her, his obvious love for Tiercelin something she didn't think could be manufactured, and her talons would keep a close eye to make sure he could be trusted. "He said they noticeably rallied after you sang to them last night."

Cuinn straightened, delight flashing over his face. "In that case, I'll go and sing to them again."

He was gone before either Theac or Talyn could say anything, disappearing in a flurry of silver-white wings.

"Never thought I'd see a winged man so thrilled by the idea he might be able to help a human," Theac muttered.

"He wants to help. It's all he's ever wanted."

THEIR SHIP APPROACHED Port Lachley docks late in the morning. Given Talyn was unexpectedly arriving on her family's doorstop with an Acondor prince and just under sixty foreign warriors, she sent a message on ahead to the castle the moment the ship made berth.

Getting themselves off the ship and lined up along the jetty took time, and soon a large crowd of onlookers was staring at the spectacle.

Talyn winced.

"They aren't going to love this idea of yours, are they?" Cuinn asked at her side. The two of them stood watching as her talons finished sorting the Wolves into neat lines, Jasper curled up at Cuinn's feet.

"They'll be fine. Are you ready?" she murmured.

"Ready to greet the family that doesn't want me anymore than my mother and brothers do?" He turned towards her. "I can't wait."

"I think you'll find the Dumnorix are a little different," she assured him, then amended. "After my uncle gets over his apoplexy."

Cuinn laughed. "What's the plan, anyway? We just going to walk in there, announce I know who I am, and demand their help?"

It was her turn to chuckle. "We might aim for a little more subtlety than that. Let's greet them first. They'll want to know why we're here—I'll put them off until Uncle can gather whatever family is in town. Otherwise, use that magic of yours to pick the right time. If we want their backing, we need to handle this carefully."

His expression turned sober. "I trust your advice, Talyn. But I don't want to be away from Mithranar too long."

"Neither do I," she assured him.

Talyn led the way down the long pier, Cuinn and Jasper at her side. Theac and Corrin flanked them, two steps behind, and the Wolves marched along in formation beyond. They made an impressive sight in their grey and white, particularly the winged folk. Everyone on the docks stared.

A familiar figure waited for Talyn at the end of the pier, a smile of welcome on his handsome face.

"Tarcos!" she said in surprise. The sight of him caused a flickering of unease that was quickly dispelled by his warm hug—his anger at her was seemingly forgotten, or at least pushed aside in his pleasure to see her. And she was glad to see him too, glad to seemingly be on better footing than she'd left things. "What are you doing here?"

"I was there when your message came, so I thought I'd come and say a proper hello before your family swallows you whole. It's so good to see you," he said.

"And you." She gestured to Cuinn. "You remember Prince Cuinn?"

"I do." Tarcos offered his hand, then his eyes widened as Jasper took a step forward. "What is that?"

Cuinn shook firmly. "Lord Hadvezer. Good to see you again. *That* is my friend Jasper. As long as you don't make any sudden moves, he won't eat you. Probably."

Jasper obligingly let out a warning snarl. Talyn hid her smirk as Tarcos took a half step backwards before recovering. "No sudden moves. Got it."

Tarcos fell into step with Cuinn and Talyn, one wary eye on Jasper, and they walked together along the main road leading east out of the city. Once they got clear and turned north up the bluff to where the castle fortress looked down over harbour and city both, the traffic on the road thinned and they made better time. The Wolves marched in neat rows, offering the occasional smile or wave to those who stared at them.

Beside her, Cuinn's gaze was wide, taking in the hulking castle sprawling across the rocky bluff ahead of them, the SkyRider base on a second bluff to the east, and the rolling, forested hills spreading out from there to the horizon—the tallest of which was Mount Fanar. Talyn had raced that mountain on FireFlare twice before, and won both times.

"You're still with Uncle's court then?" she asked Tarcos. "I thought you'd be back in Firthland by now, learning the ropes from your uncle."

"That will come later. For now I asked to be his representative to King Aethain's court," Tarcos explained. "I'm thrilled that you're back, Tal. I wasn't sure when I was going to see you again, and I didn't like how we left things."

Talyn ignored Cuinn's pointed look and smiled at Tarcos, relieved his anger at her seemed to have passed. He'd always been a wonderful friend and she was pleased not to have lost that. "Neither did I."

He glanced back at the Wolves marching behind. "What brings you both here? And with all your Wolves?"

"It's a long and complicated story, and one that I need to discuss with my family first," she said apologetically.

He frowned again, clearly knowing her well enough to pick up the repressed grief in her voice. "What's happened, Talyn?"

She smiled and forced the dark thoughts away. "Nothing that needs to worry you."

"We'll have a drink together," he promised. "Right after you've dealt with that powerful family of yours. How long are you staying?"

"Not long. A few days, maybe a week," she said carefully, not wanting to upset him.

He sighed, sounding resigned. "I knew it would be too much to hope for more." They approached the castle gates and Tarcos halted. "I might take a walk while I'm out in the fresh air. Make sure you come and find me for that drink."

"It is lovely weather for a walk." Cuinn flashed a winning smile. She didn't miss the little hint of song magic he used to bolster Tarcos's interest in leaving.

"I'll find you after," she promised Tarcos.

As soon as he was striding away, she elbowed Cuinn in the ribs. "Quit being jealous."

"I would never!" he said, scandalised.

She grinned. He grinned back.

"*Six thrices, you're ridiculous. I NEVER thought I'd see my fearless, cool-as-ice partner silly with infatuation.*"

"*You shut up.*"

A brief silence, then, "*I'm happy for you.*"

"You did notice that he pretended I wasn't here that entire conversation?" Cuinn asked mildly.

"I did."

"Very polite, Firthlanders, aren't they?"

"Enough." She gave him a look.

The gates opened and two Kingshield came out to greet them. Talyn recognised Captain Dunnil.

"Captain Dynan." He gave a short head bow to Talyn, then did a quick double-take at the sight of Jasper. "Your Highness." A more pronounced bow to Cuinn. "Welcome to Port Lachley."

"Thank you," Cuinn said graciously. "I apologise for my sudden arrival. I'm aware of the strain that must place on your guard rotations. I'm hoping my Wolves will help alleviate that."

Dunnil glanced at Talyn, then nodded. "We're preparing barracks for them inside, Your Highness. Captain, your mother is waiting for you. My men will escort your Wolves, if you and Prince Cuinn would like to come with me?"

"Captain?" Theac barked, stepping forward. He didn't seem to like the proposed arrangements.

"We're inside my family's home, Theac. There's no safer place for us," she reassured him. The words, spoken aloud, sank in for her too. Here they were safe. "Help the talons get the Wolves settled in and ask Halun to take Jasper. I'll come and find you later."

He saluted, reluctance all over his face. "Yes, Captain."

TALYN'S SHOULDERS gradually stiffened as Dunnil led her and Cuinn through the fortress hallways—she'd promised her uncle she'd never tell Cuinn who he was, and she'd blatantly broken that promise. Not to mention breaching the First Blade's confidence in telling Cuinn about the planned invasion.

Leaving Mithranar so abruptly had felt right, the only way to keep Cuinn safe until they could plan the best way forward.

But that certainty was rapidly fading under the imminent reality of not only telling her uncle and mother she'd broken her word, but then demanding they formally acknowledge Cuinn. She'd gone well beyond the remit of a Dumnorix not part of Aethain's court without any power or responsibility.

Her uncle was going to be furious with her. And her mother... worse.

"To be honest, I'm kinda glad I'm not there."

"Helpful, as usual."

Cuinn's eyes roved her face, sensing her creeping dread. He placed a brief hand on her back, and like a jolt his magic flowed into her. Steadying. Calm. A smile crept over her face.

Ahead of them, Dunnil opened the doors to one of the castle meeting chambers, and gestured for Cuinn and Talyn to enter. Alyna Dumnorix was there, seated at a table near a fireplace and frowning over some paperwork. She looked up as they entered, and for a tiny instant cold anger flashed in her eyes. It vanished as quickly as it had come and Talyn was left wondering if she'd imagined it.

"Mama." Talyn walked over, straight into a warm hug. She held on tight, her grief surging with a vengeance now that she was in her mother's arms. Alyna hugged her back just as fiercely. By the time they parted, Talyn had recovered her poise.

Alyna stepped back. "You finally came. And you brought Prince Cuinn."

Cuinn bowed slightly and offered a warm smile. "A pleasure to see you again, Lady Alyna."

"Is Uncle around?" Talyn asked. "We all need to talk."

Alyna glanced between them, a considering look on her face. "He's with Ariar actually—away from the city. They'll be back in a day or two. Is something wrong?"

"I... yes." Talyn nodded, disappointed. She didn't want to linger any longer than was necessary, but they had no choice but to wait for her uncle's return. "I'd rather wait until they're both here before we get into it. Is it all right if we stay until then?"

Alyna chuckled. "As if you even need to ask. We're already preparing rooms. Six thrices, Talyn, did you really need to bring all of your Wolves, though? The Conmoran lords are not going to be happy that so many foreign warriors have made an uninvited appearance in their capital."

"Sorry," Talyn apologised. She knew managing the lords' pride would be hard work for her mother and Aethain to manage. "But it was necessary. A detail of ten will be on Cuinn at all times—I hope that won't be a problem?"

Alyna frowned in concern. "Talyn, what's going on?"

Talyn squeezed her mother's hand. "We'd rather not tell the tale more than once." She swallowed. "It's not a happy one, Mama."

Alyna's gaze shifted to Cuinn, full of worry. "You'll both join me for dinner, I hope?"

Where she would do her level best to pry the information out of them. Talyn nodded gamely. "We'd love to. I've missed you, Mama."

Alyna stepped closer, violet gaze searching Talyn's face. "Are you okay?"

"She is." Cuinn spoke before Talyn could, using a subtle hint of magic that was just enough to relax Alyna's shoulders and smooth the frown from her face. "We've had a difficult time recently, but as Talyn said, it's a long tale best told all at once."

"If you say so." Worry still lingered in her mother's eyes, but she seemed to have let it go for the moment. "Captain Dunnil will show you to your rooms. I've put you in the guest wing if that's all right? A few lords are in residence at the moment so these walls are almost full-to-bursting."

"It's absolutely fine." Talyn hugged her mother again. "We'll see you at dinner."

THE QUARTERS they'd been given in the guest wing were luxuriously appointed, with separate bedrooms that surrounded a common area with chairs, lounges and a massive fireplace.

A fire had been lit to dispel the cold air in the room, and a tray of food and drink sat on a table by the window. As soon as the door closed behind them, Cuinn reached out to grab her hand. "Come here," he laughed, pulling her in and pressing his mouth to hers.

She crashed into him, winding her arms around his neck and falling with him onto one of the couches. Too long. It had been far too long on that stupid cramped boat with no privacy whatsoever.

His hands went to her shirt, fingers brushing her bare skin. It was heaven to feel his body entwined with hers again, his mouth raining kisses on her face and lips. She tore his shirt off, and laughed as his fingers fumbled with the buttons on her own shirt, made awkward by his urgent desire.

"I missed you," he breathed against her skin.

"I did think about you from time to time." Talyn found his belt, tugged it out of his pants, then helped shove them down and off. Her breeches were next and then they were skin to skin, finally. His mouth pressed against hers. Talyn's eyes slid shut at the sensation and she pulled him closer, closer, always closer.

NOT ENTIRELY UNEXPECTEDLY, a messenger knocked on the door a full-turn later. Talyn extracted herself from Cuinn, dragged clothes back on, and answered the door. A servant stood there holding a message, but before he could say anything, Jasper shot through the opening in the door, forcing her to jump back out of his way.

The servant stared, clearly torn between fascination and terror.

"Can I help you?" she asked.

Wordlessly, he passed her a note, then walked away. Fast.

Talyn opened the folded parchment—her mother wanted to see her.

"You didn't use enough magic on her," Talyn said wryly as she kicked the door shut. Jasper had leapt up onto the sofa and was purring as a bare-chested Cuinn stroked his ears.

"It was hard. You Dumnorix are all so strong minded," he said. "She's just worried about you."

"And she won't let it go till I've told her at least part of the story." She sighed. "I'll be back later... sometime. Would you mind checking that the Wolves are settling in okay?"

He nodded. "She loves you. Remember that when you start getting stubborn and annoyed."

Talyn leaned down to kiss him. "You're going to keep Jasper from eating people?"

"Absolutely." He grinned.

· · ·

"Mama?" Talyn knocked on the ajar door of her mother's private rooms.

Alyna turned and smiled. "Ah, you got my message. Come in, Talyn. I hope you didn't truly expect me to let your rather dire comments go without further discussion?"

"No, I suppose not." Away from Cuinn, the shadows pressed down on her again. A manageable weight, though. One she'd learned to bear.

Alyna sat by the windows, then motioned Talyn to a chair opposite. Her violet eyes were dark with concern. "Tell me what happened."

"The full story can wait, but... we lost some Wolves in an attack. One of my talons died." Talyn swallowed, having to force the words out.

Alyna reached over to squeeze her hand. "I'm so sorry. You're all right though? You weren't hurt?"

"Nothing serious." Jystar had removed the stitches in her leg, and although it was sore, she was walking normally again.

Her mother's sharp gaze searched Talyn's face for a moment, but Alyna seemed to accept she didn't want to talk about it any further. She shifted away, changing the subject. "Aethain and Ariar are due back late tomorrow. I've cleared the king's schedule for the morning after so we can discuss whatever it is you need to."

"Thank you." Talyn settled back in the chair.

Alyna was silent a moment, then, "I noticed that Tarcos couldn't get out of here quickly enough to go and meet you. I'm glad for you, Talyn."

Talyn chuckled, stretched out her injured leg without making it obvious it was aching slightly. "It's not like that, Mama."

"You don't have to worry about upsetting me. You and Tarcos were always intended to be married. It's a suitable match for us."

She lifted an eyebrow. "It would be if I was part of Aethain's court. Which I am not."

Alyna gave her a look. "He's your lover, isn't he? What's so terrible about marrying someone you already like and respect?"

"Actually, no, he's not my lover anymore." Talyn sat forward. "And I'm confused about why you're becoming so insistent on this."

"You are a Dumnorix, Talyn. It's important that you do your duty by your family—and in this case we're not asking much. You like Tarcos. There is no Trystaan in your life."

"*She has no idea.*"

"*Quiet.*"

Talyn raised her eyes to her mother's. "You know how important Mithranar is to me."

"I know you love it there. I know you enjoy leading the Wolves and it gives you a sense of satisfaction," Alyna said. "But being here with us would give you that same feeling. And you know as well as I do that we don't always get the things we want."

Talyn studied her mother's face, tried to fight the feeling that she was talking to a stranger. She'd spent most of her life away from home since turning sixteen, had rarely seen her parents after that. She loved them, yes, but she hadn't been part of their lives. And Sari's death had changed Talyn irrevocably, in ways her mother had never gotten to know or understand.

It was startling to realise that Trystaan's death had done the same for her mother in ways Talyn probably wouldn't ever understand either. Because she hadn't been there. She'd been in Mithranar.

To survive her grief, Alyna had retreated to her Dumnorix self, to the only comfort and strength available to her.

"*You tried that, but it didn't work,*" Sari murmured.

"*No. I found my solace in my father's home.*"

Talyn's heart sank. Maybe she just needed to find another way to make her mother understand. "Did you know that Da was winged folk?" she asked softly.

Alyna shifted, taken aback by the subject change, sadness filling her expression. "I asked him once, about the scars on his back. It was too painful for him to talk about. I couldn't bear the agony in his eyes so I never raised it again."

Talyn leaned forward, reaching out to touch her mother's knee in support. "For a winged person, having their wings removed is an unimaginable horror."

Alyna swallowed. "That's what happened to Trys?"

Talyn nodded. "What did he tell you about his family, the reasons he left Mithranar?"

"I know there were political reasons, that he felt he had to leave and couldn't return. But he rarely spoke of it."

"He was the heir to a very powerful family—his father was the right hand of the queen. Da had a half-brother, a human, who became a criminal." Talyn paused. "When Queen Sarana found out, she had Da's entire family executed. Da barely escaped. He had his wings removed so that he wouldn't be recognisable. That's why he was so afraid of me going to Mithranar."

"She killed them all?" Alyna's violet eyes had gone dark with horror.

"Yes. Do you understand what I'm saying now, Mama? You talk as if Mithranar is a toy I like to play with. But it's more than that. It's a part of me. I am as much Mithranan nobility as I am Dumnorix."

"No, you're not." Alyna's face hardened. "You were born and raised here, with us. We are Dumnorix—you don't get to cast that aside. We have inherent responsibilities you are shirking."

That stung. Guilt writhed—was her mother right? But she didn't want to fight, she didn't have the emotional energy for it. Instead, she just rose from her chair. "I think I'll give dinner a miss tonight. Please let me know when my uncle and Ariar arrive."

"Talyn, wait!"

"Later, Mama." She tried not to slam the door on her way out.

CUINN WAS GONE from the guest quarters when she arrived back there, hopefully still with the Wolves. Walking to her mother's quarters and back had left her healing leg sore, but she ignored the pain, crossing to the window where she could look out over the lights of the city below.

A soft knock came at the door, surprising her. Cuinn wouldn't knock, and she'd made it clear to her mother that she wanted space. Who else would be coming to see her?

"It's open," she called out.

Tarcos entered, dressed to join the family and whatever nobles were in residence for dinner in the great hall.

"Tarcos." She managed a smile. "I'm going to eat up here tonight. I'm not really in the mood for a big dinner and talking to all those people."

"I thought that might be the case. Can I join you?"

She sighed, tried to work out how to refuse without hurting him. Cuinn would be back soon, and she wanted to eat with him—wanted to just be with him. Tarcos saw the answer on her face, and stepped closer. "We're still friends, aren't we? I haven't ruined that?" His eyes were hazel warmth.

"We are," she said. "I know I hurt you, and I'm sorry for it."

He was quiet again, the frown returning. "Your mother has spoken to me formally of a potential match between us."

"I see," Talyn said quietly. "I wish she hadn't. Tarcos—"

"Wait." He raised his hand. "Please hear me out."

"All right." She wanted to give him that, at least.

"I heard what you said to me in Ryathl. It hurt, and I'm sorry that I reacted the way I did." He reached out to take her hand. "I understand that you're not in love with me. But we are friends, and you like and respect me. Isn't that a good basis for a marriage?"

"You didn't hear everything I said." She met his gaze, trying to be gentle. "It's not about that. I don't want to be married. Especially not to the warlord of Firthland. My life isn't there, Tarcos."

He took a deep, shuddering breath. "I could wait. Until Mithranar is out of your system. Until you're ready."

"I will never be ready. It will never be what I want." She spoke firmly. "I don't want to hurt you, but if I'm not honest you'll only be hurt worse in the long run."

His jaw clenched. "I need you at my side."

"No, you don't. You will be a fine warlord without me."

Tarcos stepped away then, dropping her hands. "That wasn't what I meant."

"Then what?" she asked, mystified.

"It doesn't matter. I'm sorry to have bothered you about this again." He turned and left.

The door closed with a click behind him, and after a moment's hesitation, Talyn reached for her cloak and followed him out. The heavy weight of grief was back, along with the unease and guilt over the conversations she'd had with Tarcos and her mother.

She wanted to see the Wolves. See Cuinn.

And let them help her.

MANY FULL-TURNS LATER, Talyn couldn't help the laughter bubbling out of her as Cuinn tickled her mercilessly, rumpling the sheets beyond repair as they rolled over and over. Eventually she slapped his hands away, gripped his wrists, and pinned them to the pillows above his head. Firelight glimmered over the walls, warming the room despite the cold outside.

"We should get some rest," she said, grinning. It had been not far off midnight when they'd returned from dinner, but something about several full-turns in the company of Cuinn's guards had both of them in energetic moods. Now it was drifting into the early hours of the morning.

"Do you really want to go to sleep right now?" He asked, green eyes dark as he ran a slow, seductive gaze over her naked body.

"Absolutely not." She lowered her mouth to his for a slow kiss.

Mid-kiss, she dropped her hands to his ribs and began tickling the bare skin she found there. He gave a shout of startled surprise and they began wrestling under the sheets again, laughing with delight. Eventually she dropped down beside him, breathing hard, draping an arm across his chest.

Cuinn shifted so they were eye to eye. "Where do you see this going, Talyn?"

"You want to talk about that now?" She lifted an eyebrow, not bothering to pretend not to know what he meant. "Is it because Tarcos asked me to marry him again?" She'd told him as soon as they'd had a moment alone, walking back to their rooms from dinner with the Wolves.

"Partially, but not because I'm jealous." A look of wonder spread over his face. "When we're together... you don't hide from me. I can feel everything you feel. How could I doubt you after that?"

"Then why?" she asked.

"It just made me think... you don't want to marry Tarcos. But does that mean you never want to marry?"

"I've never wanted it, Cuinn," she said softly, wanting to be as honest with him as she had with Tarcos. "I'm a warrior—I live for that. Settling down, children, family life, it's not me."

He propped himself on an elbow, clearly thinking about that. "Sari had those things and was still Callanan. It didn't hold her back from what she wanted."

She would be lying if she said it hadn't crossed her mind, even briefly, even if she'd shoved the thought away each time she thought it because...

"It's not possible," she whispered. "I can't do it to my family. I know that Mithranar's safety is at stake too, but a marriage between us would form a power base that could destabilise the Twin Thrones. Even if I wanted to marry, I couldn't marry *you*."

His mouth twisted. "I wish I didn't understand, but I do."

She sighed, pressed her forehead against his. "We probably shouldn't have started this."

"Probably not. But let's hold onto it as long as we can," he murmured, shifting to kiss her.

She kissed him harder, pushing him down against the sheets, hands sliding over his skin, gasping in delight when his wings closed around them. A happiness she hadn't felt before filled her as his touch removed every thought but him from her mind.

How was she going to let this go?

CHAPTER 41

*A*ethain and Ariar arrived the following afternoon, their approach announced by a Kingshield rider sent on ahead. A messenger from Alyna found Cuinn and Talyn in the mess with the Wolves.

Cuinn's heart sank a little at the news. This precious time he and Talyn had been able to share was about to come to an end.

Ariar—not delayed by several courtiers needing his attention— bounded into the entrance hall moments after Cuinn and Talyn managed to get there, blue eyes bright, hair rumpled from the ride. He came straight over, a wide smile of welcome on his face. Cuinn had liked Ariar from the moment they'd met, and wondered now how much of that was due to their shared blood. It was an odd thing, the knowledge that he had *other* family.

"Ariar!" Talyn grinned a greeting and threw her arms around her cousin.

"Talyn. Cuinn." Ariar hugged her tightly then stepped back to grin at Cuinn. Nobody pointed out that Ariar had unthinkingly dropped Cuinn's title, as all members of the Dumnorix did with each other. "It's good to see you both. How long have you been here? I had no idea you were planning a visit."

"We docked three days ago," Talyn explained. "Events in Mithranar prompted the trip. I'm hoping to talk to all of you about it once Uncle has settled in."

Ariar frowned. "That sounds ominous."

"Unfortunately it is." Talyn glanced at Cuinn. He hated the shadows in her eyes at the mention of what had happened. "Mama has already cleared your schedules for a family meeting first thing tomorrow. She's rather anxious to know about whatever it is that brought us here."

"That's mean of you, to keep her hanging like that." Ariar's eyes twinkled.

Talyn winced. "Part of the reason is that our story is difficult, and we'd prefer to have to tell it only once. And the rest, well, I'd rather you all get furious at me all at once."

Ariar threw back his head and laughed, a reaction that had Cuinn liking him even more. "I cannot wait. Will you at least be at dinner this evening?"

"If you are, we will be," Talyn promised.

"Both of you?" Ariar turned his attention to Cuinn, expression hopeful.

"I'd like that," Cuinn said, pleased. He looked forward to spending some more time with Ariar.

"How about we leave Uncle to his business and say hello at dinner?" Talyn eyed the courtiers still surrounding Aethain.

"That is an excellent plan." Ariar followed them as they headed out of the hall.

SEVERAL LORDS and ladies in residence, as well as Tarcos, filled the formal dining table along with Aethain, Alyna and Ariar when Talyn and Cuinn joined them for dinner that night. Darkness had fallen, but the large hall was bright—the result of several warming fires along the walls and a myriad of hanging lanterns.

The atmosphere was formal, restrained, vastly different to what Cuinn was used to in Mithranar. But he got the distinct impression that was simply the Conmoran way, and not a result of unhappiness or discomfort. He sensed nothing but respect and loyalty from the various lords when they greeted their king.

"Is this an official visit, Prince Cuinn?" Aethain asked.

"That's actually a complicated question to answer," Cuinn admitted. "Perhaps we can talk in greater detail tomorrow?"

"How's Aeris? Has he settled in well to Samatia?" Talyn asked, presumably attempting to deflect further questioning.

Aethain's severe face softened. "I miss the lad fiercely, but yes, he's doing well."

Cuinn glanced at Talyn. She was seated next to him, and they were both a little further down the table than Aethain, Ariar and her mother, who sat around the top of it. He wondered how angry her family was going to be that she'd told Cuinn the truth. Maybe they wouldn't be angry—after all, he could tell they all felt the undeniable pull of Cuinn's Dumnorix blood now that he'd stopped wearing his glamour and using song magic to deflect their attention.

The little glances they shot his way when they thought he wasn't looking were filled with fascination and unease. Most of the former were from Ariar, and the latter from Alyna. Aethain seemed distracted by other worries on his mind. Tarcos flat out couldn't stand him. Cuinn wondered if jealousy was the only reason for that.

"Talyn?" Ariar called across the table.

"Ariar?" she mimicked, teasing him.

"When are you planning on returning to Mithranar?"

"As soon as we can." She glanced at Cuinn. "There are some things we need to do here first. Hopefully with all of your help."

"I'm growing more and more intrigued." He winked. "I'll stay on until you leave then."

Talyn smiled. "Good."

Ariar leaned towards them, lowering this voice. "This dinner is getting more boring with every passing second."

"We could always stage a dramatic escape. Talyn could create a diversion," Cuinn offered in an equally loud whisper.

Ariar nodded thoughtfully. "I like your thinking. Shall we just up and run for it?"

"Absolutely. We'll have the element of surprise. They won't be able to catch us."

"Both of you will stay exactly where you are," Talyn hissed. "If I have to stay then so do you."

Ariar shrugged, but rose to move down the table to be closer to them, politely dislodging poor Lord Somner in the process. "So, tell me. Just a little hint on why you're really here? I promise to act surprised at our meeting tomorrow."

Talyn shared a look with Cuinn. In her emotions he read that she'd leave it to him to decide what to tell Ariar.

Cuinn summoned a casual tone to hide his pain. "Let's just say I'm not well-liked by my eldest brother and likely heir to my mother's throne. Mithanis tends to get violent when he feels threatened. We lost some of our Wolves."

The merriment had vanished entirely from Ariar's face as he glanced at Talyn. "Cousin, this disturbs me. Does our uncle know of it? If the threat to Prince Cuinn's life is as serious as you imply, he would want to help."

"Would he?" Talyn met her cousin's eye.

Ariar's expression turned grim. "He should."

Talyn relaxed, giving a little nod. "I hope he does. We're going to need it."

TALYN TURNED over in her sleep, moving deeper into Cuinn's arms. He lay awake, mind awhirl. The closer they came to the meeting with her family tomorrow, the more worried he was. No matter what the outcome, his life, his future, was about to change dramatically. And it was likely he was going to have to face that alone. Talyn wasn't going to be with him forever.

His arms tightened around her. He'd just about drifted off to sleep when a loud thudding sounded, distant, and slightly muffled. Talyn was already rolling out of the bed and reaching for her daggers before he registered that the sound wasn't normal.

They both stilled, waiting.

Another thud.

"Get dressed." Talyn grabbed her clothes.

He did as she bade without complaint. "What is it?"

Before she could reply, the sound of bells began ringing through the night.

"Don't tell me, those are alarm bells?" Cuinn asked as he tugged on pants. "What is going on?"

Talyn tightened her weapons' belt around her waist, brushed fingers over the hilts of her daggers. "No idea."

She ran for the door. Cuinn dragged on a shirt, precious seconds wasted as he fumbled with the extra buttons, then sprinted after her, catching up to her before she reached the bottom of the stairs. Jasper paced the stone at the base of the steps, agitated and clearly waiting for them to come down.

Wolves were spilling into the common area, Corrin in the lead. He stopped dead at the sight of Cuinn and Talyn descending together from her room. The concern on his face faded into surprise, and then embarrassment.

Silence descended.

"What's going on?" Talyn snapped.

Corrin cleared his throat. "I don't know. We heard the explosion and my first priority was to ensure the prince was safe."

"I'm fine," Cuinn shouted above the ringing bells. "Can you—"

Booted feet sounded from the corridor outside, and then Theac burst in, taking in the room in a glance before his gaze settled on Talyn. "The Kingshield have been summoned to the north-west wing. Two explosions went off."

Cuinn took a breath. "What's in the north-west wing?"

"Nothing." Talyn frowned, clearly thinking hard. "Kitchens, store-rooms. Stables outside."

"An accidental explosion then?" he suggested.

"No," Theac answered. "I overheard one of the Kingshield captains. There isn't any izerdia stored in the castle. It's kept elsewhere."

Cuinn glanced at Talyn, saw the shadows in her eyes. "Theac, take the Wolves to join the Kingshield and help with the castle's defence in case this is some sort of attack. Leave Corrin's detail here with Talyn and I."

"Right." Theac saluted and ran.

"Where are we going?" Corrin asked.

Talyn glanced at Cuinn. "Let's find my family."

"I CAN SMELL SMOKE," Corrin murmured as he scanned the corridor, hand on the hilt of his sword. They were approaching the royal wing, Talyn insisting on caution. Her emotions were coolly controlled as always, mind clear, but Cuinn could sense her underlying unease.

She thought the explosions were a distraction.

"Izerdia fumes," Roalin muttered. His purple wings furled and unfurled at his back. "I'd recognise that sweet scent anywhere."

Talyn glanced at Cuinn. "At the end of this hall is a wide foyer area with a set of steps that lead up into the royal wing. It's where my mother, Ariar and the king all have their rooms. It will be crawling with Kingshield so we need to be careful," she said. "We don't want to walk into a stray arrow because they think we're attacking."

Jasper pressed against his leg, snarling softly—his desire to hunt, to kill, was as clear to Cuinn as if a human were experiencing those emotions. "Stay, Jasper."

He let out an unhappy snarl, but remained at Cuinn's side as they edged their way down the hall, weapons drawn, a few paces behind Talyn in the lead. Cuinn summoned his song magic, surrounding them with it, trying to sense if any danger lurked.

All of them froze when the sound of fighting broke out ahead.

Talyn's gaze whipped to his, and then she was running forward. Cuinn followed, gesturing for Corrin and his detail to hold back. The talon hesitated, clearly reluctant, but obeyed Cuinn's order. Cuinn stayed behind Talyn as she pressed herself against the wall to peer around the corner, but he craned his neck so he could see too.

A handful of Kingshield fought bitterly in the open space before the stairs against a much larger group of fighters. As they peered around the corner, one of the attackers turned, glancing their way.

He wore a copper mask.

"It can't be," Cuinn breathed.

"Maybe Saniya brought her people *here* when they fled Dock City?" Talyn muttered, her expression confused.

"No." He stared. This didn't feel right. "Something else is going on."

"No time for questions." Talyn glanced down the corridor, catching Corrin's eye. Cuinn stepped away to give them time to quickly strategise and relay orders to the waiting Wolves. Jasper was like a drawn bow at his heels, claws scraping on the stone floor, body rigid with the desire to hunt.

"How can I help?" he asked as they readied themselves to move.

Talyn regarded him for a moment, then smiled. "Can you sing confusion and fear to break their concentration?"

Relief filled him at being given something useful to do, at being saved from being a liability. "I can do that."

"Without affecting us or the Kingshield guards?"

His smile spread wide over his face. "Child's play, Captain."

Her smile matched his. "Then let's fight."

Roalin threw back his head and howled. Jasper let out an ear-splitting snarl in echo.

Cuinn stepped out from the corridor, facing the fight ahead and taking a deep breath. Then, he began to sing. It was a wordless tune, haunting and eerie, a tune filled with doubt and fear and confusion. He wrapped his magic around one masked man at a time, carefully avoiding the Kingshield.

The moment Cuinn's magic touched them, they began to falter, their blows going wide, their footwork sloppy. The Kingshield didn't stop to question what was happening, instead pushing their advantage.

And then Jasper and the Wolves were joining the fray. Talyn and

Corrin led them at a run, Talyn drawing a dagger mid-sprint and throwing it. One of the masked men dropped as the blade embedded in his neck. Corrin's knives killed another three in quick succession—the speed with which he could throw was blinding—and Talyn took care of a fifth with her second dagger. Jasper dropped one man with a single swipe of his claws, then leapt onto another's back with a vicious growl.

The Wolves surged after them, taking care of the fringes and covering the Kingshield still alive. Cuinn sang, deepening his voice, making it louder, quelling the attackers with his magic, making them easy prey for the Wolves and Kingshield. He stayed well enough back that while their emotions still hit him, he could bear the strain.

In minutes the masked attackers were dead to a man.

Talyn glanced over to check he was all right, sapphire eyes bright, cheeks flushed from the fight. He gave her a little nod.

"Talyn!"

Talyn spun as Alyna Dumnorix appeared on the landing at the top of the steps, several Kingshield close behind. The sword she held was bloodied, and more blood and gore spotted her clothing. Her violet eyes were as flaming bright as her daughter's.

Cuinn spread his wings and flew the distance to land beside Talyn, the Wolves forming up around him in case of further danger. Jasper returned to his side.

"Mama, you're okay?" Talyn called. "What's going on?"

"I'm fine. My Kingshield woke me when the bells started ringing. They reported explosions in the north-west wing. We had just left my rooms when we were intercepted by swordsmen wearing those masks." Alyna pointed at the dead bodies.

"Ariar? The king?" Cuinn spoke before Talyn could. Worry surged through him. Something was going on here, something they were missing. Why would Vengeance be here? Why set off explosions…

"A distraction," Talyn said before he could. "That's what the explosions were—to draw all the castle defenders to the north-western wing."

419

Alyna was as quick as her daughter. "The opposite side of the castle from the royal quarters."

"Where's Aethain's Kingshield?" Talyn demanded.

"I don't know," Alyna said grimly. "Hopefully barricading his quarters until the threat has passed."

"Talyn?" Cuinn couldn't stay quiet any longer. The unease inside him was surging to unbearable levels. "We should go to him."

Talyn nodded. "I agree. Mama—Cuinn, the Wolves, and I will go after Aethain in case he's under attack too. You need to go and take control of the castle's defences."

Alyna baulked. "We don't know what Aethain's situation is—he might have already escaped with his Kingshield, or they could have set a trap down there waiting for one of us to walk into."

"Aethain is king of the Twin Thrones," Talyn said firmly. "I'm not leaving him. We'll be fine. Meanwhile, the rest of the castle needs defending. This could be an attack on a larger scale. GO!"

A new voice shouted out. "Talyn!"

Cuinn spun to see Tarcos running towards them, several hulking Bearmen behind him; his protective guard. He came to a halt at the bottom of the stairs. A palpable vibe of fierceness emanated from him and his men. "What's going on?" he asked.

"Don't know yet. Cuinn and I are going to take the Wolves and secure Aethain and his wife." Frustration poured from Talyn at the lack of action, making Cuinn wince and take a step back.

Tarcos nodded. "What do you want me to do?"

"Find Ariar. If he's not ordered it already, we need Aimsir riders out as quickly as possible covering all the exits to the city. Order them to shoot on sight anyone attempting to leave that is wearing a mask or holding a weapon."

"Can do. I'll leave half my guard here with you."

She shook her head. "No, I've got the Wolves. Send any Bearmen you can spare with my mother. She's going to organise the defence of the castle."

"Done." Tarcos turned and began rapping out orders to his men. They peeled off neatly, half to follow Tarcos away, the others to form up with Alyna's Kingshield detail. All the warriors were calm and focused, a soothing balm to Cuinn's song magic, helping with some of his anxiousness.

Alyna gave Talyn a warning look. "Once you find Aethain, you bring him to us in the main hall. Don't do anything risky."

"Promise." Talyn nodded.

Once her mother was gone, Talyn turned to Cuinn and the Wolves. "I'm going to take lead. You follow behind, quiet as you can, weapons drawn. Cuinn, you're behind me. Tell me at once if your magic senses any danger ahead."

"Understood," he said. "How much ground do we have to cover?"

"We take this hallway down to the end, then it's a left turn into the hall where the entrance to Aethain's suite of rooms is—a set of double doors at the end of the corridor. Clear?" she asked.

A series of confident nods.

They moved at a swift walk. Jasper seemed content to stick by Cuinn, but his mouth was open in a silent snarl, claws out and ready.

Only a handful of paces away from reaching the left turn, dread slammed into Cuinn's magic so strongly he swore, one hand reaching out to stop Talyn before he realised what he was doing. Jasper hissed.

She spun. "What?"

"We need to hurry," was all he could get out.

She ran.

He was only half a pace behind her as they rounded the corner. Cuinn's gaze went straight to the bodies of four Kingshield prone on the ground outside the double doors at the end of the hall. Blood seeped into a merging puddle on the floor from two guards lying close together—their throats had been slit.

"Two cut throats and two kidney strikes." Talyn's gaze ran clinically over the bodies. "That's not..."

"What?" he asked.

She didn't answer, instead skipping around the bodies and bursting through Aethain's doors. Cuinn, Jasper and the Wolves followed, nobody bothering about staying quiet now.

Everything looked fine in the sitting room beyond the doors. The embers of a fire almost out glowed orange in the hearth, a sofa, chairs and table untouched. A book left open was also undisturbed. Talyn went straight through without stopping, pushing open the door to another room, this one a study of sorts, and then another door, the bedroom.

Cuinn sucked in a breath of horror as he followed Talyn inside, the residual fear and pain in the room soaking into him in sickening tendrils. Aethain and his wife lay on the bed, under the covers, as if they'd been peacefully sleeping when...

The king's throat had been slit, his amber eyes wide open and staring sightlessly at the roof. His wife's body lay beside him, their blood soaking the sheets. Talyn's emotion hit him next, raw and grieving. But even before Cuinn could master his own reaction and offer comfort, her emotion receded, packed away as she fought to maintain clarity.

"Clean cuts," she said, voice cool. "Professional. Quick. Before either could raise the alarm."

Her eyes turned to his, bleak. When Corrin spoke, they both started, having completely forgotten about the Wolves that followed them in.

"A Shadow assassination, Captain?"

Cuinn swallowed. A Shadow who'd gone for the king of the Twin Thrones. Not him.

Shit.

"Can your detail stand guard here?" Talyn asked Corrin. "They deserve better than to be left alone like this."

The king of the Twin Thrones was dead.

Shit.

Corrin saluted, and with a look, his detail converged on the bed, surrounding the bodies in a watchful pose, gazes on any entrance to the room.

Talyn laid her palm over Aethain's heart for a long moment, then took a breath and stepped back, clearly trying to force her thoughts into some sort of order.

Shit.

Deep inside, he knew what Aethain's death meant, but he pushed the awareness away. There was no time for personal grief.

"We'll find Theac, and Ariar and your mother," Cuinn said after a moment. "We can take it from there."

Talyn took a deep breath. "Let's go."

TALYN LED Cuinn and Jasper through the back passageways of the castle, just in case there were more masked attackers lurking. Eventually they emerged into the main courtyard of the castle fortress where they found Theac speaking with Alyna and a Kingshield captain. A handful of Wolves and Kingshield stood at the closed gates, waiting to stop anybody trying to flee.

"Talyn!" Relief flashed over Alyna's face at the sight of them. "You're okay! Did you find Aethain?"

Cuinn glanced at Talyn, felt her grief, and answered so that she didn't have to. "We found him. He's been killed, Alyna, I'm so sorry."

A horrible silence fell as everyone in the vicinity heard and processed Cuinn's words. Alyna stared at them like they'd just told her something utterly impossible.

"Ariar?" Talyn managed. Her fear for her cousin hit Cuinn hard and he swallowed, riding it out.

"He's with the Aimsir organising a temporary blockade of the city." Alyna's voice was distant, like only part of her was engaged, the rest still trying to process the loss of her relative.

Even so, the news that Ariar was safe had Talyn's shoulders straightening infinitesimally. "What's our status?"

Theac, knowing exactly what she needed, spoke up, calm and precise. "Each Wolf detail is combing the castle for the attackers and flushing them out into the yard here. Kingshield have been dispersed to every possible exit. As of just under a quarter-turn ago, the castle is locked down. Nobody is getting out."

There was a brief silence. Alyna was still in shock, and even Talyn was struggling to maintain clarity. So Cuinn spoke, threading his voice with magic. "Alyna, you'll need to take command until something else can be organised. I recommend having Talyn lead the defence of the castle, while you gather all the lords in residence and make sure they're alive and safe."

"You're right." Clarity flashed into those violet eyes. "And I agree. I'll go and sort the lords. Talyn, you run the defence with Ariar. Once the crisis is over, we'll talk about what comes next. Agreed?"

Talyn shared a glance with Cuinn, then turned to Alyna and nodded. "Keep safe, Mama."

"You too." Alyna reached out to hug her daughter fiercely before turning to stride back towards the castle, Kingshield close on her heels. She was a fearsome sight, and Cuinn pitied any adversary they ran into.

"Liadin!" Talyn called out for the winged Wolf. "Take Roalin and Nirini and fly over to the SkyRider base—it's on the opposite bluff. Tell them they've direct orders from me to send a legion to Moth-duriem with an urgent message for Sky Chieftain Soar. He's to come here at once, and bring another legion with him."

"Captain!" Liadin saluted and leapt into the air.

"Open the gates!" a Kingshield on the wall bellowed suddenly. "Lord Ariar approaches."

Kingshield ran forward to open the castle gates, and moments later an Aimsir raced through at full gallop, reining his grey stallion in to a rapid halt before them.

"Ariar, what is it?" Talyn asked.

"We found a ship moored off the coast just east of here. Small boats are lined up on a deserted stretch of beach at the edge of the forest. The ship isn't flying any flags." Ariar's sky-blue eyes scanned the yard, wild-eyed. "Is everyone safe here?"

Talyn glanced at Cuinn, giving a little shake of her head.

"I'm sorry, Ariar. Your king was killed. His wife too," Cuinn said as gently as he knew how.

Grief leapt out from Ariar so intensely that it burned. Cuinn winced, taking a step back. A moment later Talyn's hand curled around his, calming him.

"I'm sorry," she murmured. "I keep forgetting."

"Alyna?" Ariar demanded.

"She's fine," Talyn assured him. "But we need to contain the threat so nobody else gets hurt. Have your Aimsir keep watch on the ship. If it so much as tries to raise the anchor to move, send flaming arrows into the sails, but leave the ship intact. I want at least some of those on board kept alive."

Ariar's face cleared. "Can do. I'll get down to the harbour, raise the patrol boats we have anchored there. They can surround the ship within a full-turn or two depending on the winds."

"Do it," Talyn ordered.

As Ariar galloped back out of the gates, the Kingshield moving to close it behind him, a loud screeching rent the skies. Cuinn stared up in wonder as several large shapes swooped down from the night sky, flying low over the castle before soaring back into the air.

"Liadin got to the SkyRiders," Talyn said.

Her relief was profound, easing some of the sting of Ariar's grief. Cuinn let out a slow breath.

The situation was under control.

But that idea brought his own grief surging back. Because the king of the Twin Thrones was dead. All Cuinn's plans were ashes. There would be no help from this quarter, not now.

He was going to have to face his brother alone.

CHAPTER 42

Slowly, under Talyn's command, order was restored. The Kingshield and Wolves hunted down all remaining attackers, the body count rising to almost fifty masked warriors. None had allowed themselves to be captured alive.

Two Kingshield were injured, all Aethain's guards dead. The Wolves survived unscathed.

From what Talyn could piece together, the izerdia explosions had been a distraction to draw Kingshield away from the royal quarters. Aethain's detail had stayed with him, but the reserves had gone to contain the apparent threat.

A distraction for a Shadow to kill a king.

As she was overseeing the process of bodies being carried out—attackers to an ungraceful pile, Kingshield to an honoured resting place inside one of the smaller halls—a SkyRider landed in the front courtyard. The news he brought wasn't good.

The Conmoran patrol boats had surrounded the ship anchored off the coast. Once they were in place, SkyRiders had dived on it, joining naval boarding crews to scour the ship from top to bottom.

It had been empty.

Ariar rode in a half-turn later to report that while the Aimsir cordon remained in place around the city, and SkyRider patrols covered the skies, nobody had tried to get in or out of Port Lachley.

With that news weighing on them, Ariar, Alyna and Talyn gathered in the castle's main hall, where Aethain's body, alongside that of his wife, had been laid out. Once Talyn walked in, the last to arrive, Alyna dismissed all the servants and Kingshield guards.

Talyn couldn't tear her eyes from where her uncle lay, resting peacefully, atop a bier. Someone had cleaned all the blood away from the bodies, placing freshly cut roses over their throats to hide the horrible wounds there. When she did finally tear her eyes away, trying bitterly to keep the welling tears from falling, her gaze landed on the Dumnorix banner hanging from the back wall—amber lightning wreathing the crossed swords.

Those colours would change after today. No more would the Kingshield, Callanan, SkyRiders and Aimsir wear the Dumnorix crossed swords etched from amber stars on their uniform.

Now they would be silver-grey.

"Messages have gone to the First Blade already." Alyna's voice broke the heavy silence. "A full investigation will be launched. The Callanan based in Port Lachley have already begun working."

"We don't know anything about the ship. The SkyRiders found nothing inside it to indicate the identity of those on board or where it came from." Ariar repeated what he'd already told Talyn. His voice lacked its usual energy, and even his bright eyes were dull. "It's a merchant vessel, an old one, according to the patrol boat captain that was part of the search."

Talyn ripped her eyes away from the wall hanging, forcing herself to pay attention. "There's a possibility the attackers were Vengeance," she said, explaining as concisely as she could what she knew.

"Why would they come here and attack us like this?" Ariar said.

"I honestly don't know." She hesitated. "But we shouldn't forget the fact that Callanan information tells us they work on behalf of Montagn."

"Your latest report said you'd dealt with Vengeance," Alyna said.

"We destroyed their base and we killed or arrested most of their members," Talyn said. "That's why, despite the masks, it doesn't make sense to me that the attack last night was them."

Ariar frowned. "If it was Vengeance, could the attack have been directed at Prince Cuinn?"

"No." Talyn was exhausted, heartsick, but this conversation had to happen now. "I don't think so. Looking at the scene in his bedroom last night... Aethain was killed by a Shadow. Which means—"

"He was the target." Ariar paled. "There were no Shadows breaking into our rooms."

Talyn nodded. "I believe so."

"*I agree*," Sari whispered.

A silence fell as the Dumnorix assessed Talyn's words.

And then Alyna was rising back out of the chair, life returning to her face and voice. She paced, coiled tight like a spring about to unleash. "Why would a Shadow assassinate the king of the Twin Thrones?" she snapped. "Warlord Hadvezer would never—"

"Of course not, but Talyn already learned that a Shadow mercenary is working with Vengeance in Mithranar," Ariar said.

Talyn glanced at him. "True. And we also know the warlord has been having trouble with the military, that some of the niever-flyers have gone rogue. It's not a leap to assume some Armun have too, Shadows included. We might need to question the loyalty of the Armun Council."

"Then we have to assume Montagn isn't just after Mithranar, but us too. Why else have Vengeance attack and assassinate our king?" Alyna said.

Talyn opened her mouth. Closed it. That didn't feel right. But she wasn't sure why. Instead she just pointed out, "Surely the Callanan informant would have warned us if the ahara was behind Aethain's assassination?"

Ariar ran a hand through his curls. "So we're under attack, and it's completely unforeseen. How do we fight back if we don't understand what's happening or why?" He grimaced. "And the bigger issue. We don't have a king to deal with it."

"I'll have Aeris summoned back from Samatia immediately," Alyna said crisply. "We can manage things until he arrives and is crowned by the lords."

Talyn's gaze shifted again to the wall hanging. Amber lightning turning to silver-grey.

Ariar huffed an incredulous breath. "He's fifteen, Alyna."

"He's a sensible young man. Besides, he'll have all of us supporting him." Alyna's violet gaze settled on Talyn at those words. "Won't he?"

She didn't look away. Because after all, she was Dumnorix, and they looked after their own. "He will."

LATE AFTERNOON FOUND her standing on the western castle battlement, looking down over the harbour and city below. Grey clouds scudded across the sky, and in the brisk wind was the hint of smoke from the fires that had been put out at the source of the explosions.

"Talyn?"

"Yes?"

"I'm sorry."

"Thanks." Talyn focused on her partner's presence in her mind, using it to ground herself.

A little while later, she was unsurprised to hear the rustle of wings behind her, and waited silently for Cuinn to approach and lean against the cool stone beside her. "You okay? You sort of disappeared after meeting with your family."

"I'm fine," she said. "Just thinking."

"About?"

"We're in trouble." She let out a long breath, turning to face him. "The Twin Thrones, I mean. Serious trouble. And... I have to stay here."

A thick silence fell. She forced herself to hold his gaze, to not look away, and saw no surprise in his luminous green eyes. He'd been expecting this. He'd always been expecting this. She hated that she'd proved him right.

Eventually he glanced away to stare out over the city. "Do you?"

"You know I do, Cuinn," she said, angry but not at him. "For the first time in generations, the stability of the Twin Thrones is threatened. I'm a Dumnorix. I need to stay here and help. That's my duty. It's who I am."

"I'm not surprised that you chose the Twin Thrones over us." And there was no censure in his voice either, only understanding.

"I'm not choosing—"

"Yes, you are," he said, cutting her off. "Don't pretend otherwise. Don't lie to yourself and to your Wolves. Don't lie to me." He gave her a sad smile. "But don't feel guilty about your choice, either."

"I have been pretending for so long that it would never come to a choice like this," she admitted, the words tearing out of her. "Sari kept warning me and I kept ignoring her. I'm sorry."

He turned away again. "I'm going back to Mithranar today. Your family is no longer in a position to help me, at least not until the situation here stabilises. And I can't afford to wait for that. If Vengeance was behind this… killing your king, then Montagn might be ready to move. Mithanis can't save Mithranar. But I have to try."

Fear flooded her. "You can't go back alone. You know Mithanis will come for you, or Vengeance will. We—"

He lifted a hand to cut her off. "I have a choice to make too. Either I continue hiding from my brother, or I finally stand up and fight for *my* country, *my* people. I choose to stand and fight."

She swallowed, turning back to the parapet, trying and failing to unclench her fists. If he went back alone…

"I won't be alone," he murmured as if reading her thoughts. "I'll have your Wolves with me. And I'm stronger now. *You* made me stronger."

"I'll find a way," she said fiercely, spinning back to him. "I promise you. I'll find a way to come home. You wait for me. Promise me you'll wait before you do something stupid like getting yourself killed."

"I promise." A little smile lit his beautiful face. "I promise I won't die until you're at my side, Talyn Ciantar."

AFTER SHE'D MANAGED to recover some semblance of calm following her talk with Cuinn, Talyn went to find her Wolves, dreading the coming conversation even more than the one with Cuinn.

Most of them were busy, helping with clearing away rubble and whatever else needed doing. Theac sat with Andres and Halun in a narrow hall the Wolves had been using as a mess. All three had food in front of them but none were eating. Theac glowered at his plate. He glanced up at her entrance, the forlorn look on his face telling her he'd been waiting for her to come.

Without saying anything, she walked the length of the tables, swinging a leg over the bench to sit beside Halun and opposite the other two. Theac pushed his mug towards her. She took a sip—tea with too much sugar, just as he liked it.

"I would stay with you, if I could," he said gruffly, staring at the tabletop.

"You have a beautiful family in Mithranar." Talyn tried to smile. "And who else can I trust with protecting Cuinn? It will make me rest easier, knowing you all are there with him."

Halun didn't say a word but she suddenly found herself being enveloped by a warm, brawny arm. A breath escaped her as she hugged him back, almost a sob. "You too, Halun."

"I'll do my best to keep him safe," Andres said in his sober, grave way. "And we will await your return, Ciantar."

Theac abruptly pushed his mug away and stood up. "Things to do." He hesitated, his usual scowl softening as he met her eyes. "I'm going to miss you, lass. Best thing that ever happened to me, you coming to the cells that day."

Fighting another sob, Talyn nodded, swallowed. "Theac, you have to look after him for me," she whispered. "I'll be back, but until then... promise me."

"You know I will."

Halun's hand settled in reassurance on her shoulder, and then he too rose to leave, Andres following suit, managing a little smile. "We'll see you soon then, Captain."

Then they were gone.

Corrin came a little while later. He walked in just as she was leaving the mess. For a moment they simply stared at each other in silence. When he finally spoke, there was a mixture of determination and guilt written across his young face. "I owe you a lot, Ciantar," he said in his quiet, steady voice. "You saved me, and my family, in more ways than one, and you made something of me."

"You did that for yourself, Corrin." She tried not to let her voice break. Failed miserably.

His face contorted. "I'm sorry, I can't stay with you. Prince Cuinn... he's my prince now. I won't walk away from him when he needs me."

"Oh Corrin." Talyn laughed through the tears that wanted to fall. "Don't feel guilty. As skilled a warrior as you are, you've become an even better man. I'm glad you'll be at his side."

"I won't let him down," Corrin promised.

"I know you won't," she said softly. "We'll see each other again, I swear it. I'll find a way."

He nodded. "Farewell, Ciantar."

"Good bye, Corrin."

Zamaril never came.

Talyn watched from the battlements as the glow of dusk lit up the horizon, turning the ocean orange, as Cuinn's ship slipped out into the harbour and slowly headed for the northern horizon. She stood there until the ship was only a faint speck in her vision, and kept watching until it faded completely from view.

Fighting tears and the despair settling over her, she turned away from the ocean, resting her back against the cold stone.

Sari was there then. *"How are you doing?"*

"Miserable. Terrified for him. Worried for the Twin Thrones."

"Sometimes life is just awful, isn't it?"

"Sometimes it is."

Refusing to stand there and wallow in her grief and fear and misery, she forced herself to walk along the wall to the steps leading down.

Halfway down she stopped, frozen.

A group of figures waited at the bottom, all wearing the distinctive grey and white of the Wolves. A familiar figure detached himself from the group.

Zamaril.

Of course. A hysterical laugh threatened to bubble up, and she continued down to the bottom.

"Dare I ask?" She lifted an eyebrow.

"I am afraid you may wish to expel me from the Wolves for this, Ciantar," he said. "But my loyalty is not to Prince Cuinn, or to Mithranar, it is to you. Always you. I am staying, and nothing you say can move me."

"And these others?" She pointed to the ten Wolves behind him. They were all looking straight ahead, stubbornly refusing to meet her gaze. Another smile threatened.

"When I informed Prince Cuinn that I was staying..." Zamaril straightened his shoulders. "He told me that he would trust nobody but the Wolves with your protection."

For the hundredth time in two days, Talyn teared up. She wanted to hug the thief, but it would only make him embarrassed and awkward.

"As sorely as I am tempted, I won't order you home." She huffed a breath. "Thank you, Zamaril."

He saluted again, a small smile on his face. "My Lady."

She made a face at him. "Don't even start with that nonsense. I am Captain to you."

"Not anymore." He shook his head. "Here you are Lady Talyn Dynan."

His words registered something in her. For a long moment she stared at him. He was right—she still wasn't part of court, but she would be here now, helping her family strategise, giving them support. And finally, *finally* after months of heartache and uncertainty about it, she understood where Zamaril's place was. Unlike the other

Wolves, he couldn't and would never place Cuinn's safety first. He was *her* man, heart and soul. And so…

"Fine. In that case, do you think you could take up your duties immediately?" she asked crisply. "I am expected at a meeting with my family. In fact, I'm probably already late."

He hesitated. "My duties?"

Talyn nodded. "As captain of my Kingshield guard."

Zamaril coughed. "Captain?"

"That's what I said. You want to stay, this is the capacity I am prepared to accept you remaining in."

A little smile spread over his face. "I think I can manage, Lady Dynan." Turning, he made a gesture towards the waiting Wolves to join them. At her acceptance of Zamaril, their gazes had begun flicking her way, hopeful. "Four winged Wolves—Prince Cuinn and I both thought they might be an advantage in a country with no winged folk. They are all volunteers."

"Kiran, I thought I'd finally be free of those pranks you like to play." Talyn smiled at him.

He smiled. "My life's pleasure is annoying you, Captain."

"And the rest of us." Tirina rolled her eyes, while Ehdra and Dansia chuckled.

Ehdra and Dansia. Cuinn had also left her with two Wolves who had Callanan shielding ability. She didn't know if that was a good or a bad thing. They wouldn't be able to use their ability to protect Cuinn, but they were also out of harm's way here. If Mithanis ever learned that humans had winged folk magic…

"I'm glad all of you are here," she told them, hoping they could hear in her voice how much she meant those words. "Thank you."

"It is our pleasure." Nirini smiled shyly.

"Truly, Ciantar." Roalin bowed.

"I'll get us all home, I promise you." She put as much conviction as she could into the words, needing to say it aloud, needing to *hear* them. She didn't know how long it would take, how she was going to figure it out, but she had to hold on to it. Or she would despair.

"We're happy to stay here with you as long as that takes, Your

Highness." This from Troi, and around him, the Wolves added their assurances. Then, at a barked command from Zamaril, they straight-ened up and saluted before falling in around her.

"I don't care what my position is here, you and your detail will be referring to me as Captain," she told Zamaril in no uncertain terms. Part of her couldn't bear to lose that. "Clear?"

"Very, Captain."

"Do you feel confident, Zamaril?"

"You couldn't have better protection than the Wolves." He looked insulted by the question.

Talyn smiled inwardly at his trademark cockiness. "Good."

ALYNA, Ariar and Soar were waiting when Talyn entered the war room. The Sky Chieftain had arrived earlier in the afternoon, unaware of everything that had happened. By some stroke of fortune, he'd set out from Mothduriem two days earlier on a planned visit to the capital. He was grey and tired-looking, the news hitting him as hard as it had the rest of them.

Zamaril was a comforting shadow at her back as all eyes turned to Talyn. She paused for a brief moment, gathering her thoughts and strength, then approached the large table in the middle of the room.

"You're here?" she asked Sari.

"I'm here."

The Wolves dispersed around the room to cover the various entrances while Wilfes and Talia took up a position a few steps behind Talyn and Zamaril.

"I was just assuring Soar that we've dispatched a SkyRider messenger to Samatia to summon Aeris back as quickly as possible," Alyna said.

"Wouldn't it be faster to send a full legion to fly him back?" Talyn asked.

"Given what's happened, I prefer he remain under the protection of the full Kingshield details there with him," Alyna said. "Once we know he's aboard one of Hadvezer's ships and coming home, we can send a SkyRider legion to escort him in and provide another layer of protection."

"I've also sent for more legions from the mountains," Soar added. "Along with the Kingshield already here, and the Aimsir, Callanan and Kingshield on the way, I think this will be the safest place for Aeris to be. The castle fortress is far more defensible than the palace in Ryathl."

"Agreed," Talyn said. "I also think we should send emissaries to Warlord Hadvezer, Ahara Venador and Queen Sarana today. We inform them of Aethain's assassination and let them know we're investigating with all resources at our disposal. Warn them the culprit will be identified, and when they are, they'll feel the full force of the Twin Thrones' fury."

Ariar shot a troubled look her way. "What about bringing the army, Callanan, SkyRiders and Aimsir to battle readiness, and increasing our recruitment? I don't want to get ahead of ourselves, but you don't assassinate a king and then stop there."

"I think we should." Talyn nodded. "At least until we have a better idea of what happened and why."

"Does this mean you are taking command?" Alyna asked her, direct and unflinching.

Talyn stared at her. "You've got to be kidding me! Aethain has only been dead a day, and his son is still alive."

"I meant as regent," she said coolly. "Someone needs to take control, and it can't be a fifteen-year-old boy. Especially not at a time of potential war."

"You're forgetting I'm not a member of this court," Talyn said, matching her mother's cool, shifting her gaze from Alyna, to Soar, to Ariar. "The last thing we can afford is instability on the throne. Aeris will be crowned, and we will give him as much help as he needs."

"I agree with Alyna on this," Soar said. "I'm absolutely not suggesting we take Aeris' throne away, but he's still a boy. He needs more experience before he rules a country at war. Talyn, you are exactly what we need."

"Over you? Or Mama? Or Ariar?" Talyn couldn't believe what they were saying. "I'm a *warrior*. That is all I've ever been."

Zamaril shifted at her side. If he opened his mouth now she was going to be hard-pressed not to roar at him. But he thankfully said nothing.

"I beg to differ," Alyna said. "Look at your Wolves, their loyalty to you. According to Callanan reports, you've got the human population of Mithranar following you without question. You've successfully led your Wolves through multiple offensives against superior forces, not to mention the successes you had as a Callanan. Of those here, only Ariar has anything near that kind of battle and strategic experience."

"And I will happily use that experience to help Aeris." Talyn managed to keep a stranglehold on her temper.

"I'm with Tal," Ariar said before Alyna could argue more. "The throne belongs to Aeris. You said it yourself earlier, Alyna. He's young, but he's smart and capable."

A brief silence fell, then Soar appeared to concede the argument. "Talyn, Ariar, do you really think it's necessary to bring our forces to readiness?"

"All indications point to Vengeance being the perpetrators of Aethain's assassination, but for multiple reasons I remain unconvinced it was them," Talyn said. "I find it difficult to believe they've managed to pull together so many fighters and more izerdia in the matter of weeks since we destroyed their base, let alone get themselves here and plan an attack like this."

"Then someone wants us to think Vengeance was behind the assassination?" Alyna suggested.

"Maybe," Talyn conceded, sliding into a chair. They needed to get the First Blade here, and more importantly, updated reporting from her informant in Montagn.

"Where is the First Blade?" Ariar asked, catching the drift of Talyn's thoughts.

"The SkyRider messenger Alyna sent should arrive at Callanan Tower in Ryathl in the next day or two. Then it'll be another four days to travel back here with a fresh SkyRider escort," Soar answered.

"Could Montagn be intending the same thing here as in Mithranar?" Ariar asked. "Create instability before invasion?"

Alyna frowned. "Invade the Twin Thrones and Mithranar at the same time?"

Talyn shook her head. "I've seen the resources of Montagn. They dwarf what we can muster, but even so they'd be foolish to attack two places at once. It would be more strategically sound to take Mithranar and control its izerdia production before coming after us. And Ahara Venador didn't strike me as a fool, or a reckless man."

Ariar straightened. "What are these Montagni warriors like?"

"They're disciplined and well trained, and I've seen their Berserkers fight. They're good."

Soar rose to his feet and began pacing slowly. Alyna stared at the tabletop with narrowed eyes. Ariar looked faintly ill. Talyn sank further into her chair, exhausted.

Eventually Alyna spoke. "We'll send messages to Warlord Hadvezer, Queen Sarana and the ahara as you suggested, Talyn. While we wait for their responses, the Callanan can continue to investigate and Aeris will return. In a week or so, we should have a better idea of how to proceed."

Talyn nodded. By then Cuinn would be back in Mithranar. Maybe he might learn something that could help.

If he lived long enough.

CHAPTER 43

*W*ith good winds, the return trip to Mithranar took just under a week. The thick humidity of Dock City embraced them as their ship slowly drifted into Feather Bay. Cuinn leaned on the prow railing, eyes studying the citadel. The sea breeze ruffled his silver-white feathers. Anxiety tightened in his gut.

Behind him, the sound of stomping feet echoed through the quiet morning as Theac and his talons summoned the Wolves up on deck, their crisp orders a calming sound. Jasper watched from atop the deckhouse, tail swishing.

"Your Highness?" Theac's voice interrupted his reverie.

Cuinn didn't turn. "Yes?"

"We have something to show you."

Deliberately turning his back on the citadel looming before him, Cuinn spun to find his Wolves lined up in neat rows on the main deck. The sapphire wolf glimmered on the bottom of their charcoal tunics, and the steel of their weapons shone brightly. But that wasn't all.

Seeing them, he stilled.

Where before the Wolves had worn no marking on their chests, now they wore a new sigil. It was similar to the Acondor emblem—a royal crown framed by a pair of outstretched wings—except for the jagged lightning symbol that cut through the crown.

The same lightning symbol the Shadowhawk used.

And the stitching was bright emerald, the colour of his eyes.

He couldn't summon a single word, instead looking over at Theac. The Wolf captain was smiling.

"They know?" Cuinn asked softly.

"They've known for a while now, Your Highness."

"How?"

"You stopped hiding from them," Theac said simply. "I know it's dangerous, and if you choose not to display this sigil, we'll take the vests off and unpick the stitching. But if you've decided to take off your mask, then we'd like to proclaim our allegiance to the world."

He swallowed, desperately trying to hold back the tears pressing at the backs of his eyes.

No more hiding.

Even so, it wasn't only himself he had to worry about. "It won't just be dangerous for me, Theac."

"We know. We accept the danger." Corrin stepped forward before Theac could answer. "Because we want to stop hiding too, Your Highness. And winning a better life for ourselves… we acknowledge that might not happen without a fight, without danger and loss and pain. Not in Mithranar."

Cuinn couldn't hold back the tears this time, and he summoned a hint of magic, sending his gratitude and joy washing over every Wolf standing before him. "I thank you," he said clearly, bowing his head and sweeping his wings back in deep respect.

They all came to attention, saluting sharply.

THE DOCKS WERE as hot and bustling as ever by the time Cuinn and his Wolves disembarked from the ship.

"I'll send the winged Wolves with you up to the citadel, Your Highness, and then—"

"Not necessary, Theac. I'll walk with you."

They caught the attention of those nearby immediately—no doubt the sudden disappearance of the prince of song and his WingGuard wing had caused a lot of chatter, and interest in their equally sudden return was just as intense.

But then people began noticing the sigil the Wolves were wearing. And silence fell.

As Cuinn and his Wolves walked, stares turned to whispers, and then to shock and puzzlement. Their emotions hit him—they recognised the lightning strike instantly as the Shadowhawk's, but didn't understand why the Wolves were wearing it.

"Your Highness?" Theac muttered as they approached the wall walk. The flower offerings at the wall were still there, the old ones taken away, fresh ones put down. He'd been gone weeks, and still his people honoured the dead.

"Hmm?"

"There's a bit of a crowd developing."

Cuinn glanced back, saw the streams of people following behind the Wolves. The emotion of the crowd wasn't dangerous, merely puzzled, and in some cases, quietly hopeful.

An idea occurred to him. If he wanted to be king, he needed support. From *all* his people.

If Talyn were here, she'd tell him it was a stupidly dangerous idea. But Talyn wasn't here.

These people were *his*.

And he wasn't hiding anymore.

"Highness!" Theac's voice sounded again, sharper this time.

He was pointing into the sky above the citadel, where teal-clad Falcons were lifting into the sky. Tens at least, more drifting upwards with every breath. A full flight.

They knew he was back.

Cuinn glanced around—they were almost at the wall, the Falcons still gathering. They might be coming to arrest him. Possibly to kill him. But he could put a show on for them as well. Stop them from carrying out their orders... buy himself some time.

"Theac, send Corrin and Halun up to stand with me, and hold the rest of the Wolves at the base of the wall." He didn't want to risk Errana and her girls by having Theac front and centre for what he was about to do. "We don't draw weapons unless the Falcons attack. That's an order."

Theac didn't protest. He called a quiet order to Corrin and Halun, then lifted a hand to halt the marching Wolves. They stopped in their neat rows, perfect in their discipline, unbothered by the crowds gathering around them or the Falcons massing in the sky.

He forced down his rising anxiety and scanned the stalls lining the opposite side of the street, looking for one in particular. When he found it, he smiled at the young man behind the table of wares. "Can I borrow one of the cloaks you have for sale?"

The man swallowed, flushed. "Of... of course, Your Highness. Take your pick."

"Thank you." Cuinn picked one in dark fabric—there weren't many, most of the clothing on offer was more suited for Mithranar's warm weather—then cast his gaze around. "I don't suppose you have any scarves?"

"We don't... maybe one down here." He ducked below, then popped up a few moments later holding two scarves, one red and one dark blue.

Cuinn chose the blue one. "Thank you."

More murmuring whispered through the crowd as Cuinn began walking up the wall. His song magic picked out confusion, anticipation, and an added layer of unease as more of them noticed the Falcons.

Corrin and Halun followed, hands on weapons, as Cuinn walked the wall path until he was still in clear view of those immediately below, but also visible to those filling the streets further back.

And to the Falcons now moving in their direction.

The muttering died to an expectant hush as Cuinn shook out the cloak, then reached up to tie the scarf around his face, leaving only his eyes visible. At the same moment that he drew the cloak over his tightly-furled wings, he summoned his glamour, using it to smooth over the edges, making the bulk of his wings invisible under the cloak. It was too bright a day to summon the shadows, but he didn't need to.

Slowly, carefully, he drew the hood of the cloak up. As he did so, he continued fashioning the glamour, using it to alter his features into that of a human man with stubbled jaw and untidy hair. And then, finally, he altered the appearance of the scarf, so that it looked exactly like the mask he had worn during his nights on the streets of Dock City.

Below, those gathered had turned utterly silent.

Before them stood the Shadowhawk.

Shouts sounded above—the Falcons. Halun and Corrin shifted nervously on either side of him, and he could feel the unease of the Wolves below. He steadied himself. Glanced upwards. They were dropping out of the sky towards him.

Slowly, Cuinn drew the hood back and un-wound the scarf, showing them his human visage. After a long, heavy moment, he began releasing his glamour, allowing the human features to slide back into his real face, his wings to become visible behind the cloak.

Finally, he drew off the cloak and tossed it away.

Then he bowed, wings spread wide. Anxiety tightened in his gut, along with a heady relief that, combined, made him dizzy. He had no idea how they would respond.

At first it was silent. The anxiety deepened, his chest tightening with it. Then a whisper of noise, several muttered words. Then someone laughed in astonishment. Someone else clapped. Another joined her.

Then they were all clapping. Whistling. Cheering.

For him.

The crowed was restless now, shocked and stunned and delighted, but also unsure what to make of the fact that the prince of song was their Shadowhawk. He sensed their confusion, the questions bubbling in their minds... and also the beginnings of hope stirring.

Halun and Corrin stepped closer, protective, in case the crowd became dangerous. But Cuinn wasn't worried. They weren't going to hurt him. Relief filled all the empty spaces in him, banishing the anxiety and fear. They accepted him. Who he was.

The hubbub began to die down. Those at the back of the crowd began slipping away.

Frowning, Cuinn turned, looking up at the sky. Most of the Falcons hovered above, but some were almost upon him, dropping to the wall walk.

He was surprised to see Brightwing landing before him on the path—he'd been expecting Mithanis. More Wolves were moving up the wall walk at Theac's order, but Cuinn made a gesture to hold them back.

He wasn't hiding anymore. He could handle this.

"Your Highness." Brightwing looked an amusing mix of horrified, shocked and disgusted. When his gaze landed on the new sigil on Theac's chest, the disgust deepened. "What was that little display?"

"You saw it?" Cuinn smiled. "I'm glad. What do you want, Brightwing?"

"When Prince Mithanis hears what—"

"Why isn't he here to blather at me himself?" Cuinn asked, cutting off the flight-leader's angry words.

Brightwing's jaw turned rigid. "Your family and their court has travelled to the Summer Palace. Prince Mithanis instructs you to join them there immediately."

Cuinn's heart plummeted. "It's barely spring," he said, managing an idle tone. "Why has everyone decamped to the SkyReach so early?"

"My orders were to instruct you to leave, Prince Cuinn, not to answer your questions," Brightwing said coldly. "You can be sure I will write to Prince Mithanis this evening, to let him know what happened here."

"You do that." Cuinn smiled. "After all, it doesn't do to disobey my elder brother."

"The Falcons will know by nightfall," he hissed. "Those winged folk still here, they'll all know. I'll make sure of it."

"Good." Cuinn stepped forward, using magic to cow Brightwing as he once had Ravinire. He used his newfound confidence, his relief in not having to wear any more masks, his delight in finally, finally, being himself, to bolster his strength. "Tell them all, Brightwing. Tell them how the humans cheered for me."

Brightwing wanted to say more—his contempt and shock pounded against Cuinn's song magic—but he didn't. He didn't have enough spine for it. Instead he leapt into the sky, wings carrying him quickly away. The Falcons followed him.

"What was that about?" Theac asked.

"There's only one reason the royal family and Queencouncil members go to the SkyReach outside the hottest months of summer," Cuinn said. "To formally choose an heir."

Theac scowled. "Why can't they do that here?"

"It's tradition to do it at the Summer Palace." Cuinn shrugged. "Something about the grandness of the mountains and the palace, or some such ridiculousness."

"You just won Dock City to your side, Your Highness," Corrin said carefully. "Going to the SkyReach takes you away from their support."

"I can't challenge Mithanis for heir if I'm not there, Corrin," Cuinn said. "So to the SkyReach we go."

"We'll be with you, Your Highness." Theac bowed instead of saluting.

Corrin followed suit, then one by one the Wolves of his detail did the same thing. Below, the humans still gathered bowed too, many still looking dazed, but all making it clear where their loyalties lay.

He took a deep breath, filling himself with that loyalty, that respect, and let it war with the fear within him.

Because it was impossible to pretend, even to himself, that the prospect of facing down Mithanis didn't terrify him.

CHAPTER 44

he reply from Warlord Hadvezer came first, eight days after the assassination, arriving via niever-flyer for Tarcos. The heir to Firthland's leadership echoed his uncle's sentiments when he brought the message to the war room where Talyn sat with her family.

"My uncle admits that along with several niever-flyers, a handful of Armun have also deserted," Tarcos said grimly. "He concedes they may be the ones who undertook the assassination."

"And has the Shadowlord directed the Armun Council to investigate as a priority?" Alyna lifted an eyebrow.

"Yes. We offer whatever support the Dumnorix require and will bring our army to immediate readiness." Tarcos bowed slightly. "Prince Aeris is on our fastest ship heading for Port Lachley and I've been instructed to do whatever else I can to assist. I assume you've not heard back from Queen Sarana or Ahara Venador yet?"

"No, our messages would have only just reached them—we'll be waiting at least several more days before we can expect a reply." Ariar was pacing. He didn't like sitting still, and the strain of being inside the castle rather than out with his Aimsir showed in the shadows under his eyes and his rigid shoulders. Talyn imagined she looked no different.

"We did get a missive from a Lord Tarich Swiftwing late yesterday." Alyna pointed to an opened letter on the table in front of her.

"Mithranar's foreign emissary." Talyn sat forward. "What did he want?"

"To inform us that Queen Sarana and her Queencouncil were soon to begin the process of naming her heir." Alyna rubbed a hand over tired eyes. "Then the usual flowery wording about fruitful cooperation no matter who is chosen and all that."

Fear churned in Talyn's stomach. Cuinn would challenge Mithanis for heir, she had no doubts. Nor did she doubt what Mithanis would do about that.

And she was stuck here in Conmor. If anything happened to Cuinn while she wasn't there…

"Thank you, Lord Tarcos, for bringing the message straight away," Soar said, breaking Talyn from her train of thought.

It was a polite but clear dismissal. Tarcos bowed smoothly, sent a small smile Talyn's way, then strode from the room. Once the doors clanged shut behind him, everyone relaxed slightly. Now it was just family.

"It's an easy excuse, to say these niever-flyers and Armun deserted," Ariar pointed out. "Should we be concerned?"

"No," Soar said firmly. "I know Warlord Hadvezer well. I spent several years with him in Samatia when I was a youth and he was heir. He's a good man and would never betray the Dumnorix."

Alyna frowned. "I have to agree. Aethain always spoke highly of him."

Talyn hadn't ever met the warlord of Firthland, but she trusted Soar and her mother's assessment. Besides, she knew Tarcos, his heir, and what kind of man he was. Ariar conceded with a shrug.

Alyna frowned. "The Callanan haven't made any progress into learning who killed Aethain. Montagn is the most obvious answer given what we already know about them."

"But why now?" Ariar tossed the warlord's message across the table in frustration. "And what exactly is it they're after?"

Despite the increased armed presence in Port Lachley and Ryathl, no further attacks eventuated in the days that had followed Aethain's assassination. No army had arrived on their doorstep. The Callanan and Armun reported no threats. It was as if nothing had ever happened.

A surgical strike. In and out.

But Ariar was right. Why now? And why kill the king of the Twin Thrones?

Silence fell around the table. Frustration and anger was a live creature throbbing through the air. A group of Dumnorix with a threat they didn't know how to address—it was in their bones to fix, to help, to lead, and right now they were stymied.

Was their country in danger? Or had Aethain been killed for some reason that had nothing to do with the Twin Thrones?

A sharp knock sounded at the war room door before anyone came up with an answer. A sigh of relief went through the room at the distraction and Alyna called for whoever it was to enter.

The Callanan First Blade had arrived.

Along with two familiar faces.

Talyn leapt up from her chair and a moment later was enveloped by a pair of Callanan, her breath escaping in a loud *oomph*.

"Talyn!" Leviana bellowed.

"Levs, Cynia." Talyn escaped the hug, drawing back to smile at them in mixed astonishment and pleasure.

"We are relieved to see you," Alyna greeted Shia before Talyn could ask her friends what they were doing there.

"I left Callanan Tower the moment your SkyRider message reached me, Your Highness." The same grim look was on Shia's face that Talyn had seen on everyone since the attack. "The news is beyond shocking, and I am deeply discomfited that this attack should come about without any forewarning from us or the Armun."

The air visibly deflated in the room. "So you have no information from your Montagni informant?" Ariar said.

"None." Shia hesitated. "I am sorry. He did not warn of any attack against the Twin Thrones, but we have not had contact with him in weeks. It's possible he learned of something and hasn't had the opportunity to tell us yet."

"What of Montagn's plans against Mithranar?" Soar pressed.

"Nothing there either. In our last contact with him, he said the ahara's plans were developing, but he was still some way off from moving."

"Because we dealt with Vengeance?" Talyn asked.

"We assumed so, yes." Shia nodded. "Master Ranar left for Montagn a week ago to meet with our informant in person. Unfortunately I have nothing for you until he returns."

"*Tal, this is odd.*"

"*I agree.*" Something wasn't right, but she couldn't put her finger on it.

"I'll go now and speak with my Callanan undertaking the interrogations," Shia said briskly. "Lady Alyna, will you direct me to where they are?"

Alyna rose from her chair. "I'd like to speak to them too. Warriors Seinn and Leed, you're most welcome to stay here in the castle. There's room in the guest wing and I'm sure Talyn would like the company."

As Alyna and Shia walked out, Ariar gave a heavy sigh and reached out to clap Soar on the back. "We'd best get to signing that pile of parchment that doesn't seem to get any smaller. How did Aethain ever find the time?"

Talyn turned to Cynia and Leviana, intensely curious to know why they'd arrived with the First Blade. "Tell me everything, now!"

"The First Blade brought us to assist on the investigation into your uncle's assassination, largely because we've spoken directly to the Shadowhawk and are the only Callanan aside from Master Ranar who know about Vengeance, the informant or his information." Leviana glanced at Cynia. "Was your mother serious about us staying in the castle?"

"I'm sure she was." Talyn cast her eyes upwards. "Part of her ongoing campaign to convince me, no doubt."

"Convince you to what?" Cynia frowned.

"It's a long story." Talyn dismissed the question. Her mother was nothing if not stubborn. "How long have you been back from Montagn?"

"We'd barely stepped foot back in Ryathl when the First Blade summoned us to travel here. We haven't even unpacked our bags." Leviana glared at Talyn. "This doesn't feel quite right, Tal."

"I agree." Talyn threw her hands up. "I saw and heard nothing to indicate Vengeance would act here, and against the king, not in this way."

"Why are you here?" Cynia asked. "You must have been here before the attack. Four days isn't enough time for a message to get to Mithranar and you to travel here."

"Another long story..." Talyn began, but capitulated as both Callanan glared at her. "I brought Cuinn here after we were attacked in Mithranar. I thought we could seek help here."

Leviana gaped. "Attacked by who?"

"Sibling rivalry, most likely," Talyn said lightly. "Prince Mithanis isn't the biggest fan of his youngest brother."

"And where is Cuinn now?" Cynia didn't fail to notice the look on Talyn's face.

"Back in Mithranar. After the assassination... there was no point in him lingering here. And he feels responsible for what's happening in Mithranar right now. One of his mother's lords has sent a missive to let us know she'll be naming her heir soon." Talyn tried her best to sound relaxed, but it was bitterly hard. Cuinn was in danger, so much danger, and she was stuck here instead of at his side, with her Wolves, where she belonged. She wondered if her mother could ever understand how powerfully that was ripping her apart.

"Tal, what's going on?" Leviana asked.

"I'll tell you all about it, but right now I have an important meeting." Talyn groaned as she heard herself. "Listen to me. My mother's influence is already showing. A meeting with the trade ambassador is hardly important, but there you go. Dinner later?"

"We'll be there," Cynia promised.

"Take your stuff to the guest wing. It *will* be nice to have the company."

Maybe they would help ease the loneliness she felt.

CHAPTER 45

The orange glow of dusk filtered through the arched window in Talyn's chambers as she sat in her armchair several days later, reading a letter from Theac. A smile curved her lips at her second's words. He assured her that they'd all arrived safely in Dock City, only to find that most of Sarana's court had departed for the Summer Palace.

Prince Cuinn has been ordered to get there immediately, so we'll be departing first thing in the morning. The prince suspects the travel to the SkyReach means the queen is preparing to name her heir. I'm sure you will be unsurprised to learn that the lad intends to challenge Mithanis for it.

I fear greatly for him, as we have always done, but part of me hopes too. If we could have a king like him, Ciantar... I scarcely dare imagine it. Be confident that your Wolves will protect him.

I hope you are well.

Farewell, you are missed.

Completely absorbed, Talyn allowed herself the momentary indulgence of remembering Mithranar and her Wolves. After a few moments, she cleared her thoughts and sat up, pushing the letter from her mind. Dwelling on what she missed wasn't helpful, and she needed to focus on the present.

Another meeting awaited her.

"Ready to go, Zamaril?" She greeted the Wolf outside her door.

He smiled. "Always, Captain."

"I received a letter from Theac. They're safely home." She passed him the pages. "He tells me he misses you."

The thief's face lightened. "I miss him too. Never thought I'd say that about the crusty old man."

She hesitated. "You know that you can go home anytime?"

"I choose to stay with you, and that won't ever change." He carefully tucked the pages in his pocket as they came to a stop outside a closed door.

The First Blade, Leviana and Cynia waited inside, along with Tarcos, Ariar and Allira—Soar's daughter had arrived days earlier with her husband, come to offer whatever support they could. Soar and Alyna had sent messages saying they were running late. It soon became clear though that their absence didn't matter.

They still had nothing. Nothing at all. And it was getting beyond frustrating.

"We're just going over old ground, why don't we—" Allira's voice was cut off by the bells ringing through the castle.

The bells announcing a SkyRider was approaching the roof.

By tacit agreement, they broke off conversation and waited. Maybe this was the update they'd been waiting for.

It wasn't long after that Alyna opened the door and walked in. Talyn rose from her chair at the look on her mother's face—pale and shaken. She'd opened her mouth to demand what was wrong when the sound of boots running outside echoed through the open door.

Soar burst in, almost running Alyna over. He still wore his flying beanie and his cheeks were flushed from flight. "It was Montagn."

Chairs screeched as everyone else shot to their feet. "Explain," Talyn snapped.

"The merchant vessel we captured just off the coast, the one carrying the assassination team." He took a breath. "My SkyRiders have been going over every inch of it. They found papers half-burned in the main cabin's fireplace. The vessel was registered in Montagn a few months ago. Most of the parchment of sale was burned away, but we got a name of the new owner. Venador."

Ariar spoke into the silence. "A member of the ahara's family purchased the ship?"

Talyn spun back to her mother. Soar's news was big, but not entirely unsurprising. And something told her that Alyna had news too. Worse news. "Mama, what is it?"

"We've lost contact with Aeris."

"What does that mean?" the First Blade asked when the Dumnorix appeared stunned into silence.

Alyna took a breath. "The journey from Samatia is three days at most, and he should have been here by now. Soar, it worried me, so I sent some of your SkyRiders out to scout the seas. There is no sign of any Firthlander naval ships along the route Aeris's ship would have taken."

Tarcos turned grim. "I'll write to my uncle at once. Learn what happened."

"You think he's kidnapped Aeris?" Ariar demanded.

"No," Tarcos said flatly. "We are your sworn vassals. We would never do such a thing. If my uncle says he put Aeris on a ship, then he did."

"I'll send more SkyRiders out tonight and have them fly a broader search pattern. I'll lead them myself. Maybe the ship experienced trouble," Soar said grimly. "If he's out there, I'll find him."

Nobody disputed Soar joining the search. Aeris was family. It was their duty to find him, and right now the SkyRider amongst them was best placed to do that.

"And in the meantime we have our answer." Alyna looked stronger now, steadied. "It's time to begin preparing our armies. For war with Montagn."

"I'll include this in my letter to my uncle," Tarcos promised. "We'll have our Bearmen and niever-flyers rallied at once. The Shadowlord will be directed to have the Armun Council focus on collecting intelligence on Montagni movements immediately."

Shia moved for the door. "I'll leave for Callanan Tower in the morning."

Ariar smiled, though it held no warmth. "It's been many decades since we've had to muster the Aimsir. We're in play."

And I am none of those things anymore, Talyn thought. I am Ciantar.

Tarcos approached as the others left, the meeting temporarily over.

"I know you haven't eaten today," he said. "How about you meet me in the kitchens in a half-turn after I've written this message to my uncle?"

Talyn wasn't really hungry, but knew she should eat. "Sounds good. I just want to talk to Levs and Cynia and then I'll head down there."

"Sure, I'll see you soon."

"What do you make of all that?" she asked her friends once the door closed behind Tarcos.

The partners shared a look before Cynia said, "Montagn is much more powerful than we are. Winning a war against Montagn won't be easy."

Talyn sighed, rubbing at her eyes. Her duty was to be here, helping, preventing any instability. But Cuinn was in Mithranar, challenging his brother without her help.

"Cosy dinner with Tarcos, huh?" Leviana clearly couldn't decide whether to smile or frown.

"It's just food," Talyn said tiredly.

"It looks like you need sleep more than food." Cynia looked concerned. "Talyn, is there some reason you and Tarcos are so chummy again? I thought he was upset with you."

"It's not really a mystery." Talyn sighed. "Both my mother and Tarcos would very much like me to marry him and sit the Twin Thrones as regent until Aeris is old enough. Now that he's missing, I'm guessing she'd prefer that I take the throne."

"You're going to *marry* Tarcos?" Leviana's eyes widened.

"No," she said simply. "I'm not."

"And Cuinn?" Cynia asked.

"Is far away in Mithranar, and I will probably not see him for a very long time." Talyn paused; these were two of her closest friends in the world, and she wanted to tell them the truth, but it was so hard to even say the words.

"I understand," Cynia said quietly. "I was right, wasn't I, about you and Cuinn?"

"It doesn't matter."

"Of course it does. Marry *him*." Leviana lowered her voice. "Your family can't dispute a match with another prince, surely? It will cement an alliance against Montagn at the very least."

"Even if I wanted to, I couldn't marry Cuinn." Talyn hesitated, then drew her friends over to the chairs by the fire. "What I'm about to tell you can't go beyond these walls, but... I was sent to Mithranar in the first place because Cuinn is a Dumnorix," she said, then told them everything.

"Tal." Cynia reached out to touch her arm, hearing the anguish in Talyn's voice.

At the touch, her shields came slamming up. "I'm fine."

"Oh shit." Leviana suddenly shot upwards in her chair, eyes wide as saucers. "Cuinn a Dumnorix... he's the Shadowhawk, isn't he?"

Cynia groaned. "That explains so much."

"You're right, but that's just another dangerous secret." Talyn rose. "Come on, let's go and eat dinner with Tarcos."

Leviana stood, slinging her arm around Talyn's shoulders. "How about *we* go and have dinner with Tarcos while you go and get some sleep? You're exhausted, my friend."

That actually sounded wonderful.

She smiled at them both. "All right. Apologise to him for me, will you?"

"No apologies necessary. He gets the two of us instead of you, lucky man," Leviana said airily. "Off you go now. We'll see you in the morning."

Feeling a little better after speaking with her friends, Talyn headed up to her rooms, the Wolves a faithful shadow at her back.

The moment she closed the door behind her, Sari roused in her head.

"Talyn?"

"Yes?"

"We're going to have a conversation. Right now."

Talyn frowned, dropping into the chair by the fire. *"Okay."*

"It's time to be blunt. You're trying so hard to do the honourable thing—sacrifice what you actually want and live up to your duty to your family—that you're missing something very obvious."

"What are you talking about?"

"Tal, if Montagn is truly intending invasion, then what sort of position is the Twin Thrones in if Mithanis takes the throne of Mithranar? Do you really think he can defeat Montagn?" Sari continued before Talyn could respond. *"You're forgetting basic strategy. Mithranar is a buffer for the Twin Thrones, no?"*

"Yes..." she said slowly. *"And their izerdia supplies are crucial to any war."*

"Right. Keeping that in mind, who is the one person in Mithranar that the Dumnorix can trust and rely upon? No matter what."

She let out a breath, realisation unravelling inside her with a rush. *"Another Dumnorix."*

"So if we're heading for war, strategically speaking, who is the best person for the Twin Thrones to have on the Mithranan throne? Which Acondor family member is in their best interests?"

Talyn bolted upright in her chair. *"Shit, Sari!"*

"Yes, I know, I'm a genius. You would have figured this out yourself if you weren't so caught up in the fact that you're in love with Cuinn and want to go home but feel like you have to sacrifice that for the greater good."

"Maybe I don't." Talyn breathed the words, making them alive.

"Maybe you don't."

CHAPTER 46

$\mathcal{C}$uinn wasn't surprised to find Mithanis waiting for him as he reached the main entrance of the Summer Place, a snow-filled wind ripping around them. The prince of night wasn't trying to hide his anger, his dark wings raised and stiff with fury. A handful of Falcons stood behind him.

Cuinn glanced back at his Wolves, then walked forward, keeping his stride loose and confident. "Hello, Brother."

"How dare you!" he snarled, taking a step forward, fists clenched, wings snapping outwards in the breeze.

Fury, hot and uncontrolled, hit Cuinn's song magic so fiercely he sucked in a breath before letting it recede and bracing himself as best he could. "How dare I what?"

His calm tone only increased Mithanis's fury. His brother snarled and stepped closer again, his magic buffeting Cuinn. Without hesitation, Cuinn drew upon his own magic, using it to hold the prince of night back. It took a lot of effort, matching Mithanis, whose magic was powerful and surging with his anger.

But he did.

He drew on the cool competence of the fifty-odd Wolves lined up behind him, drew upon his own strength and skill, and shoved Mitha-

458

nis's magic away with a strong punch of anger and determination. The prince of night staggered a step backwards. The anger battering at Cuinn faded. Vanished.

"How did you…?" The stunned look on Mithanis's face was almost comical.

"How did I what?" Cuinn took a step towards his brother.

Mithanis straightened, realisation crawling across his face, feeding his anger. "You've been hiding your magic from us."

"Or you were too stupid to notice it," Cuinn needled. As afraid of his brother as he still was, he was angry too. For Raya, for his dead Wolves. For Ronisin and his detail. He used the anger to hold the fear back.

"You're nothing," Mithanis spat, still not fully understanding. "A worthless pretty boy who likes wine and women too much to ever be useful."

A smile curled at the edges of Cuinn's mouth. "You are so gullible, thinking any of that was real."

Mithanis's dark eyes flickered.

"That's right." Cuinn took another step forward. "I've never been what you think. You only ever saw what I *made* you see."

Mithanis frowned, gaze cutting to the Wolves and the emerald sigil on their chests, doubt clouding his expression. When he spoke, his voice was hesitant. "I thought Ravinire an idiot, that his mind had been addled, to go babbling to our mother that you were the Shadowhawk."

His mother *had* betrayed him. It hit him hard and fast, sucking the air from his lungs, even though he'd already guessed. He forced it aside, grabbed hold of that anger, made it his strength. "And you were too stupid to notice that too, *Brother*."

Mithanis' breath came out in a hiss. His mouth opened. Closed. The racing thoughts in his head were palpable as he looked at Cuinn now, felt his magic, put the pieces together. "He *was* right…"

"Yes, the Shadowhawk was me. This whole time." Cuinn smirked. "Right under all your noses."

Fury and frustration battered at Cuinn suddenly, Mithanis losing all control. Cuinn stood there, shoulders straight, and weathered it, enjoying for once seeing his brother well and truly beaten. Even if only for a minute.

When he spoke, Mithanis's voice was low and bitter. "You have to realise that you are giving me no choice but to act against you. Join my side, like Az, and you can live, Cuinn. We are brothers. I don't wish for your death."

"You haven't succeeded in killing me yet. What makes you think you ever will?"

Frustration overtook Mithanis then, fist clenching and unclenching at his sides. "Despite your ridiculous accusations, I've never tried to kill you before. I've never acted against you. I didn't kill Raya and I didn't set off an explosion to kill your Wolves."

Lies, all lies.

Mithanis stood back, shaking his head. "The crown is mine. You are foolish if you think you can defeat me."

"Am I?" Cuinn closed the distance again. "The humans are loyal to me; how many of the WingGuard do you think are loyal to me also? How many would see you wanting to murder your own brother as a good reason to destroy you and follow me instead?"

"All words, Cuinn," Mithanis murmured, his confidence returning rapidly. "And you and I both know it."

With that he was gone, streaking up into the sky and leaving Cuinn to stand there and stare after him.

The anger vanished as quickly as it had come. Before he could let himself give in to the fear that trembled in his limbs—could he really do this without her?—Willir came dropping out of the sky above, young wings flapping fiercely to keep him in the air. The fear that leaked from him suggested he'd overheard most of that conversation.

"Welcome back, Prince Cuinn." The boy bowed.

"Thank you, Willir." Cuinn cleared his throat, fought for an even tone of voice. "What has you hovering here waiting for me?"

"When I heard you'd arrived, I wanted to come straight away." Willir looked anxious. "It's your mother; she's unwell."

Cuinn sighed and rubbed a weary hand over his forehead. "I'll go and see her now."

"Your Highness?" Theac asked as he turned.

"My mother is ill. I'm going to see her." Cuinn paused. "You'll come with me?"

The veteran scanned Cuinn's face, his scowling features softening slightly. "I'd be happy to take command of your current detail, Your Highness."

"Good." His eyes roved the Wolves, falling on a familiar figure with sea-grey wings. "Jystar, a word please?"

"Your Highness?"

"You were one of our most senior healers until recently. Is my mother truly ill?" Cuinn asked as they walked.

Jystar's grey wings rustled but he remained expressionless. He was nothing like his expressive, light-hearted younger brother, but Cuinn knew the man's reputation. He was considered the most powerful healer amongst the winged folk. "She began feeling unwell almost a year ago. I was one of two healers summoned to attend her. Nothing nefarious is going on, Your Highness. It's a wasting sickness that we have been able to slow down, but not cure."

Cuinn's stride faltered and he sucked in a breath, shocked. Jystar's gaze was sympathetic but he didn't say anything further.

He'd been distant from his mother as long as he could remember. He'd accepted she didn't love him the way he'd seen other mothers love their children, the way Alyna Dumnorix loved Talyn. And he'd had to hide himself from her along with everyone else, never giving her an opportunity to know him. Still...he'd had no idea at all.

"How long does she have?" He fought to keep his voice steady.

"Weeks, maybe months," Jystar said.

"Why didn't she tell anyone?"

"I believe she was afraid, Your Highness, that her declining health would be seen as a weakness." Jystar hesitated. "I believe even Princes Mithanis and Azrilan had no idea."

Cuinn nodded, hiding his surprise as best he could as they came to a stop outside his mother's rooms. The Falcons on guard at the door didn't seem to know what to do, but when Theac barked at them, they stepped aside to let Cuinn in. He paused, looking at Jystar. "That's why she's naming her heir now? She knows she's going to die soon."

Jystar nodded, bowing his head. "I think so, Your Highness."

Cuinn left him and walked through the open door. His mother lay in her bed, skin pale, blue shadows under her eyes. Thankfully neither of his brothers were there, and he was able to dismiss the Falcons in the room to wait outside.

"Hello, Mother." He sat by her bed, reaching out to take her hand.

"Cuinn." She smiled faintly. "You're back."

"I came straight here. I was told you're unwell."

"Yes." She spoke slowly, as if it took a lot of effort. "I thought I was getting better, but…"

Cuinn's heart sank as her voice trailed off and she coughed. "Is there anything I can do?"

"No. It will pass."

"That's not what Jystar says," he said gently. Something about the way she was lying there made dread fill his every bone. He'd never seen his powerful mother look so vulnerable. Not once in his entire life.

Her eyes slid closed, opened. "Please don't go away again," she whispered. "I feel better when you're close."

"That's never been true."

"It has…" She coughed. "You're the child I shared with the love of my life. So precious."

"Are you ever going to tell me who he is?"

Sarana smiled faintly. "Safer not to know. He's gone, Cuinn. Keep him gone."

He thought about telling her that he knew his father was a Dumnorix, but she looked so weak lying there, and there were other things they needed to discuss. He squeezed her hand. "I know that I've never allowed you to see it, but I'm stronger than you think, Mother. I'll talk to Azrilan, maybe together we can…" His voice trailed off as sadness filled her face. "What?"

"Azrilan left. He fled, fearing what your brother would do before the formal nomination." She gripped his hand tightly. "You should leave too."

"No." Unbidden, anger filled him and he took his hand away. "If I run, then I leave every person in Mithranar at Mithanis's mercy. If I do nothing, he will rule here. Because *you* have done nothing, he will rule here."

"So passionate," she murmured. "You have more of your father in you than I realised... but... you've hidden that so well, haven't you? I've missed so much."

"You have." He tried to keep the accusation from his voice, but it was hard.

She rallied, meeting his gaze. "They are not worth your life, Cuinn. They were not worth mine."

"I am their prince," he said, voice shaking with conviction. "They are worth everything I can give them. Where did Az go?" Maybe he could catch him, convince him to come back. Together they might be able to form a strong enough base against Mithanis and the fear he held over everyone.

His mother's eyes slid closed. "Gone," she whispered. "Gone to Arataire, where he's safe with his family."

Cuinn's heart sank as her breathing slowed and she fell asleep.

And then he took a deep breath.

He could do this without Azrilan. He had the Wolves at his back.

CHAPTER 47

*I*nstead of going to bed, Talyn sent messages out that night. Soar had already left to search for Aeris, and she needed his legions, so she had to wait for him to come back. But that was fine —she used the time to pace her quarters, thinking, planning. Sari joined her, the two of them going back and forth, considering and improving the plan. In the early turns after midnight, she brought Zamaril in.

His eyes widened at the sight of her. She hadn't slept or washed, and no doubt looked a sight with her manic energy and bright sapphire eyes. "I'm going to do something drastic," she said. "But I want your thoughts before I present the plan to my family."

He listened patiently as she laid it out for him. Once she was done, a short silence passed. He reached up, scratched his nose. Tilted his head.

Then a wolfish smile spread over his face. "I like it."

"It doesn't solve our problem, not even close. But it means both of us can..." She trailed off as his smile widened.

Talyn was about to ask whether he saw any flaws in the plan when the bells signalling a SkyRider approach began ringing through the castle.

"Soar's here!" She ran for the door.

Zamaril was barely half a step behind her, calling orders for his detail to keep up. Wings rustled as the winged ones launched into flight down the cavernous hall. Roalin's song magic picked up on her and Zamaril's manic excitement, and he almost flew into a wall before he managed to control it.

The castle bells were still pealing through the still dawn air as Talyn took the steps to the SkyRider landing platform two at a time, Zamaril close behind, the winged Wolves soaring into the sky above.

A thick fog had rolled in during the night, restricting vision to only a few inches. She stopped at the edge of the yard, peering into the thick mist. Her hearing picked up the high-pitched screeching of an eagle, and seconds later the magnificent creatures were descending around her through the fog.

Gusts of cold air from the flapping of the great eagles' wings swept her hair back and chilled her skin. She could make out the shadowy forms of dismounting SkyRiders through the fog, and then Soar's tall figure jogged towards her. His flight beanie was pulled down firmly over his ears, and his skin was flushed from the cold, luminous blue eyes snapping with the joy of flying.

"McTavish is just behind us," he said as they fell into step, referring to Ariar's second. "I found his Aimsir command on my way back to the capital as you asked. Is something wrong? We only just left Port Lachley."

"I know you need to search for Aeris, but I won't keep you here beyond a full-turn or two, I promise," she said. "Let's get inside. Hopefully Ariar and Mama have heard the bells and will be waiting for us."

"What's happening?" Ariar strode towards them as they emerged from the stairwell into the main castle corridor, dressed as always in his Aimsir leathers.

"Our cousin summoned me," Soar said. "And a full division of your riders."

Ariar made a comical face at Talyn. "You summoned my Aimsir?"

"I did." Talyn grinned, still infected by the same manic energy. "McTavish's division. I have a plan." McTavish ruled the northern

Aimsir, all riders stationed in Conmor. All those that could converge on Port Lachley in a matter of days.

Her cousin considered that. "Your mother's not going to like this, is she?"

"Not at all." Talyn shook her head. "Not even a little bit."

Rior McTavish's copper hair was windblown and rumpled as he jogged towards them from the direction of the main castle entrance, cheeks flushed with the thrill of a long, fast ride. "Sky Chieftain, Horselord, Lady Dynan." He acknowledged them all. "I am here as requested."

"Let's take this into the hall—best I lay it out to all of you at once," Talyn said, pushing the doors open. "Zamaril, with me."

As Talyn had hoped, Alyna was already in the great hall with Allira —in fact it looked like both had already been there despite the early hour, working away on a large pile of parchment with a pot of steaming tea between them. Talyn waved Soar, Ariar and Rior to chairs but stayed on her feet, taking up a position at the head of the table. Zamaril halted a pace behind at her left shoulder.

She took a deep breath. "I've come up with a way forward. A way to secure our position, and at the same time warn Montagn off, or at least stall them while we prepare."

Alyna lifted an eyebrow. "Do tell?"

"Are you sure this is what you want?"

Talyn's heart thudded. *"It's not entirely, but... yes, more than any other option available to me."*

"Then go for it, partner."

She took another long breath, forced herself not to shirk from looking them all in the eye, one by one. "I'm going to join the Dumnorix court, take up all responsibilities of being a member of the family. And then you will marry me to Cuinn Acondor. After that, Cuinn and I will take the throne of Mithranar."

Ariar coughed. Soar looked bemused. Allira puzzled.

McTavish glanced between them dubiously, finding himself in the middle of an uncomfortable situation. "I'll... wait outside until you need me." He rose and walked quickly from the hall. The moment the doors closed behind him, Alyna swung towards Talyn.

"You can't." Alyna's voice shook. "You two married... that could be the death knell of the Twin Thrones."

"I know that's what it *seems* like, but think about it," Talyn said. "You know me, you trust me. I would *never* move against the Twin Thrones. Would you prefer Cuinn married to me, or a Montagni princess like his mother wants? Which of us do you think is the safer choice for the stability of the Twin Thrones?"

"Your children..."

"Don't have to know. Nobody beyond this room has to ever know about Cuinn's Dumnorix blood." Talyn's hands pressed against the cool stone of the tabletop. This was the right choice. It had been in front of her all along but she hadn't seen it. "Put us on the throne of Mithranar and *use* me as a strategic tool against Montagn. With me as Cuinn's wife, *you* have control of the izerdia. More, you have a Dumnorix ally on the Mithranan throne if Montagn truly intends invasion."

"We would have that in Firthland if you married Tarcos," Alyna said.

"Firthland is already sworn to us, and they do not control the izerdia supply," Talyn countered. "This way all three kingdoms are allied against Montagn. We might actually be able to counter their military might that way."

"You talk of putting yourself and Prince Cuinn on the Mithranan throne, but it's not as simple as that. He's the youngest prince. What you're saying is you want to start a civil war there," Soar said grimly.

"No." Talyn shook her head. "Queen Sarana is about to name her heir. If we put Cuinn in an unassailable position, by giving him and me the full backing of the Twin Thrones, we can force the queen and her nobles to name him as heir without a fight. Their army is weak, it can't stand up to us any more than it can stand up to Montagn."

"An alliance such as you're suggesting works both ways," Alyna said. "If Mithranar allies with us and gives us control of their izerdia, that means we are duty bound to help them too."

Ariar jumped in before Talyn could. "What's so bad about that? Talyn is right. We have Firthland as firm allies already. If we formally ally with Mithranar via marriage, Montagn would really have to think twice about coming for any of us."

Soar glanced between Talyn and Alyna. "How would you propose to do it, Talyn?"

"I'll take a force of Aimsir and SkyRiders to Mithranar. The Aimsir will encircle the SkyReach from the north and cut off the Causeway to Montagn. The SkyRiders will take the Summer Palace and cow the WingGuard there into submission. We make it clear to Queen Sarana and her Queencouncil that the Twin Thrones wants Cuinn to be named heir. No matter how angry Mithanis is, there will be little he can do about it." Talyn paused. "The WingGuard can't fight us and win, and they know it."

It meant taking Mithranar against the will of its queen and her Queencouncil, there was no getting around it. But this way they could do it without hurting anyone—Mithanis might want to fight but the WingGuard wouldn't stand against a powerful enough showing of SkyRiders.

"And what do we do until Sarana dies and Cuinn can take the throne?" Alyna asked.

"We exile Mithanis and Azrilan to Montagn to live with their families—that is part of the deal we make," Talyn said coolly. "Without their presence, Cuinn and I can build enough influence in Mithranar to keep Sarana aligned with us." She was confident in Cuinn's song magic. And her ability to win the Falcons to her.

A heavy, thinking silence filled the room. Ariar looked convinced, as did Allira, who'd also married for strategic gain. Even Soar's frown was fading.

Alyna saw the mood shift. "Talyn, no. Even if we agreed to this insane plan, you can't lead our forces."

"Mama, enough!" Talyn rounded on her. "I am not a regent. I am a warrior. There is no one else better suited to lead this than me. Ariar will come with me while Soar searches for Aeris and you and Allira manage our armed forces here."

Alyna rose from her chair, facing Talyn down, words careful and clear. "And when do you intend to come back?"

The answer was burned into Talyn's brain, and it was as if a lamp had suddenly been lit inside a dark room, illuminating what before had been darkness and confusion. And as she accepted that realisation, despite its consequences, she felt as if a huge weight had been lifted from her shoulders. No matter that she was a Dumnorix; she belonged elsewhere. She was Ciantar.

And like she'd promised, she'd found a way to go home.

"Talyn?" Her mother's voice was sharp, cutting through her sorrow.

"I'm sorry, Mama." Talyn spoke just as slowly. "I won't be coming back."

Alyna's mouth was set in a thin line. "While I concede a strategic marriage could work, we still need you here in Port Lachley. A royal marriage like this does not mean you need to stay with him."

"Maybe not," she said softly. "But I choose to stay. I am Ciantar as much as I am Dumnorix, and Mithranar is my home."

Ariar glanced between them. "Talyn—"

"Ariar, I know what you're going to say." Talyn raised a hand. "I—"

"No you don't," he said in frustration. "Look, we're in a mess. There's a good chance Montagn is planning war and our king is missing. Even if he wasn't, he's a boy who is too young to rule. That's the reality."

"Thanks for the overview," she said dryly. "I didn't quite understand the severity of the situation before."

"I'm saying go back to Mithranar," he said in a rush. "Because that's where you belong."

Talyn stared at him, tears filling her eyes. "Really?"

"Really." He smiled slightly. "It's what your father would have wanted. Zamaril has told me a lot, and I think the Mithranan people deserve someone like you to fight for them. And once I've helped you and Cuinn, I will come back here and I will help fight for our country, I promise."

She gave him a shaky smile. "Thank you."

469

Soar spoke into the silence that fell, pushing sadness from his face and speaking in brisk tones. "Right. Let's go over the plan for putting Talyn on the throne of Mithranar. And then I have a search to conduct."

A fierceness sprung up then, one that Talyn didn't attempt to restrain. The Dumnorix were expanding their power... it instinctively pleased all of them.

That was fine. Because it meant she could go home.

TARCOS FOUND her that night as she packed what she needed into a single duffle. Leviana and Cynia were 'helping' by sitting on her bed and grinning like fools. At the sight of Tarcos they shared a look, then filed over to give Talyn a warm hug each.

"You take care, friend," Leviana instructed. "And write often."

"I will," Talyn promised. "And once things are settled in Mithranar I'll come up with a reason to get both of you there on Callanan business."

"You'd better." Cynia gave her another hug and the two Callanan left. A pang went through her as they disappeared from sight. She was going to miss them.

Tarcos waited until they were gone before speaking, still leaning casually against the doorframe.

"Ariar filled me in on the details of your plan. You're going to marry Prince Cuinn?"

She stilled. "Tarcos—"

He lifted a hand. "I don't want to keep being an arrogant idiot about all of this. You being willing to marry, after what you said to me... this isn't about saving the Twin Thrones, is it?"

"Not entirely," she admitted.

He gave a sad little smile. "I can't say that I understand, from what I've seen of Cuinn Acondor. But he's a lucky man."

"Thank you for saying that."

He cleared his throat. Straightened. "I get the impression you're expecting trouble in Mithranar, and I have a detail of Bearmen stationed here with me. Would you consider allowing me to come with you?"

She huffed out a breath. "Your uncle would kill you."

"On the contrary, as I'm to be next warlord, I think it's in Firth-land's best interest for me to assist our sovereign to improve our relations with Mithranar," Tarcos countered. "Particularly since one of my closest friends is about to be queen there and we're going to form an alliance against Montagn."

"You're serious?"

"Deadly," he said, then smiled. "So, can I come?"

A grin escaped her. She'd been on a high ever since her family had agreed to her crazy plan. "Welcome aboard."

The more the merrier.

CHAPTER 48

*S*houts filled the morning air as an alleya ball was kicked from one Wolf to another. Sweat trickled down the back of Cuinn's neck, his lungs panting for breath, muscles warm.

When the ball came back in his direction, he spread his wings wide, stretching them, the cold air running delightfully through his feathers. At just the right moment he leapt into the air, intercepting the pass and tossing the ball downfield to his teammate, Corrin.

Mixed cheers and cries of disappointment rang out as Corrin scored.

The physical exercise was a welcome distraction, and not just for him. They were all as wound up as he was, not just from anxiety, but from the air of unease that hung over the Summer Palace. Not once in the recent history of the winged folk had a nomination for heir been such a dangerous time.

And the queen was dying.

Two weeks of waiting, most of that spent cooling his heels in the palace. Sparring. Skimming. Playing music when the unease became unbearable. Surrounding himself with Wolves at all times.

And all the while the queen insisted she was getting better, that anytime now she would be strong enough for the nomination to happen. Jystar confided to Cuinn that while she might rally for a time, her illness wasn't one they could heal.

He visited her each day, never staying long, struggling with her weakness and her refusal to talk about anything important, like his father or the fact she could choose to name Cuinn heir if she wanted to. His identity as the Shadowhawk lay heavily between them, unspoken, unresolved.

He was startled from his thoughts when play abruptly came to a halt, gazes turning past Cuinn's shoulder. He turned to see Ravinire landing lightly on the opposite side of the yard, red wings a bright splash of colour against all the white.

At a gesture from Cuinn, Corrin sent the Wolves away, leaving only his current detail watching protectively.

Cuinn waited for Ravinire to come to him. "What brings you by, Falcon?"

Silence followed his question, and Cuinn let it sit, waiting patiently.

Ravinire glanced away, then back. "I came to ask you why I'm still alive."

A bitter laugh of surprise escaped him. "Shouldn't I be the one asking you that question?"

Ravinire shifted his feet. "I'm sure Captain Dynan informed you that I—"

"Betrayed me to my mother?" Cuinn cut in, deliberately calm. "Who then told Mithanis what she knew? Resulting in an izerdia explosion that left seven of my Wolves dead."

Ravinire's gaze cut to Corrin standing a short distance off, to the sigil on his chest. "You are the Shadowhawk. It was my duty to tell my queen."

"Flea-bitten rubbish!" Cuinn snarled, wings flaring as he took a quick step toward the Falcon. "You had no proof, no evidence. You had *nothing*. And you still served me up on a platter to my brother, knowing what the consequences would be. Well congratulations, you killed seven innocent men and women."

Ravinire's jaw tightened. "All of that is true. So why aren't I dead?"

Cuinn huffed a breath in astonishment. "What have I ever done to make you think I'm capable of cold-blooded murder? If I were the type of man to do that, you'd have been dead before you had a chance to say anything to my mother."

Ravinire said nothing, face turning bloodless.

"That just makes it worse, doesn't it? You don't get to justify your actions by telling yourself I'm just as bad as my mother and brother." He stepped closer again, staring the Falcon down, ignoring the bitter guilt pouring off him. "Let me be utterly clear—I would never have executed the Ciantar and his family. I would never have executed Ronisin Nightdrift and his detail. You chose the wrong side, Ravinire, and you know it."

Ravinire's jaw clenched, but he said nothing.

"I intend to challenge my brother for the crown." Cuinn paused. "Will you support me or him?"

"I will do as my queen commands," Ravinire said with quiet dignity. "I don't change sides or loyalties, Your Highness."

Cuinn wanted to push harder, to confront Ravinire over his mother's worsening illness, but he couldn't. He knew how much pain it would cause the Falcon and he couldn't willingly inflict it on him, no matter how angry he was. Talyn wouldn't have hesitated. Cuinn had to.

"Get out of here. I'm not interested in talking to you any longer."

Corrin approached after Ravinire had disappeared into the sky, but before he could say anything, Halun's bear-like form appeared. His brow was furrowed, tightening the top edges of his slave tattoo. Jasper paced at his side.

"What is it?" Cuinn asked him.

"The Falcons are talking in the mess, Your Highness," Halun said. "The Queencouncil has called an extraordinary session for tomorrow afternoon. Your mother says she is well again."

Cuinn stilled. "They're going to decide on the heir."

Halun bowed his head in affirmation.

CHAPTER 49

*C*uinn paced back and forth, running a hand through his hair to push it back from his forehead. Jasper prowled at his heels, almost tripping him a number of times. A fire crackled in the hearth, giving light as darkness settled outside.

"Your Highness, there's time to re-think this."

He had his talons gathered with him. *Her* talons, once. And of course Theac was the one to advise caution. Lyra and Liadin shared a glance. They wouldn't verbally gainsay something their captain said, but their emotions told Cuinn they strongly disagreed.

"It's a bit late for that, Theac," Cuinn said. "I've already told Mithanis I'm going to challenge. Even if I don't go through with it tomorrow, he'll never let my challenge lie."

"Jystar says none of the Queencouncil members are going to vote with you," Corrin added. "Except maybe Tirin Goldfeather, but his whole family is warning him against it—they know what will happen to them if he votes against Mithanis."

"That doesn't change anything," Cuinn said.

"Your Highness," Andres pushed, quietly persistent. "What makes you think Mithanis is going to let you walk out of there alive tomorrow, no matter how it goes?"

Her humans. So cautious. So worried for him. Just like she would be.

"My mother is still alive. That might be enough to hold Mithanis back." A faint hope, but one he clung to. As determined as he was to do this, he didn't want to die. Not without seeing Talyn again. Anyway, he'd promised her he wouldn't die. "I know that I'm risking your lives, too, so if you want to leave before—"

"Never," Corrin said with steely determination. Around him, the talons nodded.

"I think we should leave the SkyReach and go back to the citadel after the nomination is official. Get away from your family." This from Theac. "We could even go to Sparrow Island."

Lyra started saying something, but her words were drowned out when the door slammed open and Tirina ran in. The warrior Wolf was agitated, her scarlet wings rustling, flaring and furling in a hurried rhythm. Jasper snarled but they all ignored him.

"What is it?" Theac barked at her.

"Just got a message from Captain Strongswoop. Brightwing has been given orders for the Falcons stationed here to arm themselves and form up."

"Flea-shitting bastards!" Theac swore, turning to Cuinn. "Mithanis isn't going to let you get as far as attending the council tomorrow."

Dread opened up a pit in his stomach, and he felt like a fool. "I should have expected this."

Jasper snarled, the sound loud and vicious, as if he didn't like Cuinn's tone.

Nobody bothered arguing with Theac and Corrin that Brightwing's orders might have nothing to do with him—there was no other reason the WingGuard would be forming up. He turned to Theac. "Where are the rest of the Wolves?"

"They'll be in the mess for dinner."

"Tirina, did Strongswoop tell you how long we had?"

"The orders just came. Falcons aren't the most efficient lot... we have a full-turn, maybe a little less."

That steadied him. "Then they're not going to find us when they come." He moved for the door. "Tirina, keep an eye on the Falcons' progress. The rest of you, with me!"

Theac and the talons followed, a step slow. He ignored them, Jasper a blur at his side, as he sprinted down the corridors and stairs until he was outside, boots sinking into fresh snow as he ran for the cluster of chalet huts used by the Wolves. Two thudding steps and he was bursting into the mess hut.

The Wolves stared at him for a heartbeat.

And then they were rising to their feet, backs straight, arms loose at their sides. Awaiting his orders. More boots thudded outside and then his talons were filing in, instinctively taking up flanking positions around him.

"The prince of night has decided not to play fair." Cuinn spoke briskly, allowing a curl of magic through his words that spoke of confidence, calm. "The Falcons have been given orders to form up and arm themselves. No doubt Mithanis would like to prevent my attendance at the Queencouncil session tomorrow."

It washed over him then. Their anger. Worry for him. Determination to keep him safe. To do as their captain had trained them.

He turned to the men and women at his side. "Talons, assemble your details. Once everyone is accounted for, head for the tunnels to the caverns below the palace. Just like the morning wall run, you're going to go fast. Take weapons and nothing else."

Theac stepped up to him, voice lowered. "We're running?"

"We're keeping ourselves alive," Cuinn said. "I don't want to kill Falcons, Theac. And there are too many Falcons stationed here for us to stand and fight without Wolves dying. I won't have that either."

"And what do we do once we're down in the mines?"

A thud as someone landed outside. It was Tirina, face flushed, eyes glittering. "It's all a bit chaotic—there hasn't been an order for such a large form up before. We've got a half-turn, I reckon, before they move on us."

"How many?" Halun asked.

"A full flight, it looks like."

Almost three hundred Falcons.

Mithanis wasn't messing around.

"One step at a time, Theac," Cuinn said to his captain. "We get out before they hit us. Then we decide what comes next."

Theac saluted, then turned to the Wolves staring at them, letting loose with his distinctive parade ground bellow. "Right, you heard him. That is an order from your prince. GO!"

A sharp ringing resounded over and over through the four walls as the Wolves in the room drew weapons and began forming into their details. They were no less efficient under pressure than in drill, and in moments they were across the room and lined up in ranks before their talons.

At an order from Theac, Liadin took his detail first, then Corrin's went next. Halun's came after.

"I'll be right behind you," Cuinn promised Theac.

The man's scowl deepened. "What does that mean?"

"I need to see my mother before we leave. She's dying, and I can't..." He cursed himself. "I need to say goodbye."

"Then my detail will come with you."

"No. I can hide in the shadows. You can't. You need to get clear into the tunnels. Hopefully it will take some time for the Falcons to work out where you've gone. I'll meet you in the main cavern down there. Jasper, go with him!"

"If you think I'm letting you go alone—"

"You don't have a choice." Cuinn wreathed his voice with magic. "Go, Theac."

He wavered, but an order was an order. In a sharp movement he turned and ushered his detail out the door, one warrior at a time, moving in a steady jog for the cavern entrance.

And then, with a final look at Cuinn, Theac was gone too. Jasper followed with a hiss of displeasure.

HE MOVED ON FOOT, hugging the shadows around the ground level buildings, making his way towards the sprawling corner of the palace where the royal quarters were.

The night was quiet. Too quiet. Somewhere hundreds of Falcons were arming themselves, ready to kill. Elsewhere, those of the court had probably caught a hint of what was about to happen and were sticking to their rooms.

Quiet was good. It made it easier for him to move around.

By gathering the darkness around him and using glamour to darken his wings, he easily evaded the single Falcon keeping watch on the outer wall of his mother's rooms. The window was unlocked, and all he had to do was wait, pressed against the wall, until the Falcon looked away. Then he was lifting the sill and furling his wings to clamber inside.

The room he landed in was her sitting room, dark and empty, but orange light flickered from under the door of the bedroom. He took a deep breath, summoned his magic, and spread it out as far as he could, seeking the emotions of anyone else present.

She was alone. Awake, but tired.

The moment he stepped into the room, Sarana sat up against her pillows, fear flashing over her face and hitting him with her song magic. "Mithanis is coming for you. I couldn't stop him, Cuinn. He knows you're the Shadowhawk and he—"

"I know." He filled the room with calm. "The Wolves are already out of the palace, and I'm going to follow. But I couldn't leave without saying goodbye."

For a long moment they stared at each other, betrayal and pain wreathing the space between them. All this time, her son had been the Shadowhawk. And she'd betrayed that knowledge to his brother.

"He overheard me talking to Ravinire. I didn't tell him," she said eventually. "How *could* you, Cuinn?"

He ignored her question. "When Mithanis told you he was going to have me killed, you didn't stop him?"

"I tried." Her shoulders sagged then, his magic telling him everything he needed to know. She'd failed. Her strength was gone. Her ability to outmanoeuvre her son was gone too. He ached for her as much as he was hurt by her failure.

"I became the Shadowhawk because our people needed help, and you wouldn't give it to them."

Another silence fell. She didn't understand. Probably never would.

"I know who I am, Mother," he said into the silence. "I know what blood my father carried—Acondor and Dumnorix both. I have a better claim to your throne than Mithanis, and I'm going to use it. I wanted you to know that. I'm going to do better than you did."

"You can't defeat him, Cuinn."

He smiled. "I'm going to try anyway."

For a moment her old snappishness appeared on her face. "How are you going to do that by running?"

"I'll figure it out. A way to beat him without killing Falcons or Wolves. Without killing him, if I can help it." Cuinn crossed to the bed. He'd been here too long already—he needed to leave before someone found him. He needed to get to his Wolves. "Goodbye, Mother."

Her hand came up to press against his jaw when he leaned down to kiss her cheek. "I do love you, Cuinn." Her weakened song magic showing him the truth of her words. She'd loved him, but never been able to understand him. Never tried hard enough to. Part of her regretted it. But she'd loved the strength of her eldest son most, his power and similar outlook on the world.

They stayed like that for a long moment. He tried to show her his love for her while holding back his disappointment and regret she'd never loved him as she could have. He showed her the strength of his purpose.

Then he squeezed her hand and left.

He took three steps across the sitting room beyond, only to have the main door open abruptly before him.

Anrun Windsong stood there.

"I thought I might find you here," the man said. "Strongswoop's warning reached you, I take it?"

Cuinn readied his song magic, just in case. "What are you doing here?"

Determination shone in the man's sea-green eyes. "I want a Mithranar where *you* are king, Prince Cuinn."

Cuinn's magic read sincerity in every note of Windsong's voice. And not just sincerity, but respect. Admiration. A combination of emotions Cuinn had never experienced in his life before Talyn and the Wolves. There was no time for hesitation or doubt, so he simply trusted his magic. "We're retreating down into the caverns."

"I know," Anrun said. "And I can help."

"Then you'd best come with me."

BACK OUTSIDE, both men stilled at the sight of hundreds of Falcons lifting into the air above the palace, massing in the skies for several minutes before slowly moving off towards the Wolf barracks.

"Stick close to me," he told Windsong quickly. "I can keep us hidden."

No hesitation or questions from the older man. Just a nod.

They moved on foot, shrouded in Cuinn's shadows, hidden from anyone watching, until they reached the western edge of the palace grounds. Then he dropped the shadows, glamoured his wings to darkness, and looked at Windsong. "Now we fly. Fast."

"I can keep up, Your Highness."

It was the fastest he'd ever flown, using every downdraft he could find to drop him lower, plummeting through some sections of the mountains, guiding himself down towards Darmour. Sweat slicked his skin, weariness burned his muscles, but the rest of him delighted in the speed, the rush of air over his face.

And Windsong kept up admirably, just as swift, just as strong, his darker wings keeping him as well-hidden as Cuinn's glamoured ones.

They almost landed right in the middle of them—a mass of Falcons gathered at the entrance to the mines from the coastal road.

Shit. Mithanis had planned ahead—planned for the Wolves to try and escape through the mine tunnels. That meant the mine entry in Darmour was likely blocked with Falcons too.

At the last moment they veered away, landing out of sight around a turn in the road.

"Can you hide us well enough to sneak past all those Falcons?" Windsong murmured.

"If you stick really close… like touching me close. And we move *really* slowly," Cuinn said. There was no other choice. They had to get inside, warn the Wolves that an ambush was awaiting. "And keep a tight control on your emotions in case any of them have secondary song magic like you."

It took every bit of shadow magic he had to hide them both from sight, and even then, he pressed as hard back against the rock as he could, inching his way, slow shuffling step by slow shuffling step, along the edge of the road. Windsong pressed close, his shoulder and arm solid against Cuinn's side. His emotions were impressively hidden; not even Cuinn could read them.

Falcons were barely paces away from them. All one had to do was stretch out a wing, stumble sideways, and they would be discovered. And the shadows surrounding them couldn't move too quickly or it would look odd… so he had to keep his movements painfully slow. His heart thudded in his chest, anxiety curling in his gut. He paused to focus his song magic and ensure the emotion stayed buried. The effort was draining.

And then they were at the tunnel entrance. Slowly, painfully slowly, they edged their way inside, moving further away from the gathered Falcons.

The moment they were out of sight, Cuinn dropped the shadows and he and Windsong ran.

By the time they reached the main cavern at the base of the palace, sweat slicked his skin and breath rasped in his chest. Magical and physical exhaustion dragged at his bones.

But none of that was any different to the myriad long nights he'd been the Shadowhawk. He had more to spare.

The Wolves waited, watchful and focused. They straightened in relief when Cuinn appeared, and the talons came straight over to report.

"What's he doing here?" Theac barked at Windsong.

"Helping," Cuinn panted. "Listen, there are Falcons posted at the road entrance. Probably at the Darmour mine entrance too."

"The horses are gone as well, Your Highness," Andres said. "Mithanis must have had them cleared out."

"He isn't taking any chances," Corrin said, calm despite the news that they were essentially trapped in the caverns.

"We'll have to make a stand here, Your Highness." Theac was grim.

"There's another tunnel." Anrun's voice rang with confidence bolstered by song magic. All eyes turned to him. "One that leads through to the northern edge of the SkyReach. It's narrow, so we'll have to go on foot, but few people know of its existence. It will take a while for Mithanis to work out where we've gone."

"How do you know about it?" Cuinn asked, trying to push down the hope growing inside him at Windsong's words. Despite the sincerity he was reading from Windsong, he was wary of another trap.

"I've been assigned to the SkyReach flight for nearly thirty years, Prince Cuinn. It's my responsibility to know about all accesses to the Summer Palace."

"We can't just keep running without a plan, Your Highness." Halun spoke firmly, arms crossed. He was unhappy.

"If we stay here, then it becomes a fight between Wolves and Falcons," Cuinn said. "Both will get hurt, die, and I can't accept that. Those Falcons are following orders, and not all of them believe in Mithanis, or think like Mithanis. I am their prince too, Halun."

"We're eventually going to have no choice, Your Highness," Andres said. "Because they're coming to kill us, and unlike you, they won't have any hesitation about doing so."

Cuinn took a long breath, trying to steady his mind. Weariness tugged at him. "We'll take Windsong's tunnel, head north. If we get clear, we can head for Montagn. That's where Azrilan fled—he might be able to help us."

"Or at least give us passage to the Twin Thrones," Corrin added.

All options. All possibilities.

But he doubted Mithanis would make it that easy. The Falcons were going to keep chasing them until they caught up. And then the Wolves were going to have to fight.

The best he could do was hold them off as long as possible. And maybe they could reach Montagn, if they moved fast enough, if Mithanis took long enough to figure out where they'd gone, if they could survive the journey without supplies or proper cold weather gear...

Theac's gaze was on his, as if the grizzled warrior knew exactly what he was thinking.

"I suggest we take things one step at a time, Your Highness," Windsong broke in. "Let's take the tunnel north. It leads into larger caverns at the base of the SkyReach, and I have provisions stocked there in case of emergency. You and your Wolves will be able to rest and get some water and food. Then, with clearer heads, we can plot our next course."

The man sounded exactly like Talyn. Cuinn smiled suddenly. "I like the way you think, Windsong. All right. We go north to the Ice Plains."

Theac began rapping out orders and the Wolves moved moments later, one detail at a time, their talons in the lead. With one mighty beat of his wings, Windsong flew across the cavern and landed before one of the several tunnels leading away. He lifted a torch from the wall, then without a word, he furled his wings and broke into a run.

The Wolves followed.

CHAPTER 50

The manic energy that had filled Talyn once she'd made the decision to go back to Mithranar faded rapidly once they were on ships heading north. The ten-day journey, despite being helped by surprisingly strong winds, was interminable.

Her gaze frequently swept the five Conmoran naval ships following in their wake, all outfitted for carrying Aimsir horses and mountain eagles. Two hundred Aimsir and six legions of SkyRiders. Five hundred elite warriors in total. She was going home with a powerful force at her back to win Cuinn his throne.

If she got there in time.

By the time they reached the eastern coast of the Ice Plains it would be nearing a month since Cuinn had arrived home. Factoring in the time it would have taken him to travel north to Darmour, two weeks at least would have passed. The Queencouncil session to formally nominate Sarana's heir could already be over.

"You can't do anything about that. You're moving as fast as you can," Sari pointed out.

"I should have done this sooner."

"Maybe. Maybe not. But you're on your way now."

Talyn tried to let Sari's words reassure her, but the anxiousness building inside her made it hard to do anything but pace the deck in frustration.

The ship's bell began ringing then, a steady beat. Across the ocean around them, the other ships in the fleet echoed the ringing.

Talyn scrambled across the deck, moving lithely over the rocking surface, joining Zamaril on the opposite deck, facing west.

They were approaching the coast.

SIX SKYRIDER SCOUTS LIFTED off open decks into the sky, tasked with ensuring there was nothing waiting for them along the isolated coastline. They reported back quickly, confirming it was safe to approach, to the great relief of everyone on board.

The Aimsir were ferried ashore first, their restless and highly-strung horses making it a difficult task. More SkyRiders lifted into the air, swooping low overhead, screaming their pleasure in the icy breeze and freedom of flight. Talyn's winged Wolves did the same, the humans keeping a watchful eye on her.

Once they were all ashore, Tarcos and his Bearmen gathered together, snug in their bearskins and bushy beards. Ariar sent his Aimsir scouts inland to make sure there were no unwelcome surprises waiting.

There wouldn't be. Talyn was confident of it.

The tallest peaks of the SkyReach were too cold, the air too thin, the winds too severe for Falcons to travel over them from Darmour or the Summer Palace. And they didn't have scouts patrolling the northern areas of the mountains.

Fools.

"Swept says there's nothing out there but ice and snow." Ariar joined her in watching the Aimsir assemble themselves to ride, giving her the report from the SkyRider in command of the legions with them.

"I'm not surprised," she said. "Nobody lives out on the Ice Plains, or on the northern face of the SkyReach. Too inhospitable."

"It's beautiful. Stark, but stunning," he murmured.

"And cold." She smiled. "But yes, I completely agree."

"I'm beginning to see why you love it so much here."

Talyn made a face. "You might change your tune if you ever get the chance to go to the citadel. The air's as thick as soup and you literally cannot escape the heat."

He chuckled.

She sobered. "Are you sure about this?" She hadn't yet had a chance to talk to him privately about her decision. Ariar had travelled on the ship carrying the Aimsir riders, Talyn on a different one with Tarcos and his Bearmen and her Wolves.

His luminous blue eyes studied the dark landscape as he replied. "I like your plan. And even if it wasn't about assuring our security by putting Cuinn on the throne... he's one of us. He deserves our help."

"He does," she agreed.

A moment of comfortable silence fell between them, then Ariar gave her a teasing glance. "You didn't just suggest this because it was strategically sound though, did you?"

Talyn scowled at him. "Don't be awful."

"I'm not trying to be." He met her gaze. "I'm going to miss you, Cousin, with you living so far away."

"I'm going to miss you too." She touched his arm. "Let's hurry this along."

Tarcos walked across the snow to meet her the moment he saw her approach. He was tall and imposing with his bearskin over his broad shoulders. "What a fascinating place. What's the plan, Tal?"

"We're going to have to leave you behind, I'm afraid." She dug a map from her tunic, passed it to him. "Your horses won't be able to keep up with the Aimsir. Follow that route and catch up as quick as you can."

He made a face. "I hate the idea of missing a fight. My boys will too."

"If everything goes as planned, there won't be a fight."

"We'll come after you as fast as we can," he promised. "If there's any trouble, we won't be far off."

"I'll see you in a few days."

"Count on it." A fierce smile lit up his dark face.

THEY SPED west throughout the night without stopping, two hundred Aimsir riders at full racing gallop. The human Wolves rode double with riders on the strongest mounts. Those with wings were almost invisible in the night sky above them. Flying such a distance and so quickly would exhaust them, but they had heart and will and would manage.

And higher again flew the six legions of SkyRiders, born for flying in these conditions.

The WingGuard wasn't going to stand a chance.

Talyn's hair and cloak flew back with the wind, and FireFlare's speed sent familiar exhilaration coursing through her blood. Finally they were off the damned ships. For the first time in months there was something to do, some action to take, and she felt better than she had since Cuinn had left.

Ariar and Greylord rode at her side—he didn't have to say a word for her to know that he was enjoying this equally as much.

They continued through the daylight hours, the Aimsir horses able to run and run and run, needing rest and water only when they stopped to camp the following night. Each time, the winged Wolves would drop from the sky, eat something, and then collapse into exhausted sleep.

Late morning on the fifth day, the outline of the SkyReach grew closer to the south, the peaks lit by the orange glow of the setting sun. With the fading of daylight, so dropped the temperature.

McTavish called a halt and the horses slowed, breath steaming, coats lathered. Talyn's entire body was tense with anticipation. She stood high in the stirrups, gaze focused on the mountains. Zamaril appeared at FireFlare's side, giving Talyn a quick nod.

"How far from the coastal road?" Ariar asked.

"It's hard to tell for certain, but I think less than a half-day's ride west," she replied. "Zamaril?"

He huffed a breath. "I'm a Dock City gutter rat, Captain. But that sounds right."

A handful of SkyRiders dropped out of the sky, circling lazily before landing on the snow nearby. Talyn, Zamaril, McTavish and Ariar waited patiently as Swept dismounted and crossed the snow towards them.

"Orders?" he asked, saluting.

"Send a few scouts in to see if there's any activity around the coastal road or the mountains around the Summer Palace," Talyn instructed. "Stay high if you can. I'd rather nobody spot you. Send some more northwest, towards the Causeway. I'd like to know if there are any Montagni lurking around."

Swept nodded and jogged back to his eagle. A short time later, individual SkyRiders broke free of the huddle above and shot westwards.

"What's the plan, Cousin?" Ariar asked.

"Swept makes sure there are no surprises waiting for us, then we take the legions in and surround the Summer Palace, force the Wing-Guard out of the air." They'd already discussed this, but as an experienced warrior, Ariar liked to go over it multiple times. Make sure there was no uncertainty.

"While I take the Aimsir and hold the ground between the coastal road and the Causeway, make sure no Montagni surprises creep up on you from behind," McTavish added. "You'll leave a couple of SkyRiders with me in case I need to send a warning?"

"I will."

Ariar glanced at her. "When the WingGuard are cowed, you and I have to lead the delegation in. Once fighting is off the table, it becomes a diplomatic representation from the Twin Thrones to the Acondor crown."

A smile teased at her mouth. "Our favourite thing in the world, Ariar. Diplomatic representations."

Ariar made a face. "I brought my nice tunic and everything."

Talyn laughed.

"So what do we do now?" Zamaril asked.

"Now we wait," she murmured.

CHAPTER 51

*C*uinn decided that if he ever managed to become king of Mithranar, he would gift Anrun Windsong with riches, influence and whatever position in the WingGuard he wanted.

Maybe he'd even make him a Queencouncil lord.

After a full day and a half of running, before slowing to a swift walk and then finally stumbling along in complete exhaustion, Windsong led Cuinn and his Wolves out of the dark tunnels and into a wide cavern. Directly ahead an archway—which was dug into the rock— opened out on the bright white snow and whistling winds of the Ice Plains.

"Dry food supplies are stored through there." Windsong pointed to another tunnel leading off the main cavern. "Talon Skywing, your detail is in charge of gathering and distributing food. Talons Dariel and Arasan, take your details through that tunnel to the left where you'll find blankets, enough for everyone. Talons Songdrift and Tye, please have your details get started on fires and collecting snow outside—we'll boil it for water. Captain Parksin, apologies, but we're going to need scouts back along that tunnel. Pick the freshest Wolves, get them something to eat and drink, then send them back down there. We'll relieve them in three full-turn shifts. Any questions?"

Six pairs of eyes turned to Cuinn. Windsong's mouth opened, then closed, as he realised he'd just given orders to soldiers who weren't his own.

"Do it," Cuinn said.

The Wolves scrambled.

Windsong looked at Cuinn. "Five full-turns of rest, then we move again. We can't afford to linger longer than that. With your leave, I'll assign some Wolves to packing enough supplies to get us to the Causeway."

"Do it. And I'll help with packing supplies. I don't need as much rest as the others."

CUINN'S faint hope that Mithanis wouldn't quickly figure out where they'd gone proved hopeless. The Wolves managed food, water and about three full-turns of sleep before the scouts Windsong had sent back along the tunnels came running out. He and a handful of others were just putting the finishing touches on filling satchels with basic food supplies. The scouts' obvious agitation had Jasper leaping into the space in front of Cuinn and letting out a warning growl.

"Quiet, Jasper," Cuinn said sharply.

"Your Highness, the Falcons are coming," Leta warned. "They'll be here inside a quarter-turn."

"Up and in your details! Now!" Theac bellowed without missing a beat. "Weapons ready."

"You're certain you don't want to stand and fight, Your Highness?" Windsong asked.

Cuinn hesitated. "I'm sure. We make for the Causeway."

"Falcons can fly," Theac barked. "They'll be on us well before we get there."

"We only fight if we have to," Cuinn insisted. Maybe they were further behind than Leta thought. Maybe there wouldn't be many of them and they wouldn't want to engage the well-armed Wolves. All probably useless hopes. It didn't matter.

He was going to try anyway.

. . .

THEY MARCHED out into the snow, turning northwest in the direction of the Causeway. Cuinn flew with the winged Wolves and Windsong, his wings stretching wide to catch the cold air, a food satchel hanging down his back. Below, the Wolves moved in a steady jog across the snow, getting clear of the cavern, holding loose formation.

Any hope Cuinn had of outrunning the Falcons turned to ashes in his chest when he turned back and saw turquoise-clad figures streaming out of the cavern entrance and leaping into the sky to give chase.

They'd been even closer than he thought.

Below, Theac's voice barked out and the marching Wolves came to a halt. More orders sounded and they shifted into a fighting formation, facing back towards the mountains. Exchanging a brief look with Windsong, Cuinn furled his wings and dropped out of the air to land beside Theac. Jasper immediately prowled over, green eyes flicking between Cuinn and what lay behind them.

"Prince Cuinn, you need to fly on ahead with the winged Wolves," Theac said "The rest of us will stay here to give you time to get clear. You make for the Causeway and—"

"No."

"Your Highness, you can't—"

"I'm not leaving the human Wolves behind to die for me." He spoke clearly and firmly, without emotion. "If it has to come to a fight, then I'm standing with you."

"That's not fair." Corrin strode over, breath steaming. "You are Mithranar's prince. You're the only one who can replace Mithanis. None of us can do that. You're the one who says he'll bring us a better Mithranar... dying here won't do that, Your Highness."

The words pummelled into him, all the more painful for how true they were.

"You promised us," Liadin chimed in, eyes bright. "So save yourself. Please."

"I—"

But shouts interrupted him. All the Wolves were staring at where hundreds of Falcons were pouring out of the mine entrance.

Beside him, Corrin's shoulders sagged and the light faded from Liadin's eyes.

"No!" Cuinn snarled at them. "We are not lost. You are Wolves. Each of you can fight ten times better than any Falcon coming towards us. And if I stay with you, use my magic, we can win."

Mithanis had left him no choice. He would have to help kill Falcons. The knowledge was a bitter pill to swallow, but he pushed aside his fear and his doubt and the knowledge of what this would do to his song magic and summoned every bit of resolve he had.

"The prince is right. Wolves, arm yourselves!" Theac bellowed. "We fight."

Cuinn could only watch as the cloud of Falcons swarmed towards them. He could only sink into his magic, draw up everything he had, and ready it to sing for his life, to protect himself and his Wolves.

They drew closer and closer, until the metal of their drawn swords flashed in the afternoon sun gleaming off the white snow.

His brother might finally succeed in killing him.

"Can you hear that?"

Cuinn barely registered Liadin's words, his entire focus on preparing his magic, readying to sing fear and confusion and dread. But then he caught Liadin's own confusion, and that of the other talons gathered around him, sensing it growing stronger as it spread through the waiting Wolves.

"Hear what?" he asked.

Theac raised a hand. "Silence!" he bellowed.

As one they stilled. Silence fell over the Ice Plains.

Cuinn heard it then. A distant rumbling.

Jasper snarled, body turning rigid. His green eyes flashed, but Cuinn didn't sense anger or threat from his tawncat... instead it felt more like anticipation.

Corrin frowned. "Is that an avalanche?"

Cuinn glanced back at the oncoming Falcons. So close now. Then he shook his head. "No, it's coming from the north."

The rumbling grew louder. Turned into something resembling thunder.

Then the Wolves stopped being still and quiet. One of them spotted something on the north-eastern horizon and pointed excitedly. A black smudge. The source of the sound.

Halun hazarded a guess. "The Montagni?"

"Wrong direction. Whatever that is, it's coming from the northeast," Andres said.

Cuinn spun back to the oncoming Falcons, barely moments away now, and then to the horizon.

"It's not an avalanche or the Montagni," he breathed.

"The Falcons are almost on us!" Lyra shouted a warning.

But suddenly the Falcons were pulling up mid-flight, sharp eyes staring into the distance, shouts of alarm drifting through the sky.

Cuinn stared, stared until his vision turned blurry and tears ran down his face.

The thunder resolved into galloping hooves. Then the whoops and catcalls of Aimsir riders as they rode directly for the Wolves at blistering speed, snow flying in a cloud around them.

Cuinn watched, awestruck, as the Aimsir barrelled towards them, whooping and screaming, their bows out and drawn, pointing up towards the Falcons.

Two riders were in the lead, a copper mare and a big grey stallion. Two Dumnorix, sapphire and sky-blue eyes luminous as the stars.

She'd come. And brought an army with her.

And then the riders split apart, Ariar leading one half around to the east, Talyn the others to the west, until the Wolves were surrounded by Aimsir. They galloped in circles, in constant motion, never pulling up or slowing down.

Making a moving target if any Falcons decided to attack.

His brother's warriors hung frozen in the sky, all one hundred of them. More began emerging from the tunnels, winging swiftly towards the frozen tableau.

And then a loud screech sounded above the clouds.

And another.

494

And another.

Until the screams were deafening. The Falcons stared as out of the clouds above them swooped SkyRiders, their great eagles' talons extended in threat and warning. The Falcons froze into utter stillness as warning arrows fired into the space around them.

The SkyRiders flew rings around the gathered Falcons, their eagles screaming in challenge, tighter and tighter until, utterly cowed, the Falcons began dropping to the ground. One by one, until every single Falcon was out of the sky and standing in the snow. Screams of triumph echoed through the sky as the eagles banked and flew back above the clouds.

Cuinn began walking, pushing forward out of the pack of Wolves, heading towards the grounded Falcons. Jasper padded behind, looking suitably terrifying for anyone that might take it into their heads to make a move on Cuinn.

The encircling stream of galloping Aimsir parted effortlessly to let him through and then two riders were approaching him. Talyn was just in front, FireFlare stepping lively under her, Ariar on a grey stallion at her side. Both were flushed, their excitement hitting him in a wash of exuberance.

"Captain Dynan," he drawled, coming to a halt, wondering if his eyes were glowing with the same joy as hers. She'd come back. He wasn't sure if he could contain what he felt about that. "You've been busy."

Her gaze shot straight to him, sapphire darkening. Then she was off FireFlare and running for him. He caught her up in his arms, holding her close, not saying a word as they held each other for a long moment.

Eventually she stepped back, and Cuinn gave her a little smile before walking over to greet Ariar. "Prince Ariar. Nice to see you."

"I did promise to come and visit sometime." Ariar grinned, shaking his hand warmly. "I brought some friends. I hope that's okay?"

"It most certainly is." Cuinn's gaze shifted to the Falcons. It was hard to credit how suddenly and drastically the situation had reverted in their favour. Moments ago he'd been convinced he was about to die. And now... "Let's go and accept their surrender, shall we?"

Talyn took the lead as they headed towards the Falcons, strides long and sure, and he let her have it. If she'd truly come back, bringing the might of the Dumnorix behind her, then this moment belonged to her.

After all, she was Ciantar.

By the time they crossed the snow, Brightwing had barked enough orders that the Falcons had formed into almost neat lines behind him. They were terrified. Cuinn could feel the waves of it beating at him, and tried not to wince.

They thought they were about to die.

"Go easy," he murmured to Talyn. "They're frightened."

She glanced back at him, realisation that he was going to let her handle this flashing over her face. Those sapphire eyes brightened, then her attention shifted back to Brightwing. "He's not."

No, he wasn't. He stood, scowling with frustrated anger. It practically vibrated from him.

"You're beaten, Brightwing," Talyn said as they came to a halt, Cuinn and Ariar on either side of her.

"You're invading us!" he hissed, his anger white-hot. "Traitor!"

"You want to talk about playing fair?" Cuinn asked, using magic so that his voice rang out over the plains. "Who tried to kill me before I could attend the formal Queencouncil to name an heir?"

"Prince Mithanis is heir to the throne. It has always been so." Brightwing's eyes narrowed. He glanced at Jasper, then back at Cuinn.

"Not anymore." Talyn lifted her gaze from Brightwing, ran it over the assembled Falcons. "I am Ciantar. Who here is loyal to my father's family? To *me*?"

For a long moment there was silence.

Then wings rustled as a Falcon close to the back began pushing forward through the ranks until he emerged to stand before Talyn. Astonishment swept through Cuinn at recognising Ravinire's second, Firas Grasswing, his emerald wings bright against the stark white snow.

496

"Ciantar!" He saluted.

Hundreds of pairs of eyes watched as Talyn nodded to him, then Grasswing walked past her and went to stand with the Wolves lined up behind them. Another heartbeat, then Darian Strongswoop stepped forward, striding over to stop, salute Talyn, then continue past to stand with Grasswing.

Strongswoop's decision broke the dam. Within the space of heartbeats multiple Falcons were breaking ranks and moving to join the Wolves. Not many. But enough to make a point.

Brightwing stood and watched it unfold before him, hatred written all over his face.

"I'm not going to kill any of you," Talyn said once everyone had stopped moving. "That's not how Prince Cuinn does things. You're free to go."

They didn't believe her. He could feel the doubt seeping through the cold air. So Cuinn stepped forward, filling his voice with magic. "You are free to go. I am not my brother."

Wings rustled. One Falcon took several steps back and lifted into the air. When nothing happened to him, others followed. Soon they were all gone, winging their way back to the mine entrance and the dubious safety of Mithanis.

WHILE TALYN and Ariar sent SkyRiders and Aimsir out to ensure nobody approached the mine entrance, Cuinn and the Wolves, along with the newly loyal Falcons, headed back into the disused mines.

It was chaos for over a full-turn as Aimsir found somewhere for their horses and SkyRiders trickled in after ensuring their eagles were settled in roosts in the lower slopes of the mountain above. Once again, Cuinn found himself promising Anrun Windsong whatever he wanted once this was all over. The supplies he'd had stored away, not to mention the upkeep of the unused mine caverns, meant there was space for everyone.

Cuinn came from checking the Wolves were sorted—even Jasper had finally settled to sleep—and returned to the main cavern in search of Talyn and Ariar. Tiredness tugged insistently at him, but Mithanis would soon be receiving a firsthand report about what had happened from the Falcons they let go, and they needed to decide what to do next. Rest could come later.

The two Dumnorix were on the opposite side of the cavern, speaking with a small group of men and women whom Cuinn presumed were the Aimsir and SkyRider captains, along with Theac. Ariar caught sight of him first.

Oddly, the Dumnorix prince straightened his tunic, adjusted his swordbelt, then took off his Aimsir slouch hat and ran a hand through his hair to tidy it. Beside him, Talyn caught what he was doing, spotted Cuinn approaching across the cavern, and turned red. If Cuinn had been sitting on a chair, he would have fallen off it. As it was, his steps slowed. He could count on half a hand how many times he'd seen Talyn flush.

"Ariar, we don't need to do this now," she said, her words drifting to him on the breeze coming from the cavern opening. Outside the sun was setting over the snow, a wondrous sight.

"Yes we do. Come on." Seemingly satisfied that he looked neat and tidy, Ariar strode across the cavern to meet Cuinn halfway. Talyn, waves of mortification flooding from her, reluctantly followed in his footsteps.

What was going on?

As if sensing something important was about to happen, those in the cavern cleared the centre space, moving back to line the walls. There were Aimsir, SkyRiders, the Wolves of his detail, all of her talons. Footsteps sounded as more Wolves filed in—either woken up or not fallen asleep yet, sensing that something was up.

Then suddenly it was just Cuinn and Ariar, meeting in the centre of the open space, Talyn a step behind her cousin. The attention of the room was a weight on his shoulders, all that interest and curiosity focused on them. And he didn't even know why.

Cuinn opened his mouth to ask what the hell was going on when Ariar cleared his throat, taking on a serious expression that was almost entirely undermined by the twinkle in his blue eyes. He glanced at Talyn—she couldn't meet his gaze.

"Prince Cuinn Acondor." Ariar spoke clear and firm. "The Twin Thrones offers you a formal alliance. We will provide whatever military or other support you need to see that you take the throne of Mithranar. If it comes to it, we will fight for you. Consider our assistance earlier a gesture of goodwill."

"And in return?" Cuinn asked, because such offers never came without strings.

"You marry Talyn Dumnorix." Ariar paused, eyes glinting. "One of us will be your queen."

His eyes had turned to Talyn before Ariar had even stopped speaking. She was looking at him with that cool calm of hers, the one she wore to hide her stronger emotions. The cavern around them had gone deathly silent. He was astonished none of them could hear his heart thudding. Could it be…?

"It has to be her choice, Ariar," he said softly. "Always her choice."

Ariar cleared his throat in a way that sounded suspiciously like he was stifling a laugh. "It was her idea, Cuinn."

His breath caught. She smiled at him then, gave a little nod. "It was."

For a moment he wasn't sure he'd heard right. But her gaze was steady on his. She was giving him her hand and the might of her family's army in one fell swoop. He swore to himself then and there that he would work the rest of his life to deserve it. To deserve her and the happiness she gave him.

"Then I accept your offer of formal alliance, Prince Ariar." Cuinn somehow mustered the ability to sound firm and formal—his first act as future king of Mithranar. "Put me on the throne, and I will marry Talyn and swear to support and fight for the Twin Thrones if called upon."

A grin spread across Ariar's face, breaking his serious demeanour. He stuck out his hand to shake Cuinn's enthusiastically. "Welcome to the family. Now, we have some pressing matters to discuss. Not the least of which is that your brother is soon going to find out what happened to the feathered idiots calling themselves soldiers he sent after you."

"Agreed. Plus, you did just promise to help me with the throne." Cuinn waved over Theac and the talons, all hovering nearby and wearing expressions ranging from astonished to burgeoning hope. As they approached, a disturbance sounded at the main entrance. SkyRiders and Aimsir peeled away to welcome the new arrivals.

In that moment, Cuinn didn't particularly care if they were invading Montagni. Taking advantage of the momentary distraction, he spun to Talyn, taking her hand and tugging her to him. "Are you sure?"

Her blue eyes were aflame as she looked at him. "I am."

"And Sari's okay with you marrying a dissolute third prince from Mithranar?"

"Are you kidding me? She's practically doing cartwheels in my head right now," Talyn grumbled. "It's extremely annoying."

He was going to kiss her. There was absolutely no way he could stand there with her looking at him like that any longer and not kiss her senseless, the cavern full of people be damned. Her gaze darkened as she read his intent, but right at that moment, Theac cleared his throat *very* loudly.

"What?" Cuinn snapped.

"Your Highness." Tarcos Hadvezer stood there, intimidatingly tall and muscular in his bearskin and dark plaited hair. More bodies had filled the room, these men even more hulking than Tarcos.

Firthlander Bearmen.

"Welcome to Mithranar, Prince Hadvezer." Cuinn offered his hand, did his best not to tighten the grip when he felt the man's intense dislike for him. So he'd come for Talyn then, and not because of the alliance.

"Ariar was right, we need to discuss what comes next," Talyn interjected. "Talons, Ariar, Tarcos, let's find a space."

THIS WAS his country and he wanted to be its king, so rather than let the intimidatingly competent leaders around him begin the discussion, Cuinn spoke before any of them could. "The immediate issue for us to address is what to do about the pursuit Mithanis will no doubt send after us once he learns what happened. Then we need to decide how we go about putting me on the throne without starting a war. I won't have innocent Mithranans killed."

"I've already sent Wolf scouts into the tunnels," Windsong said.

"You ordered my Wolves?" Talyn asked coolly.

"I did." Not a shred of remorse on his face.

"We've also sent SkyRider scouts over the SkyReach to keep an eye on the palace." Ariar's mouth twitched. "We'll be warned if Mithanis makes a move."

"They might attack," Cuinn said. "Mithanis controls close to two thousand Falcons and he's an angry man who doesn't always see reason."

"I don't mean to be picky, but doesn't your mother still control the army?" Talyn asked. "Surely we just have to make her see reason and nominate you as heir."

A heavy silence fell. Windsong looked down, wings sagging. Cuinn met her eyes. "Mother is ill. She won't live much longer, and she has little power or influence left."

Shock rippled over her face, and she reached out to touch his hand. "Cuinn, I'm sorry."

"We have time." Windsong cleared his throat. "Mithanis will have to summon more Falcons from the citadel if he wants to fight your Aimsir and SkyRiders."

"I want to resolve the situation sooner." Cuinn shook his head. "Before Mithanis gets so angry he thinks his Falcons can defeat SkyRiders."

Talyn, who'd half been paying attention and half frowning in thought, spoke up then. "I have a plan to do that."

Cuinn couldn't help his smile. "Just like that?"

"Of course just like that." She gave him a look. "Don't you know me at all?"

"Do tell, Cousin," Ariar drawled. He leaned back in his chair, legs up on the table, despite the formal war council taking place.

"I'll challenge Mithanis to a duel on Cuinn's behalf. That will end this, once and for all, without anyone else getting hurt."

"No!" Theac shook his head.

"You've just come home, we can't lose you again!" Corrin protested.

"Are you sure this is a good idea, Tal?" This from Tarcos.

She raised her hands as they all spoke simultaneously. "I do thank you all for your great faith in my abilities."

"I know you can take him." Cuinn spoke. He worried for her, but he knew Talyn inside out, and he knew his brother too. "But I'm not sure if it's the best approach. Can I demand that the lords follow me as king if I can't fight my own battles?"

"I'm not just anyone. I'm your Ciantar," she pointed out. "And the only other way to do it is by force, using the Aimsir and SkyRiders. And that means good soldiers dying on both sides. Neither of us want that."

He nodded, looking at nobody but her. "Then we do it your way."

"Ciantar." A smile broke out on Theac's weathered face. "Remember our first drill session, when you told me if I beat you, I could have command of the Wolves?"

"I remember," Talyn said.

"I thought I would take a strip of a girl like you in under ten seconds."

"I remember that too," she said dryly.

"That's the day I learned never to underestimate you, lass." He smiled. "You can take him."

"Windsong, we'll send you to Prince Mithanis to deliver the challenge," Cuinn said. "If Mithanis refuses, you can enlighten him regarding the two hundred Aimsir and six legions of SkyRiders camped on his doorstep."

"And warn him that we can get more where they came from if he decides to push the point." Ariar smiled.

"A week from today, at the alleya stadium in the citadel," Talyn said. "I want all of the noble families there to witness. And the humans from Dock City too."

"That's too soon," Tarcos said. "Tal, you need to get some rest."

She waved him off, not noticing how his face darkened at her dismissive gesture. "First we wait for Mithanis's response. If he agrees, we'll head to Darmour immediately, get the Wolves and Falcons on ships south."

Ariar sat up, legs sliding off the table. "I'll remain here with the Aimsir and SkyRiders. We'll send two SkyRiders with you to the citadel, the rest will nest up in the SkyReach. They can be at your side in the citadel inside a day if needed. The Aimsir can protect your rear in case Montagn tries anything—like venturing across the Causeway."

Cuinn rose, smiled at the room and infused his words with confidence. "Let's get to it."

WITHIN A QUARTER-TURN, Cuinn found himself alone with his newly-betrothed in a small cavern that had its own door and tiny fire. An old mine-overseers office, he presumed. Or maybe it had even been the man's sleeping quarters—after all, anyone working a mine this far north wouldn't exactly be able to go home to Darmour for the night.

Great, he was so tired his mind was starting to wander.

He closed the door behind him and leant against it, half of him wondering if at some point during the day he'd wandered into a dream.

But then a soft smile lit up her face as she looked at him, and he knew it was real. Tears welled in her eyes, and he no longer tried to hold himself back from her. She went straight into his open arms.

"You have no idea how much I missed you," he murmured into her hair, crushing her to him so tightly it must've been almost painful, but she didn't complain. "You came back."

"I came home," she whispered. "I promised you I'd find a way."

"Are you sure about marrying me? You're not just doing it because you think it's what's best for me, or the Twin Thrones?" He stepped away and framed her face in his hands. "I want *you* to be happy. I don't care about anything else. We can find another way to make an alliance work."

"What about you?" She pushed gently on his chest, breath huffing in a laugh. "I'm the one that sprung this on you. Do *you* want to marry?"

"Talyn, I..." His throat closed over and it was a long moment before he could get any words out at all. "You have no idea."

All his life spent alone. Nobody to trust. Nobody who loved him enough to protect him or put him first. Then, to have the only person willing to love him like that murdered. He simply couldn't put into words how it felt to know that Talyn Dynan wanted to marry him.

"I feel the same," she whispered fiercely, pressing her forehead to his. "I swear it, I do. I want to marry you."

Then he was surrounding her with his arms and wings and they were laughing and crying, refusing to let go.

After a long moment, he took a breath and stepped back, a stupid grin on his face. "Well then, future wife, we'd best go out there and organise a trip to the citadel."

CHAPTER 52

*T*alyn walked out onto the green grass of the alleya stadium.
A hot sun lit up the morning, a sheen of sweat already
slicking her skin.

She wore the grey breeches and sleeveless vest of the Wolves, their
new sigil gleaming emerald over her chest. Mithanis's weapon of
choice was a sword and so today she wore one too. It hung between
her shoulders, Sari's daggers nestled at the small of her back.

Around her the stadium was rapidly filling.

News of the duel, of Cuinn's alliance with the Twin Thrones, that
SkyRiders and Aimsir were encamped on their northern border, had
spread through Dock City like wildfire. When their ship had docked
two days earlier, there had been literal crowds on the streets waiting
to greet them.

The humans were excited.

Talyn Dynan was back and had claimed her place as Ciantar. The
youngest prince had revealed himself as Shadowhawk and claimant
for the throne. A foreign power was backing them both.

But there was worry too. Cuinn had sensed it, and told her of their
fear. News had also spread that the queen was dying. Her health had
worsened, Cuinn suspected after learning what had happened, and

the healers had insisted she remain behind at the Summer Palace, that her health was too fragile for travel. It hurt him, leaving her behind, but he was resolute.

A duel with Mithanis was the one way to ensure nobody else died in a fight over the crown. But it also meant that if Talyn lost, she would likely be dead, and Cuinn soon after. Mithanis would take the throne unassailed.

And nobody had any doubts he would punish those who supported Cuinn.

The stadium had started filling up from early morning, even though the duel was set for midday. The humans sat in the western side of the stands, crammed into the tiers of seating, far outnumbering the winged folk seated in the eastern side or hovering in the sky above.

The Wolves lined the western arena wall, along with Strongswoop and some of the Falcons that had broken ranks to join the Ciantar. Windsong had volunteered to remain in the SkyReach with Grasswing and the rest to keep an eye on the queen.

Tarcos had wanted to be there, but Talyn had asked him to remain in the Summer Palace with his Bearmen. If the fight didn't go the way she hoped, well... she liked the idea of a unit of fierce Bearman covering their backs if they needed to flee north.

Falcons loyal to Mithanis lined the opposite wall. Ravinire stood with neither party, alone at the top of the field.

In stark contrast to the alleya game the Wolves had won, the crowd was silent. Human and winged folk alike would be heavily affected by the outcome of this fight. There was no enjoyment here, only unease, fear and faint hope.

For the humans, if Mithanis won, their lives would only become worse. For the winged folk, if Talyn won, their futures and elevated position in Mithranan society were thrown in doubt. Cuinn as a ruler was an unknown quantity. They knew him only as the indolent, playboy prince. If she won today, he had a lot of work ahead of him correcting those beliefs.

She had no doubts he would succeed.

Calm, confident as always before a fight, she walked to the centre of the field and stopped to wait. A tiny breeze kicked up, pleasurably cool as it skimmed across her heated skin. She breathed deeply, glad beyond words to be breathing Mithranan air once again.

A murmur rippled through the human crowd. Curious, for Mithanis would not make his appearance for another few minutes, she turned. The whisper of sound spread through the tiered seating like a wave, until even the winged folk rustled in surprise.

Looking at the Wolves, Talyn saw that they were all looking upwards. She followed their gaze, her breath catching in her throat.

Cuinn spiralled down from the sky toward her. His silver-white wings shone brilliantly in the sun, and his golden hair was framed in its light. His emerald eyes held hers as he walked the few paces towards her, then offered her his hand.

She took the hand, shook it. Then raised her fist to clench over her heart. He did the same. A formal acknowledgement between an heir to the throne and his Ciantar. An audible gasp swept through the stadium.

"Burn bright and true," he murmured.

She smiled. "Burn bright and true."

Cuinn stepped slowly backwards, eyes never leaving hers. Then, he spread his wings and leapt into the air. The human crowd cheered him as he returned to land beside the Wolf talons.

The winged folk were silent.

With that, Mithanis walked out into the stadium. He came with long, measured strides, ebony wings held stiff behind him. His aura screamed with magic that he made no attempt to hide and his eyes were alive with menace and a confidence that rivalled Talyn's. Neither of them doubted who was going to win this fight.

One of them was going to be wrong.

Talyn stood calmly as he approached. She didn't doubt her abilities, would never doubt them again after Mithranar and the Wolves had taught her how to heal, but this adversary would be the sternest test she'd ever faced as a warrior.

"You're going to own him. And not just because you're the best fighter I've

ever seen. He underestimates you, he always has, and it's going to be a fatal weakness."

A smile curled at her mouth. *"Thanks, Sari."*

"Let's make the terms of today's duel clear." Mithanis spoke loud and clear, his voice carrying at least as far as the Wolves and Falcons lining the stadium. It was hard to tell how he felt, but there was anger and frustration there, burning under his façade. He must hate that his youngest brother had challenged him, that he hadn't seen it coming, that he was now facing a Twin Thrones military force that his Wing-Guard could not match. That he'd been left with no choice but this duel.

"A good idea," she said, simply.

"I am here to kill you," he said. "And when you are dead, I will kill your Wolves and my brother, and I will be king of Mithranar."

"And when *I* win, you will be arrested and Prince Cuinn will take the throne of Mithranar," she said coolly.

Mithanis's eyes narrowed. "Arrogance isn't going to help you. You will die just as quickly as your grandfather."

"Then let's get to it, shall we?"

Mithanis stepped back as Brightwing approached—the duel's referee.

Brightwing held his hand high, a small cotton flag fluttering in the breeze. "When I drop this flag, the fight begins."

Talyn focused her entire attention on Mithanis. She calmed her breathing and her thoughts. The menace seeping from him was as palpable as the thick humidity of the air. But Sari was also right. He was facing an opponent he didn't fully understand, his winged folk arrogance making him incapable of seeing her for what she was.

The prince of night attacked the moment Brightwing let go of the flag. He lashed out with his song magic, wrapping her in the darkest of emotions, despair and failure, using them to squeeze and crush her.

For a moment he had her.

She hadn't expected such a quick magical attack. But then, cold fury swept through her. A deep, focused breath, and she *ignored* his magic, using the cool self-control she'd mastered years ago to focus on the fight rather than on what she was feeling.

Then she raised her hands and sent two sapphire energy bolts right at him. He only barely avoided them by leaping into the air, his song magic cutting off as his focus collapsed. The drain on her magic was instant and noticeable. She wouldn't be able to do much more of that.

It didn't matter. She smiled. Cuinn had told her Mithanis didn't have the level of skill necessary to use multiple magics concurrently. He came at her a second later, snarling, drawing his sword with a loud ring of steel.

Good. That was the kind of fight she wanted.

Talyn drew her sword and countered Mithanis's downward strike with ease. Using his momentum against him, she danced sideways and swung at his head. He dodged aside and thrust upwards. She brushed the thrust aside and went for his head again.

He twisted away, dropping low to the ground, wings flared for balance. She ran at him, wanting to keep him engaged in the physical fight, prevent him from gathering the focus needed to throw magic at her again.

They fought without respite, feet moving in a blur over the grass, blades clanging together over and over. Mithanis was a skilled fighter but he also used small bursts of magic to assist him. More than once, Talyn almost cut through his guard, only to slip at the last moment as a flare of his song magic would shift her focus *just* enough to send her strike off target.

She didn't back away, not for one second, not even for a breath. Their swords slammed over and over and over, feet dancing, ducking and rolling whenever he leapt into the air or flew at her. Sweat slicked her skin, dripped from her hair and the hilt of her sword.

Mithanis was a match for her. His skill was superb, his strength and conditioning equal to hers. And he had wings to aid him, not to mention his magic. Talyn gritted her teeth and kept going.

They went back and forth for what began to feel like an eternity. Their focus was entirely on each other, and everything around her faded, everything but those dark eyes and the hunger to defeat her written all over his handsome face.

And then, after a furious flurry of clashing blades, they broke off, a tacit agreement for a breather. She was reluctant to concede the need for a break, but the air burned in her lungs and her sword arm was beginning to tremble. His blows were powerful, delivered with the superior power of the flight muscles in his shoulders, and countering them had drained the strength in her arms.

Around them the stadium was utterly silent. Even through her focus she'd noted the quiet. Not a single cheer. No cries of support. It was like the entire population was holding its breath on the outcome of this fight.

Which they probably were.

Taking deep, gulping breaths, Talyn tossed the sword away and drew both her daggers. These were lighter, smaller, and they were her weapon of choice. Her heart thudded in her chest, and the familiar burn of effort sang in her bones and muscles, sweat slicking her skin —this was what she lived for.

"Talyn, I have an idea."

Talyn heard Sari out, then drew another deep breath. Mithanis shifted. He was about to attack again. *"That's risky."*

"When was anything we ever did not risky?"

"You make a good point."

Talyn and Mithanis both moved at the same time, meeting in the middle with a renewed clashing of blades. Talyn deflected his thrust with a dagger, shoved it aside, then slashed her other dagger at his throat. His wings flared and he leaned away, the blade sliding harmlessly through the air.

When he came at her again, she forced herself to be a step slower, reduced the intensity of her attacks. Nothing too obvious or overt. She just wanted to give him a bit of confidence, let him settle into the fight, feel like he had the upper hand. So then he could...

It happened slowly. His dark eyes gleamed when she stumbled slightly, when one of his thrusts sliced a shallow gash in her left arm after she was too slow to get fully out of the way. It stung. She ignored it.

Then he used his magic again. Stepping back with a flare of his wings, thinking her tiring too quickly to come at him, he opened his mouth and roared, the sound infused with the full depth of his magic.

She cried out as it hit her, enveloping her in an onrushing wave that she was helpless to resist. It left her body vulnerable, and he took full advantage, leaping for her, thrusting his sword straight at her heart.

Gathering every bit of magic she had, Talyn lifted a hand and erected her shield. The sapphire light glimmered brightly, crackling and hissing. He backed off, switching to using his magic to attack her mind, her spirit. His voice sang, deep and powerful.

Which was what Sari had wanted.

With an effort, Talyn relaxed her self-control and allowed him in. She sensed his surprise, then his triumph as he barrelled through her emotions, exploding through her with fear and doubt and despair.

Until his magic hit Sari, surging through Talyn's mind to slam into him.

And then, for the first time in three years, Talyn and Sari were back together, fighting side by side with their Callanan magic, seamless and ruthless.

And invincible.

Mithanis screamed. His powerful roar turned into a thing of shock and infuriated puzzlement.

Sari and Talyn entangled his magic with theirs, chasing him out of her emotions and throwing them back at him like a mirror. He cried out and staggered backwards. Talyn's eyes snapped open. Mithanis's hair was plastered to his head with sweat and his wings were limp at his sides. He was looking at her with stunned horror.

She dropped her shield. Stood before him knowing the balance of the fight had just tipped her way.

And in the background now there was a steady roar. The crowd she'd completely forgotten about. They began chanting her name in a steady, thumping rhythm.

The humans of Dock City screaming for their Wolf captain. Their Ciantar.

Buoyed by the crowd and Sari still with her, she lifted her daggers and went for the prince of night, a blur of blades, *sabai* and cold, deadly purpose.

Mithanis fought back bitterly, but his magic was depleted and Talyn the superior fighter. In the end, her right dagger curled around his blade, sending it flying with a sharp twist of her wrist, and then her left dagger was slashing in, turning at the last moment to slam hilt-first into the side of his head.

Mithanis swayed, blinking, then crumpled to the ground and lay there, stunned. Talyn crouched over him and placed Sari's dagger at his throat, pressing it in enough so that a trickle of red ran down to the grass. For a long moment, she crouched there, muscles trembling as she fought not to drive it home.

A better Mithranar. That's what she and Cuinn would build. And it didn't begin with death.

"Do you concede?"

He didn't want to die. He was furious and cowed and beaten, but he didn't want to die. So the prince of night nodded once, his dark eyes sliding away from her face, unable to look her in the eye.

"*Thanks, partner.*"

"*Anytime.*"

She stood up, stepped away, and lifted both arms into the air, claiming victory as the roar of the crowd swept around her.

Finally, it was over.

CHAPTER 53

*E*xhaustion was setting in, the adrenalin of the fight fading, as Theac and her talons came over to escort Talyn off the field. Strongswoop and several Falcons went straight to Mithanis, binding his wrists firmly and dragging him to his feet. Ravinire had vanished.

"Ciantar, what do you want us to do with him?" Strongswoop flew over to ask.

"Lock him up, and make sure he can't use his magic on the guards to escape. Have them wear something to block their hearing when they're outside his door," she said. "It will be up to Cuinn to decide what to do with him."

"Ciantar!" Strongswoop saluted sharply, then turned to relay her orders to his men.

She swept her gaze over the stadium, looking for Cuinn, finding him landing amongst the winged folk, where the Queencouncil families had their viewing platforms.

Good.

"You'll let Jystar take a look at you at once, Ciantar." Theac's barking voice caught her attention, brooking no refusal.

She acquiesced. Mithanis hadn't landed any crippling blows, but she had numerous gashes that were bleeding and sore and it would be wise to get that dealt with before she keeled over from blood loss.

"Bring him to my quarters." She mustered a smile.

With Theac and Zamaril at each side, and Lyra, Liadin, Halun, Andres and Corrin encircling her completely, they walked to her old quarters in the Wolves barracks. It was a slow trip. While she refused to lean on any of them, the wounds and exhaustion had her almost stumbling by the time they reached her front door.

Afternoon sun flooded her room with heat and light, Zamaril carefully checking the space to ensure it was safe as she dropped onto the edge of her bed before her legs gave out completely. Theac went to open the glass balcony door in an effort to ease some of the stuffiness in the room.

By the time Zamaril assured himself the area was safe, Halun appeared at the top of the spiral staircase, a steaming mug in his hand. Jystar was a step behind, carrying his healing bag. Halun handed the mug to her with a little smile. "This will help."

Talyn sipped the liquid, which turned out to be kahvi. The drink left a trail of warmth down to her stomach, and gave her a renewed jolt of energy.

"Halun, I love you," she breathed, closing her eyes in bliss.

Theac hovered like a mother hen. "Are there any wounds we need to worry about?"

"I'm fine, Theac, just a few scratches and bruises. Nothing life threatening."

Jystar gave her a brief smile then got to work. Once he was done cleaning and bandaging her cuts, he knelt at her feet, eyes closed, palm on her knee, and used his magic on her. By the time he stood up, she felt almost normal again. "Thank you, Jystar, you're wonderful."

"Ciantar." He nodded tersely, but a little smile hovered on his face. "You'll let me know if any of those cuts turn more painful than they should, or don't look like they're healing properly?"

"I will," she promised him.

"There you are." A musical voice came from the doorway. All of them turned as Cuinn walked in. He looked tired too, like he'd been using his magic, but his face was relaxed, calm.

"How did you go with the lords?" she asked, coming to her feet.

He let out a sigh. "They are severely unhappy. But most of that stems from fear. They don't know how to deal with a world where Mithanis is gone and I'm potentially their next king."

"Potentially?" She lifted an eyebrow.

"Mother is still alive, as is Azrilan. It's not a guarantee they'll choose me as heir," Cuinn pointed out. "They don't like that I have the backing of a foreign kingdom, nor that I spent most of my life convincing them that I was worthless. And it makes them extremely uneasy that I was the Shadowhawk, though I've been at pains to point out that I never willingly hurt a Falcon. I will need to prove myself. It will be the same for you, I fear, despite Ravinire willingly handing over the reins of the WingGuard."

Theac looked astonished. "He did?"

Cuinn nodded. "He left the orders with one of his flight-leaders and then disappeared."

"The Ciantar has truly returned," Halun's eyes were bright.

"Can't the Dumnorix insist Azrilan stands down too?" Theac asked.

"We could," Talyn offered. "Ariar is still here."

"No. I'd like to have as much legitimacy as I can. I need to beat Azrilan, if he wants to be heir, in front of the Queencouncil." Cuinn was firm. "Now that Mithanis is dealt with, we need to take the throne without any further interference from outside."

She shrugged, wincing as the stitched wound on her arm pulled. "I have no doubt they'll eventually choose you. Azrilan was always in Mithanis' shadow, as terrified of him as everyone else."

"We should send Ariar home too. Being chosen over Azrilan won't mean anything if two hundred Aimsir and six legions of SkyRiders are shadowing the whole thing," Cuinn added.

She nodded slowly. Cuinn was right, and Ariar was needed back in the Twin Thrones. "I'll send the SkyRider scout back to Ariar and

Tarcos tonight. Let them know we won, and they should leave it to us from here."

He studied her a moment, green eyes steady on hers. "Wolves, give us the room please."

Theac straightened with alacrity before moving to the door. When Jystar and Halun did not instantly follow, he barked at them to hurry up. Their boots thudded on the iron stairs and then Theac's voice drifted up from below, banishing everyone from her quarters and ordering Halun's detail to take up Cuinn's guard shift.

Zamaril's voice sounded then—presumably arguing he would need to ensure Talyn was guarded properly—and the two men's voices murmured back and forth until the front door closed behind them.

"Are you hurt?" Cuinn's eyes were soft with worry as he crossed to stand before her.

"Just a few scratches." She smiled, leaning forward to press her forehead against his chest. "I'm fine."

"Are you sure?" Worry hit her then, *his* worry. For her. He hadn't even made a murmur of complaint when she'd suggested fighting Mithanis, yet he knew his brother's strength and power better than anyone alive. He'd had faith in her, as always, to make her own choices. To win her battles. And he'd hidden his worry, to prevent it being a burden on her.

"Cuinn," she whispered, reaching up to frame his face with her hands. "I love you. I'm sorry I've never said it before. You deserve better than that. Better than my fear."

"You didn't need to say it." He gently pulled her into his arms.

"I still should have said it. I love you. With everything I am."

He smiled. "I'm glad you're home, Talyn Ciantar."

And then he kissed her.

CHAPTER 54

*T*he following day, Talyn convened the WingGuard leaders, calling upon the title of Ciantar to get all the captains and flight-leaders into the Falcon's war room.

Right now, Cuinn's first priority was winning the lords, being named heir and establishing firm leadership. Hers was winning the WingGuard and preparing them for a Montagni invasion.

The fact they showed up was promising.

Still, the majority of Ravinire's flight-leaders and captains had never liked Talyn, and that hadn't changed despite the previous day's events. And until Cuinn was confirmed as heir, or the queen rose from her sickbed to give a direct order, those who disliked Talyn most would resist her leadership.

She faced a table of captains and flight-leaders who all wore expressions like they'd eaten something sour for breakfast. Brightwing had apparently resigned his position with the WingGuard in a furious rant in the WingGuard barracks. Only a handful of those present looked pleased to see her there—and all but one or two of those were her talons. The Falcons who'd sworn loyalty to Talyn and Cuinn, she'd already sent back to the SkyReach to report to Windsong.

She wanted loyal soldiers manning the north in case of a sooner-than-expected invasion.

Theac, standing at her side along with Strongswoop, leaned over to murmur in her ear. "You won us over. You can do it with this lot too."

"Thanks," she muttered. "Any ideas on how to go about it?"

"Absolutely none," he said cheerfully.

"My thoughts," Strongswoop offered. "Make too many changes too quickly and you'll never win them. They'll simply wait until Azrilan reappears from Montagn and flock to him. Whether the prince of games wants the throne or not, it will only make trouble for Prince Cuinn."

She nodded acceptance of that.

"You don't like me or trust me." She addressed the room. "But despite all that, I know that you can't have missed the effective force I have built the Wolves into. If you haven't noticed, then you don't have the right mindset for being a soldier." She paused. "I can make you and your wings just as effective as the Wolves."

Muttering broke out, some rustling feathers. Most of it was indignation that she'd suggest the Falcons weren't as good as the Wolves. She swallowed a sigh.

"You're not good right now," she said bluntly. "But you will be. I will make it so that next time Aimsir and SkyRiders breach your borders, you won't need to submit. You'll be able to fight back."

More dark looks and muttering. That was fine. Theac was right. It had taken months to win the Wolves, and she'd done it with actions, not words.

"For now all of you will keep your ranks, but you'll attend training with the Wolves over the next weeks—you *and* your warriors," she told them. "You will be assessed during that time, and if you demonstrate your ability to lead, work hard, and treat your fellow warriors with respect, you will keep your ranks."

"I'm not going through any test," one captain said angrily.

She was tempted to tell them that they might be facing war at any moment, that they *needed* to listen to her because they might have very little time to develop into a capable army. But she held back. That might panic them. She needed to win their trust before she laid all that on them.

"That's fine," Talyn said evenly. "I don't want anybody in the Wing-Guard who doesn't want to be here. You're all free to resign without consequence."

Two Falcons did get up and leave, slamming the door behind them. The rest muttered under their breath and directed dark looks her way.

But they stayed in the room.

ONCE SHE ENDED the meeting and the Falcons had filed out, leaving her with the talons, Andres shifted in his chair. "You want us to assess close to two hundred Falcon officers in a few weeks?"

"I know it will be difficult, but we're going to need a competent army sooner than we'd like." Talyn sat too.

He nodded. "We'll get it done, Ciantar."

"Theac, you'll now be the Wolf captain. Does anybody have any objections to that?"

All shook their heads.

"Zamaril, you'll stay in your position as captain of my detail, just a small one. Say twenty warriors, with five on shift at any one time." The idea of having a guard made her itch with frustration and bruised ego, but if she was going to be marrying the king of Mithranar, she needed to look the part. At least Zamaril she could trust with anything.

Theac cleared his throat. "Not meaning to pry, lass, but you and the prince...?"

"Me and the prince what, Theac?" She lifted an eyebrow.

"Getting married," Zamaril said bluntly.

Talyn chuckled and rose. "Yes, that is the agreement underpinning our new alliance with the Twin Thrones." She paused. "Not that I'm displeased by the idea."

"Nor are we, Ciantar," Corrin said gravely, a smile twitching at his mouth.

LATE IN THE AFTERNOON, Talyn went down to Dock City. She ordered a cup of kahvi from Petro and sat down with him for a chat. Not long after she'd arrived, the mayor showed up and joined them.

She directed a sour look at Petro. "You tattled on me?"

"He's been wanting to see you." Petro lifted his hands helplessly. "And he *is* the mayor."

"Can you blame the mayor of Dock City wanting to speak with the country's new Ciantar and future queen?" Doran lifted both eyebrows.

"I suppose not." She sighed inwardly.

"*You're going to be a queen,*" Sari said in glee.

"*Don't start,*" Talyn warned.

"I couldn't believe it when Prince Cuinn revealed himself as the Shadowhawk," Petro said wonderingly as he served hot kahvi to the mayor then sat down. "To think the man I'd been helping all this time was an Acondor prince. I'm still struggling to understand it."

"We had wondered about your devotion to his protection," Doran added, then gave her a sober look. "You already know this, but he has the support of every human in Mithranar."

"As do you, Ciantar," Petro said. "You have to know that this is a dream come true for us. Real change has become a possibility—it's hard to believe."

"Don't be too happy," she said quietly. "We still have troubled times ahead."

"Too true," Doran said gravely. "But if there is anything we can do to help, don't forget you have allies here, Ciantar. Allies a winged ruler of Mithranar has not had for decades."

BEFORE RETURNING TO HER QUARTERS, Talyn walked up the barracks stairs to the hallway that held the talons' private rooms. Tiercelin's remained empty, his things still scattered around, untouched since the explosion.

She went inside, sitting carefully in the chair by the small window, smiling at the messy stacks of parchment on his desk lit up by the afternoon sun.

She stayed there a while, eyes closed, breathing in the combined scents of parchment and his healing herbs lining a chest nearby and revelling in the rightness she felt—no matter what came ahead, she was where she was supposed to be. There was no fear of having to go back anymore. She was home.

"Thank you, Sari."

"What are partners for? I'm glad you listened to me, Tal. And look at you, agreeing to marry someone! I genuinely never thought I'd see the day."

"A wedding like this... to seal an alliance... we'll have to do it properly. Pomp and ceremony and all that." She hesitated. *"I'd like Roan and Tarquin to be there for it."*

"So would I," Sari whispered.

CHAPTER 55

$\mathcal{T}$alyn found Cuinn at the railing of the royal pool, soaking up the fading sun of the day. Jasper was sprawled on the marble at his feet, sound asleep. He didn't even twitch at Talyn's approach.

"I'll never understand you Mithranans' enjoyment of this ridiculous heat," she grumbled half-heartedly.

"It grows on you, no?" He turned with a wink.

"I just got a message via SkyRider from Ariar." She showed him the creased parchment with Ariar's messy handwriting. "Confirming they reached the ships safely and were boarding as he wrote. They'll be on their way home by now."

Cuinn's smile widened as he read her cousin's parting words.

I look forward with great delight to the oncoming battle between you and Alyna over whether this wedding is held in Port Lachley or Mithranar. Either way, I can't wait to see you both again. Stay safe, Cousin. Cuinn too.

Ariar

"I got a message too," Cuinn said, smile fading. "Azrilan should be here in a few days. I've called a formal Queencouncil meeting for when he arrives. The lords have agreed to confirm one of us as heir at that meeting."

Ah. This explained finding him alone staring off into the distance.

She frowned. "No message from your mother? Should we wait until she's well enough to travel here? Or we could go there."

Cuinn swallowed. "She's too ill to participate... her healers say she's mostly unconscious now. And I want the decision to happen here, where my support base is, not far to the north. If the lords choose Azrilan..."

"They won't," she assured him. Cuinn had been working furiously, not just with the Queencouncil lords, but the rest of winged folk nobility too. And it was already becoming clear to them how he intended to rule. Mithanis sat imprisoned, ready to be ruled upon once someone was on the throne, not dead. His supporters were still alive and free and had been actively included by Cuinn in the first Queencouncil meeting since Mithanis's defeat.

"I'm glad." A troubled expression crossed his face. "We need this sorted so we can start preparing for what comes next. Your king was assassinated, Talyn, and your Callanan still believe Montagn wants to invade."

"With such turmoil of leadership here, they may decide this is a good time to do it, too," she said softly.

"What if it *was* Montagn behind Aethain's death?" Cuinn turned to her, worry in his green eyes. "What if they want everything? Can we stand against that?"

"We can and we will," she said simply. "Us, Firthland, the Twin Thrones. We all fight together now."

Shadows crept into his eyes. "It won't be easy. There will be war. People will die."

"I know." She dreaded the thought too, even though she didn't have his magic. "But if war comes for us, we have no choice but to fight."

He smiled then. It was a fragile thing, but it was there. "Together?"

"Always together."

"Ciantar?" Zamaril interrupted the little bubble of warmth that had built up between them. He'd appeared without her realising.

She turned to him. "Something wrong?"

"Savin contacted me," the thief said. "He wants you to meet him down in Dock City now, on the corner near Petro's café. He says it's urgent but extremely sensitive. He wanted to meet with you alone, but I insisted on being with you."

She let out a breath of relief. "Then we'd better go meet him. Hopefully he has something that can help us." Maybe he could confirm Vengeance was gone, and hadn't been in Port Lachley murdering her uncle and his wife. If they could do that, it meant someone or something else was behind the assassination. Maybe it wasn't an indication that Montagn was about to unleash its mighty armies on the rest of the world.

Cuinn caught her hand as she turned to walk away, tugging her back in for a kiss. "Don't stay away long."

"Don't worry," she leaned up to murmur in his ear. "I'll be back later to warm your bed, Prince Cuinn."

"I love you," he whispered.

"And I you." She kissed him once more, then turned and walked away.

Halun, in command of Cuinn's current detail, offered her his quiet smile as she and Zamaril passed him. "Stay safe, Captain."

"I will. You just concentrate on keeping my future husband protected." Her mouth quirked in a smile.

He bowed his head, serious despite her joking words. "Always, Captain."

SAVIN FELL into step with them as they approached Petro's, appearing out of the growing shadows of dusk without warning.

"Nice of you to join us," she said dryly, refusing to show him she'd been startled.

"You've been busy," he said. "Word came a week ago of your formal alliance with Prince Cuinn. The Shadowlord himself has instructed me to place all the Armun resources in Dock City at your disposal."

"Orders from Warlord Hadvezer?" she confirmed.

"That's right." A smile ghosted over Savin's bland face, an oddly triumphant note to it. "The Shadowlord's orders come direct from him."

"And it's taken you this long to come to me?" she asked with a hint of annoyance. They could have been using those Armun resources.

"I've been in the middle of something." He waved a dismissive hand. "Vengeance are back."

Her gaze snapped to his. "What? Are you sure?"

"The report of your alliance included information on the assassination of King Aethain. The moment I read that the attackers had been wearing copper masks, I dropped everything else I was working on," he said. "It took me almost the entirety of last week, because they've been hiding their tracks so well. But I found them—one of my informants spotted a Vengeance member and followed him."

"Where?"

"He was heading back to their old compound beyond the wall." Savin slowed as they approached the izerdia workers' tunnel entrance. "We need to get in there and find out how many of them remain, how much strength they've rebuilt. But we don't want them to know we've found them, so rather than using their tunnel, I figured we could take this one."

"You want to go beyond the wall now?" Zamaril glanced up at the fading light. "That's a decent hike through tawncat infested forest, Savin."

"If Vengeance are back, do you think confirming it should wait until tomorrow?" Savin asked. "If they were behind the assassination of King Aethain, we need to take care of them sooner rather than later."

Zamaril glanced at Talyn. "Then maybe we should go back and get your full detail to take with us?"

"And have Vengeance hear us coming a mile away?" She shook her head. She was Callanan trained, Savin was a Shadow and Zamaril a thief. They'd do better slipping in and out alone. Once they had a thorough look and understood numbers and defences, Talyn would come back tomorrow with the WingGuard and raze them to the ground. It would be a good test for them.

They waited until all the day's workers had climbed up out of the tunnels, then Zamaril held the grating open while Savin and Talyn climbed down before following.

"No lights," Savin said when she reached for one of the lamps left behind from the workers.

"Not all of us can wrap ourselves in shadows like you can, Savin," she grumbled.

"Stick close and you'll be fine."

So she followed him into the darkness.

CHAPTER 56

"You're dining with Lord Nightdrift tonight, Your Highness?" Corrin asked as Cuinn emerged from his tower. His detail had just taken over from Halun's. Behind him, Jasper snarled, tail whipping around angrily, upset as always about being left behind. Cuinn adored the tawncat, but the last thing he needed was Jasper trying to eat Charl Nightdrift in the middle of dinner. That wouldn't help his efforts to get a powerful Queencouncil member on his side.

"Yes." He'd been making time to eat with all the lords in recent days, using his mother's formal dining room, a room that would hopefully soon be his. "As sour and grief-stricken as Charl is, I think he might actually vote for me."

Corrin nodded and fell into step with Cuinn as they walked. He flew less now, so that his full detail could accompany him at all times, and he always had the talon of his detail walking at his side. A mark of respect to those dedicated to keeping him alive.

He hoped Talyn hurried back from her mysterious chat with Savin. He vastly preferred having her with him at these dinners. Warrior to her bones, she nonetheless understood the niceties of court behaviour. Plus, he enjoyed watching for her subtle tells when she got bored, which on average was about a quarter-turn into the dinner.

"I'll try and keep this one short so you all don't have to stand around too long," he said to Corrin as they approached the dining rooms.

"Do what you need to do, Your Highness. We'll be fine."

Cuinn opened the door and walked inside, stopping dead in surprise at the sight of Azrilan sitting at the head of the dining table, alone. Nightdrift was nowhere to be seen. "Az, you're back. I didn't expect you for a few days yet."

Azrilan stood slowly. "News of our elder brother's humiliating defeat spurred me on. You did well, Cuinn. Or should I say, your Ciantar did."

Cuinn met his stare. There was no point prevaricating—best to get the obvious issue out of the way immediately. "I want to be named heir."

"I thought you might." Azrilan smiled faintly.

A knock thudded on the door, then Theac entered, scowling. He paused in surprise at seeing Azrilan, but then continued straight to Cuinn. "Your Highness. One of Talon Strongswoop's scouts on the south-eastern headland just flew in. He reports ships approaching Feather Bay. They're flying the Firthlander flag."

Cuinn frowned in confusion. "Merchants?"

"He wasn't sure, Your Highness."

"Then get Strongswoop to send more scouts to find out."

"No need." A tall, imposing figure stepped out of the shadows on the other side of the room. "You'll find there are twenty ships. Carrying Bearmen and six legions of niever-flyers."

Silence filled the room. It was heavy and full of creeping unease.

What was Tarcos Hadvezer doing here?

"Tarcos." Cuinn glanced between him and Azrilan. His magic rose unbidden, warning him with a sharp thrill of unease and danger. "Why are twenty of your ships approaching my harbour?"

"*Your* harbour?" Azrilan asked with a little smile.

"They're here to blockade it." Tarcos took another step forward, voice calm with a hint of surprise, as if Cuinn had asked a silly question. "And help my friend take the throne of Mithranar. From you."

Cuinn's gaze narrowed, heart beginning to thud. Ice curled through his veins.

The sickening realisation was far, far too late in coming. All three brothers—all three Mithranan princes—were song mages. All three were equally powerful. But Cuinn had thought *he* was the only one who was using his magic to fool the rest.

When this whole time...Azrilan had been too.

And Azrilan was clever. Smarter than Mithanis. More rational. Which meant this wasn't a spur of the moment decision. This was planned. A long time in the building.

And he would know Talyn was his greatest threat.

Terror gripped Cuinn.

Where was she?

CHAPTER 57

hey walked through the dark tunnel, Savin in the lead and barely visible, Zamaril a shadow at her side. A tiny amount of light filtered down from the grates in the city street high above, but once they reached the wall it would be gone completely.

"*Talyn.*"

She stopped dead. She'd only ever heard that tone from her partner a handful of times before. The Callanan lauded Talyn's instincts, her sharp strategic awareness, but Sari had never been wrong, not once, when the two were about to make the wrong move. Except for that one day.

"Captain?" Savin's voice, slightly irritated as usual, floated back.

"Sorry, just a stone in my boot," she said, continuing to walk after rubbing at the leather for effect. Her heart thudded and she began scanning her surroundings, fear creeping through her chest despite her best efforts.

Zamaril was suddenly there then, pale blue eyes glimmering up at hers. He felt it too. That confirmation of her instinct hit her like a punch in the stomach.

"Tell me more about your informant, Savin," she asked lightly. "How credible are they?"

"They've never given me wrong information in the past."

"Talyn, stop now."

So she did.

Zamaril remained at her side, not even asking what she was doing. Ahead of them Savin stopped, turned back. "What's wrong?"

"Talyn. I'm sorry. I didn't see this."

"That's okay," Talyn said helplessly. *"I didn't either."*

"It was you." She whispered, the sense of impotent frustration and despair building in her so strongly she could barely get those words out. "This whole time. I missed it." And now she was going to die for it.

Because that's why Savin had brought them down here. Using his Shadow skills of manipulation and trickery to draw them in. To die.

Navis. Savin. Navis. Savin.

The same man. She'd missed the obvious. It had been right in front of her face. The Shadowhawk's informant, using him to find Saniya, to turn her group into Vengeance. But how had a Firthlander Shadow become a Montagni agent?

"Your instincts really are remarkable," Savin said, moving back towards them. "A tad too late in this case, I'm afraid."

"Why?"

"Like you, Talyn Dynan, I am loyal to my leader."

"The warlord of Firthland didn't order this." She shook her head. "Which makes you a traitor."

"Ah, but the warlord of Firthland *did* order this."

There was no humanity in Savin's face now that he was no longer hiding from them.

"Zamaril, you have to get out. You have to warn Cuinn." She kept her voice composed, breathing steady. Her mind worked overdrive to figure some way out of this.

"I'm not leaving your side." The thief's lips were curled in a snarl as he eyed Savin.

The Shadow smiled, made a sharp gesture. Steel rang and boots crunched. Someone lit a torch, tossed it onto the ground between Talyn and Savin. It cast an orange glow on the multiple figures in the shadows. They were surrounded. She'd known it from the moment Sari's voice had sounded in her head.

Talyn swallowed, drew both her daggers.

"I think I preferred your way of dying, Sari. Not knowing what was coming."

"You're going to get out of this," her partner hissed fiercely.

"I don't think so. Savin knows me. He will have brought enough men to take us down."

Talyn turned. She couldn't make out the details of any of those encircling them, they were too much in shadow, not quite close enough for the light to reach them. That was good. It would give her the time she needed.

"Zamaril, my friend, it's been an honour."

He flashed her his cocky smile. "Ciantar. I would die no other way."

Savin barked a bitter laugh. "It's been hard to keep a straight face around all your touching sentiment, Talyn Dynan."

"Savin?" Talyn asked, fingers sliding around the cool grips of Sari's daggers. "You don't think you're actually getting out of this alive, do you?"

He blanched as he read the intent on her face. "Take them, now!"

But she was already launching into movement, sprinting after him as he turned to run, sacrificing any chance to get out—because she wasn't getting out of this—to take Savin with her.

She collided with him, shoved him hard into the ground, then crouched over him. His face contorted in a rictus of anger and helpless frustration. "Goodbye, Savin," she snarled, and buried her dagger in his heart.

Then they were behind her, Zamaril desperately trying to hold them off, but failing from sheer weight of numbers. Talyn's eyes widened, shock coursing through her at seeing who was attacking them. She pushed off, leapt towards the closest Bearman, but was hauled back mid-jump as a brawny arm wrapped around her from behind.

A burning hot line of pain erupted from her right side—a blade driving in deep. A scream escaped her, and she turned, writhing out of his grip, only for another arm to wrap itself around her throat, cutting off her air.

And then she was done.

CHAPTER 58

*H*ow had he missed this?

Cuinn faced Tarcos and Azrilan across the room, not knowing what to do, or say. The world had spun on its axis and the new reality—the reality that had been there all along—had him undone.

Tarcos smiled. There was no warmth in the smile, only cold enjoyment. "There's no use getting upset. I'm doing nothing different than what Talyn did. Using force to get what I want. It was probably a little early to send Ariar home though, wasn't it?"

The mention of Talyn's name on the prince's lips sent another stab of terror ripping through Cuinn. Heart thudding, he turned to the Wolf captain. "Theac, where's Talyn?"

"I don't know." Grim lines settled into the veteran's face.

"She hasn't come back from her meeting with Savin?"

Theac turned to Corrin, lifting an eyebrow. The young man shook his head. "I haven't seen either of them."

"Go find out where they are," Theac barked at him.

Corrin was out the door before anyone could move or respond.

Fear gripped Cuinn's chest in a vice so strong it was an effort to remain standing. Wherever she was, Azrilan and Tarcos knew too well the threat she posed. They wouldn't be confronting him like this, wouldn't be making their move, unless they thought she was contained.

Then the citadel alarm bells starting ringing.

He swallowed, managed to rasp out the words, "You're attacking us, *Prince* Hadvezer?"

"Tarcos is just blockading the harbour until your Wolves and any rogue WingGuard agree to stand down," Azrilan said lightly, conversationally. "There's no need for unpleasantness. Let's just sit down and talk."

"Why are you helping him?" Cuinn stared at Tarcos. "You're her friend."

"She was my way to a Dumnorix bride and an easier way of taking what I wanted," Tarcos said flatly. "Until she refused me. Now she's just in the way."

That wasn't true, not entirely. Cuinn's magic told him that. Tarcos may have had ulterior motives, but he felt something for Talyn. Despite the fact Cuinn was out of his mind with fear, he pushed at the crack in Tarcos's armour, seeking a way out of this. "So you're fine with my brother killing her? You know that he won't let her live. He can't afford to."

Tarcos blinked, appeared to hesitate, then that fierce look filled his features again. "She refused me, repeatedly. I'm done with her."

Cuinn swallowed, mind racing. It didn't make any sense. Why was Tarcos helping Azrilan? How did they even know each other?

Focus. He had to focus. The why could come later. Right now he needed to figure out a way to survive this.

"So what?" Theac barked suddenly, moving in a blink until he was standing before Cuinn. "You kill them and then hand your feathered friend the Mithranan throne. What do you get out of it?"

He was stalling for time. Cuinn scanned the room, mind racing. First step was getting out, finding Talyn. Maybe they could stop the ships—

"Careful how you address me, human filth." Azrilan's form blurred as he spread his wings to leap across the room and stand before

Theac. "You aren't just addressing the king of Mithranar. You stand before the new ahara of Montagn."

Silence draped like a cloak over the room. Tarcos was smiling slightly. Azrilan's charcoal eyes were flushed with triumph. Matching emotion slammed into Cuinn like a runaway horse. Azrilan wasn't lying.

"You..." Cuinn's voice trailed off. The plans forming in his head faded away. Ahara?

"I didn't *flee* to Montagn, Brother." Azrilan chuckled. "I waited until Mother finally made the decision to name her heir, and then went to Arataire to start the spill. My House had everything in place, ready for the right time."

The magnitude of what Azrilan had pulled off was astounding. Realisation was slow, too slow in coming. He'd missed all of it. Guilt and shock and fear writhed through him, scattering his thoughts, making it hard to figure out a countermove.

"You're not the only one who can use song magic to hide from everyone and pretend to be what he isn't, little brother," Azrilan said softly.

He swung to Tarcos. "Your uncle won't stand for this." Maybe he could sow division there, try to fracture whatever this partnership was, draw the Firthlander to his side.

Tarcos laughed. "The niever-flyers and Armun have been mine for months and the Bearmen now too. My uncle is under guard, and as soon as I return to Samatia I will be taking his place as warlord. Then, with the might of Montagn behind him, Azrilan will help me take the Twin Thrones." Something fierce and awful took over the Firth-lander's face. "It's time the Dumnorix learned what bending the knee is like."

More horror piled atop terror. An alliance between Tarcos and Azrilan? Talyn's family were in trouble and they didn't even know it. Talyn... *she* was in trouble. She had to be. Shit. He didn't know what to do.

Azrilan glanced at Tarcos, and the man called an order. Four hulking Bearmen appeared from the adjoining room. With one look at Cuinn, Theac dove for the door—he was much closer, only three steps away.

"GO!" Cuinn bellowed. It was the smartest play the Wolf could make. Theac couldn't keep Cuinn alive on his own, but if he could get more Wolves here quickly enough, they might have a chance. Talyn's warriors could take four Bearmen any day.

And Cuinn had to survive if he wanted to ever fix what he'd ruined.

"Let him go," Azrilan said to Tarcos before he could order the Bearmen to follow. "The Wolves have to be destroyed, and it will be easier if they come to us."

"I'll summon more Bearmen," Tarcos replied, then called an order to one of his warriors. The brute bowed his head and left the room. "They will have dealt with Talyn by now."

The mention of Talyn distracted Cuinn long enough for the remaining Bearmen to surround him. He struggled uselessly as they forced him to the floor, facedown. Once he was pinned there, unable to move, Azrilan knelt by his head. "I'm not Mithanis. You don't need to die, not if you swear loyalty to me."

"No." He ground out the words, filling them with his song magic, throwing determination at Azrilan.

A dark smile graced his brother's beautiful face. There was the scrape of a knife sliding out of a sheath, then the cool kiss of a blade running along the skin where his wings emerged from his back.

"You will swear to me, Cuinn. I could use your powerful gifts."

"No," he repeated, forcing his terror down, allowing none of it to surface strongly enough that Azrilan could pick it up.

The knife bit in, driving deep, slicing into the skin and tendon along the edge of his right wing. The pain was excruciating and he screamed, unable to stop himself. Hot blood poured down his side onto the floor. The Bearmen held him still, and he was unable to do anything other than cry out in agony.

Then it stopped.

"Swear to me, and keep your wings and your life." Azrilan used magic now, threading it into his voice, compelling Cuinn to agree.

His heart raced, his skin slick with sweat and blood. He was sick with fear for Talyn and the flooding agony through his back. But he'd spent his whole life hiding, pretending weakness, and he refused to ever go back to that. He would be strong. And he would *never* bow to Azrilan, not ever, no matter what happened. He could master pain. He'd been doing it his whole life.

"No," he gritted out.

The pain started again, unending, a line of fire digging deep into muscle and tendon. Cuinn writhed on the ground, screaming.

"Swear to me!" Azrilan demanded.

"NEVER!" Cuinn roared it, throwing his magic at Azrilan, filling it with his determination. He would figure out a way to fix this. He would never bow to either of his brothers. Never again.

The knife dug in again, this time on his other wing, but stopped when the doors slammed open. Theac was in the lead, axe drawn, the other talons behind him, snarling.

Desperate, Cuinn took advantage of Azrilan's distraction and flung every bit of song magic he had at the Bearmen holding him. It didn't do much, but sowed enough momentary confusion in them that he could wriggle free of their bloodied grasp and crawl towards the Wolves.

The Bearmen followed, reaching for him, but then Halun was there, the big man roaring his fury. He stood in the middle of the room, axe swinging, forcing the three hulking warriors to halt. Liadin and Corrin surrounded Cuinn, helping him up, Andres and Lyra holding off Tarcos and Azrilan.

"More Bearmen are coming, Your Highness." Theac was admirably calm. "The Wolves are holding them off for the moment, but if we don't go now we won't get out."

Tarcos snarled, drawing his sword and swinging at Andres. The Wolf countered the blow, pushed him back. When he came again, Corrin shouted, his green energy shield lighting up the room and forcing Tarcos even further back. Liadin slipped an arm around Cuinn, helping him stay upright. Azrilan began singing, throwing doubt and fear at Corrin. The shield wavered, held.

"Take them!" Tarcos bellowed at his warriors.

"Go! Get out of here before it's too late!" Halun shouted.

Cuinn caught the Wolf talon's gaze, the former slave, the man with a bigger heart than anyone he knew. Halun smiled, and there was nothing but resolve and acceptance in his eyes. "She told me to protect you. Allow me to do that, Your Highness."

And then Halun turned to throw himself at the Bearmen. Cuinn nodded, then summoned enough magic to send love and respect and gratitude Halun's way, wrapping him in it, forcing out any fear or pain the big man felt. Then he filled him with confidence and pride.

"Goodbye, my friend," he whispered.

A moment later the talons were hustling him out as fast as they could. The sound of fighting crashed through the hallways outside. Blood loss made his legs unsteady. He could feel it trickling down his back, feel the odd weight of both wings as they hung at an awkward angle. His vision turned blurry.

When he staggered, almost falling, Liadin, Corrin and Theac were forced to half-carry him, trying to jolt him as little as possible but causing stabbing pain with every step. Grief tore at him. Halun. He feared desperately for Talyn. And more Wolves would die tonight getting him out.

He swore to himself that he would be worthy of it. The wounds on his back were bad. The pain and blood loss told him that, along with the increasing weakness coursing through his trembling muscles.

It didn't matter.

He would honour the sacrifices the Wolves would make for him tonight. And he had to be alive for that. He wouldn't give up. Not ever.

THEAC HAD MADE a series of quick and clever decisions. While he and the talons had come for Cuinn, the full force of Wolves were battling a path down to the wall walk leading to Dock City. Bearmen and Falcons lay dead, Cuinn's groggy gaze running over them as he was carried out of the citadel and down the wall.

Wolf howls echoed through the night, full of pain and grief, but fierceness at the same time. When they reached the bottom of the wall, Jystar shoved his way forward, horror filling his face at the sight of Cuinn's wounds. "We have to stop. I need to stop the bleeding," he shouted.

"We can't stop. They're right on our heels. And once that flea-bitten piece of shit sets his niever-flyers loose… we need to get off the streets," Theac barked.

"If I don't staunch the bleeding, he dies within a quarter-turn," Jystar snapped back.

"Do it!" Cuinn somehow found enough strength for the order. "Get me on my feet, even if just for a short time."

"Your Highness, if I don't…" Jystar hesitated. "If I don't do a thorough healing now, if you let the damage linger… you'll lose your wings."

His eyes slid closed. Opened. "I don't need wings, Jystar. I need to be alive. Staunch the bleeding only."

Jystar snapped orders to the nearest Wolves and they began tearing strips off their shirts and stuffing them into the open wounds. It was agonising. The healer worked feverishly, hands making quick movements, and the scary weakness began fading. His mind cleared. The grief continued to tear at him.

Another order, and he was gently lowered to his feet, Corrin and Andres with an arm each around him. Jystar began binding something around his chest and wings, holding tight the cloth packed into the wounds.

"Has anyone found Talyn?" Cuinn asked Theac, the desperate hope fading when the man shook his head. He swallowed, forced back the terror.

"Okay. I'm done," Jystar said.

Theac bellowed an order for them to get moving, but they'd only just formed up around Cuinn when shouts came from the Wolves up front.

"What are you doing here?" Theac stepped smoothly in front of Cuinn as Saniya appeared, weaving her way through the throng. Unbelievably, Jasper paced at her side, green eyes flashing with anger when they landed on him and saw how hurt he was. Cuinn blinked, not confident he wasn't hallucinating. Had Vengeance come to finish the job? With Jasper?

"You don't look so good, Your Highness." She ignored Theac, running her cool gaze over Cuinn instead. "Your pet thinks the same, he came looking for me."

"I'll be fine." He swallowed. "What are you doing here?"

"Thought you might need a hand getting out of the city, Shadowhawk." She shrugged. "After all, we've helped you with that sort of thing before."

He met her gaze, those sapphire eyes as cool as Talyn's, just without the Dumnorix luminosity. Then he sagged in Corrin and Andres' grasp, relief flooding him. She meant it. She was here to help. He didn't know why, but that didn't matter. "Thank you."

Andres scowled. His dark skin was filthy with blood and sweat and his grief over Halun was a live thing in his eyes. "We're going to trust Vengeance?"

"We're going to trust Talyn's cousin," Cuinn said. "Do what she says. That's an order."

A thought occurred to him. It was so hard to think, but he fought through the dizziness. "Corrin, Theac, take your family and Evani and find one of Halun's friends, someone who can slip the Firthlander blockade before it's settled in place." Resolve filled him. It wasn't only Mithranar he had to try and protect. "Go to Port Lachley. You have to warn Talyn's family... about Tarcos and Firthland. He'll be going for them next, with the might of Montagn behind him."

Theac looked at Saniya. "Can't you get all of us on a ship south?"

"Not right away. Not for so many of you, not with him hurt like this." Saniya's gaze was darting around, looking up the wall where they'd come from, her collected demeanour fading. "We really need to go."

"Go, Theac. Corrin. Do as I say." It was harder to focus now, blackness swirling at his vision.

"Prince Cuinn." Theac looked horrified at the idea of leaving him. "You cannot..."

541

"We obey our orders, Captain." Corrin gently slid away from Cuinn, giving up his place to Liadin. "We'll do as you ask, Prince Cuinn, and then we'll come back for you."

"Good." He swayed in their grip.

"Come on, let's move." Saniya snapped. "Who's in charge with Parksin gone?"

"I am." Andres' voice sounded. "What do we do?"

"You follow me and do everything I say without complaint or hesitation. We're not safe yet."

"Wolves?" Lyra's voice called.

As one, the Wolves howled.

* * *

The story continues in A Duet of Sword and Song

* * *

Want to delve further into the world of *A Tale of Stars and Shadow*? By signing up to Lisa's monthly newsletter, *The Dock City Chronicle, you'll get* exclusive access to advance cover reveals, book updates, and special content just for subscribers, including:

- A short ebook - *A Tale of Two Callanan*
- Maps to download
- A download of *We Fly As One* - a song written and recorded for A Tale of Stars and Shadow by Peny Bohan

You can sign up at Lisa's website
lisacassidyauthor.com

ABOUT THE AUTHOR

Lisa is a self-published fantasy author by day and book nerd in every other spare moment she has. She's a self-confessed coffee snob (don't try coming near her with any of that instant coffee rubbish) but is willing to accept all other hot drink aficionados, even tea drinkers.

She lives in Australia's capital city, Canberra, and like all Australians, is pretty much in constant danger from highly poisonous spiders, crocodiles, sharks, and drop bears, to name a few. As you can see, she is also pro-Oxford comma.

A 2019 SPFBO finalist, and finalist for the 2020 ACT Writers Fiction award, Lisa is the author of the young adult fantasy series *The Mage Chronicles*, and epic fantasy series *A Tale of Stars and Shadow*. The first book in her latest series, *Heir to the Darkmage*, released in April 2021. She has also partnered up with One Girl, an Australian charity working to build a world where all girls have access to quality education. A world where all girls — no matter where they are born or how much money they have — enjoy the same rights and opportunities as boys. A percentage of all Lisa's royalties go to One Girl.

You can follow Lisa on Instagram and Facebook where she loves to interact with her readers. Lisa also has a Facebook group - Lisa's Writing Cave - where you can jump in and talk about anything and everything relating to her books (or any books really).

lisacassidyauthor.com

ALSO BY LISA CASSIDY

The Mage Chronicles

DarkSkull Hall

Taliath

Darkmage

Heartfire

Heir to the Darkmage

Heir to the Darkmage

Mark of the Huntress

A Tale of Stars and Shadow

A Tale of Stars and Shadow

A Prince of Song and Shade

A King of Masks and Magic

A Duet of Sword and Song

Consider a review?

'Your words are as important to an author as an author's words are to you'

If you enjoyed this book, I would be humbled if you would consider taking the time to leave an **honest** review on GoodReads and Amazon (it doesn't have to be long - a few words or a single sentence is absolutely fine!).

Reviews are the lifeblood of any book, and more reviews help my books achieve greater visibility and perform better in Amazon's ranking algorithms. This is a MASSIVE help for an indie author. Not to mention a review can absolutely make my day!

Printed in Great Britain
by Amazon